9/9/13
$29.99
6650
CHF

9/13

LOVE IN A BROKEN VESSEL

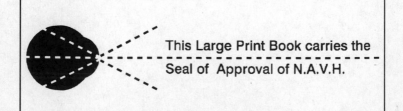

This Large Print Book carries the
Seal of Approval of N.A.V.H.

LOVE IN A BROKEN VESSEL

MESU ANDREWS

THORNDIKE PRESS

A part of Gale, Cengage Learning

GALE
CENGAGE Learning·

Detroit • New York • San Francisco • New Haven, Conn • Waterville, Maine • London

LIBRARY OF CONGRESS CATALOGING-IN-PUBLICATION DATA

Andrews, Mesu, 1963–
    Love in a broken vessel / by Mesu Andrews. — Large print edition.
        pages ; cm. — (Thorndike Press large print Christian historical fiction)
    ISBN-13: 978-1-4104-6020-2 (hardcover)
    ISBN-10: 1-4104-6020-7 (hardcover)
    1. Large type books. I. Title.
PS3601.N55274L685 2013b
813'.6—dc23   2013014071

Published in 2013 by arrangement with Revell Books, a division of Baker Publishing Group

Printed in Mexico
1 2 3 4 5 6 7 17 16 15 14 13

To my forever best friend,
Joni Edwards Jones.
You saw me at my worst —
and you refused to leave.
You saved my life —
and then I met Jesus.
How do I thank you for eternity?

NOTE TO THE READER

When you think of reading the story of Gomer and Hosea, what novel comes to mind? *Redeeming Love* by Francine Rivers, right? I think I've read it at least four times. It's tied for first place in my all-time favorites, and Francine Rivers is hands down my favorite author. So why would I dare write a novel that might be compared to such a classic? Because *Love in a Broken Vessel* is biblical fiction, and *Redeeming Love* is a biblical story set in a prairie romance. Trying to equate the two stories would be like comparing apples and oranges — both are fruit, but very different yummy flavors. My hope is that readers will enjoy each one for the unique story it is.

Engaging fiction must be believable, but let's face it — a righteous man of God marrying, loving, and repeatedly forgiving a prostitute is hard to grasp. However, as you immerse yourself in the ancient days of

7

Hosea and Gomer, remember that the Bible says Hosea married a harlot named Gomer, and the story mirrors God's desperate attempt to turn the hearts of Israel back to Himself. The story may not have happened exactly as I've written it, but it did happen. It was the mystery of Christ's love and mercy before the incarnation of our Savior.

Now, regarding the parts that are fiction, there is no historical data linking the prophets Jonah, Amos, and Hosea. However, Amos was indeed a fig picker from Tekoa, and it was feasible that Jonah was still living during the time of Amos's prophecies and Hosea's ministry. I've chosen to weave their lives together in a prophets' camp — a sort of school for aspiring messengers of Yahweh. Though, again, I found no factual basis for a prophets' camp in Tekoa, the Bible often refers to a community of prophets beginning as early as the tribes themselves. Shiloh was the gathering place for prophets with the ark of God. In 1 Samuel 19, Saul sent messengers to Naioth to seize David from a company of prophets, and 2 Kings 6 gives an account of some cantankerous prophets complaining that their living quarters are too tight.

Scripture also describes the details of King Uzziah's leprosy but gives no location of the rented house where he lived out his life while Jotham ruled from Jerusalem. Neither does the Bible declare Uzziah's exact relationship to Isaiah and Amoz. Scripture tells us that Isaiah was the son of Amoz (2 Kings 19; 20), and according to Talmudic tradition (ancient Hebrew text), Amoz was Uzziah's uncle (*Meg.* 10b). This dilemma encapsulates the beauty and challenge of biblical fiction — piecing together Scripture's truths with historical supposition.

Hosea's ministry began approximately 180 years after King Solomon's death. Solomon's son, Rehoboam, angered the northern ten tribes with high taxes and hard labor, so they rebelled against the young king's authority. The kingdom of Israel split into two nations. Israel comprised the northern nation of the ten rebelling tribes, while the tribe of Judah formed a new nation, maintaining its capital in Jerusalem and claiming the tribe of Benjamin as its sole support. The Canaanite people dispersed among both Israel and Judah continued worshiping pagan gods, drawing false parallels between El, the father of gods, and the Hebrews' God, Yahweh. The northern nation of Israel set up golden calf idols in Bethel and Dan, drawing Israelites into idolatry and stoking Yahweh's wrath. But more profoundly — Israel broke His heart. God's chosen people rejected His love. And that is where Hosea and Gomer's story begins.

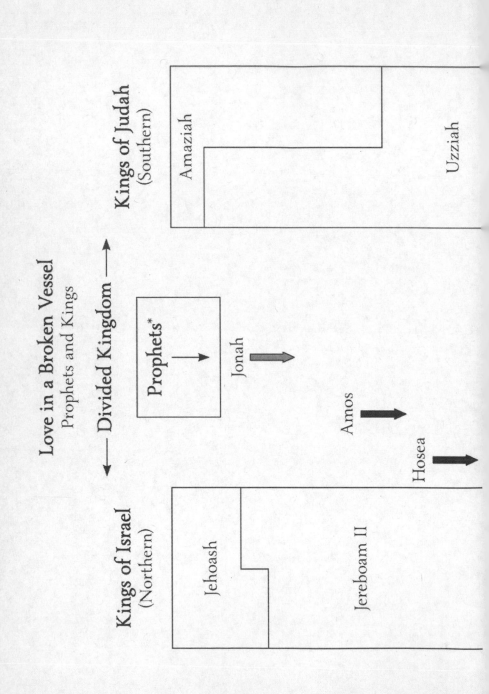

Love in a Broken Vessel
Prophets and Kings

←— Divided Kingdom —→

Kings of Judah
(Southern)

Amaziah

Uzziah

Prophets*

Jonah

Amos

Hosea

Kings of Israel
(Northern)

Jehoash

Jereboam II

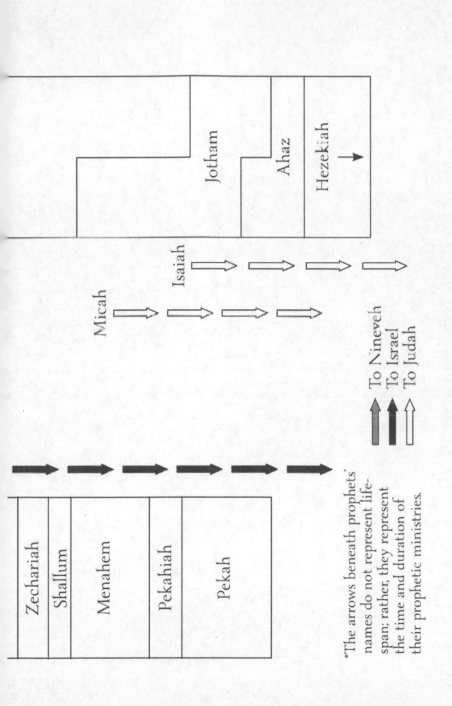

Zechariah

Shallum

Menahem

Pekahiah

Pekah

Micah

Isaiah

Jotham

Ahaz

Hezekiah

To Nineveh
To Israel
To Judah

*The arrows beneath prophets' names do not represent life-span; rather, they represent the time and duration of their prophetic ministries.

PART 1

PROLOGUE

When Yahweh first spoke to Hosea, Yahweh told him, "Marry a prostitute, and have children with that prostitute. The people in this land have acted like prostitutes and abandoned Yahweh."

Hosea's empty house throbbed with sweet silence. He soaked it in, letting it nourish him like the last bite of warm, fresh bread soggy with lentil stew. His stomach rumbled, and he realized it was past time for his evening meal.

The stone worktable stood like a sentry in his main room. Covered baskets hung on the wall, filled with day-old bread and hard cheese. The meager fare would suffice until he could soak lentils for tomorrow's meal. He approached the table, noticing dust dancing in a shaft of dusk's golden light.

A second look at the glow drew him deeper into contemplation. *I only see the dust when light shines through the window.* Hosea waved his hand through the light, stirring the dust, but felt no resistance. Visible and real, yet without recognizable sound or weight, the dust was present but immeasurable. A slow, satisfied smile crept across his lips. *Now, that is a good topic for the prophets' class tomorrow.* Jonah would enjoy the —

A breeze swept through the house, startling him, swaying the hanging herbs. Hosea turned to the front door, confused. Had the wind blown it open?

The door was closed.

"What was that?" he whispered to no one. The wind stirred inside the house again, this time not a breeze but a gale that whipped his robe around his legs.

The wind spoke. *Marry a prostitute.*

Hosea gasped. *Yahweh?*

Marry a prostitute, and have children with that prostitute.

The wind grew stronger, and Hosea covered his face, fell to his knees, listening.

The people of Israel have acted like prostitutes and abandoned Yahweh.

The wind stopped. All was silent. Tranquil again.

1

HOSEA 1:1

Yahweh spoke his word to Hosea, son of Beeri, when Uzziah, Jotham, Ahaz, and Hezekiah were kings of Judah and when Jeroboam, son of Joash, was king of Israel.

Gomer hurried from her private room, through a connecting breezeway, and into the brothel's kitchen. Jarah, one of the servant girls, grabbed a few dried figs and, with a trembling hand, held them out to Gomer — an offering. Gomer took two and closed the girl's hand around those remaining. "Eat them yourself, Jarah. Don't let Tamir find them and give them to someone else." Gomer walked away, noticing the girl slip one into her mouth, and tried to remember the last time she smelled warm bread baking in that kitchen. Her stomach

19

rumbled at the thought.

She emerged into the sunlit courtyard of Tamir's brothel, spotting old Merav tending three toddlers playing in the dust. Gomer glanced left and right, hoping to avoid a confrontation with the owner. The wealthiest businesswoman in Samaria, Tamir had built her business on determination, cunning, and the favor of the gods.

And Gomer.

Yes, Gomer had been Tamir's most lucrative harlot since she'd been dumped on the woman's doorstep after Gomer's twelfth year.

"Why do I have to go to the sacrifice this morning?" Gomer ranted while stomping toward Merav. "Why can't the younger girls go without me? I've had only a moment's sleep, and I'm tired, Merav."

The old woman pressed a single finger to her lips and nodded at the sleeping infant in her arms. Merav, the brothel's midwife, loved all the children inside the gates, whether born within or abandoned at the threshold.

Gomer adjusted her volume but not her tone. "Why does Tamir demand I accompany the girls? They are quite capable and can work the crowd just as well as I." Disgusted, she gathered one of the toddlers in her arms, giving her a little spit bath to clean her smudged cheek.

"Tamir knows you represent her house well, and the other girls look to you for leadership while they're on the streets." Merav's voice was gentle, and Gomer wondered how much of her soothing was for the sleeping baby boy in her arms and how much was meant to calm Gomer's foul mood. "Here, eat your pomegranate skin." The old midwife held out the dried rind and offered a wry smile. She was done listening to Gomer's complaints.

Gomer planted the toddler back on the ground and reached for the pomegranate rind — but captured Merav's hand and kissed it before letting go. The old woman brushed her cheek. "Now, take some pomegranate seeds with you. I don't want to be holding your baby next year."

A wave of emotion washed over Gomer at the thought. "Well, I wouldn't know if it was my baby, now would I?" The question came out more accusatory than she intended, and when she saw the hurt on Merav's features, she knelt beside the old woman. "I'm sorry. You know I didn't mean anything by that. It's just that, well . . ." She fumbled for words, trying to unravel the knot of feelings she'd awakened with this

21

morning. "You know me, Merav. I try to forget yesterday and not worry about tomorrow. If it wasn't for you and these pomegranates, I might have a dozen children by now."

The old woman met her eyes and stroked her cheek. "What troubles you this morning, my little Gomer?"

"I awoke with a terrible sense of dread. Perhaps one of the gods is warning me of danger."

"Or maybe you drank too much wine last night." Her eyes twinkled with mischief.

"I'm serious!" Gomer shouted, causing the sleeping infant to stir. A warning glance from the old woman reminded her to lower her voice. "I'm getting older, Merav. I've lived through two childbirths and one rue-induced drop. No matter how many pomegranates you feed me, I'm almost certain to get pregnant again with the number of clients I see each night. Tamir says she'll teach me how to run the brothel, but so far . . ."

"But so far she hasn't begun teaching you the *business* side of harlotry." The old woman finished Gomer's sentence.

"That's right." Their eyes locked in understanding. "She hasn't taught me *anything*! Only you have taught me, Merav. You've taught me what herbs, roots, and teas prevent a man's seed from growing inside me. You've taught me how to bring forth a child on the birthing stones. But I've watched the other girls long for the babies of their womb and become less human with each child that's taken from them. I must know *why* Tamir sends all the male babies away but has decided to keep this one."

"Even I don't know the answer to that, my little Gomer. I've known Tamir since she purchased this house, yet she hides what's special about this boy." The old woman caressed his downy black hair and snuggled him closer to her heart.

"Then tell me why she refuses to let an ima know which babe is her own." Gomer glanced at the little ones playing with sticks and stones at Merav's feet. "Are any of these mine?"

Merav's eyes welled with tears, but her voice was solid stone. "You know I cannot answer that." She raised her chin and swiped her tears. "And you know how hard I try to keep any of Tamir's girls from conceiving. If they would eat the seeds I give them and drink the tea regularly, we wouldn't have to take the babies or give them rue to induce —"

"I know," Gomer said, laying her head in

Merav's lap. "I'm not accusing you, my friend. I'm just frustrated, and for the first time I'm trying to see my future — but the path is very dark."

Merav stroked Gomer's hair and began humming a familiar cradle tune while still holding the infant in her other arm. Gomer's mind wandered to her childhood in Bethel. It seemed ages ago. She saw her three younger sisters cowering in the corner during one of Abba Diblaim's drunken rages. He was a priest at Bethel's temple — and a pig at home.

Then she saw Hosea's face. He'd been ten when she last saw him; she'd been six — that day in the temple, when she fell from the rafters. She didn't even get to say good-bye when his abba took him from Bethel. Hosea had been her one friend, her protector.

When Abba Diblaim sold her to an Asherah priestess from Samaria a few years later, she learned the bitter days of a priestess and the lonely nights with drunken men. She'd believed one of the Baal priests when he said he loved her. What a little fool she'd been. Stripped of her ritual duties, she was labeled a harlot and dropped at Tamir's gate. Merav had soothed her broken heart and tended the whipping wounds on her back. The poor woman didn't deserve the tongue-lashing Gomer had given her this morning.

"We've been together almost seven years now," Gomer whispered, letting her tears wet Merav's robe. "I know better than anyone how you love the girls in this house, and I want to make sure we *both* have a place to live after I'm too old to provide food and shelter as a street harlot." She lifted her head, holding the woman's gaze intently. "I need to know who Tamir talks to at the temple when one of our young girls reaches the age for service in Asherah's grove. And how does Tamir decide which girls become priestesses and which ones work as street harlots or serving maids? What other ways does she bring in food and income for this house besides the street harlots' pay?"

"Well, well," came a silken voice from behind them. "It appears I've happened upon an important conversation this morning."

Gomer saw the fear in Merav's eyes and realized Tamir had heard too much. She leapt to her feet and faced the brothel owner. "I was telling Merav the questions I intended to ask you when I returned from the sacrifice today." She could hear the quiver in her voice and cursed herself for it. She'd perfected her conniving with men but still struggled when lying to Tamir. "Is there anything I can help with before I leave? Any special instructions?"

Tamir's eyes narrowed, and she placed balled fists on slender hips. "Yes, in fact, there is something you should know before you leave this morning. Today's sacrifice will be the first of its kind in Israel. The drought we've experienced for the last two years has affected even King Jeroboam's grain stores." She glanced right and left, lowering her voice. "He's finally desperate enough to show real devotion to the gods. Perhaps he'll live up to the glory of his namesake, Israel's first Jeroboam, who gave us the golden calves at Bethel and Dan. He's built a new altar for the special sacrifice."

She twirled a lock of Gomer's auburn hair around her finger. "The altar fire will glisten off your curls, and the beating drums will arouse the worshipers. Make sure you and the rest of the girls are near the altar at the moment of sacrifice. I expect a full day of celebration, and I want all payment in grain." She dropped Gomer's hair and shooed her away like a fly. "We're low on grain here, and the servants can't make bread from silver."

Everything within Gomer screamed indignation, but what other choices did she have? Where else could she go? "Of course, Tamir. I'll do exactly as you ask." She swallowed hard and tempered her voice, determined to find a way of escape. "Is there any other way I might serve you, my lady?" She bowed, hoping to hide the rage her expression could not.

"Yes. Get to the sacrifice. Now!" The owner of the house stormed away, shouting instructions at one of the serving maids across the courtyard.

Gomer trembled with pent-up fury and whispered to Merav, though she dared not look in her direction, "I will go as she commands, but when I return tonight, my friend, I will have enough silver for us both to leave this hen house."

Merav reached for her hand. "Just be careful, little one. I've seen that look in Tamir's eyes before. King Jeroboam isn't the only one who is desperate."

2

AMOS 8:11 NIV

"The days are coming," declares the Sovereign LORD, "when I will send a famine through the land — not a famine of food or a thirst for water, but a famine of hearing the words of the LORD."

Hosea's thighs burned with each step up Samaria's rocky hill, and he noted the faltering gait of his old teacher. Jonah leaned heavily on his walking sticks. Why hadn't Hosea asked Isaiah to stay and help Jonah rather than sending him ahead to await their signal north of the city?

"Let me help you." Hosea placed a supportive arm around Jonah's shoulders, but the crusty old prophet issued his familiar reply.

"Yahweh and my walking sticks are all the help I need, thank you." He shrugged off

Hosea's arm, offering half a smile, assuring his student of his gratitude — and refusal. They'd left Amos's farm in Judah four days ago. Jonah's stamina had weakened. His good humor hadn't.

Hosea sighed, shook his head, and let Jonah lead. In the man's younger days, he'd traveled to Nineveh and back, survived three days in a fish's belly, and turned a generation of Assyrians to repentance. Who was Hosea to insist he needed help? *Yahweh, give him strength. You know how much he means to me.*

Hosea released his teacher to the Lord's care, focusing on the gleaming white palace, awed at the capital city of his homeland — a city he'd never seen, a homeland he'd left twelve years ago.

He cast a sideways glance at Jonah and noticed him shivering. Hosea unwound his mantle and wrapped it around his friend's shoulders. This time Jonah offered no protest but tugged the woolen garb closed at his neck. The winter breeze must feel cooler to an old man's thinned blood. Jonah was now covered head to toe, hiding his milky-white clumps of skin — the enduring evidence of his three-day lesson in the belly of the fish.

"How far from Samaria is your hometown,

Jonah?" Hosea decided to make conversation instead of gawking at the poor man, waiting for him to collapse.

"About the same distance north as your hometown Bethel is to the south." His voice quaked like his shoulders.

Hosea nodded but remained silent. He squeezed his eyes shut, mentally kicking himself for letting Jonah come at all. He'd feared the journey from Amos's farm in Tekoa would be too much for him, but Jonah insisted on accompanying Hosea on his first prophetic mission. The night of Yahweh's first revelation had been the beginning of a three-day holy windstorm, giving Hosea insight into where, to whom, and how to deliver Yahweh's message. But the instructions hadn't included Jonah's presence on the mission.

"Do you need the blanket from my pack?"

"Enough! I'm fine," Jonah said, his voice muffled beneath the folds of his robe. "Stop fussing like an overbearing ima." Hosea noted a slight twinkle in his eyes. "I'm not sure whether I'm cold or nervous for you, but I can't seem to stop shaking." He pulled back his mantle just enough to issue an encouraging wink.

Hosea saw pride in Jonah's eyes, and he threw his arm around the man's shoulder.

30

"Don't tell me you don't want help," Hosea said before his mentor could protest. "I'm resting my arm on you because *I* need the support."

Jonah chuckled, and they walked in companionable silence up the steep and rocky path. Hosea's mind wandered to the first time he'd seen "the fish prophet," as Gomer had called him when they were children. She had convinced him to sneak into the temple rafters again, spying on their abbas' priestly duties, when Amos, accompanied by Jonah, had arrived to deliver Yahweh's message of judgment on Israel. Hosea would never forget Amos's words: "A famine of God's Word is coming to Israel." The high priest Amaziah had scoffed at the threat. But the words rang true in Hosea's abba Beeri, and he left Israel with other faithful Yahweh followers and took Hosea to Amos's farm to be taught with other would-be prophets.

"Have I ever thanked you and Amos for beginning the prophets' school in Tekoa?" Hosea kept his eyes forward, afraid his emotions would choke his words if he met Jonah's gaze.

"I'm sorry your abba Beeri isn't here to see you prophesy. I think he'd be pleased that you are the first prophet to speak in

Israel since Yahweh's declared famine of His word twelve years ago."

Hosea's heart squeezed in his chest. He missed his abba at moments like this. Jonah had been his guardian since Abba died two years after they arrived on Amos's farm. Jonah had been both spiritual and earthly mentor since.

"I miss Abba Beeri, but you have been a faithful abba to me, my friend."

Jonah stopped his trudging and straightened, forcing Hosea to meet his gaze. "The day you told me of your first Yahweh encounter — I think it was the happiest day of my life. Remember? I danced for joy — without these walking sticks!"

Both men chuckled, recalling the spectacle. "I remember," Hosea said, wiping happy tears. "Did Yahweh tell you He would command me to take a wife? Before you left that day, you said I shouldn't take a wife unless Yahweh commanded it. Did you know He would speak to me?"

Jonah's merriment faded to growing intensity. "Yahweh hasn't spoken to me directly for quite some time. I receive nudges — leanings. But you, Hosea — you are Yahweh's prophet for this moment in Israel's history. Speak boldly, my son. Speak with the authority Yahweh has given to you." His piercing eyes set in that eerie white skin would make any man wince.

Silence lingered between them as weary travelers walked past. Hosea felt like a child but needed to ask. "Yahweh told me to marry a prostitute, but He didn't say exactly how to find one or how to go about — well, securing her agreement." Feeling heat rise in his cheeks, he scuffed his sandal in the dusty path. "What if I find a harlot but she refuses me? I'm not as handsome as Isaiah. He would have no trouble winning a woman's heart. He's already won Aya." He lifted his gaze, voicing the deepest fear of his soul. "What if I can't even attract a *harlot*?"

Still standing amid the tide of travelers, Jonah gathered Hosea under his arm and started trudging up Samaria's hill once more. "Your harlot may refuse you."

"What?" Hosea stopped, but Jonah yanked his robe and drew him back under his arm to continue their walk.

"I said she *may* refuse you, but you must remember why you're here. Yahweh's heart has been broken by Israel's unfaithfulness. You must become vulnerable to the affection of the one you seek to marry. You must publicly declare your intentions to her and thereby risk rejection."

"This is not making me feel better, Jonah."

He kept replaying Isaiah's happy dance after Aya's bride negotiations, cringing that he'd never feel that sweet triumph.

"It's not my intention to make you *feel* better, my son. It's my hope to prepare you for the calling Yahweh has given. Your struggle, your emotions, your joys and sorrows will often mirror Yahweh's own."

Hosea fell silent once more, glancing again at Samaria's white limestone palace. He realized his days as a student in the prophets' school were over, but the days of learning to be Yahweh's prophet had just begun.

He swallowed hard, gathering courage to venture another question, glad Isaiah wasn't with them. Though Hosea and Isaiah were raised together at the prophets' camp, Isaiah was four years his junior and could be as annoying as any younger brother. And because Isaiah was born into royalty, he might not understand Hosea's concerns.

"What if I don't want to obey Yahweh's calling, Jonah? What if I don't want to marry . . . a harlot?" Even the word tasted bitter on his tongue.

Jonah smiled, and Hosea was humiliated. "I don't see what there is to smile about!"

Jonah lifted one crinkled eyebrow. "You're asking *me* about disobeying Yahweh?"

Hosea realized the irony of posing his

question to the runaway prophet, and his defenses weakened.

"God will have His way — with or without our participation. If we're unwilling to obey, He'll use another circumstance or find someone else to serve His purpose. But God *will* have His way because ultimately, His way is best."

Hosea nodded, and they continued their walk in silence, caught in the swell of humanity approaching King Jeroboam's city. Samaria, like Jerusalem, was chosen as the nation's capital by a long-ago soldier because of its military advantage. King Omri had valued Samaria's position high atop a steep hill and carved its rear walls directly into a mountainside. Omri's son, Ahab, added to the city by building extensively; in fact, it was Ahab's extravagance and gifts to his wife, Jezebel, that caused merchants to muse about Samaria's ivory palace.

Hosea halted, shielding his eyes from the glare. He stared up at the palace and its grounds that occupied nearly one-third of Samaria's hill. The two-story mansions east of the royal properties testified to the luxury and excess of all Israel's leaders. Hosea's heart squeezed inside his chest.

Jonah stopped, anxiously watching those

who hurried past, and tugged at Hosea's sleeve, "What are you doing? If merchants' reports are true, the sacrifice could begin at the temple any moment."

But Hosea turned in a circle, drinking in the sights. "I'm an Israelite by birth, Jonah, but I've never seen Samaria."

A man tilled the soil with his mule and plow. Children ran through an olive grove, laughing.

Hosea's throat tightened with emotion. "This will be destroyed if Jeroboam doesn't listen to my message from Yahweh."

"Remember your training, Hosea. You are God's prophet. You are not God."

Jonah placed his arm around Hosea's shoulder and leaned into his support as the two walked through the city gates. Once inside Israel's capital, they turned west, climbing up Samaria's famed hill. In the center of the street flowed the city's drainage ditch. Even two prophets from the country knew to stay as far from its foulness as possible. The smell nearly made Hosea retch. When the crowd slowed, he looked behind him and saw poorer dwellings at the bottom of the hill, the natural drainage destination for all the garbage and refuse of the city. *Another reason the rich and powerful live at the top of the hill in two-*

story mansions.

"It looks like we may have to separate," Jonah said, nodding in the direction of the stalled crowd. "You'll need to get as close to King Jeroboam as possible, and you won't be able to get as far if you're dragging an old cripple." Hosea started to protest, but Jonah silenced him with a raised hand. "Yahweh has chosen you to deliver this message, my son. He will make the way clear and give you wisdom. Now go." Jonah shoved Hosea's shoulder, leaving no room for argument.

With his heart thundering in his chest, Hosea took his first steps toward a large building connected to the palace's east side. Above the apex of the portico was perched the Phoenician god Melqart — no doubt built by Ahab for his queen, Jezebel. Hosea glanced behind him several times, watching more and more people separate him from Jonah — until finally, he could see his teacher no longer. The stunning white, two-story temple loomed before him. Immaculate gardens trimmed its outer edges, and stone images of every size and persuasion dotted the courtyard. He commanded his feet to keep moving, and the crowd pushed him forward.

Delivered into the main sanctuary, Hosea

gasped. Unlike the simple golden bull from his childhood home in Bethel, an enormous idol consumed much of Samaria's temple. The shining bronze image of a man with a bull's head nearly reached the peak of the temple. Its belly was aglow, belching smoke from a blazing fire. Hosea had heard stories of this god — to the Moabites, he was Chemosh; to the Ammonites, Molech. The Canaanites called him Mot and taught the Israelites that he must be appeased when drought threatened their land. Their stories told of Mot conquering the rain giver, Prince Baal, and taking him to the underworld until a sacrifice was made. No matter which god was named in this abomination, Hosea knew what that altar meant.

A child was about to die.

3

Listen to the word of Yahweh, you Israelites. . . . "There is no faith, no love, and no
knowledge of Elohim in the land. . . . That
is why the land is drying up."

Gomer sliced through the temple crowd
with a skill borne of experience and purpose. The girls trailing behind her had
maintained the pace admirably, and she'd
noted their kohl-rimmed eyes followed her
every move. "You, dance at the left of the
king's platform," she instructed the youngest. Then, motioning to a tall, more experienced girl, Gomer added, "Stay near her
until you see the customer pay an agreeable
grain price." Both girls nodded and hurried
away, bronze bells jingling around their
ankles with each step. Gomer assigned loca-
tions to the rest of Tamir's girls — far

enough from other harlots to avoid confrontation, close enough to the altar to attract eager worshipers.

Finally, having placed all the others, Gomer surveyed the temple sanctuary to find her favorite spot. The precise site varied with each event, but her guidelines were the same: the most discreet location near the highest-ranking officials. An elder or judge — even a priest — had no qualms about taking a harlot to his bed. But an official could be ridiculed if he paid for pleasure too often. Or if the woman was ugly. Gomer knew she wasn't ugly; some of the most powerful men in Samaria had told her so. Repeatedly. So discretion was vital if she hoped to lure those who could provide enough silver for her escape tonight with Merav.

The temple drums began a slow bass pounding, vibrating Gomer's soul, setting her feet into motion. She began to dance and sway, moving with the beat toward a shaded area near the king's platform. Jeroboam was seated on his temple throne with Israel's newly appointed general at his side. Menahem was a ruthless soldier and an exacting leader. Like King Jeroboam, he demanded unquestioning loyalty from those he commanded. Gomer had felt the sting of the general's whip two nights ago when she'd been slow to serve his wine. She'd never make that mistake again.

Seated at the king's right was Amaziah, Bethel's high priest during Gomer's childhood. She'd seen him a hundred times since she'd arrived in Samaria, resenting his promotion to Israel's high priest. But today she felt six years old again, and in her mind's eye she saw Amaziah rage at the prophet Amos, who had come from Judah to prophecy against Israel — and Amos brought that fish prophet with him.

The fish prophet. He's the one who took Hosea away. A fresh memory of Hosea's kind face squeezed her heart. She hadn't thought of her childhood friend for years — until this morning. Why had he plagued her thoughts today?

Gomer covered her ears, shutting out the memory, concentrating on the flute and drum of the celebration to come. But she could feel Hosea's arms around her. He was just a little boy, but he was like a big brother, strong and protective. When his abba Beeri declared he was taking Hosea to Judah — away from Israel's pagan worship — Gomer remembered screaming, falling from the rafters. Her world went black. When she'd awakened, Hosea was gone —

and soon her innocence was taken as well.

The drums in King Jeroboam's temple kept beating, but Gomer stood like the blazing idol before her, staring at Amaziah. Somehow he was responsible for her life of pain. Deep, writhing hate rose within her as she watched the pompous fool clap off beat. She had been ten when her abba Diblaim sold her to Samaria's priestess — the same day Amaziah was made Israel's high priest. The same day Abba Diblaim became high priest at Bethel.

Some men's careers were built on little girls' beauty. The thought that she had been bartered for her abba's political favor consumed her with alternating hate and despair. A shiver worked through her. Gomer shook her head, trying to clear the memories. She must be at her best if she hoped to earn enough silver to escape with Merav tonight. She closed her eyes, willing herself to enjoy the drums, to feel the vibration of the beat beneath her feet.

She resumed her dance toward the king's platform, passing the new altar, an image of a man with a bull's head, seated with legs crossed. Flames burned amber and white in its belly, the heat nearly singeing her. She gave the brazen beast a wide berth, marveling at its size and intensity. Twice as tall as a man, the image was wide enough for a camel to stand inside its fire chamber. She'd never seen anything like it in Samaria — or in Bethel, for that matter. The Canaanites had many gods, and Gomer felt cheated by her simple Israelite worship of El and Asherah, Baal and Anat.

Asherah was her patron goddess, blessing and cursing the fertility rites of men and women. Gomer had given Israel's gods the respect they'd been due, but something about this brazen furnace drew her, aroused her. The drums beat faster, and she flung her arms wide. She tipped back her head, abandoning herself to laugh and dance. The bells around her waist, ankles, and wrists tinkled in time with the bass *thrum-pumming* of the drums, and she was lost in the thrill of all this new god might offer.

"Listen to the word of Yahweh, you Israelites." A deep, male voice scraped her nerves, resounded over the drums, and hushed the noisy crowd. "Yahweh brings these charges against you."

Gomer's spell was broken. *Yahweh?* She hadn't heard of that god since Bethel, since Hosea . . .

"Who dares interrupt the king's holy sacrifice?" Amaziah rose from his gilded couch and stood at the edge of the king's dais, searching the sea of faces. The crowd writhed and stirred until one man stood alone — encircled by curious but cautious spectators.

"There is no faith, no love, and no knowledge of Elohim in this land," the intruder continued, but Gomer couldn't get close enough to see his face. "There is cursing, lying, murdering, stealing, and adultery. *That* is why the land is drying up, and everyone who lives in it is passing away — your animals, birds, and fish are dying too, are they not?"

"Don't lay blame on Israel's leaders when it's the people who commit these heinous crimes." The high priest's volume rose, as did the small humps where his shoulders belonged. Gomer had always thought Amaziah's physique was more serpent than man.

She weaved through the crowd. *One more fat Israelite to pass, and I'll finally see the Yahweh prophet.*

"It is Yahweh who says to *you,* Amaziah: My case is against you priests. I will destroy My people because they are ignorant. And because you have refused to learn and teach, I will refuse to let you be My priests. You have forgotten the teachings of your Elohim, so I will forget your children, Israel."

Finally! Gomer emerged from the crowd and found herself standing face-to-face with the prophet. *By Asherah's bosoms — no!*

"Hosea?" The word escaped in a whisper, and thank the gods, he didn't hear her.

But it was him.

She'd always been the bold one on their childhood adventures. *Now look at him.* Her timid friend, now Yahweh's fiery prophet. Her heart pounding louder than the drums that set her feet dancing, she watched her long-ago friend. In many ways he was the same. Curly hair. Soft brown eyes — as round and innocent as they were twelve years ago.

Then he met Gomer's gaze. And she saw his innocence shatter.

Hosea bent forward, clutching his gut as if he'd taken a blow. Murmurs rose from the crowd, and he knew he had to continue with God's message, but how? *Maybe it's not her.* He allowed his eyes to wander across the mosaic floor tiles to the henna-dyed feet of the prostitute before him. Slowly, almost painfully, his eyes traveled the length of her scantily clad form. Every bangle, veil, and bell had been expertly placed to accentuate the smooth skin and perfect curves of the little girl he'd known in Bethel.

She reached up awkwardly, covering the scar on her forehead from her fall out of the temple rafters. But she couldn't hide the beauty mark beside her left nostril. She'd hated it as a child and tried to scrub it off with mashed cucumber and pine sap. It hadn't worked, and now it distinguished her as a rare and exotic beauty.

Hosea felt a hand on his shoulder and jumped like a frightened little boy. The crowd laughed, then gasped, but before he turned, he saw hatred in Gomer's eyes when she glimpsed the old prophet behind him.

Jonah had removed his hood, revealing his curdled skin and, subsequently, his identity. "My son, you must continue," he whispered. "I realize you've become distracted —"

"You don't understand, Jonah. She's —"

"Yahweh understands, Hosea. Not even the smallest detail escapes His knowledge or plan." He stepped back then, giving his student the freedom to choose. Ministry or distraction. He glanced again in Gomer's direction, his heart breaking when she turned away.

And then his anger flared.

"Thus says Yahweh: the more priests there are, the more they sin against Me. So I will turn their glory into shame. They will eat, but they'll never be full. They will have sex

46

with prostitutes, but they'll never have children."

He saw Gomer's head snap in his direction, a wicked stare warning him to stop. He could not — even for his beloved friend.

"Israel has abandoned Yahweh, and a spirit of prostitution leads them astray. They commit adultery by giving themselves to other gods."

Amaziah began to laugh and said to Jeroboam and Menahem, "It appears this young man does not approve of our lovely Gomer." The crowd joined the mocking, pawing and lunging at the young prostitutes sprinkled among them.

Hosea shoved the man who had taken Gomer into his arms. "Stay away from her!"

"No! *You* stay away from me!" she shouted and nestled into the man's barreled chest. She glanced over her shoulder at Hosea, almost daring him to defend her again.

What had they done to her? Why would Gomer run into the arms of a man who would misuse her when Hosea could help her and restore their friendship? His chest ached at the pain of her betrayal.

"Yahweh understands," Jonah had said moments ago, when he thought Hosea had simply been distracted by a harlot's lovely form. Well, finally, *Hosea* understood. He

47

grasped Yahweh's indescribable pain of a nation who refused His attempts to woo them, choosing instead to worship other lovers. Indignation fueled his passion.

"My people offer sacrifices on mountaintops and burn incense on hills and under oaks and poplars. That is why your daughters become prostitutes and your daughters-in-law commit adultery." His last words seemed to quiet the crowd. Evidently the mention of adulterous daughters-in-law strummed heartstrings that remained silent for lowly prostitutes. " 'Yet I will not punish your daughters when they become prostitutes,' says Yahweh, 'or your daughters-in-law when they commit adultery. For it is the men who go to prostitutes and offer sacrifices with the temple prostitutes. And Israel herself acts like a prostitute!' Lord God, let not Judah become guilty too!"

Barely had the word *Judah* escaped when King Jeroboam sprang from his throne. "Enough! I've heard enough from this seer. I recognize you, Jonah. You old conniver. How dare you hide behind a pink-cheeked boy to pronounce doom on a kingdom you helped build?"

Jonah stepped forward and bowed while soldiers marched closer. "You are right, King Jeroboam, it is I, Jonah. But you are wrong when you say I helped build your kingdom." A serene smile stretched the old man's mottled skin. "I delivered Yahweh's message to you and your abba Jehoash. Elohim is the one who restored Israel's boundaries from Hamath to the Dead Sea. Not King Jehoash. Not you. And certainly not me. Give Yahweh alone the glory — or prepare this nation to face His wrath."

The guards arrived just then and grabbed Jonah's arms roughly.

"He's an old man," Hosea said, shoving one soldier away. "You needn't force him. We'll leave." He placed a protective arm around Jonah's shoulders and walked toward the courtyard, shouting, "Israel is as stubborn as a bull. How can Yahweh feed you like lambs in open pasture? The people of Ephraim choose to worship idols, so we will leave you alone for now, but when you're done drinking your wine and lying with your prostitutes, the wind will carry you all away. Your sacrifices will bring you shame!"

"Remove them from my sanctuary!" Jeroboam shouted. "Resume the drums!"

Hosea heard the pounding begin again and glanced at Jonah, worried that the guards might have harmed him. Instead, he was met with a satisfied grin and a nod of approval.

"Nooo!" A woman's scream split the amiable moment.

Both prophets were shoved from the sanctuary while an old woman clawed and kicked at the soldiers leading her in. Blood streamed from her nose and a cut above her eye. She'd been beaten — probably by the massive soldier walking ahead of her. He held a squalling infant, swaddled and raised high above his head like an offering. Who was this woman? Too old to be the baby's ima, was she the savta, protecting her daughter's child?

Panic fueled Hosea's strength, and he made a final attempt to escape his captors. One of the soldiers landed a blow across his cheek with the hilt of his sword, and Jonah grabbed Hosea's forearm before he could fight back.

"No, my son," Jonah said. "We have been obedient to Yahweh's will. Now Israel must choose to repent and obey or engage in the single most abominable act of humankind. If they sacrifice that child in the fire, they'll be no better than the Canaanites, and they'll be driven from Yahweh's Promised Land into exile."

Hosea was given no time to think, no time to decide. The soldiers dragged both prophets outside the temple courtyard and threw them into the drainage ditch of Samaria's main street. They sat in the stench, listening as the drums beat faster and the crowd shouted louder.

It seemed to last an eternity. And then the drums stopped.

A single wail split the air, and Hosea pictured the beaten old woman. When the voice was snuffed out abruptly, he wondered what fate had befallen the only one who dared defy her nation.

4

[Yahweh said to Moses,] "You must give me your firstborn son. . . . They will stay with their mothers seven days, but on the eighth day you must give them to me."

Gomer watched in horror as Menahem's captain paraded through the frenzied crowd, holding the swaddled infant above his head. She'd been with many of Israel's most influential soldiers, but this man, Eitan, was second in cruelty to Menahem alone. The drums beat louder, faster, and she measured the guard's pace with his obvious destination. She angled through the crowd, arriving at the altar moments before Eitan.

"Please, please . . ." She knelt before him, the heat from the furnace nearly igniting her veils. But before she could continue, he swept her aside with a casual kick, and she

52

landed awkwardly on her side.

Merav saw her lying there and seemed torn about whom to protect — the babe destined for the fire, or Gomer, the girl she'd cared for so long. The moment passed and Gomer knew. Merav was saying good-bye.

Eitan held the infant aloft, facing the brazen image. He stood just a camel's length from the roaring flames while two guards held Merav between them. She had stopped struggling, but the blade of a dagger still glinted against her left side. Gomer bowed her head and wept.

"Do not let a bitter young man and a vindictive old prophet disillusion you, Israel." Amaziah raised his arms and shouted above the noise. The crowd quieted, but the drums kept pounding. "The priests of Israel know the Law of Moses as well as Jonah, but he selects the laws that serve his purpose. For didn't El also say to our great prophet Moses, 'You must give me your firstborn sons; they may stay with their imas for seven days, but on the eighth day you must give them to me'? It is El, the benign one, who has allowed Mot to overpower Prince Baal and keep the rains from us. So be warned, O godly Mot, that the fearsome Anat contemplates the battle. We will finally do as we've been told and offer a firstborn to the gods. Let our tidings stir Anat's fury, the desire for her lover, Baal. Let the rider of the clouds again grace the skies with thunder and lightning. Receive, O Baal, this offering, and pour down rain from the window of your palace." Israel's high priest dropped his arms, and the drums fell silent.

Eitan lofted the swaddled babe in a perfect arc into the altar flames, and in the same moment Merav lunged forward. Gomer watched the guard's dagger sink deep into her friend's side. Merav wilted where she stood, unable to make a sound.

"Nooo!" Gomer wailed and tried to crawl to her, but Eitan grabbed Gomer's hair and brought his knee into her belly. All breath left her.

"Get the old woman out of here," he whispered to his men through clenched teeth. "I'll take care of the harlot."

Music began playing again, and the crowd roared in celebration. Flutes and lyres joined the drums, reviving the frenzied worship, while Gomer lay gasping for breath. All around her, feet were dancing and harlots' bells tinkled.

"Rejoice," Amaziah exalted. "Rejoice with me, people of Israel! Surely our gods have heard our prayers and will answer us quickly. Take your pleasure where you find it, and may Asherah's fertile groves fill your every desire."

"Get up." Eitan jerked Gomer by her hair and trapped her ear against his lips. "You should know better than to detract from Amaziah's big moment. I'm afraid you'll have to pay for your poor judgment." He held her under one arm and dragged her toward the courtyard exit. She tried to struggle free, but he crushed her to his side.

Barely able to catch her breath because of the stabbing pain in her ribs, she croaked out the words, "What will happen to Merav's body?"

Eitan didn't answer. She assumed he was ignoring her concern, but after clearing the crowded courtyard, Eitan turned down a deserted street beside the temple and asked, "Who?"

"Merav, the old —"

Before she could finish, understanding lit his features. "You were wailing about the old hag, not the child? I should have known a woman like you would have no maternal instinct." He chuckled and shoved her into a corner.

The street ended at the courtyard wall. She had nowhere to run. "Please, Eitan. I'm the only family Merav had. I need to wash

55

and wrap her body for burial."

He raised an eyebrow. "So you remember my name? I'm flattered."

She saw an advantage, stepped toward him, and reached up to caress his cheek. "Of course I remember you. You're the only man —" White-hot pain seared her cheekbone, and she found herself on the ground looking up at the giant.

He yanked her to her feet and drew her close. "I'd love to hear all the wonderful things you would say about me, but I cannot let your actions go unpunished. Because I like you, I'll have the old woman's body sent to Tamir's brothel." He smiled, and Gomer's stomach knotted. "Unfortunately, I doubt that you'll be in any condition to prepare her for burial."

Then the blows began, and Gomer waited for sweet darkness to rescue her.

"I can't do it, Jonah." Hosea cut a slice of hard cheese and offered it to his friend. "Besides, Yahweh didn't say I must marry *Gomer*. He said I must marry a prostitute and have children with her. I didn't even know Gomer was a prostitute." Hosea's heart was in his throat at even acknowledging the fact.

Jonah cut a slice of cheese, placed it on a

piece of bread, and took a bite. Nodding. Chewing. He stared at the afternoon sun from their shady hillside outside of Samaria. They'd escaped the city when they heard the worship resume in Jeroboam's temple and waited here for Yahweh's instruction.

Jonah took another bite. Chewed. Watched travelers pass by on the road beyond. Took another bite.

"Say something!" Hosea's frustrated shout drew the attention of a nearby family, who quickly gathered their supplies and started toward town. "I know you have an opinion, and perhaps the Lord has even given you a message for me?"

Jonah set aside his meal and rested his elbow on his bent knee. "I believe everything you've just said is wishful thinking. First, you wish Yahweh would speak to me because you want someone else to tell you what's right. But *you* are God's prophet for this moment in Israel's history, my son. And then you wish for a prostitute you don't know because if you love her, she'll hurt you. But isn't the point of God's prophecy that you should feel His love and His pain? It seems to me this Gomer is the only woman who holds the same place in your heart that Israel holds with God. Who else could you ever love as you love this girl?"

"I don't love Gomer," he said, indignation rising.

"More wishful thinking." Jonah reached for the cheese and knife and began eating again.

"She was like a sister to me in Bethel. We were inseparable after our imas died during childbirth one month apart. Her abba and mine were priests, but her abba had a reputation for drink and violence. She was the girl who fell out of the rafters the day Amos prophesied, remember?"

Understanding dawned on Jonah's features. "She was the girl you begged your abba to betroth to you and take to Tekoa, but her abba wouldn't allow it."

Hosea's throat tightened, and he swallowed his warring emotions. "She was six when I left Bethel, Jonah. What happened to her?"

"She is a beautiful woman, Hosea, and she was a beautiful child." Jonah cleared his throat, keeping his head bowed. Hosea knew his tenderhearted friend was fighting to control his emotions. "If her abba refused Beeri's betrothal agreement and bride-price, we can assume he was certain of a better offer to come."

Hosea fell silent, allowing the terrible possibilities of Gomer's past to unfold. "I don't even know her anymore. The anger in her eyes was startling. And did you see the bells around her waist, on her hands and feet? Where did she get all those gold bangles and the ring in her nose and —"

"It seems to me," Jonah interrupted, "you did a lot of inspecting for a man who wasn't interested in that particular prostitute."

Hosea stood abruptly. From this angle, his mentor looked frail on the blanket they often shared — but he still held the power to unmask Hosea's soul. "What if she won't have me? What if she refuses to marry me?"

Jonah stood to face him. "We've been over that." He searched the windows of Hosea's soul, speaking more gently. "If she refuses you, then you'll experience Yahweh's broken heart for harlot Israel. But you'll pursue Gomer again — until she comes to you willingly." He wrapped the remaining bread and cheese in a small cloth and stuffed it into his shoulder bag. "That's what faithful prophets do. We keep obeying, and Yahweh works out the details." He patted Hosea's shoulder and then picked up his walking sticks. "We need to find your Gomer, signal Isaiah at the tombs, and get out of Samaria before they close the city gates for the night."

Hosea had nearly forgotten about Isaiah.

"What if someone has found Isaiah and stolen all of our provisions? Shouldn't we make sure he's safe before we promise a price for Gomer that we can't pay?" His heart began racing with his thoughts. "And where do we even *begin* to look for Gomer? We don't even know —"

"The Lord has led us this far, my son. Do you think He'll abandon us now?" Jonah hoisted his bag over his shoulder and started up the hill. "We'll find her and signal Isaiah to bring our silver and grain. We'll pay for Gomer if need be, and then we'll leave Samaria. Now come."

They joined the steady stream of travelers, walking the winding path toward Samaria's gates for the second time that day. Fifty cubits from the city entrance, musicians and dancers spilled into the streets. Hosea found himself staring at every scantily clad woman they passed. None of them were as beautiful as Gomer.

"Perhaps we should go to Asherah's grove," he said, uncertain if Jonah could hear over the laughter and noise.

"She was not dressed as a temple priestess, Hosea." The old prophet kept walking, turning right on the city's main street, the opposite direction of the temple. Hosea had worried that those walking sticks would tangle in the crowd and Jonah would go tumbling down the eastern slope of Samaria's main street, but he weaved and bobbed between revelers. Hosea barely kept up.

"Wait! How do you know we're headed in the right direction?" he shouted from behind the old prophet, who had seemingly been strengthened by the meal.

Jonah's answer came when he stopped a little girl on the street. Her robe was worn and tattered, but it was her face that distinguished her as a brothel servant. A bronze chain connected a small ring in her nose to an earring.

"Here, little one," he said, retrieving the hard cheese and bread from his shoulder bag.

She looked up with the eyes of a frightened bird caught in a fowler's snare. "What must I do to earn it, my lord?"

Hosea thought his heart would break in two.

"You must tell me the truth." Jonah's voice was stern, but the girl seemed no more fearful than before. "First, I must know your name."

She glanced right and left and then squared her shoulders. "First, I must have a bite of bread."

Hosea hid a smile and watched Jonah buy

his first portion of truth.

"My name is Jarah," she whispered, "and I'll tell the full truth if you give me the full portion of bread and cheese."

Jonah rubbed his milky-white chin as if deep in thought, and Hosea marveled that a frightened girl could be so resourceful. A worthy haggler, this one could be trusted.

"All right, Jarah, I've seen a certain harlot, and I wish to find her."

The girl giggled. "My lord, there are plenty of harlots all around you. Choose one."

Jonah's stern gaze sobered her into silence. "I want the harlot with copper-colored hair. She has a beauty mark on her left cheek and is known by the name Gomer."

Jarah's smile fell and took Hosea's hopes with it. She pushed away the bread and cheese Jonah had offered. "The woman you seek won't be seeing customers for a very long time — if ever. She belongs to my brothel, and Mistress Tamir has sent me to fetch the physician. If he can restore Gomer, my mistress will pay for her remedies. If not . . ." She shrugged her shoulder as if Gomer's life was as regretful as the lost bread and cheese.

5

HOSEA 8:5–6

Get rid of your calf-shaped idol. . . . Samaria's calf-shaped idol was made in
Israel. . . . It is not a god. It will be smashed
to pieces.

"Take us to her!" Hosea shoved Jonah aside
and shook Jarah's shoulders. "What happened to Gomer? Why does she need a
physician?"

Jonah stepped between them and shielded
the girl, who looked almost as pale as the
old prophet.

"I can't return to the brothel without the
physician or I'll be beaten. I've already
wasted too much time and will probably feel
Tamir's strap." With a final longing look at
the bread and cheese, she slipped past them
into the bustling crowd.

Hosea reached out to stop her, but Jonah

swatted him. "Move your feet and not your mouth," he whispered, already falling into step behind the girl. "We'll watch her until she returns to the brothel with the physician. Then we'll go in and talk with the owner. It's this Tamir that holds Gomer's future in her hands, not Jarah."

Keeping pace with the serving maid wasn't an easy task. Several times they lost sight of her in the crowded streets. Hosea skirted around corners, running ahead of Jonah to find her. Finally, they spotted Jarah hurrying back down the hill, accompanied by a stooped old man carrying a shoulder bag. *Yahweh, give him wisdom,* Hosea prayed, assuming the man must be the physician. He and Jonah slowed, observing from the shadows as the girl led the man through a brothel gate.

Jonah stopped, his breathing erratic and panting. "Wait, my son." He leaned over, bracing himself with the walking sticks.

"Are you all right?" Hosea steadied him and felt the old man's sweaty tunic.

Nodding, Jonah stood and leaned back against the wall. "I just need to catch my breath and be sure you are listening to Yahweh and not to your heart alone." He reached up and placed a firm hand on Hosea's beating chest. "Consider God's

64

purpose in all that is happening before you react out of fear or anger, or both. Remember you are in Samaria to marry a prostitute. We came prepared to buy a woman's freedom from her owner, but if Gomer has been injured beyond usefulness, this Tamir may give her to you, and then we can use the funds to stay in Samaria until Gomer is well enough to travel. Either way, you will need a clear head to negotiate and hear Yahweh's instruction."

Hosea tried to steady himself with a deep breath. Jonah was right. He would have marched through the brothel gates and done anything, said anything, paid anything to get Gomer away from this place. But then what?

Yahweh, if Gomer is the prostitute You would have me marry, let her heart be softened enough that she'll become my wife willingly. He glanced at Jonah and found his mentor's eyes just opening. It seemed their prayers had ascended as one to God's throne.

"At least now I'm certain I want to marry Gomer." Hosea offered a rueful smile, and Jonah nodded his approval.

"Hail the gatekeeper, and let's negotiate for your bride."

"Shalom this house!" Hosea shouted and

peered through the gate, its cedar planks reinforced by iron plates and a single barred window at eye level. Hosea peeked inside and found the inner courtyard deserted and disheveled. Contents of water jars and food baskets had been toppled over and spilled out. He pounded harder. "I've come to inquire after one of your harlots!"

The brothel was a two-story dwelling with several hallways converging on the open courtyard. Hosea thought he sensed someone stirring in one of the darkened walkways. "You! Whoever you are. Go tell your mistress that I come to bargain for Gomer. I might help pay for her care." At this, he saw the swish of a robe and heard footsteps running away.

"Well done." Jonah squeezed his shoulder, and they waited in silence.

But not for long.

A middle-aged woman emerged from a shadowy hallway, her head covered with a purple scarf and a circle of black braids extending from an intricately woven headpiece. She walked with quick, choppy steps, carrying a mug of something steaming — as if Hosea had interrupted her leisurely afternoon with a friend.

"What is this about someone paying for Gomer's care?" she asked. A hulking male servant accompanied her and opened the gate. Hosea stepped forward, leaving Jonah hidden behind the stone wall. The woman examined the young prophet from head to toe and lifted one corner of her red lips. "I am the owner, Tamir, and you must be one of Gomer's regulars to be so generous. Perhaps you would be willing to enjoy one of my other girls while Gomer is recovering from today's mishap."

The offering of women as though they were trinkets made Hosea's blood boil. A coarser man would have slapped the painted smile from her face. Instead, he said with strict control, "I will know every detail of today's events before you see one shekel of my silver."

Tamir leveled her gaze, meeting the challenge. "I will tell you what pertains to Gomer and nothing more." She stepped back and extended her hand in welcome, laughing without humor. "But as usual, what pertains to Gomer is more than enough to make a compelling story."

Hosea motioned to Jonah, and he slipped through the gate, unnoticed by the brothel owner. The servant locked the gate, and Tamir led her guests across the courtyard.

"I want the details now, before I see her," Hosea said, stopping short of the hallway.

"I'll assume you were at the temple sacrifice this morning," she said, turning casually.

Then she saw Jonah.

"You!" she said to the pale-white prophet as her mug slipped from her hand and shattered into pieces. "Get out! Both of you! If the high priest or king discovers you've been here, they'll shut me down."

The servant reached for the old prophet's arm, but Hosea shoved him away and glared at Tamir. "Give us Gomer and we'll leave. From what we hear, she's of no use to you anymore."

She signaled her servant to stand down and pinned Hosea with a stare. "From what you hear? Well, let me tell you the *facts* about your pretty little harlot, Prophet. After you and your ghostly friend here were dragged from the temple, I saw my midwife fight to save an infant that meant nothing to anyone. And because Gomer cared too much for that midwife, she foolishly disrupted Jeroboam's first real sacrifice to the gods. So General Menahem's captain had to teach Gomer a lesson."

She shoved Hosea's shoulder, moving him back toward the gate. "Now for all our sakes, get out of my house, and get out of Samaria. If you involve yourself with Gomer, you interfere with the royal house and its officials. And if you continue to spout ridiculous predictions of Israel's demise, you'll bring down Mot's fury on everyone you hold dear." She nodded toward her gatekeeper, and the hulking servant seized the back of Hosea's neck.

Nearly immobilized, Hosea turned where he was aimed and walked where he was pushed. His last attempt was a single shout. "She is worthless to you if she dies, and I have come from the company of Judah's prophets with enough wealth to buy a bride." He heard no response, but the servant stopped pushing, so he added another plea. "She'll drain your resources if you have to pay a physician. Why not give her to me and get her out of your house?"

Still in the giant's grasp and facing the gate, Hosea heard Tamir's voice like a trumpet at daybreak. "Because if I give her to you, I'll be on the wrong side of this quarrel between you and the high priest. I've built my business on a relationship with Amaziah. Temple priestesses, street harlots, and now male babies for sacrifice." Suddenly freed from the hand on his neck, Hosea turned and found Tamir waiting at the hallway entry. "Why would I destroy my golden calf?"

A quick glance at Jonah confirmed that the old prophet had caught the irony of her question. Yahweh had foretold that He would someday destroy Samaria's idols: the corrupt national leaders, the spiritually unfaithful Israelites, and the literal golden calf images in the temples of Bethel and Dan.

Yahweh, did You just use a brothel owner to assure me of Your presence in this moment? Hosea breathed out his wonder.

He took one step toward Tamir, speaking with renewed confidence — extending his hand, coaxing. "Let us accompany you to talk with the physician. If he says Gomer will recover, we'll leave, but if she's of no further use as a harlot, then allow me to pay you a bride-price."

The woman stared at him for an interminable moment — and turned abruptly, walking down the dark hallway from which she'd come. He cast a victorious glance at both Jonah and the hulking servant and prayed a new prayer, following the mistress through winding hallways.

Yahweh, let Gomer's injuries be severe enough to save her life.

Gomer sensed movement around her. She heard voices, hushed. Men and one woman.

Then pain — but only her head. Oh, but her head felt as if it would shatter into a thousand pieces. She tried to adjust her position.

Nothing moved. Her arms and legs felt like giant boulders attached to her lifeless body.

Panic seeped in as memories of being beaten assaulted her. Eitan. His enormous fists. His repeated kicks when she curled into a ball. Trying now to focus her eyes, she saw four blurred figures standing near her sleeping mat. She peered through one slit, identifying Tamir — but who were the others?

"I won't know how severe her injuries are until she wakes up," an old man was saying. "The blood from her ears is a bad sign. The extensive bruising on her neck and back could also mean permanent damage."

"What . . ." Gomer's voice sounded like a croak, but it was enough to bring all four blurry figures to her side. Tamir knelt at her right, and Gomer now recognized the old man kneeling on her left as Samaria's physician. Her breath caught when she saw Hosea and that fish prophet, Jonah, positioned just beyond the others. Panting, gasping, she tried to move away, but all she could do was cry out, "No! No!" Surely they'd come to pronounce judgment on her just like they'd condemned Israel's king and priests.

Hosea shoved Tamir aside and cradled Gomer, pressing his lips to her forehead. "Shh, little one. I know you're frightened, but Yahweh has sent us here to rescue you." He'd spoken in a whisper, but now he raised his voice to the others. "What must we do to determine the extent of her injuries?" She felt his warm breath on her face but had no sensation of his arms around her.

Gomer watched Tamir standing over Hosea's shoulder. She looked angry. Gomer turned to see what the physician was doing. He was kneeling beside her . . .

"By the gods, get him away from me!" she screamed.

All eyes focused on the doctor crouched at Gomer's side, cradling her arm, where he'd made a single, long cut with his dagger. Blood was flowing onto her sleeping mat, but she felt nothing. Her momentary panic was replaced with a sort of morbid fascination. "How can I not feel that?" she whispered.

"That's enough!" Hosea snatched the dagger from the physician's hand and threw it across the small room.

The physician, too, seemed eerily intrigued. "I've never seen anyone survive a beating this severe. I can't imagine any hope of this girl regaining the use of her arms or legs, but I'll need to continue regular visits in order to keep record of her progress."

The room spun, and Gomer felt as if she might lose what little breakfast she'd eaten. The edges of her vision grew dark, and a loud roar consumed her. Perhaps she would die after all.

"I wish to have her as my bride."

Hosea's words were like a cold splash of water, reviving her to the dark present.

"How much are you willing to pay for such a beauty?" Tamir loomed over his shoulder, tension stretching her lips into a forced smile.

"Wait," Gomer whispered, but everyone heard.

Again Hosea pressed a kiss to her forehead. "I have waited too long as it is. I wanted to arrange our betrothal before I left Bethel, Gomer, but your abba wouldn't allow it. Now I wish to make you my wife."

Her head spun. The lamplight faded. Surely she was dreaming. Would Hosea be gone again when she woke?

6

HOSEA 5:4

The wicked things that the people have done keep them from returning to their Elohim. They have a spirit of prostitution, and they don't know Yahweh.

Gomer's head lolled back, eyes closed, and Hosea's heart stopped beating. "Gomer?" He drew her to his chest and rocked her. "You can't die! I've just found you again." Violent sobs shook him as he buried his face in her blood-caked curls. A low moan escaped her lips, and he gasped.

"Lay her back on the mat." The physician reached out to help but recoiled at Hosea's threatening stare.

Hosea sat with his legs outstretched and cradled her in his lap. "Gomer?"

She moaned again, her swollen eyes fluttering. Her right eye too bruised to open, she peered through the narrow slit of her left eye. "Am I dreaming?" she whispered, a single tear rolling into her copper hair.

He choked on his answer, part sob, part chuckle. "Well, that depends. Did you dream that I asked you to be my wife?" He brushed her tear away, but instead of the welcome he'd hoped for, she turned her face from him.

"Leave, Hosea. Forget you saw me, and pretend I'm still the innocent girl you once knew." She lay in his arms because she couldn't push him away.

The physician reached for Gomer's arm. Hosea hugged her close and shoved the man away. "You'll not touch her again."

"The wound needs dressed," he said, motioning to the bandages in his hand. "I must pack it with herbs to stop the bleeding."

Hosea nodded permission and laid Gomer back on the mat. While the physician worked, Hosea leaned over her and whispered, "When we were children, I let you lead in our adventures, and we often found ourselves in trouble for it." He smiled, hoping her spirit would lighten with the memory. When she didn't respond, he leaned closer. "This time I can't let you lead, Gomer. I must obey Yahweh, and you must obey me." He saw a spark in her eye — a little rebellion that told him the fiery Gomer he once knew still lived behind those beautiful hazel eyes. "I command you to live, Gomer, and I plan to make you my wife tonight."

She closed her eye, squeezing out another tear, and released a long sigh. At least she didn't refuse.

He planted a kiss on her forehead and turned to Tamir. "I will give you a fair bride-price, but I will not haggle. I realize the drought has hit Israel hard, so I will give you fifteen pieces of silver plus the equivalent in barley. It is my one and final offer."

He noticed perspiration forming on the woman's top lip. "But what about —"

Hosea lifted a hand to silence her negotiation. "It is my one and final offer." He turned to the physician, noting Gomer's arm had been tended and bandaged. "I will pay you a fair price for your service today, but you will never touch my wife again. She will be under my care from now on."

"I require five shekels for the care she received today."

Hosea raised one eyebrow. "You'll get three shekels and realize that we are generous but not fools."

Both greedy Israelites sputtered their

discontent, suggesting counteroffers and arguments for more and better terms. Hosea's stubborn silence won out, and the physician packed his supplies, muttering curses under his breath. He stormed from the room without an escort — evidently familiar with the brothel's winding hallways.

Tamir hovered behind Hosea and then leaned over his shoulder. Gomer opened her left eye, seeming to sense her owner's presence. Tamir spoke to Hosea but aimed her sharp tone at Gomer. "I will accept your offer, but I do not want to know anything about her. When she leaves my gates, she is dead to me."

Gomer closed her eye and turned away.

Tamir straightened, standing over them both. "Are we agreed?"

Hosea nodded, a cold chill racing up his spine. "Agreed." He glanced down at Gomer, and seeing another tear roll from the corner of her eye, he felt renewed pity. *Has anyone ever loved you, Gomer?*

Tamir turned to leave, but Jonah stopped her at the door. "We'll need to stay in Samaria until Gomer is recovered enough to travel. Would you be so kind as to send someone to sit with Gomer while Hosea and I search for a house to rent?"

"No," she said flatly. "I would not be so

kind. Everyone in this house works for their living." Tamir pushed past him toward the door.

"What about the girl —" Hosea began, but Jonah cast silent daggers at him before he mentioned Jarah's name.

Tamir stopped, turned slowly, like a predator luring prey. "And what *girl* would you suggest, Prophet?"

Hosea's mind reeled to protect Jarah. "Uh . . . perhaps the girl you offered me when you thought I was one of Gomer's paying customers?"

Her eyes narrowed as she measured his answer. "If you'd like to pay for another girl's services, I don't care what you do with her. Otherwise, Gomer waits alone." Tamir stormed from the room, and both Jonah and Hosea released a simultaneous sigh.

"I will go alone," Jonah whispered. "I'll use our blanket to signal Isaiah at the tombs as we had planned. This is about the time of day we told him to be watching." The old prophet laid a comforting hand on Hosea's shoulder. "The circumstances are different than we imagined, but Isaiah will still get to serve as friend of the bridegroom while I recite your wedding blessing. Yahweh is faithful, my son." He nodded his farewell and slipped from the room, closing the curtain behind him.

"You should have gone with him." Gomer's voice was low and scratchy. "An old man alone isn't safe in this city." She kept her good eye closed so she didn't have to look at Hosea. She couldn't look at him.

"Jonah traveled alone to Nineveh and back. I think he can manage Samaria's streets."

She heard mocking in his voice, and it made her furious. She opened her eye as far as the swelling allowed, gritting her teeth against the burst of pain. "Why are you doing this? Just let me die."

The emotion on his face was unreadable. He'd been kneeling, awkwardly hovering, but now he sat back. Perhaps he'd finally given up.

She bit back a small gasp when he repositioned and lay beside her, pulling her closer. "What are you doing?" Her body was dead weight, numb and motionless. "You heard the physician. What if I never regain the use of my arms or legs? I can't be a wife, Hosea."

He propped himself up on an elbow, leaning over, breathing his promise on her cheek. "I won't let you die because as soon as Jonah returns with the bride-price, you *will* be my wife." His lips brushed her ear lightly. "Yahweh has spoken to me, Gomer. He told me to go to Israel, to marry a pros —" Hesitating, he stumbled over the word.

"How do you expect to marry me when you can't even say the word?" Emotion seized her, but she forced the words past her lips. "You don't know what I am — what I've *done*!" Her stomach churned; bile choked her. She cursed her lifeless limbs, wishing she could run far and fast from this godly man who couldn't fathom what a woman must do to survive.

The caress of his long, slow sigh against her neck was both excruciating and enticing. He leaned down and whispered, "Yahweh said, 'Marry a prostitute, and have children with that prostitute.' I believe the Lord plans to heal you and give us a houseful of children, Gomer. From this moment forward, I will love you — as Yahweh loves Israel." He leaned back, searching her face, his yearning so innocent it pierced her. "Do you understand what that kind of love means?"

"I understand that you've been swindled." Her voice was becoming stronger, perhaps fueled by anger born of hopelessness. "You paid a bride-price for a harlot who will never feel your touch or satisfy your desire.

How dare you appear from the great beyond after leaving me in Bethel at the mercy of my abba? Do you expect me to trust you now, Hosea? If you're lucky, I'll die before Jonah returns with the bride-price, and you can go back to your holy prophets in Judah, marry a boring wife, and raise fat babies!" Her final words escaped on a torrent of sobs.

Hosea's arms consumed her, and her useless arms couldn't even push him away. Oh, the utter humiliation of being at the mercy of another! When would *she* make the decisions? When would *she* have a choice?

With a voice as stony as her heart, she said, "Get off me."

Startled, Hosea held her at arm's length. She must have appeared quite a paradox with her granite countenance and tear-streaked face. Hosea's confused expression brought her a measure of satisfaction.

"You asked if I understood a marriage relationship. The answer is yes. I'm a harlot, not an imbecile."

She saw the first walls erected around his heart. He sat up, leaving his intimate repose. *Good. Maybe he's not as slow-witted as I feared.* She averted her gaze, not trusting her emotions if his compassion should return.

"I'm sorry, Gomer," he said, his voice

controlled, "but you misunderstood my question. I said nothing of a marriage relationship. I asked if you understood the kind of *love* Yahweh feels for Israel."

Oh, by the gods, was this to be her life? A tedious treatise on Hosea's tiresome god? "I'm familiar with the marriage of the gods," she said, hoping to cut short his explanation. "I was trained in the temple of Asherah at age ten when Abba Diblaim sold me. I know that when El married Asherah, they respected one another but maintained their independence." Guilt nibbled at the edges of her heart. "I realize I may have been less than respectful to you . . ." Her words trailed off into silence. Finally, wondering why her talkative companion had gone mute, she was more than a little surprised to see a storm gathering on his features.

"Independence?" Hosea said, his voice bearing subtle remnants of his adolescent squeak. "You think this holy relationship is about *independence*?"

"And respect," she added.

"No!" he said before she could spout any more nonsense about her silly gods. "You have no idea what Yahweh's love entails. He adores Israel and calls her His treasure. He wants nothing more than to be the object of her singular love and devotion. His heart breaks when she runs after other gods or is deceived by false priests and prophets into believing that other gods can offer the same blessing He longs to pour out on His people."

Gomer closed her good eye, curving her lips into a mocking grin. "If your Yahweh loves Israel so much, why did I hear you tell Amaziah that He is going to destroy us all? Face the truth, Hosea. Sometimes people have wandered too far to return." Her wry smile died on that beautiful, bruised face. "Sometimes people don't deserve to be loved."

In that moment, God's voice resounded like a ram's horn in Hosea's spirit: *The wicked things My people have done keep them from returning to their Elohim.* And he knew Gomer's callousness was the armor of a warrior who thought herself too scarred from life's battles to ever be loved. He brushed her cheek with the back of his hand, all fury melting away.

Gomer recoiled, but this time he wasn't angry. "Rest now," he said. "When Jonah returns, I want to make you my wife."

She didn't respond.

He lay down beside her again but didn't

hold her. Instead, he tucked a blanket around her and kissed her cheek. "Sleep. I'll be right here when you wake up."

Gomer woke to the sound of men's voices in her room, dim lamplight, and chilly night air. The coppery taste of blood lingered in her mouth, and her head still throbbed — now a dull ache rather than clanging cymbals. Someone was dabbing a cold cloth on her forehead.

"Hosea?"

"No, it's me," came a little girl's squeak.

She tried to open her eyes and discovered both were in working order. Jarah, the kitchen maid, knelt beside her, washed and dressed in her finest robe and tunic.

"What . . ." But before Gomer questioned the girl, Hosea knelt at her left side.

"You look better. The swelling is down and both eyes are open."

"Who is that?" Her gaze motioned to the handsome young man standing with the fish prophet.

Hosea seemed to understand and swept the hair off her forehead. "Jonah brought my friend Isaiah back from the tombs. We've paid Tamir the agreed price, and Jonah rented a small house on the other side of town." He paused, gazed into her eyes with some undecipherable emotion. "Everything is in place to perform a simple wedding ceremony. Isaiah will serve as friend of the bridegroom. Jonah will pronounce the blessing, and Jarah" — he motioned to the girl kneeling a cubit from them — "will be your virgin attendant." He leaned close, a wry smile creasing his lips. "We had a little trouble finding a maiden among your . . . *associates* . . . who qualified for the honor."

Gomer smiled in spite of herself and noted Jarah's pink cheeks. "I'm glad you chose her. She's my favorite."

The girl stifled a small gasp. "Thank you, Mistress Gomer."

She returned her attention to Hosea, noticing his smile had fled.

"I believe Yahweh has chosen you to be my wife, Gomer, but I will not force you to marry me." He lifted his voice for all to hear. "Before Yahweh and these witnesses, do you *choose* to be my wife?"

Gomer's heart thundered in her chest, its beat resounding in her ears like the drums at the temple this morning. She had lamented her lack of choices, demanded her opportunity to decide. How did Hosea know what she needed — when she needed it? Suddenly, a strange calm swept over her, as it often had when they were children.

Hosea used to take her hand in his and strum her fingers like a harp. Just like he was doing now . . .

"Hosea!" She lifted her head and looked at her lifeless hand lying at her side. He had indeed been strumming her fingers. "I felt your touch! Strum my fingers again!"

He laughed and cried and strummed her fingers, rejoicing with her at the hope of recovery. While the others celebrated, Hosea lifted her into his arms and kissed her. Not the friendly peck of a ten-year-old boy, but the sweet passion of a bridegroom longing for his bride.

Breathless, she whispered, "Yes, I will marry you."

7

ISAIAH 2:1

This is the message which Isaiah, son of Amoz, saw about Judah and Jerusalem.

Gomer sat in the narrow shade of their small rented house on Samaria's northeast side, listening to the birdsong — and to Jonah's snoring. The fish prophet said he'd seen seventy summers. Gomer felt certain he'd slept through fifty.

"You must cinch it tighter, Hosea. Here, let me do it." Isaiah snatched the leather strap from his friend's hand, and Gomer's slow boil rose to full steam.

The bossy young messenger had taken over the two-wheeled cart project that Hosea was building and Gomer designed. Her injuries had healed nicely in the past three Sabbaths, but she still wasn't strong enough to saw or tie or lift. So Hosea let

Isaiah "help."

"Hosea was doing just fine," she shouted across the courtyard. "If you make the strap too tight, the baskets won't flex as a back support, and the strap will break."

Jonah expelled an enormous snort and startled himself on his teetering stool. Hosea chuckled, but Isaiah leveled a challenging stare at Gomer. "If you think you can do better . . ." He stepped back and invited her with a sweep of his hand.

She refused to be cowed and grabbed one of Jonah's walking sticks to push herself to stand. Hosea rushed to help, but she shoved him away. "Leave me alone." She hardly noticed the hurt in his eyes anymore. What did he expect? A street harlot one day, a loving wife the next?

A few excruciating steps, and she was face-to-face with her husband's handsome friend who despised her. "Say what you wish to say to me, and then I see no need for us to speak again." She lifted her chin, pleased at his shocked expression.

"Isaiah . . ." Hosea stood between them, sweat beading his brow. "She is my wife."

"She is a *prostitute.*" The word spewed from his mouth like vomit. "She is a symbol of everything Yahweh despises in Israel, and yet you treat her as if she is fine pottery

88

from Egypt." He turned his mocking smile on Gomer. "I am grateful to you for one thing. Your black heart has shown me all that my lovely Aya is not. I will marry a pure and holy maiden when we return to Tekoa, a woman whose heart is right with her God and who knows how to love."

Gomer had no words. She began to tremble and knew she must escape or lose all control in front of this *child* who had peeled away layers of carefully placed armor. A nod was her reply.

She turned and started for the house. Jonah stood at the door, his eyes full of tears. *No! I don't want your pity!* she wanted to scream. And then she felt Hosea's hand on her arm. "No! Don't touch me!" He obeyed, stopping in the courtyard while she retreated into the lone private chamber of their rented house.

Was life as a prophet's wife supposed to be better? At least as a harlot she had the respect of her peers. She knew she didn't deserve love, but had she given up all hope of friendship as well?

"How could you, Isaiah?" Hosea asked when Gomer disappeared into the house. He spun on his heel and rushed at him, grabbed the collar of Isaiah's robe, and lifted him off the ground. "How could you say those things?" he screamed.

"I am a prophet, and we've been taught that prophets must say hard things sometimes."

Hosea released him, breathless, wordless. He felt Jonah's hand on his shoulder, pulling him aside.

"How did Yahweh's voice manifest to you, Isaiah?" the old man asked. "What proof did Yahweh's Spirit give you that you could grasp when others questioned your motives — like we're doing right now?"

Isaiah's face shaded deep crimson. "I didn't hear Yahweh's voice word for word, but —"

"That was not prophecy, Isaiah," Jonah's voice thundered. "It was your jealousy speaking, wishing you'd been given a prophetic mission before Hosea."

"I'm not jealous of him. Why would I want to marry a prostitute?"

Hosea's heart shattered into smaller pieces.

Jonah paused, allowing silence to stress his words. "You've made your disdain for Gomer clear. Your childish tantrum and inability to comprehend Yahweh's heart has revealed your immaturity. You're not ready for Yahweh's call, Isaiah."

All color drained from Isaiah's face. He and Hosea watched Jonah hobble to the house with one walking stick. Hosea folded his legs and sat, too numb to fight.

His humbled friend sat beside him. " 'I'm sorry' hardly seems enough — but it's where I'll start."

Hosea nodded but couldn't yet bring himself to accept Isaiah's apology. How would he ever unsay the hurtful things Gomer had heard? "You were wrong. She's not the symbol of all Yahweh *despises* in Israel. She's all that He seeks to redeem — the brokenness, the confusion, the lost lamb that needs a shepherd." Isaiah rubbed his face and sighed deeply, nodding his head in what Hosea hoped was a vow to see her afresh. "But you were also right about Gomer. She doesn't yet know how to love. I think Yahweh wants me to teach her."

Isaiah cocked his head, furrowed his brow. "It seems you've already started. Please don't misinterpret what I'm about to say, but . . . she hasn't said a civil word to you since we moved her from that brothel. Yet you seem to care for her. How can that be?"

Hosea shook his head, a slow smile forming. He looked at his reckless young friend and clapped a hand on his shoulder. "I must have a soft spot for people who need forgiveness."

Gomer glanced at the wool and spindle lying on her sleeping mat and then cursed the lumpy thread beside it. What was Hosea thinking? A harlot didn't spin wool. If he'd like her to paint his nails with henna or line his eyes with kohl, she'd be happy to oblige.

Today marked her fourth day in the private chamber, and she'd be content to die there. If she ever saw Isaiah again, it would be too soon. How could he describe her so accurately after knowing her for only three Sabbaths? She *was* everything this Yahweh god despised, if all Hosea had said at Jeroboam's sacrifice was true. But when Isaiah exposed her utter inability to love — *that* was the dagger to her heart. Her black heart.

"Gomer?" Isaiah's voice sliced through her from the other side of the curtained doorway.

She said nothing, hoping he would think she'd died.

"Gomer, please. I need to talk to you. I want to apologize."

Her heart pounded. If she allowed him in, where could she escape? This was her sanctuary, her only retreat. He drew back the curtain, and indignation replaced her fear. "I did not give you permission to enter!"

"I know, but —"

"Who do you think you are — a king? I am no longer a harl —"

"No, but I'm the cousin of Judah's king."

Her mouth went dry, and words failed her. She hated the satisfied grin on his face but didn't dare heap more condemnation on her already long list of offenses. If Isaiah was royalty, she would undoubtedly be executed the minute they arrived in Jerusalem.

He walked in and seated himself across from her. "Hosea loves you." A slight pause. "And I love Hosea like a brother. I see that the way I've treated you hurts both of you — and I'm sorry, Gomer."

She tried not to roll her eyes but evidently failed at hiding her disdain.

"Why do you do that?" Mounting frustration tightened his jaw. *Cousin to the king, cousin to the king.* She must try to be respectful. It hadn't been long since she'd played the harlot with many men. This would be no different. She softened her tone, painted on a smile, demurred. "Please forgive me, my lord. I have not been myself since the beating. I ask your patience and will make a better effort in the future." She kept her head bowed to hide her unmasked anger.

Silence stretched into awkwardness. Finally, Isaiah's voice quivered as he spoke. "That's why you frighten me."

Gomer snapped to attention, finding the young royal staring at her — as if she were Mot from the underworld. "I frighten you?" she asked, mocking. "You're the righteous one, raised in the security of your perfect prophets' world."

But Isaiah didn't draw his verbal sword this time. His expression seemed almost . . . vulnerable. "You so easily deceive, and I've witnessed the destruction that deceit and idolatry bring to a nation — to a family."

"What would a *royal* Yahweh student know of idolatry?"

"King Uzziah is my cousin, my abba's nephew. But because their ages are similar, they grew up more like brothers. Abba Amoz hated deceit and palace politics, so he moved to Lachish and learned the pottery trade. When Uzziah's abba, King Amaziah, turned to idolatry, conspirators in Jerusalem sought to take his life, so he fled to Lachish for Abba's shelter. Assassins followed Amaziah there and killed him. Abba has always felt responsible."

"But he wasn't responsible," Gomer protested. "It was the zealots — those men who wouldn't allow King Amaziah to worship other gods."

"No, Gomer. Uncle Amaziah was responsible. Each one of us must choose whom — or what — we worship."

Gomer's blood ran cold. "How can you be so narrow-minded? So certain Yahweh is the only god?"

"Because He proves Himself to each one of us — if we are willing to set aside the distractions and desires that draw us away from Him. That's why Uzziah commanded Abba Amoz to move closer to Jerusalem. He feared Abba would succumb to Lachish's idolatry while mourning my ima's death — she died while giving me life."

"I'm sorry, Isaiah." Gomer's sympathy was stirred, but she wasn't yet ready for a truce. Besides, some of his story didn't make sense. "If King Uzziah commanded your abba to move to Jerusalem, why were you raised with Hosea at the prophets' camp?"

A slight grin began but died before it reached his eyes. "Yahweh had blessed Uzziah's reign in both military and building campaigns. He purchased land in the foothills around Jerusalem and then began building towers and cisterns in the wilderness to fortify the nation of Judah. He'd spent some time in the Tekoan wilderness and knew there was plenty of clay soil to supply a workshop. Knowing Abba hated politics, Uzziah asked the prophet Amos if he could build a pottery workshop on his farm. An agreement was struck, and I grew up at the camp." A sad smile creased his lips, and Gomer saw a thousand unspoken words behind his eyes.

"I'm sorry you never knew your ima, but it sounds like a pretty perfect life to me, Isaiah."

He held her gaze, pondering, and then he stood, holding out his hand. She accepted, feeling somewhat better about Hosea's hostile friend.

He reached for the curtain, pulled it aside, but stopped just before they left her self-imposed prison. "I have a good life, Gomer. But at least you knew why your abba gave you away. Mine lives in the same camp, but he let others raise me — and I have no idea why."

8

HOSEA 6:3

Let's learn about Yahweh. Let's get to know Yahweh. He will come to us as sure as the morning comes.

Hosea glanced behind him to ensure he wasn't being followed before entering their courtyard. They had lived in Samaria undetected for two full moon cycles. Tomorrow they'd leave for Judah. After closing and locking the gate, he took a single step . . .

Crash!

He flinched, glancing down at the clay pitcher that now lay in shards at his feet, thankful he'd leaned right to latch the gate instead of left. The familiar verbal battle raged between his wife and best friend.

"You will not treat me like a stupid cow!" Gomer's fists were balled on her hips, her face as red as her hair. "You're a year younger than me, and you have no right to instruct or command me."

"I have *every* right to instruct you in the ways of Yahweh," Isaiah fired back. "And I'll stop treating you like a stupid cow when you stop acting like a —"

"Enough!" Hosea barked from where he stood, causing both combatants to fume in silence. "Isaiah, you will speak respectfully to my wife." He saw the look of triumph she cast in Isaiah's direction. "And Gomer, that's the second pitcher you've broken since last Sabbath. We can't afford your little tantrums." Her triumph turned to seething, and she aimed her anger at him.

"I might not indulge these little *tantrums* if I hadn't been held captive for two full moons."

Hosea recognized the pain beneath her anger. When her injuries were still severe, she'd been satisfied to sit in the courtyard, enjoying the spring sunshine. Now that she was almost recovered, she was as restless as a lion on the prowl.

"I know it's difficult to remain hidden, but you know if any of Jeroboam's men recognize you, we could all be arrested — or worse."

Her expression remained like granite, unmoved by logic or reason. He reached into his shoulder bag and drew out the sky-blue piece of linen he'd purchased at the market. It was the length of two camels, finely woven, as smooth as silk from the east — but much more practical for daily wear.

Her lips softened into a begrudging grin. "It must have cost you dearly. Who is it for?"

He laughed, but felt a twinge of sadness when Isaiah slipped into the house. Hosea would talk with him later about his relationship with Gomer. He had asked Isaiah to teach her Yahweh's Law since Gomer was still wary of Jonah. Even after these long Sabbaths in the same house, she still referred to the old man as "the fish prophet." He'd hoped Isaiah's chats with her would spark a friendship between them. His hopes had been in vain.

"Are you saving that veil for your next wife?" Gomer's question drew him back to the moment.

He closed the distance between them, and she stepped back. *Still afraid I'll force myself on you?* The thought pierced him. He'd promised himself — and Yahweh — he wouldn't lie with her until she invited him. "I bought the veil for you to wear in the market. You're a married woman now," he said with a slight grin. "You must never appear in public without a veil."

99

"More rules," she muttered.

Anger stirred, his patience wearing thin. "This *rule* might cover your hair and hide your appearance enough to visit the market before we go back to Tekoa tomorrow. But if you don't feel like wearing the veil . . ." He let the words hang, waiting with wicked delight as his stubborn wife submitted to the reality of her circumstance.

She grabbed the cloth from his hand and limped resolutely toward their courtyard gate. "I'm going to the market alone," she said. "Don't you dare follow me."

Hosea caught her arm and whirled her to face him. She winced in pain and stumbled, but he scooped her into his arms and curled her into his chest. "Are you all right?" he whispered. "I'm sorry."

She shoved him away, and he nearly dropped her. "Put me down!"

He gently placed her feet on the ground, and he saw her wince. His heart twisted. Her legs and hips hadn't fully recovered after the beating. *Yahweh, remind me that she's fragile.*

The commotion must have summoned Jonah and Isaiah. They stood at the doorway of the house, watching.

"I'm going to the market *alone,*" Gomer said, staring at each of the male faces before her. "I have done everything you've asked of me for eight Sabbaths. You can at least give me an afternoon to say good-bye to the city I called home."

Gomer fought with the silly blue veil Hosea had purchased for her, wrapping it to hide her copper curls and distinctive features. She wondered if her regular customers would recognize her. The bruises were gone, but she no longer wore paints on her eyes, cheeks, and lips. No more bangles or bells, and her dowdy brown robe covered the long scar on her forearm from the physician's blade. Hosea said she was still . . . Well, he always said she was beautiful, but who could trust a man's opinion?

Hosea. What did he want from her? Didn't he expect what all men took from their wives? So why hadn't he forced her? He wasn't shy. Each time they were together, he stood too close, touched her cheek, whispered on her neck.

"Watch where you're going!" A grousing old crone shoved Gomer aside and interrupted her brooding.

Gomer stepped over the drainage ditch and winced at the pain in her hip. Would the effects of Eitan's beating remain for a lifetime? Would she ever escape the scars of harlotry? Could she ever be a true wife — and ima?

Hosea kept insisting he could love her. How? He may have known her once, but he had no idea who she was now. She'd tried to show him who she was.

"My recent customers called me the lady of invention," she told him one day while he was working alone on that silly two-wheeled cart meant to carry her back to Judah. She'd intended her words to wound, but his pained expression pierced her soul.

"Gomer, when will you let me love you?" he said.

Emotion strangled her. "When will you let me go?"

"Never," he whispered.

"My answer is the same."

The memory brought unexpected emotion, and she swiped at the tears on her cheeks. Someone in the crowd bumped her, and she realized she was standing at Tamir's brothel gate. She studied the cedar planks and iron bars and wondered what they'd done with Merav's body. Who had washed her? Had they buried her with the beggars, or had Tamir given her a proper burial in the tombs north of the city?

She knew the answer. Tamir was a businesswoman, after all.

Another sigh, and Gomer walked on, determined to think happier thoughts. The city streets were alive. Merchants haggling in the market, children scurrying at her feet. The stench of the drainage ditch never smelled so sweet. She wished she'd planned her escape more carefully and brought a few pieces of silver with her.

Hosea had purchased a small parcel of cloves for her during their first days together. She'd made it clear to him that she could live without face paints and perfume, but she refused to endure life with foul breath. He made sure she had a whole clove to suck on each day since.

She gathered her veil around her face, covering every wisp of copper hair. Did Hosea think she was stupid? She wouldn't let anyone know she was alive in Samaria. *But can I really go to Judah and live on a farm?* It all sounded so mundane. Asherah didn't endow her with beauty and fire and life to be a pandering prophet's wife.

"Asherah!" She stopped in the middle of the street, earning more than one backward glance. Asherah's groves. That's where she'd go! She reached into her pocket, fingering the nose ring, gold chains, and earrings she'd taken from the brothel — Tamir owed her that much. Perhaps if she offered them to Asherah, the great goddess of abundance would show her the right path for her life.

Gomer hurried toward the city gates, struggling against the flow of incoming travelers. The grove would be deserted this time of day. All the better for an anonymous offering from a married woman. The veil would cover everything except her eyes so the priestess wouldn't recognize her. She found herself suddenly thankful for Hosea's gift.

She strayed from the main road, following the path lined with oak trees south of the city. The lush green leaves reminded her that Baal had responded to the child sacrifice — in spite of Merav's foolish heroics. The old woman had given her life to save a baby that wasn't even her own. How senseless. Now Gomer had lost her friend, the baby was dead, and the leaves were green. Why not give the gods what they wanted and hope they left you alone? Unlike Hosea's incessant deity who wanted to badger humans into some sort of continual conversation. How exhausting to worship a god so needy.

The path spilled into a clearing surrounded by poplar, oak, and terebinth trees — Asherah's sacred grove. The most beautiful place on earth. She inhaled a cleansing breath, enjoying the sweet aroma of fresh sacrifice. *Lamb,* she thought. Though she'd served at the temple for only two years, she'd learned the distinct aroma of each sacrifice — each scent sending a unique message to the holy queen of heaven. Occasionally, she missed the grandeur of the temple, but never the routine.

Once inside the clearing, she looked up, listening to the breeze tickle the leaves. Silver and green boughs greeted her. *Welcome home.* Lifting her arms, she danced in a circle, laughing with a freedom she hadn't known since Merav's death. *But I hear no bells.* She would never again wear bells around her ankles and wrists and waist. The realization slowed her dancing, quenched her joy, and then she realized — her veil had fallen to the ground.

Instinctively, she reached down to grab it, but another hand snatched it away first. Gomer met the stare of Asherah's high priestess. "I taught you at a very young age what the punishment would be if you were caught wearing a veil in public, Gomer."

"But I'm married! I'm supposed to wear that veil!" She reached for it, but the priestess yanked it away.

"Guard! Take the harlot to the elders." A slow, satisfied smile creased her lips. "I'm sure many of Samaria's leaders will observe your trial with interest."

Hosea sat on the completed two-wheeled cart, packed and ready for tomorrow morning's journey. Leather straps secured baskets stuffed full of supplies, creating a seat suspended between two wheels — a brilliant design by Hosea's missing wife. *Where could she be?* Gomer had left for the market just after midday, and now the sun was sinking in the west.

"I can go look for her," Isaiah offered for the third time. "No one in Samaria has seen me with Gomer. I'm the safest choice."

"I'm not sure she'd come back with you." Hosea tried to muster a grin, but it died when he glimpsed his friend's face.

"I'm sorry, Hosea." The words were whispered, a struggle for composure.

"What do you mean? Why are you sorry?"

"I'm sorry for a lot of things," he said, taking a deep breath and beginning to pace. "Jonah was right. I *was* jealous when you received Yahweh's call before me. I tried not to be, but I was. And when I saw Gomer, I was jealous again because she's so beautiful, and she was so lost and needed a protector." Isaiah stopped pacing. "But I'm most sorry because I thought Gomer was beneath us — unworthy of love or forgiveness."

Hosea bristled, but he let his friend finish. "I basically said Yahweh's plan was wrong, and we were too righteous to obey it."

Remaining silent, Hosea measured his lifelong friendship against the protective love he felt for Gomer. Why must he forgive — again? "I love her, Isaiah. You've got to stop judging her. My love goes beyond obedience to Yahweh's command. I don't like what she's done or who she's become, and she's not pure like Aya, but Yahweh has given me a love for Gomer. If you can't respect Gomer, at least respect me enough to treat her kindly."

Isaiah nodded, extending his hand in truce. Hosea stood and embraced him, and Isaiah held tight, unwilling to let go. "Please, brother, let me search for her. I promise I'll bring her back to you."

Hosea swallowed the lump in his throat. "I'm afraid of where you might find her."

Jonah appeared at the doorway and nudged the young men apart. "I'll wait here while both of you search for Gomer. Everything is ready to leave in the morning, so go."

Hosea kept his head bowed, unable to look at his teacher. "What if . . ."

"Hosea, my son. Look at me."

Grudgingly, he lifted his gaze and saw the man's soft heart in his eyes. "Go find your bride. I'll stay here and pray for Yahweh's favor. We'll set out for Tekoa tomorrow as we planned."

Isaiah rested his hand on Hosea's shoulder. "Come on. We must find her before dark."

They hurried out of the courtyard, turning west toward the temple. *Surely she wouldn't walk right into the lions' den.* Hosea's logic warred with his emotions. Gomer knew the danger of being seen by anyone who could report to Menahem's captain. And if anyone discovered she'd married the Yahweh prophet, King Jeroboam would humiliate all of them as he'd been humiliated when Hosea challenged him at the sacrifice.

As they approached the temple, Hosea noticed a steady stream of people hurrying inside. He stopped one of the men and asked, "What's happening? Is there another sacrifice?"

"No, this is just the quickest way to the king's audience chamber." The man leaned close, whispering as if they were old friends sharing a secret. "I heard the elders at the gate passed judgment on a prostitute, but when King Jeroboam found out *which* prostitute was on trial, he wanted a piece of the action." The man nudged Hosea with his elbow. "Know what I mean?" He hurried away, clearly amused.

Hosea lost all sense of time and space. He needn't take another step or hear a witness to know it was Gomer. "The elders at the gate passed judgment on a prostitute," the man had said. Hosea knew she'd been wearing her veil when she left, which meant she must have returned to prostitution and been accused as a married woman committing the crime. His stomach lurched, and he bent over to steady himself. He felt Isaiah's hand on his back.

"What is it?"

Hosea took deep breaths until he could stand and then met Isaiah's gaze. Cowardice overtook him. He turned without a word, starting back to their house. He would tell Jonah — and leave for Tekoa. Isaiah didn't need to know Gomer had returned to her harlotry. He'd hate her forever. *But why do I care? I hate her too!* He let one foot fall in front of the other, plodding aimlessly. Hopelessly.

"Hosea! Stop!" A strong hand gripped his shoulder, nearly pulling him to the ground.

Staggering, he caught himself, and his

anger erupted. "Get your hands off me, Isaiah! We're going back to get Jonah, and we're leaving Samaria tonight! I'm done. Finished."

All color drained from his friend's face. "So Yahweh didn't speak to you? He didn't tell you to marry this prostitute and have children with her? This whole journey has been a lie?" The accusation in his voice slapped Hosea from his self-pity.

"Yahweh did speak to me. I mean . . ." But how could it be true if Gomer had returned to prostitution? Perhaps he'd been mistaken and Yahweh didn't mean Gomer.

In that moment, a gentle wind blew on Hosea's spirit: *Let's learn about Yahweh. Let's get to know Yahweh. He will come to us as sure as the morning comes. He will come to us like the autumn rains and the spring rains that water the ground.*

Isaiah's face lit with wonder. "I felt a cool breeze, and you grew still. Did you hear Yahweh's voice?"

Hosea nodded, unable to speak while the balm of God's voice soothed his wounded heart. Could knowing more of Yahweh really satisfy the emptiness he felt at Gomer's betrayal?

Isaiah assaulted him with questions. "How does it feel? Do you hear a *real* voice, like a human sound? Is He —"

"Isaiah," Hosea interrupted, "all I know for now is that we must find Gomer. She's been arrested."

With a resolute slap on Hosea's shoulder, Isaiah grabbed his arm and dragged him through the crowd toward the king's hall.

Hosea prayed urgently as they shoved their way through the temple and into the king's audience chamber. *Oh my Elohim, I need to know You more just as Gomer needs to learn of You. I've been taught Your Law, but in order to teach Gomer who You are, we must learn of You together in moments like this — through sunrise and rainfall. Thank You for making Your calling clear again. Give me wisdom to reveal Your steady heart through my enduring love.*

They arrived at the royal hall, and Isaiah stood on tiptoes to see over the crowd. Hosea knew his friend wouldn't like what he was about to say. "Isaiah, I need you to go back to the house, get Jonah, and wait with the cart outside the city gates before they close for the night. I have a feeling we'll need to leave quickly if we're to save Gomer and get out of Samaria alive."

9

Let's return to Yahweh. Even though he
has torn us to pieces, he will heal us.

Two guards paraded Gomer through a
courtroom full of Israelites. Women spit on
her, men pawed — this time for free. "Kneel
before the king," said one of the guards,
pushing her forward. She landed hard on
her knees and tipped onto her face, unable
to stop her momentum with her hands
bound behind her back. Those in the courtroom laughed, and she waited until one of
the guards grabbed her arm.

"Kneel!" said the other guard, yanking her
upright. She winced but refused to show
weakness. Perched on her knees between
her captors, she glanced up at King Jeroboam's specially appointed tribunal. Amaziah, the high priest, joined the king and six

advisors to judge a simple harlot. Each of the tribunal members — with the exception of the king — had paid for her services, repeatedly. But she'd never darkened the inner sanctum of the palace. She examined the long, narrow courtroom, etching every detail into her memory. Exquisite ivory and ebony inlaid furniture filled the room, and landscaped wood panels lined the walls.

Of course, she should be concerned about her sentencing. When a prostitute veils herself in public, her punishment is humiliating, costly, painful. But she was beyond humiliation, she owned nothing of value, and pain was no stranger. This was her second trial today and would undoubtedly result in another conviction. Her energy was much better spent remembering this glimpse of glory than brooding over certain defeat.

At her first trial, the guards from the grove had led her to the city gates. The elders had recognized her almost immediately, even without jewelry or cosmetics. They'd been regular customers too, and seemed intrigued — almost sympathetic — when she told them of how Eitan had beaten her the day of the great sacrifice. But their interest turned to rage when she defended veiling herself and mentioned her new husband's name. It seemed a reformed harlot was less than popular, but one married to a rebel prophet was downright distasteful.

The elders would have carried out their judgment immediately had it not been for General Menahem's guards, who whisked her to the palace for more questions and this trial. Menahem questioned her personally, seeming overly interested in Hosea's contacts with Judean spies in Israel. She laughed at the absurdity, which earned her more bruises. *Men will be men.* She was weary of the lot of them.

At least she wouldn't have to see Hosea again. He was no doubt halfway to Judah by now, or at least he would be when he discovered she'd been found in Asherah's grove. Yahweh's fiery prophet would never stomach an idolatrous wife.

"The king's tribunal will now hear testimony from two witnesses: Asherah's high priestess and the guard at the grove." The royal herald howled like a wounded dog, and Gomer wished her hands weren't bound so she could cover her ears. "They will testify that the harlot Gomer was found veiling herself in public. Should the harlot be found guilty, she will surrender all her jewelry, be stripped naked, and flogged with rods forty times minus one."

The high priestess stood, offered a perfunctory bow to the king, and addressed the full courtroom. "I saw this woman enter Asherah's grove, covered with this veil." When the woman lifted the blue linen cloth into the air, a wave of regret seized Gomer. Why couldn't she have been happy with Hosea's gift?

"The harlot tried to look respectable," the priestess continued. "She'd covered her copper hair, leaving only her eyes exposed, but when she danced before the goddess, her veil fell away. I recognized her as the filthy harlot Gomer." She spat the name, her mouth twisted in disgust. "She should reap the full penalty of her crime."

The herald stepped forward once again and drew a breath to announce the second witness, but he was cut short by a bass voice from the gallery. "This woman is no longer a harlot. She is my wife."

Gomer's heart leapt to her throat. She heard the soft swish of leather sandals on the marble floor behind her. Approaching. Then Hosea stopped beside the guard on her left.

Without lifting her gaze, she whispered, "What are you doing here?" But the words echoed in the tomb-like courtroom.

He ignored her and took another step

forward, drawing two of the king's guards off the royal dais. They stood regally like a wall between Hosea and the king. Their spears were poised at an angle, as if their fierce presence wasn't enough to discourage further advance.

"The charges brought against Gomer are unfounded because she is no longer a street harlot but rather a married woman. And as a married woman, she has the right — actually, the obligation — to veil herself in public." Hosea's tone was respectful but direct. He met each council member's gaze, moving down the line, and finally landed on the king's icy stare. Hosea's hands clenched and released the sides of his robe as he awaited the answer.

Moments passed that felt like days. Gomer kept her head bowed, unable to decide whose eyes she wished to avoid most.

"I was wondering if the king has had sufficient time to consider Yahweh's warning," Hosea said.

Gomer gasped with the rest of the audience. *Enough, Hosea!* she wanted to scream at him, but she knew he wouldn't listen. She lifted her head to peek at Jeroboam's reaction.

A wry grin appeared on the king's face. "I have thought very little of you or your supposed god, Prophet. As you can see by our budding trees and blooming meadows, the sacrifice you so vehemently condemned has pleased the true gods of Israel."

Hosea took another step forward and was met by the points of the guards' spears. He casually looked down at his belly, where the spearheads rested, as if pondering a pesky insect. "I have come to reclaim my rebellious wife, King Jeroboam."

Gomer turned away. She couldn't watch.

But instead of the sickening sounds of death, she heard the king laugh. "I haven't personally experienced the pleasure of your wife, Prophet, but if retrieving her is worth walking into a spear, perhaps I should add her to my harem!"

The audience erupted, Gomer's past customers yelling vulgar comments. For the first time, she saw Hosea's posture grow rigid. And for the first time, she felt the humiliation of a common whore.

"I have come to reclaim Gomer because I love her, King Jeroboam," Hosea shouted over the raucous crowd. "I said," he kept shouting, "I. Love. Her."

And the room fell silent.

Jeroboam's eyes narrowed, all folly gone. "Then you are an even bigger fool than I imagined."

"My love tells a story. Serves a purpose."

Jeroboam lifted a single eyebrow. Gomer was equally intrigued. Who was this warrior-prophet willing to risk his life for her?

"The king's tribunal has heard enough to rule on the harlot." Amaziah's harsh interruption startled Gomer — and the king.

"If you think, Amaziah, that you can raise an army and take my throne by force, then you may pass judgment in this courtroom." Jeroboam's anger was as pointed as the spears aimed at Hosea's belly, and Gomer wished her hands were unbound so she could applaud. Jeroboam returned his attention to Hosea. "You have one last chance to speak for your wife's freedom, Prophet. The veiling of a prostitute is punishable by beating. The prostitution of a married woman is punishable by death."

Gomer swallowed hard and studied Hosea's silhouette. He hadn't looked at her since he'd entered the hall, yet he said he loved her. He'd shouted it. She'd lived in his house for two new moons, and he hadn't once tried to lie with her. Not even a kiss after that impassioned first taste. Why? What game was he playing? She had once known a boy named Hosea. Would she die before knowing the man?

"My love for Gomer is much like Yahweh's

love for Israel," he began. "I love a woman who knows nothing of the height and depth, width and breadth of my love. She believes love is bought and sold, that it's a physical act or a fleeting fancy. She blames me when things go wrong and gives other lovers credit for her happiness."

Jeroboam's sardonic smile returned. "I can see why you want her back so desperately."

Oh! And why don't I get to stand before an audience and talk about Hosea's faults? Gomer seethed but knew better than to intervene.

"Now, King Jeroboam" — Hosea's voice was gentle — "please listen to Yahweh's heart for your nation, Israel, His bride. He loves Israel with a height and depth, width and breadth that no idol of wood or stone could match. Israel has believed the lie that she must buy the love of false gods with shrine prostitutes, divination, and human sacrifice. But Yahweh is the giver of life, not the taker of infants. He wishes to bless Israel for obedience, not punish her for rebellion. Any punishment given to a beloved wife is meant to heal, not to alienate." He turned toward Gomer now, pinning her with a stare that sent a cold chill through her. "Let's return to Yahweh. Even though He has torn us to pieces, He will heal us. Even though He has wounded us, He will bandage our wounds." He returned his attention to the king. "Return to me my wife, that we may bandage our wounds."

Gomer couldn't breathe, and it seemed everyone waited breathlessly too. Only the heartbeat in her ears convinced her it wasn't a dream.

The king stared, motionless. "Take your wife and get out of Israel, Prophet."

Hosea wasted no time. He rushed to Gomer, untied her hands, and the two hurried toward the rear door. Still, no one spoke. No one moved.

"Prophet!" Jeroboam shouted.

Hosea and Gomer stopped short of the inlaid-ivory doors. They turned slowly, bowed, and waited.

"Out of *Israel,* not just out of Samaria."

Hosea rose to meet the king's gaze. "We'll leave immediately."

"Wait! My veil!" The words were shouted before Gomer realized she'd spoken. A collective gasp filled the room, and she squeezed her eyes shut — certain three impulsive words had ruined Hosea's fine arguments.

She gathered her courage, opening one eye, and saw Jeroboam point at Asherah's high priestess and then at her. The priestess rose from her couch and delivered the veil to its rightful owner. Gomer nodded her thanks to the king, whose grin returned momentarily. "Now go."

Hosea gripped her hand firmly, and Gomer wound the veil around her head as they exited the courtroom and ran through the adjoining temple and past the grand altar. They reached the main street, and Gomer's legs failed her. She cursed her weakness, but Hosea hoisted her into his arms, racing to the city gates. Jonah and Isaiah waited with the two-wheeled cart. She'd never been so happy to see the two men in her life. Whatever waited in Tekoa couldn't be worse than what she'd endured in Samaria.

10

HOSEA 6:2

After two days he will revive us. On the third day he will raise us so that we may live in his presence.

Gomer rolled over and heard someone snoring beside her. In a rush, the events of the evening washed over her, and she rubbed her face, wiping away the instant perspiration. Fully awake, she became aware of the rock poking into her ribs. She rose on one elbow, swept away the offending stone, and peered at the sleeping form beside her. Hosea.

Moonlight cast its glow on his face. He looked like the boy she remembered. She reached out to curl a lock of his dark brown hair around her finger — but stopped. He might wake up, and then she'd have to explain the longing in her heart. Who was this courageous man who spoke boldly to a king? She'd always been the daring one, the warrior rushing into battle. When had he become brave? What had his life been like while she struggled to survive? Unable to resist any longer, she touched his cheek. His beard was soft and curly. Her hand lingered on his face, and for the first time in a long time, she was intrigued by a man. *Who are you, Hosea?*

"Gomer?" He woke suddenly, startled, and grasped her hand. "Are you all right? Is something wrong?"

The concern in his eyes stirred her. "I didn't thank you for saving my life." She cupped his face, kissed him gently, and leaned back, drawing him toward her. A cloud shadowed the moonlight, and she wished for a tent. She glanced over her shoulder, ensuring Jonah and Isaiah were well hidden behind their distant boulder.

The clouds cleared, and she found Hosea studying her. "You are so beautiful." He brushed her cheek, and she turned a kiss into his palm.

His eyes went wide, and she felt him tremble. And then she realized . . . "You've never been with a woman before, have you?"

"No. I've never been married before." His answer was so naive, a lusty giggle escaped before she could restrain it. He withdrew his hand, turned away.

It had been so long since she'd seen such innocence. How could this virile man never have known a woman? Her intrigue stirred to passion. The idea of firstfruits made the marriage bed more enticing — even if it was a wilderness path under the stars. She rose to her knees, drawing near and kissing him again. Still gentle, unwilling to frighten her little lamb. "Everyone should have an experienced teacher," she said, feeling him respond to her kiss.

"No!" he said suddenly, gripping her shoulders and pushing her away.

She landed hard on her backside, breathless and confused. "What? What do you mean, *no*?"

He sat there panting, eyes round and blinking. "We're not doing this tonight. Not like this. We must first talk about what happened between us in Samaria."

"Samaria? *Nothing* happened between us in Samaria!" she said, feeling more exposed than if he'd stripped her naked. "You never touched me, and I vow on Asherah's bosoms, you'll never taste my fruit unless you pay like all the others!" Tears burned her eyes, but she would not release them. She wrapped herself in the blanket and curled into a ball on her side. Let him grow old wondering what he missed.

"Gomer, talk to me." He laid a hand on her shoulder, but she shrugged it off. "Please."

She ignored him. Moments lingered, and the desert silence screamed her defiance.

Finally, he lay beside her, curling his body around her, his breath warm on her ear. "I'm sorry, my wife. Everything that makes me a man wants to satisfy my desire for you. In Samaria, I thought I'd go mad. And tonight, well . . ." His grip on her shoulder tightened, and he nuzzled her neck. "I feel desperate for you. But I need to *know* my wife, and I want my wife to *know* me. The Gomer I knew as a six-year-old girl holds my heart with fond memories. The woman I married has given me no reason to hope that she could ever speak a civil word to me, let alone grow to love me someday. And I'm guessing you have similar questions about the ten-year-old boy you once knew in Bethel."

He let his hand trace the length of her arm and whispered against her cheek, "And I want to teach you about Yahweh. Not just His rules, but the ways He loves and blesses His people. There is so much more to love than you realize." He paused and kissed her cheek lightly. "Sleep now. Dawn will come too quickly, but our journey will be worth the effort. Tomorrow we cross Mount Gerizim and walk the beautiful hill country of Ephraim. By the second day, we'll all feel somewhat revived, and hopefully, when we reach Tekoa on the third day . . ." He let his hands wander the length of her and kissed her cheek again — this time lingering, then reluctantly pulling away. "You will know Yahweh and your husband better by the time we reach our new home. Perhaps then we can enjoy each other's presence." He turned over and lay with his back toward her. "Good night, Gomer."

Good night? She wanted to scream at him but didn't know where to begin. Her mind reeled, and her emotions were in knots. How could she sleep when the only man on earth to deny her lay a handbreadth away? *Good night, indeed.* He was wrong about it being *good* and wrong about dawn too — it would not come too quickly for Gomer.

"There it is, Wife. Jerusalem. Isn't it beautiful?" Hosea crested the hill north of Judah's capital city and released the handles of the two-wheeled cart. He wiped his brow and waited for Jonah and Isaiah to join them.

"It's smaller than I imagined," Gomer

126

said, shading her eyes, "but Solomon's palace and temple are spectacular. Even from this distance, the gold gleams in the sun." She giggled and clapped her hands like the little girl he'd known in Bethel. "Can we visit the market before we continue to Tekoa?"

Feeling torn, Hosea wanted to please her but felt a sense of urgency to return to Amos's farm. "I'll make a deal with you," he said, slipping his arm around her waist. His heart nearly burst when she didn't recoil. "We'll spend equal time in Jerusalem's market and in Yahweh's temple."

Her smile dimmed immediately. "But what is there to do at Yahweh's temple? From what you've told me, there are no prostitutes, so why would anyone worship there?"

Jonah sputtered a chuckle. "Your wife asks a valid question, my son. I can't wait to hear your answer."

Isaiah rolled his eyes and began walking the busy path toward Jerusalem's north gate.

"Wait for me, young Isaiah!" Jonah's walking sticks raised the dust on his way toward the city.

Hosea grabbed the two-wheeled cart handles and resumed his march. Gomer fell in step beside him. "Worship isn't about what *we* receive. It's about what we give from our grateful and obedient hearts." He noticed wrinkles appear on her forehead as they often did when he talked of Yahweh or the prophets' camp. "I plan to use the last of our silver to purchase a lamb and loaves of bread in the market. We'll offer the loaves and sacrifice the lamb to Yahweh as a thank offering and then share a fellowship meal in His presence."

"Why waste your silver on a sacrifice when I could buy a kinder god in the market?"

The venom in her tone startled him, and he wondered why she felt such contempt for Yahweh. Before he could form his question, Gomer covered her mouth to stifle a gasp, seemingly terrified.

Hosea dropped the cart handles, glanced right and left, ready for a fight. His heart twisted when he recognized the enemy.

They'd approached the pagan high place. An Asherah pole stood mocking — on the hill overlooking Yahweh's temple.

Gomer turned to meet his gaze, arching an accusing brow. "Why do you pronounce Yahweh's judgment on *Israel* when I see the same goddess on Judah's hill?"

It was a question he'd asked himself, a question he'd asked Jonah. "Yahweh commanded me to warn Israel. If — or when —

He instructs me to condemn Judah, I will obey. It is my calling to speak God's words, not to question His ways." The words sounded trite, tasted bitter. They were true but hard to swallow — even for Yahweh's prophet.

Gomer's expression turned to stone. "What did you mean when you said we would share a fellowship meal at Yahweh's temple?"

"As an expression of thanks for our safe and successful journey, we'll offer various loaves of bread and an unblemished yearling lamb according to the Law of Moses. The priests will sacrifice the lamb and arrange the burnt offering on the altar and then return the prescribed portions to Jonah, Isaiah, you, and me so we can eat a fellowship meal in Yahweh's presence."

She began to tremble, slowly at first and then violently. "I don't want to eat the meal," she whispered, her wide, hazel eyes reminding him of the frightened girl he'd known in Bethel. "What if I break a law without knowing it? Your god sounds arbitrary and angry. What if He strikes me dead, or the priests discover I worship Asherah and try to kill me like they did Uzziah's abba?"

Hosea gathered her into his arms, but she

stood as stiff as the pagan pole that hovered above them. Isaiah said he'd told her about his uncle and the conspiracy of the zealots. How could Hosea now convince her that Yahweh wanted her love, but He was indeed a God to be feared? They'd grown so much closer in the three days since leaving Samaria, but her heart had remained a sealed scroll. Now that she'd finally trusted him with a small piece of it, how could he prove trustworthy to his wife *and* to Yahweh?

She pushed him away. "Don't coddle me. Tell me if I must go to the temple, and I'll abide by your decision." She stood there, waiting, eyes fastened on her sandals.

Hosea longed to make things easier for her. She was tough as granite yet fragile as a rose. *Yahweh, give me wisdom to love this woman.* "We will go together to the temple. And it's good to be a little afraid of Yahweh. King Solomon said to fear Him is the beginning of knowing Him." He tilted her chin, but she closed her eyes. Chuckling at her stubbornness, he kissed her nose and drew disapproving stares from passing travelers.

Gomer noticed the glances too. "You'd better stop that, or they'll think you married a harlot." She tried to smile.

He loved her humor but was saddened by her self-branding. She had no idea how precious she'd become to him. "My wife is not a harlot. I married the little girl who was my best friend, and we're getting to know each other again."

11

But when [Uzziah] became powerful, his pride destroyed him. . . . He went into Yahweh's temple to burn incense on the incense altar.

Hosea waved good-bye to Jonah and Isaiah at Jerusalem's northernmost gate after making plans to meet them at the temple later. Gomer was already focused on Jerusalem's busy market. Its main street lined on both sides with booths, the market overflowed with everything practical and exotic. The finest goods from all over the world — spices from Sheba, ivory and gold from Africa, silk and pottery from the East — glistened, clanged, and filled the air with all the excitement Samaria offered and more.

"Look at this vase, Hosea!" she said, lifting an intricately designed clay vase from its silver pedestal. "I've been in the finest homes in Samaria and never seen anything like this." The moment the words escaped, she regretted them. Her husband needed no reminders of her past lovers.

"I see nothing in this market as beautiful as my wife." His eyes seemed consumed by her.

She turned away, replaced the vase, and moved on, unwilling to let Hosea have any more of her heart. Why had the gods given him back to her? Or was it really this Yahweh god of whom he spoke? Why would Yahweh care about her? But she could almost believe it after hearing Hosea's stories during their journey from Samaria. Almost. The thought of trusting only one god seemed completely . . . well, irresponsible. How could the rest of the nations be wrong?

"That vase was made at Amos's farm." Hosea's voice startled her from her thoughts, and she jumped. "Are you nervous in this crowd?" he asked, concern shadowing his features.

"No, I enjoy the city, and I love walking through the marketplace." Then the import of his earlier statement settled in, and she stopped abruptly. "Did you say that vase came from Amos's farm? So Isaiah's abba made it?"

Hosea chuckled and clasped his hands behind his back, strolling through the market as if they hadn't a care in the world. "Yes, Amoz runs the pottery workshop on Amos's farm. He makes all the finest pieces."

Gomer squinted and tried to make the distinction. "Amoz, Amos — doesn't that get confusing? How do you tell them apart?"

Hosea laughed and whistled through his teeth. "You wouldn't have to ask that if you'd met the two men. You remember Amos the prophet? He came to Bethel when we were children and prophesied in the temple."

Gomer's stomach tightened at the memory. "He's sort of burly and rough-looking, isn't he?" She was being polite. According to her six-year-old memory, his long, unkempt hair and beard seemed as wild as the sheep and goats he herded.

"Amos can be abrasive, but he's got a kind heart. He's a farmer and a merchant, so he's always with people. Isaiah's abba, Amoz, is very quiet, withdrawn. He's tall and handsome like Isaiah, but he keeps to himself and works long hours at the pottery shop."

Gomer remembered Isaiah's sad countenance when he talked about his childhood and Amoz's absence. "Why doesn't he spend more time with Isaiah?"

Hosea pulled her under the canopy of a cloth dealer, drew her close, and brushed her cheek. "Now, that's a question we should let Isaiah ask his abba — right?"

She received the gentle caution with a begrudging smile and a raised brow. "I'll try to be good. Tell me more about Amos's farm." She turned to inspect the bolts of cloth lying in neat rows. Scarlet, blue, yellow, and white. Lovely wool and linen weaves.

"The farm produces a huge sycamore fig crop twice a year. Plus we raise sheep, cattle, goats — even chickens. There are a hundred ways you can choose to earn our wages at the camp."

Gomer's throat went dry. "Why is this the first I've heard of fig crops, goats, and earning *our* wages?" She kept her back to him and pretended interest in one of the bolts of cloth.

"What's the matter?"

"I thought everyone on Amos's farm was a prophet." She rubbed the airy cloth between her fingers, realizing it must be the famed gauze from Gaza. *Not the kind of thing I'll wear if I'm herding goats.*

"Most of the men are Yahweh's messengers," Hosea was saying, "but there are other families at the camp too — shepherds, farmers, and potters — who help generate income. All the women work to produce salable goods so that Yahweh's prophets aren't susceptible to bribes from royal officials. Those who call themselves prophets in Israel live like kings because they tell Jeroboam what pleases him." Hosea paused. The silence became awkward. "Does earning wages bother you?"

She spun around, driving him back a step. "Why would I be bothered that you sit and talk with your prophet friends all day while I work at some mundane task so that someone else can buy that beautiful vase back there?"

He smiled down at her with his infuriating grin. "You left out the part about feeding me grapes and fanning me with ostrich feathers."

"Oh!" She stomped her foot.

He leaned close, backing her up a step. "What had you imagined you'd be doing?" His tone was light but serious. When she tried to turn away again, he gently embraced her shoulders. "Tell me, Gomer. What did you think a prophet's wife would do?"

"Well, I . . ." How could she explain that she'd anticipated complete boredom? "I didn't know what to expect." She had wanted to escape her life at the brothel, but she hadn't considered what kind of life she'd want instead.

Hosea released her shoulders and nodded at the cloth merchant, who had become interested in their conversation. "Come, let's walk."

Gomer grudgingly complied, falling in step beside him. Hosea reached for her hand hidden beneath the folds of her robe. "We'll try to make sure whatever task you're assigned on Amos's farm will be something you enjoy, something Yahweh has gifted you for. Just as I know He created me to be His prophet."

If Yahweh had created Hosea to be a prophet, had Hosea's god created her to be a harlot? Instinctively, she pulled her hand away and wrapped her arms around her waist. "Tell me the jobs I might do at Amos's farm."

"Well, Amos oversees the livestock when he's not traveling to sell goods for the camp. If you like animals, we could find something for you to do in the barns or meadows."

Gomer wrinkled her nose.

He grinned and continued. "His wife, Yuval, is in charge of the sycamore fig crops. She's a kind woman and manages every-

137

thing from planting and harvesting to the cooking and even the medicinal uses of the figs."

"I helped my friend Merav with herbs and midwifery at the brothel. Maybe I could help Yuval with my knowledge of herbs." She relaxed her arms, feeling for the first time that she might have a purpose in her new life.

Hosea found her hand again, bolstering her spirits with his approving smile as they continued through the market. "There are many women and children, so a midwife's skills are always welcome. But you could also learn something new — maybe how to make a vase like the one we saw a few moments ago."

"A potter? Really?" She halted abruptly, causing several market-goers to stumble into them. "I don't know anything about pottery, Hosea, and who would take the time to teach a harlot such a valuable skill?" She shook her head to dislodge the foolishness, and they resumed their walk through the market. Cooking, grinding, spinning — these were the skills she would be forced to learn, not the fanciful dream of a harlot creating beautiful vases. "I'll do whatever I must."

Hosea laid his arm around her shoulders

and leaned close to whisper through her veil, "The Creator made you creative, my wife. You've always been good at designing things. If you'd like to work with Amoz, I'll see if he needs an apprentice."

Gomer's heart raced, but she refused to give in to false hope. She still wasn't sure she could trust her husband — or his god — but at least Hosea had proven reliable so far.

"Jonah!" He waved at the fish prophet, and Gomer recognized the peak of Solomon's golden temple straight ahead. Too quickly they arrived at the corrals where the sacrificial animals awaited purchase.

"Do you want to purchase the lamb, or should I?" Isaiah asked Hosea, motioning to the sheepfold where two priests sat at a table waiting to receive payment from temple worshipers.

Before Hosea could answer, an uprising on the temple stairway stole everyone's attention. Shouting turned to screams when a small circle of priests hurried down the stairs with a prisoner in their midst. When they reached street level, their circle opened to reveal not a captive but a king. Dressed in royal garments and a gold crown, the man Gomer assumed to be Judah's king appeared deathly pale with terrible-looking

139

sores on his face.

"Yahweh, what has happened to King Uzziah?" Hosea's prayer was spoken aloud and expressed the heart of every onlooker.

The crowd parted, every man, woman, and child running from the approaching regent. Everyone except Jonah and Isaiah. The old prophet's sticks clicked on the cobblestone walkway, and Isaiah ran with him toward the panic-stricken king.

"My lord," Jonah shouted, "what has happened?" Isaiah seemed ready to embrace the king, but the old prophet held him back and chastened him with a cautious stare. "King Uzziah, how can we help you?"

Hosea squeezed Gomer's shoulders and held her gaze. "I need to help Jonah with Isaiah. Don't approach the king or priests until I know what's happened."

Gomer watched her traveling partners bow to Uzziah, though they remained ten cubits from him. The priests directing Uzziah now hurried toward the prophets to speak privately, while the king stood alone — a spectacle for the gawking, frightened Judeans.

She knew the humiliation of forced display. It's why she had learned to perform, to take charge of a crowd, to denigrate before others could demean. King Uzziah had no such luxury. He was imprisoned by decorum to await the priests' verdict. Gomer was bound by no such captor, nor was she intimidated by his title. Uzziah was a man like any other, and she knew her talents could soothe him. Compelled by his pain and fear, she felt her feet move of their own accord.

She knelt, bowed her head, and said in a voice smooth as butter, "My lord Uzziah, I am Gomer, Hosea's wife, and I am honored to meet you." She looked up to offer a kind smile.

Seemingly bewildered, the king glanced from the priests to Hosea and back to Gomer again. She rose and reached out her hand.

"No!" Hosea rushed to her side, and Uzziah stepped back, as startled as Gomer. With a penitent bow to the king, Hosea wrapped Gomer's hand in his own. "Forgive me, my lord. My wife doesn't know the laws about becoming unclean by touching someone with a skin disease. We meant no disrespect."

The pain Gomer saw on Uzziah's face was all too familiar. *Unclean.* She might not know any laws about such a word, but she knew what the king was feeling at this moment. She set her jaw and withdrew her hand from Hosea's grasp. "If the king needs care for his wounds, I am willing to become *unclean* to help him."

Before Hosea replied, a deep, resonant voice said, "Thank you, lovely Gomer, but I believe one of my physicians will accompany me outside the city." He looked at Jonah, adding, "As I'm sure the priests have reported, this is Yahweh's judgment for my arrogance while offering incense. I must find a place to dwell outside the city until His mercy relieves me of these sores. Do you think Amos would allow me to stay at the camp in Tekoa?"

Isaiah stepped forward, and Gomer noticed his red-rimmed eyes. "He could stay with Abba and me."

Jonah's expression softened, and he placed a comforting hand on Isaiah's shoulder. "The Law is clear, my son. King Uzziah must live outside the camp, but I'm sure Amos would be blessed to offer him the small stone house in the clearing outside the gates."

Uzziah nodded and exchanged a meaningful glance with Isaiah. "And I would be blessed to be near my family during this unsettling time."

Gomer saw the exchange between the cousins and felt their frustration. "Hosea, can't this law be set aside for the king?" she whispered. "Isn't there a way we could let the king stay in a house close to Isaiah, or perhaps we —"

He pressed a finger to her lips, his eyes full of kindness yet stern. "We will indeed help our king, my wife, but we must allow Yahweh's judgment to do its work as well as let His Law protect us and the king. We don't know if the disease is contagious, and remember — the Lord has aimed His wrath at King Uzziah. We do not want to stand in the way if more wrath is forthcoming."

Gomer was horrified. "You mean your god could turn on you for helping this poor man?"

Hosea sighed, appearing exhausted and frustrated with her question. "It's more complex than that, Gomer."

"Don't talk to me now," she said, equally frustrated. Holding back tears, she pressed Hosea to rejoin the priests. "You can explain to me later why your *loving god* afflicted a faithful king for offering incense in His temple." Venom dripped from her tone, and Hosea winced as if physically wounded. Let him wince. He had almost tricked her into believing his god was different than others.

She must be more careful. Hosea was convincing. Too convincing.

12

EXODUS 20:3–6

Never have any other god. Never make your own carved idols or statues. . . . Never worship them or serve them, because I, Yahweh your Elohim, am El Kanna [Jealous God]. I punish children for their parents' sins to the third and fourth generations of those who hate me. But I show mercy to thousands of generations of those who love me and obey my commandments.

Hosea felt as if his heart twisted in his chest. Why would this faithful king do such a foolish thing? He knew only Aaron's descendants were allowed to burn incense before the Lord's altar. The priests continued their discussion with Jonah, but Hosea stole a glance at his wife. Isaiah stood with Gomer, talking quietly halfway between the priests' huddle and the lonesome king. For once, Isaiah seemed to be calming her. The fury in her eyes at the mention of God's judgment had been staggering. Would she always be so quick to accuse the righteous and defend the condemned?

"Hosea, what do you think?"

Hosea returned his attention to the priests and found Jonah waiting for his answer.

"Hosea? Yahweh has gifted you with administrative skills. How should we proceed?"

"I'm sorry, what exactly are you asking?"

After a silent reprimand, Jonah summed up their questions. "Can we travel to Tekoa after nightfall with both Gomer and the king in wheeled carts?"

In the span of a lightning flash, Hosea considered a thousand problems. "Uzziah's condition is worsening before our eyes. The distance between here and Tekoa is normally covered in a morning walk but becomes a half-day journey with two carts on the rocky terrain. And we all know the folly of traveling at night in the wilderness. If we're not attacked by wild beasts, bandits will try to lighten our load." Hosea watched the priests' eyes grow larger with each potential problem. He'd better give them solutions or they'd shed their vestments and pray for the mountains to fall on them. "One of you will need to follow Jonah to the palace to inform the king's officials of our plan. Prince Jotham will also need to be told about his abba's illness." He glanced at Jonah. "Perhaps Isaiah would be the best one to speak to the prince."

Jonah nodded, hurrying to where Isaiah and Gomer stood.

Hosea recited the list of remaining considerations, and the priests divided the responsibilities. He left them with a final instruction. "Remember, we'll need to wash any wood and break any pottery that King Uzziah touches on the journey." He hesitated, emphasizing his next words. "We will follow Yahweh's Law to the letter — both to remain holy and to be safe. We don't know if the king's condition is contagious. Make sure you apprise all the guards who might have direct contact with the king of that risk."

"His two primary bodyguards are built like stone watchtowers," one priest offered. "I'm sure they'd carry the king on their shoulders if necessary."

"Let's hope no one has to touch our good king," Hosea said, remembering his wife's hand extended to Uzziah. "To knowingly make oneself unclean is to willingly separate oneself from Yahweh. It's not to be taken lightly."

Gomer watched Jonah lead Isaiah away from the looming gold temple of Yahweh. Hosea's young friend was shaken. He'd even deigned to speak a civil word to her. "Thank you for your kindness to Uzziah," he'd said.

She was startled that he hadn't come over to chastise her for humiliating herself and Judah's king, but something in his demeanor told her Isaiah's world had been turned upside down in the moments of chaos she'd just witnessed.

"Are you all right?" Hosea's hand cupped her cheek, and she turned to meet his warm brown eyes.

She looked past him, noticing the priests clearing a wide path through the crowd, directing the stunned and wobbly king to follow Jonah and Isaiah. "Are they all going to the palace?"

With his hand still warm on her face, he said, "Yes, and I must go with them."

Startled, she met his gaze. "And me?"

"I thought you might like to barter for that vase we saw in the market." A weary smile turned up one corner of his lips. "I'm sure Amoz would be pleased to know you appreciated his work."

"You'd trust me to walk the market alone?"

He pulled a pouch from his belt. When she held out her hand, he dropped it, and she felt the weight of a few silver pieces, heard the familiar jingle. "I trust you," he said. "It's important that you meet me back here before the sun reaches the top of the palace roof." He pointed to a tall building west of where they stood. "Do you see it? You must be here before the sun touches that roof."

"I understand." She felt wicked for the little grin she couldn't suppress. King Uzziah had been stricken. Isaiah was hurting. But the thought that Hosea trusted her and she was free to walk in the market . . .

Hosea turned to go, but she grabbed his arm. "I'll need your dagger," she said, tucking the silver into her belt.

"What? No!" Hosea stared, seemingly amused. "How do you know I have a dagger?"

"I saw it strapped above your left sandal the night you took me from the brothel. Now give it to me so I can protect myself in the market." She held out her hand and waited.

Hosea measured the remaining crowd and led Gomer toward a more private place near the sheepfold. "First of all, it's not common knowledge that God's prophet carries a dagger. Secondly, are you sure you know how to use this? I don't want you to get killed over a silly vase." Hosea glanced side to side, knelt down as if adjusting his sandal strap, and then transferred the blade into Gomer's hand.

She tucked it into her pocket. "I've been a street harlot since I was twelve, Hosea. I could cut you from nose to navel before you realized it." A quick peck on his cheek. "Thank you, Husband. I'll meet you back here shortly."

As she melted into the crowded Jerusalem market, Gomer stole a glance over her shoulder. Hosea was watching her, his lips moving in silent prayer. She giggled, wondering, *Is he praying for me or a foolish merchant who might try to cheat me?*

Gomer hurried through the crowded streets. People everywhere were talking about the king's affliction. Some spoke unkindly of Uzziah, of course, as even the best of leaders have enemies. But the overall consensus was one of bewilderment. If Yahweh would strike out at faithful Uzziah, who was safe from His wrath?

One voice rose above the rest, and Gomer

was drawn to a large crowd near a canopied booth on the east side of the upper city. A woman stood on crates to be seen above the gathering. Her clear, smooth voice ran over Gomer's soul like spring water. "Our Lady Asherah offers life to her worshipers, not sickness and death as Yahweh gives." She presented a gleaming replica of the carved poles in the groves. "Asherah's alabaster altar can accompany you to your home, bless your household with life and health. Why travel to one of the groves in Judah or to Yahweh's temple to offer sacrifices when Asherah lives here, and Baal here?" She picked up other carved items, lifting them above the crowd to display the quality of her workmanship. "And here I have Anat and Mot." She stepped off the crates in order to meet the demands of the worshipers at her feet. "Yes, yes, I have plenty of gods for you. Wait your turn, and I'll help you decide which god or goddess will meet your needs."

Gomer watched in awe. These people had allowed themselves to be bullied into worshiping one god. The Asherah pole she and Hosea had passed on the high place looked forgotten and unkempt, but Yahweh's tantrum with Uzziah had awakened their need for the real gods of Canaan.

As she watched, a terrifying thought occurred to her. She would soon be whisked away to a small farm in the Tekoan wilderness with a leprous king — without any god of her own. To what god would she pray for protection?

Driven by fear, Gomer forced her way to the front of the crowd and inspected the woman's carvings. She chose a small alabaster Asherah and reached into the pouch for a piece of Hosea's silver. "I'll take this one."

"A fine choice, my lady."

Gomer nodded, took the goddess, wrapped it in a cloth, and placed it in her pocket beside the dagger.

Hosea stood by the sheepfolds in front of the temple while Jonah and Isaiah waited with the king and his men. *Where is she?* He was trying not to worry, but why was she late? What if she was arrested again? What if . . . *Yahweh, what if she gave herself to another man?* His chest ached as he imagined her in the arms of another, when she'd never let him love her as a husband.

He pressed balled fists into his eyes. "Stop this," he whispered, chastising himself.

"Hosea?"

He spun around at the sound of Gomer's

voice and embraced her as if he were drowning.

Looking shocked, she nearly dropped the cloth she was carrying. "Hosea, what's wrong?"

He released her and realized his explanation must include a confession. "I was worried about you. Where have you been?" The words sounded more accusatory than he'd intended.

Instead of the anger he expected, his wife seemed distracted, picking at some lint on a piece of cloth she'd purchased. She seemed nervous, fidgety. "Are the others waiting at the cart? We should hurry. I decided on cloth instead of the vase. It seemed more practical."

"Gomer." He watched her fraying the edges, smoothing the folds, avoiding his gaze.

"Do you think someone could teach me how to sew? The servants made all our robes at the brothel." She still hadn't looked at him.

"Gomer." He cupped her cheeks and held her gaze. "What happened in the market? Why are you upset?"

She turned away. "Let's go, Hosea. Please. I don't want to talk about it."

Dread returned like hot iron in the pit of

his stomach. Which of his imaginings had come true? "I need to know."

Her chin rose, and her back straightened like a rod. Anger lit her eyes. "Why? Why must you know? Must I count out each piece of silver to prove I didn't cheat you?"

"I don't care about the silver. I want to know why you're upset." He suddenly remembered the dagger. He stepped forward and reached for the pocket of her robe. "Give me the dag —"

She backed away, eyes wide with panic, and covered her pocket. "Why must you see the dagger?"

"Because if you had to use my dagger, I placed my wife in danger sending her to the market alone. Please, Gomer." He held out his hand. "The dagger."

She fumbled in her robe pocket and produced the dagger, slapping it into his hand. "Here."

The blade was clean. No blood.

"But why were you upset? Why . . ."

Tears welled on her bottom lashes, but she seemed desperate to hold them captive. "So much for your trust, Hosea." With a sneer, she walked toward the two-wheeled cart and the king's escort that awaited them. She looked over her shoulder and added, "I bought a gift for you that I have hidden in my pocket. That's why I didn't want you fishing for your dagger."

Hosea dropped his head, defeated. The scent of cloves still lingered in her wake. She was constantly sucking on the little morsels. Her breath, her hair, her clothes were steeped in the aroma. Perhaps it wasn't important to know the details of her market excursion. She was safe and in his arms, and no blood on the knife meant no damage done.

"Come, Wife. Let's go home."

Guilt chewed at the edges of Gomer's heart. They'd left Jerusalem just before the evening meal and traveled in darkness through the wilderness — a perfect condition for the black heart of one who lies to her husband about a gift when she's hiding a pagan god in her pocket. Isaiah had been right about her. She was everything despicable and didn't know how to love.

"You've been moping since we left Jerusalem," Isaiah grunted, pushing the cart with all his might. "One would think you were the one with leprosy."

Gomer issued him a sidelong glance and dug the walking sticks into the dusty path. "I'm concentrating on using these silly sticks. I don't know how Jonah gets around so well."

The old curmudgeon had collapsed north of Bethlehem, but he refused to take her place on the cart. She silenced his protests by stealing his walking sticks and kissing his cheek. Now he slept atop their makeshift wagon through the bumpiest terrain Gomer had ever traveled.

The cart creaked as one wheel dipped into a deep rut on the uphill path. Gomer stifled a cry, watching Jonah nearly topple from his perch. Isaiah pushed, Hosea pulled, and the cart moaned on its way again.

Relieved, Gomer chatted with Isaiah to distract herself from the ache in her hips. "How much farther to Tekoa?" She was trying not to complain.

"We're almost there." He must have been exhausted too. He'd been leaning his whole being into pushing uphill. He glanced over his arm, concern evident. "Do you need to stop? I can have the soldiers signal to Uzziah's guard."

"No. I'm fine."

Isaiah's brow furrowed deeply, and he tucked his head between his arms again. "You're not fine, but it's best to keep going if we can. We are very close, and when we get to camp, you'll be able to rest in your own home."

Your own home. The thought energized her. She had little memory of a real home. She would arrive in Tekoa with a leprous king and an entire detachment of Judean soldiers holding torches aloft on both sides of the path — not the way she envisioned the entrance to her first *real* home, but it would certainly be memorable. A spark of excitement pushed her onward.

She heard a shofar in the distance and looked up, noticing a soft glow in a valley below them. They crested a hill, the cart stopped, and Hosea joined them.

"That's home, Gomer," he said, pointing to the village aglow. "King Uzziah must have sent runners to let them know we were coming. They've got torches lit for us."

"I haven't been kind to you in the past." Isaiah's voice split the night air, and Hosea reached his arm around Gomer's waist, giving her a gentle squeeze. "But I saw a different side of your heart today."

A lump formed in Gomer's throat, the goddess in her pocket accusing her loudly. "I know how it feels to be an outcast, Isaiah. No one likes to feel alone."

"We will remember your kindness," Jonah's reedy voice interrupted from atop his perch. "You will need friends in your new home."

Gomer saw Hosea and Isaiah exchange an unspoken message, and her blood ran cold. Their worried expressions doused her spark of excitement and settled a blanket of dread over her weary bones.

13

LEVITICUS 13:2–4

If anyone has a sore, a rash, or an irritated area on his skin that turns into an infectious skin disease . . . the priest will examine the disease. If the hair in the diseased area has turned white, and the diseased area looks deeper than the rest of his skin, it is an infectious skin disease. When the priest has examined him, he must declare him unclean. But if the irritated area is white and does not look deeper than the rest of the skin, and the hair has not turned white, the priest must put him in isolation for seven days.

Gomer perused the lovely stone house where Hosea had asked her to wait while he helped settle King Uzziah in a home outside the camp gates. She was exhausted, and her pride was still bruised after having to be carried from the hilltop where she'd first spied Tekoa. The short rest sent a false report to her legs that the journey was over. Her weakened body refused to take another step on the rocky terrain. Isaiah took sole duty of Jonah's two-wheeled cart, and Hosea hoisted her into his arms as if she weighed no more than a sack of barley. His strength astonished her. Many things about her childhood friend surprised her these days.

Her stomach growled loudly, and she groaned a little, wishing for a hot meal and a warm bed. But Hosea had plopped her down in this house just inside the camp's gate without a word about their provisions. He'd rushed out the door to join Isaiah and the others to care for King Uzziah.

The main room was simple yet elegant. *This must be a guest house for visiting royalty.* Perhaps Uzziah stayed here when he visited Amoz and Isaiah. She fell onto a stack of curly goatskin rugs and snuggled into the softness.

But Asherah poked at her hip and pricked her conscience..

She adjusted the alabaster goddess and then scanned the room, wondering where she might hide her treasure when Hosea took her to their home. Here she could find plenty of hiding spots. Beautiful vases, jugs, and bowls were stacked on shelves over a worktable and washbasin. This home even boasted a private oven, not shared with the farm or other houses around a courtyard. In fact, she noted on passing through Amos's gates that most of the houses stood alone and were built into the surrounding mountains and hills. She'd felt a significant temperature change when she entered this large room and realized the natural-rock walls must help maintain a cool temperature in Tekoa's desert climate.

She closed her eyes and curled onto her side. Her body needed rest, but her spirit felt alive. Perhaps it was change that brought hope, but she felt more alive than she had since . . . well, since she and Hosea were children. The boy she'd thought abandoned her had reappeared and seemed to sincerely care. A slight flutter tightened her chest. Was this love? A wry smile creased her lips. What was love anyway? But she did care for Hosea. She'd be sad if anything happened to him.

Then the familiar fear strangled her. What would she do if Hosea abandoned her again? Everyone abandoned her at some point.

She reached for the alabaster goddess in

her pocket, stroking the smooth, cool stone. *Great Goddess Asherah, abundant mother of life, open my womb that I might have children one day to provide for me in my old age.* She'd never before imagined such a prayer, but the thought comforted her. As a harlot, she'd dreaded children, done everything in her power to keep her body from producing them. Squeezing her familiar goddess, she felt a strange warmth move up her arm. Yes, she was ready to give herself to her husband. If not for love, then for her future.

A knock at the door startled her from her thoughts. She sat up too quickly, and her head swam. *I must eat something.* She steadied herself and moved toward the door, wishing she hadn't returned Hosea's dagger and left herself unprotected. "Yes? Who is it?" she said through the thick wooden panels.

"Shalom, dear. My name is Yuval. I'm Amos's wife, and I've brought a small meal for nourishment."

Gomer glanced around the room, not sure what she was looking for, but equally unsure why the owner's wife would bring her food in the middle of the night. "Hosea isn't here. He's helping King Uzziah."

A slight pause. "I know, dear. Amos is with them. I thought you might be hungry and we could share a meal. Would you be will-ing to let me in?"

Now Gomer felt utterly foolish. "Of course. I'm so sorry . . . ," she said, opening the door. But the face that waited outside shocked her into silence. "Merav?" Gomer began to tremble and covered her mouth to stifle a cry.

"What? What's wrong, dear?" The old woman rushed past her and set the tray of food aside. "Sit down. You look pale."

The face, the voice, even the hands — this old woman was Gomer's midwife friend from the brothel. "Merav, I watched the guard kill you," she whispered. She couldn't take her eyes off the haunting face.

"Tell me who you think I am, Gomer." The ghostly matron led her to a rug beside the tray of food. "Your name is Gomer, right? You're Hosea's new bride?" She stroked Gomer's hand as she talked, sooth-ing, reasoning.

"Yes, I'm Hosea's wife." Gomer shook her head and squeezed her eyes shut. *This must be a dream.* But when she opened her eyes, Merav's ghost was still there. "Oh, has Mot sent you back to punish me?" She began to cry, fear seizing her.

"Shh, little one. Don't cry. We'll figure this out." The old woman wrapped her in a ferocious hug. "You see? I'm real. Mot has no dominion among Yahweh's people. I am Yuval, and no false gods will torment you here." She rocked Gomer back and forth until her tears subsided.

Finally feeling a measure of peace, Gomer released the soft, warm woman who had held her so tightly. "I'm sorry. I've made a fool of myself, but you look exactly like the midwife and nursemaid at the broth —" She stopped, horrified that she'd almost told Yuval she'd been a harlot! It was bad enough she undoubtedly thought Gomer a madwoman. "My childhood nursemaid and the midwife who trained me — her name was Merav. I watched King Jeroboam's guards stab her to death when she tried to save an infant from a temple sacrifice. You look remarkably like her."

Tears welled in Yuval's eyes. "Oh, Gomer. I'm sorry you witnessed such a tragedy. Merav sounds like a brave and caring woman. I hope my life reflects her character as strongly as my face reflects her features." She patted Gomer's hand and leaned close. "Now, may I join you in the meal? And when we're finished, I can help you unpack if you like." She waved her hand as if shooing away a fly. "Who knows how long before our husbands come home."

"Unpack?" Gomer watched the dear old woman arrange warm bread and steaming stew on the leather table mat. "Are you taking me to Hosea's house after we eat?"

Yuval's hand stopped midair, full of dates. "This *is* Hosea's house, dear. Didn't he tell you? This is your home now."

Hosea left the small stone house Amos had provided for King Uzziah and swirled his walking stick on the path in front of him. The vibration would warn off snakes, and the noise would alert any large predator of human presence. Once inside the camp's gated compound, he no longer stayed vigilant for wilderness beasts. Now his mind could settle into the matters that weighed heavy on his soul. He trudged up the rocky path toward home, wondering if the world would ever make sense again. Judah's righteous king — afflicted by Yahweh. He shook his head and sighed, his heart as heavy as his leaden feet.

The priests had inspected every affected area on Uzziah's body as the Law prescribed. Though the skin was white like leprosy, the hair in the affected area had not turned white, nor did the sores look more than skin deep. The decision — confinement for seven days — had wrought a piteous expression from the king. The Law required

Yahweh's priests to examine him every seven days to determine if the skin lesions were a simple rash or infectious. If at any point the lesions were determined infectious, he would be deemed unclean and must live outside any community indefinitely. The priests' decision would determine Uzziah's long-term living arrangements.

Hosea read terror on the king's features — a man who had thrived on activity, people, and accomplishment now sequestered in the stone-walled house no larger than his palace dressing room. With each requirement the priests listed, Uzziah's shoulders sagged lower.

"Your outer garment must be torn at all times as if mourning. Your beard must be covered with a mantle. And if anyone approaches the house, you must warn them to keep their distance by shouting, 'Unclean, unclean!' And we must shave your head, my lord."

At the final pronouncement, the king's eyes grew round. "Surely you can set aside the bald head for your king. It is unheard of for Judah's ruler to shave his head for *any* occasion."

It was Hosea's first glimpse of the arrogance that had landed Uzziah in a rented house on Amos's farm. Still, how did a king who offered all the right sacrifices, won all the right battles, built all the right towers . . . still fall under Yahweh's most severe judgment?

It was Uzziah's arrogance that separated him from Me. Outward adherence is not inward devotion. I have shown through leprosy the outward sign of his inner corruption . . .

Hosea.

A cold chill crept up his spine. Hosea heard God's words as if they were spoken aloud, but he'd never heard Yahweh call him by name. It was both tender and terrifying. Hosea fell to his knees on Tekoa's rocky soil, laying his forehead on the ground, palms up to receive whatever Yahweh would give.

Love your wife, Hosea. Love her as I love My people Israel. Love her as I love Uzziah.

A cool desert breeze swept over him, and the moment was over. Hosea lifted his head, heart racing. *As You love Uzziah? What do You mean, Yahweh?* But his spirit was silent. Would Yahweh send Jonah to help him understand? He glanced all around but saw no one stirring on Amos's compound. Even the animals were bedded own for the night. He looked to the cloudless sky. The moon was bright, stars shining.

There would be no explanation tonight.

He stood and dusted off his robe. With a deep sigh, he let the exhaustion of the day settle into his bones. "I do love her, Yahweh." He felt some of the sadness lift as he said the words aloud. His steps quickened. "I do love her." With each step, he let thoughts of his wife draw him toward the stone house he'd once shared with his abba. Gomer had come so far in the three days since they'd left Samaria. She'd shared her fears, cried in his arms. She even seemed willing to submit to the fellowship meal at the temple — until she saw King Uzziah. Perhaps Yahweh had meant Hosea must teach her faithfully, love her consistently, and, if she rebelled, somehow discipline her.

He wiped his tired face with a long swipe of his hands and looked up, judging the moon at past its midpoint. Gomer would be sound asleep. Tonight hadn't been all that he'd hoped for together in their new home, but perhaps there would be space for him on the mattress beside her. He smiled at the thought.

Anticipation pressed him onward, and he swung open the waist-high wooden gate of his small courtyard. He checked the stable, noting the new livestock he'd purchased for his household. The donkey and now two goats had fresh hay. He listened for the soft, contented clucking of hens on their nests. *I must remember to thank Micah.*

Micah had become Hosea's shadow since news of his prophetic message had filtered through the camp. He was a good boy, brought by his abba to study at the prophets' camp three years ago, and Jonah took over his guardianship. Though Hosea didn't feel the same kinship with him as with Isaiah, Micah was another little brother with whom he felt a special bond.

Isaiah. A wave of melancholy swept over Hosea. *Will You call him to ministry, Yahweh? Will he be called to sacrifice like me?*

He shook his head, scoffing inwardly. What sacrifice had he really made? He'd been married two full moon cycles and had never bedded his wife. Granted, considering Gomer's beauty, that was a sacrifice. A wry smile creased his face. But waiting for her love was worth it. He stood for a moment outside his front door, rubbed his face again, and lifted the iron latch.

A fire glowed in the oven, and lamplight flickered from the bedchamber.

"Hosea?"

His heart slammed against his chest, his mouth instantly dry. Nervous. Why was he nervous? "Yes, it's me," he said, standing rooted to the floor.

A sound from the bedchamber, and then she was there. Gomer stood silhouetted in the doorway, lamplight illuminating perfect curves through her tunic. All breath left him.

"Is the king all right?" she asked.

Silence.

"Hosea? Is he . . . is he . . . Oh!" She gasped, looking horrified.

He realized she must think Uzziah dead.

"No, the king is fine." He rushed to her and wrapped her in his arms. Her hazel eyes searched his face. "The priests have confined Uzziah for seven days, and then they'll inspect his wounds again . . ." He let his fingers slide up the back of her head, entangle in her copper curls. "I don't want to talk about the king." He kissed her, tasting the cloves he'd come to love. Tentative at first, he waited for her to stop him, to pull away — but she didn't resist. She was intoxicating, filling every part of him with a joy and pleasure he'd never known.

He lifted her into his arms and carried her to the wool-stuffed mattress he'd purchased before going to Israel. He'd been so uncertain then, questioning God's plan, doubting Yahweh's calling. He had no idea he'd find the little girl he'd cared for in Bethel. Now the little girl was the woman God had chosen as his wife.

"Gomer, I will love you all my life," he said, laying her gently on the bed.

Her eyes blazed with a fire from within. "And I will make you happy you chose me." She pulled him into an impassioned kiss, and Hosea was lost in a rapture he thought impossible this side of paradise.

14

A wife with strength of character is the crown of her husband, but the wife who disgraces him is like bone cancer.

Gomer lay beside Hosea in the first rays of dawn, studying every detail of her husband. No man had ever treated her with such gentleness, nor had she felt such tenderness toward any man. He'd been gentle yet strong. She'd lain with soldiers whose arms weren't as defined as those she saw in the morning light. How she longed to trace her fingers over his heavy brows, narrow nose, and round eyes. His lips were deep red and soft — no doubt from the small vial of sheep fat he used while traveling through the wilderness. She smiled, remembering how he slipped it out of his pocket, coated his lips, and returned it to its hiding place.

Oh my! The memory of the sheep fat in his pocket reminded her of the nonexistent gift she'd promised Hosea in Jerusalem. She'd successfully hidden her Asherah when they arrived in Tekoa, but how would she ever find a pocket-sized gift for her husband to make her lie seem true? Perhaps she could barter for something from Yuval without Hosea's knowledge. Yuval could send Amos to purchase something from a nearby market. It seemed a harmless request.

Hosea's long, black eyelashes fluttered, and she laid her head on her arm, pretending to be asleep. When he didn't stir again, she opened one eye and found him still sleeping. Leaning on her elbow, she watched his eyelids continue their dance. Merav said that when a baby's eyelids fluttered, the gods were tickling them in their dreams. *Oh, Merav.*

The thought of her old friend reminded her of the miraculous connection with Yuval. Amos's wife had been as comfortable as an old pair of sandals, and Gomer wondered if her demeanor would change if she knew of Gomer's past. What tricks were the gods playing to have sent her a new friend that so closely resembled her old nursemaid? After learning that Yuval was an orphan

172

from the land of Israel, they pondered the exciting possibility that Merav could have been an unknown relative. Gomer knew nothing of Merav's family, so they would likely never know. *How extraordinary that I would travel so far and find someone like Merav in such a place.*

"You're up early," a husky voice said while strong arms rolled her to her back.

She was consumed by Hosea's presence. More than his physical form that loomed above her, it was the fullness of his presence that left her breathless.

"I think I love you," she said haltingly.

He searched her expression but remained silent, and she cursed her foolishness. His elbows rested beside her head, and he combed his fingers through her hair. "Tell me what love means to you," he said gently.

She felt fire rise in her cheeks and turned away.

He kissed her lips, then her neck, and whispered, "I love you and have promised to always love you. Now, please, my wife . . ." Another kiss. "Tell me why you *think* you love me."

She kissed him thoroughly, no desire to talk. But he eased away, grinned, and raised one eyebrow.

"Uhh! I should never have said anything!"

Her frustrated quip dowsed the fire in Hosea's eyes. He rolled onto his back and stared at the ceiling.

Gomer squeezed her eyes shut. Why must they talk like old women at the well? Why couldn't he be satisfied with her passion as other men had been? *He's not other men. He's Hosea.* She felt the gentle strumming on her fingers and couldn't suppress a smile. He always knew how to calm her.

"I'm sorry," she said finally, still lying beside him looking at the ceiling. "It's hard for me to tell how I feel because it's like giving you a part of me that you can destroy." Her throat tightened with emotion, and she considered stopping there. Surely that was enough to satisfy him. But then she remembered last night. Perhaps she could trust him — just a little. "I think I love you because I don't want any other man to touch me." There. She'd said it. It wasn't eloquent. It didn't smell of roses. But it was the truth.

Neither of them moved. She wondered what he was thinking but was afraid to ask.

"Thank you for trusting me and for telling me you love me." He leaned on his elbow then, hovering over her, and traced the line of her nose, her mouth, her neck. "I went to Israel because Yahweh told me to marry a prostitute and love her as He loves Israel. I thought that kind of love would be . . . I don't know . . . practiced, strictly an arrangement. I never dreamed I would love this woman with every fiber of my soul." Tears gathered on his long lashes. "I'm awed that God could love His people this way, and I'm beyond thankful that He gave you back to me after all this time."

"Oh! I just remembered!" Gomer's sudden jolt startled her husband, and they both giggled.

He pecked her nose with a kiss. "What could you possibly remember at such a moment?"

She felt her cheeks burn again, but this time adoration, not shame, lit the spark. "When you said your god gave me back to you after all this time, it reminded me of Yuval. She brought a small meal last night, and I thought Mot had sent the ghost of my old friend Merav." Hosea frowned, and Gomer wondered if he was confused or unhappy at her mention of Mot. "Do you remember the old woman who tried to stop the sacrifice in Jeroboam's temple?"

Hosea nodded slowly, recognition dawning. "I didn't see her clearly, but I do seem to recall she resembled Yuval. But Gomer, you are among Yahweh's people here. You need not fear the pagan gods while —"

"I know," she interrupted, hoping to skip the Yahweh lesson. "But while Yuval and I were talking, she told me that Amos's abba bought her as an orphaned slave from Israel. She has little memory of her life before coming to Judah, and when Amos fell in love with her and claimed her as his wife, she was accepted into his family and has thought little of her Israelite roots." Gomer realized she was sitting up, gesturing wildly, and Hosea was watching with an amused grin.

"So you've been in camp less than a day and already have found a friend?"

She squealed and pounced on him. They rolled over and over, wrapping themselves in the blanket. "Yes! And she's the owner's wife!" Gomer settled atop her husband, resting her chin on his chest.

"We care very little about status and wealth here on Amos's farm. Yuval is one of the most caring women you'll ever meet. She may be the owner's wife, but she works harder than the poorest serving maid."

After the slight reprimand, Gomer treaded lightly on the next subject. "While we were in Samaria, we never discussed my wifely duties." She paused, not sure how to proceed.

Unexpectedly, Hosea tumbled her onto her back and hovered above her, smiling. "I don't think we need to *discuss* anything. You do very well without any discussion."

She giggled. "I was talking about cooking." His smile disappeared, and she laughed aloud. "Didn't you notice that I never cooked a meal in Samaria?"

"I thought it was because you hated me." They laughed together at this.

"Well, I suppose that was part of it," she said, "but the complete truth is that I've always had servant girls cook for me. So Yuval is going to teach me to cook!"

The tenderness in his eyes staggered her. "I'm so proud of you."

Her throat constricted. No words could describe a man who was proud of his harlot wife who didn't cook. She pulled him into her arms and wept. "I *know* I love you."

Hosea basked in his wife's delight during their morning exploration of Amos's farm. He remembered the fascination he'd felt when arriving with Abba Beeri twelve years ago. Seeing Tekoa's rugged beauty through Gomer's eyes was like gazing out a window through a silken sash.

"Look at the endless fig trees! And those sheep — they're tiny!"

Hosea laughed, watching his wife scatter the shepherds' carefully herded sheep. "Yes, they're a special breed of desert sheep. Amos travels to markets and festivals from Beersheba to Damascus to sell their wool and the cloth our women weave." One of the shepherds rose from his shady resting spot, a scowl on his weathered face, while his whole flock broke into a bleating frenzy.

"Hello, little sheep! Come here and let me see how soft you are."

Hosea captured her hand. "Come, Wife. Let's get to the pottery workshop and meet the king's uncle Amoz." He glanced over his shoulder, noting two shepherds whispering and pointing. He hoped they were simply angry about Gomer's lack of animal husbandry.

"But I saw a lamb over there . . ." She pouted as he pulled her away.

"The shepherds are a bit protective of their flocks. Have you spent much time around animals?"

"No, in fact, I was a little frightened when we were traveling through the wilderness. I'd heard there were lions between here and Samaria, but I've never really been around animals since I've lived in cities."

Hosea watched his wife wander and chatter as if she hadn't a care in the world.

"Of course, I've seen smelly old donkeys, and I know goats are a nuisance and will eat anything you put in front of them."

Hosea laughed out loud, thoroughly entertained. "Well, *we* own a smelly donkey and two bothersome goats. We also have several chickens, but the rooster you hear crowing each morning belongs to Yuval and Amos next door."

"I have chickens?" Her voice was filled with wonder. Then she raised her arms and shouted, "I have chickens!"

They passed two women who stared at Gomer as if she'd grown two heads. They'd been busy weaving an intricately designed fabric on a large loom but stopped when the couple passed by. One whispered to the other behind her hand, and then both scowled in Gomer's direction.

Hosea glanced at his wife, relieved to find her taking in the lush canopy of sycamore figs above them. Another distraction was in order. "And because we have chickens, my wife, we also have snakes."

"What?" All mirth disappeared. "Snakes?"

He reached for her hand and lifted it to his lips. "But Amos bought a useful gift for Yuval on his last market run to Beersheba."

"We have snakes?" Gomer couldn't seem to get beyond that news.

"Amos discovered a new kind of animal called a cat — from Egypt. He bought two of them for Yuval, and, well . . . they multiply quickly because now we have fifteen."

She wrapped her arms around her waist, searching the path before her. "Are there snakes everywhere? Are they just after the chickens, or are they out here with people too?"

Hosea stopped walking and held her at arm's length. "Listen. Tekoa is southern Israel, and we have snakes. And yes, there were lions in the wilderness through which we traveled, but they remain outside Amos's gates. Most wild animals are more afraid of you than you are of them."

"I doubt that." Then almost pleading, she said, "I know the larger beasts won't come into the compound and they prowl at night, but snakes frighten me, Hosea."

He brushed her cheek with the back of his hand. "Our chickens eat small snakes, and the cats prey on the larger vipers. Snakes sleep between rocks most of the day, so just stay on the main path and you'll be fine."

"What about the house? Are they in the house?"

"How about if we ask Yuval to borrow one of her cats?"

His wife's quick and emphatic nod told

him she approved.

"All right, as soon as I introduce you to Amoz, I'll have Yuval introduce you to a new cat."

Her smile returned, and they resumed their walk, ambling along the farm's main path. They passed homes, stables, storage barns, and the prophets' hall, where students gathered for Jonah's lessons. They veered off the main path that circled north and continued south toward the pottery workshop. The large, two-story building stood a stone's throw away, belching smoke from two chimneys.

Gomer inspected the shop from foundation to rooftop. "Why is it so far from the rest of the camp?"

Hosea directed her gaze to the smoke rising above them. "When Amos agreed to let the king build his uncle's workshop, they knew the kilns would produce significant smoke and fire hazards. So they situated it in the farthest southern corner of the property, away from our homes, the livestock, and the wool and fig operations. They also built a southern gate to make transporting the raw clay and drying pottery more convenient."

He placed his hand at the small of her back, nudging her forward. She seemed hesitant, a little nervous to embrace this new adventure. The woman he married wasn't so different from the little girl in Bethel. She still blustered of big adventures but needed his reassurance to take the first step. He held open the curtain on the workshop doorway, and they stepped inside.

"Hosea!" Amoz's cheerful voice greeted them from the potter's loft. One word and a lifted hand would suffice from the man of frugal speech.

Hosea saw Isaiah's betrothed rushing down the loft stairs. "Aya!"

"Hosea, welcome home. It's good to see you."

He felt Gomer tense, and she leaned close to whisper, "Who's the lovely maiden that blushes at the sight of you?"

He chuckled quietly. "That's Isaiah's beloved Aya. The one to whom he compares every other woman on earth."

Aya arrived with an empty basket dangling from her arm. Amoz wasn't far behind, his beard littered with crumbs, presumably from the contents of Aya's basket. The potter reached out his hand, and Hosea locked his forearm in a friendly embrace.

"It's good to be home," Hosea said. Stepping aside, he placed his hand at Gomer's back and felt her trembling. "Amoz, this is my wife, Gomer. She thinks she might enjoy learning to work clay. Would you be interested in an apprentice?"

The kind eyes of the quiet man sparkled. "Isaiah mentioned it this morning." He turned to Gomer and offered a slight bow. "Come tomorrow, after you break your fast."

A small gasp betrayed Gomer's excitement. "Thank you, Master Amoz."

He nodded, acknowledging her respect, his cheeks pinking at the attention.

"And this is Aya."

The girl stepped forward like an eager playmate. "I saw Isaiah when I brought Amoz's midday meal. He told me you were beautiful." She perused Gomer like a trinket in the market. "I had no idea a harlot would be so beautiful."

Hosea couldn't breathe. Gomer went rigid.

Aya continued chattering, seemingly oblivious to the pain she'd just inflicted. "Isaiah and I are to be married in a year. Perhaps we'll raise our children together. We'll cook and weave toge—"

"What fun we'll have," Gomer interrupted, venom dripping from her voice.

"Gomer, stop." Hosea wrapped his arm around her trembling shoulders and tried to guide her toward the door. "Come, we'll talk about this at home." He kept his voice low, though every sound in the workshop had fallen silent and all busy hands had stilled.

She shrugged off his arm and stood regally, addressing her audience. "You can teach me to cook and weave, and I'll teach you how to please a man in ways a wife cannot fathom."

A collective gasp sucked all air from the shop, and Hosea squeezed his eyes shut.

Gomer turned to Amoz with the grace of a leopard on the hunt. "I will understand if you don't wish to train a *harlot* in the art of pottery." She offered a cursory nod and took a step to leave.

"I am not training a harlot," Amoz said softly. "I am training my friend's wife."

Gomer met his gaze, expressionless. "As you wish." She reached for Hosea's arm with a trembling hand, glancing at the women workers who now stared openly. "We must go for now. Yuval is teaching me to cook. A harlot has so little time for such mundane tasks before becoming a wife."

Hosea tucked her hand into the bend of his elbow and led her out of the workshop. The moment the late morning sun kissed their faces, she jerked her hand away as if he'd contracted Uzziah's leprosy. Without a word, she started walking, her posture stiff as a rod, her chin lifted in defiance.

And Hosea knew. All the trust he'd built since leaving Samaria had been shattered, left in a heap like the shard pile at the pottery shop.

They passed the women at the loom, but Gomer's focus never wavered, her eyes fixed on some distant point straight ahead, jaw set. They were a few cubits from the first row of houses when she finally stopped and challenged him. "How many people know?"

He took a deep breath. "Everyone."

She staggered to the edge of the path and collapsed to one knee, hiding her face. When he tried to comfort her, she pushed him away.

Patient. He must be patient. He sat next to her there. Waiting. She rocked. No sound. No words. He lost track of time. People passed by, but he ignored them. Someone offered water, but Hosea waved him away.

Finally, Gomer looked at him, eyes swollen but with no other remnant of tears. "If I am to be your whore, I expect to be paid."

The words sliced him, as they had undoubtedly been intended to. "You are my wife, Gomer. Almost two full moons have passed since I heard Yahweh's voice telling me to take a wife. It was the first prophetic mission the Lord had given since Amos's journey to Israel twelve years ago."

"Congratulations." The hatred in her voice chilled him.

"No, listen!" Frustration overtook him, but he shook his head, calming his voice. "Please, just listen. After the Lord spoke on the wind, I told Jonah that I was to go to Israel and marry a prostitute. The whole camp rejoiced that Yahweh had spoken to His people." She turned away, and he was tempted to embrace her, make her listen. But he continued talking to her back. "I assumed I'd marry some nameless harlot out of obedience to Yahweh — an arrangement."

He paused, waiting for a reply. None came.

"Don't you see, Gomer? We prophets talked about God's command, and the whole camp celebrated the event. Even the nation of Judah celebrated Yahweh's message."

She turned, horror on her features. "King Uzziah knows? He knew I was a harlot when I approached him in the street?" He watched her draw the linen veil over her face, hiding her humiliation.

He ached for her.

"Please, my wife. Hear and know that you

are a miracle in my eyes. The camp sent me to Israel to be obedient, but when I found you, I understood that Yahweh wanted more than my obedience. He wants me to help Israel understand His love. Until I fell in love with you, I had no idea how deeply Yahweh's heart is moved by His people. Others know our marriage began as a command, but now it's up to us to show them the miracle of love it's become."

She removed the veil from her face, her expression once again void of emotion. "There is no miracle, Hosea. There is only a prophet married to a prostitute." She stood and sneered. "And prostitutes don't cook."

15

HOSEA 5:5–6

The people of Israel's arrogance testifies against them . . . and Judah stumbles with them. They go . . . to search for Yahweh, but they can't find him. He has left them.

Gomer couldn't stop shaking. Hosea had tried to distract her with idle chatter as they walked home from the pottery workshop, but she'd seen every sideways glance and huddled whisper. How had she missed it before? *You're a fool, Gomer.* She'd become complacent, forgotten the first rule of the streets. *Always be aware of your surroundings.* Why had she allowed herself to trust him? Men always betrayed.

"Shalom, Gomer." Yuval's voice accompanied a gentle knock on her front door.

Why had Hosea sent her? When they'd arrived home, Jonah had been waiting and said Uzziah wanted to meet with both prophets immediately. Hosea had looked at her as if she were a helpless cripple and promised to send Yuval. She'd told him not to bother. He was evidently deaf *and* stubborn.

"Gomer?" Another knock.

"Yes, yes. Coming." She stomped to the door, any pain from Eitan's beating numbed by Hosea's betrayal. With a deep breath, she tried to calm herself, adopting a pleasant air. *I must be hospitable to the owner's wife.* She opened the door — and Merav's ghost smiled back.

"Oh, there you are, dear," Yuval said. "I wondered if you'd gone out for a walk this morning."

A wave of grief washed over her. She stepped back. "Please, come in." Then she saw the creature in the old woman's arms. "What is *that*?"

Yuval chuckled and stepped over the threshold, stirring the air with the fresh scent of coriander. "Hosea said you might be interested in meeting Sampson. These Egyptian cats may not look ferocious, but you should see them go after the little snakes that crawl under the bed."

Gomer shivered at the thought — then considered asking if the cat would go after the big snake who slept *in* her bed. She refreshed her practiced smile. "Perhaps you should tell me more about living in Judah, Yuval. We never had to worry about snakes and wild beasts in Samaria." At the mention of her old life, Gomer was stricken with renewed humiliation.

"You knew last night," she whispered, "yet you were still kind to me." Yuval held her gaze, and Gomer measured the old woman in silence, suspicion coiling around her heart like the deadly vipers she feared. "Why did you bring me food when you knew who — what I was? And why are you being nice to me now?" A slight pause, and then she understood. "You wanted to see for yourself what Israel's filthy harlot looked like. Now you'll have plenty of details to share with your friends in camp, is that it?"

The old woman swallowed hard, and her eyes grew damp. "I'm being nice because — well, because you're like a newly planted fig tree, Gomer. You need a little extra care or you'll runt out and die in this climate." She transferred the cat into Gomer's arms and stepped toward the worktable and oven. "Everything in life can be learned from fig farming, child. Now pull out one of those rugs and sit down while I put on a pot of lentils to soak."

Gomer held the furry creature at arm's length, a little stunned that Yuval stayed. She studied the cat, inspecting its hypnotic green eyes, black stripes, and speckled, light-gray coat. "Will it bite me? What's that sound he's making?"

"That means he likes you. He won't bite you, but his tongue is rough, so the first time he licks you, it may feel like a little bite."

Gomer was smitten. She held him under her chin and stroked his silky fur. She danced with him toward the stack of goat-skin rugs and reached for the one on top. "So, tell me, Yuval, does Sampson scare the snakes or does he —" An iron pot clanged, and panic shot through her. "Yuval, no!"

Gomer's shout startled the old woman, and a wooden spoon clattered to the floor. "Blooming fig trees, child! What's the matter? I was just going to soak the lentils."

Gomer dropped the cat, her mind whirring for any excuse to move Yuval away from the shelf where her Asherah lay hidden. "I refuse to cook for Hosea. He told everyone I'm a harlot, so I told him harlots don't cook." Her cheeks flamed. It sounded so childish when she heard herself say it. Perhaps it would have been less embarrassing to let Yuval find the goddess.

The old woman set aside the cooking pot and joined Gomer on a rug while Sampson curled up at their feet. "I know it's hard to live with a past you're not proud of. I felt unworthy to be Amos's wife — an orphaned servant girl marrying the son of a wealthy landowner. Many of the women were unkind to me at first, and even more when our betrothal became widely known. But what matters most is the way our husbands treat us, not the opinions of a few jealous gossips on the farm."

Gomer felt tears burn. She didn't want to cry in front of the owner's wife, but the compassionate face looking back at her seemed so familiar, the voice so much like the woman who had raised her. She fell into Yuval's arms and wept. Tired. Confused. Angry.

"Why do the gods hate me? Why won't they leave me alone and let me live in peace?"

Yuval rocked her back and forth, removing Gomer's blue veil, stroking her hair. "There is only one God, child, and He doesn't hate you. Yahweh chose you as Hosea's wife."

"To make me a mockery among the people of Judah!"

"To make you the example of His divine

love." Her words were soft-spoken but firm. She coaxed Gomer to sit up. "Look around you. In what other home do you see such fine pottery? And how many baskets of grain do you count?" When Gomer didn't answer, Yuval grasped her chin and delved into her eyes. "How many baskets of grain?"

"Three."

"Yes, three baskets of grain. Do you know how many baskets of grain Hosea purchased last year — for the whole year?"

Gomer shook her head.

"He purchased one basket of grain for himself, and he slept on one of these goat-skin rugs. Who do you think he bought all these supplies and that beautiful wool-stuffed mattress for? He was preparing his home for a wife, Gomer."

"He was preparing for a harlot."

"Listen to me, little Gomer. Hosea prepared his heart to obey Yahweh and marry a prostitute — yes. But the man I saw return with you in his arms was a man in love. He loves his *wife,* Gomer." Yuval released her chin but held her gaze. "Only you can make yourself a harlot in his eyes." She transferred a kiss from her finger to Gomer's nose. "Now, I intend to teach you how to cook today, so you'd best find a better spot for whatever you've hidden over there by the cooking pot while I go to the well for some water."

The door clicked shut behind Yuval, and Gomer grabbed the Asherah, hurrying to secure a new hiding place before her perceptive friend returned. She had planned to involve Yuval in securing a gift for Hosea — something to make the lie she'd told him in Jerusalem seem true. But Yuval would almost certainly discern Gomer's duplicity. Like her old friend Merav, Yuval seemed to have an inner sense about Gomer that was both comforting and frustrating.

Allowing herself one last glance at the Asherah before hiding her under the mattress, Gomer felt renewed anger bubble up. Hosea didn't deserve a gift. If he asked what happened to the item purchased for him in Jerusalem, she'd tell him she destroyed it — just as he had destroyed any hope of their happiness.

"I've been praying all night for King Uzziah," Jonah said, allowing Hosea and Isaiah to support him as they walked the rocky trail between the king's rented house and the fenced compound of Amos's farm. "I've had no relief from this wariness in my spirit."

"I spoke with him this morning," Isaiah

194

said, "and he seemed in good spirits, though his wounds are worsening." He shook his head, seeming as puzzled as Jonah. "I left him just after the midday meal as his three chief advisors were arriving."

Hosea felt a little guilty. He hadn't given King Uzziah's troubles much thought since arriving home last night. He'd been consumed with his wife — both her ecstasy and her agony. Sighing, he tried to refocus. How could he be of worth to this struggling king?

"Uzziah knows we're of little help until the priests examine him again in seven days." Hosea was so engrossed in guiding Jonah's footing, he felt the prophet's nudge before he noticed the changes.

"What's wrong?" Isaiah glanced from the prophets to his cousin's makeshift royal city. Surrounding the little stone house was a sea of royal tents, spaced the prescribed ten cubits from the leprous king's abode. Guards and priests scurried at Uzziah's command, while he sat on a mat in the doorway of the house. It seemed the king had moved his throne to Tekoa.

"I don't think King Uzziah is learning Yahweh's intended lesson on humility." Jonah's voice reflected the dread Hosea felt. This would not be an easy meeting. Isaiah's confusion was evident, but they left his questions unanswered, hoping he'd see the spiritual significance of the meeting through the veil of his family devotion.

"Shalom the house!" Hosea shouted, trudging toward the royal clearing.

"Ah, the prophets have arrived!" Uzziah waved them over like old friends.

"My lord, remember the Law!" the high priest shouted.

"Oh, yes, yes." Uzziah cleared his throat and belted out, "Unclean! Unclean!" and then checked for the high priest's approval. Yahweh's priest nodded, and Uzziah regained his amiable smile. "I'm not used to the regulations of a leper yet. Please, Hosea, Jonah, be seated in my new audience chamber. Isaiah can show you." He winced when moving his arm to direct them. Isaiah's report of intensified suffering had not been exaggerated.

The audience chamber, as he called it, was a set of fine tapestries on the ground, two camels' lengths from the king's front door. The sun had reached midday, and thankfully, both the tapestries and the king's entry would be shaded by mighty sycamores.

The two younger men bowed to the king and his officials and then helped lower Jonah on the tapestry between them. Uzziah charged ahead with introductions.

"Have you met my officials, Jeiel, Maaseiah, and Hananiah? Jeiel is my chief scribe and Maaseiah my most trusted advisor. Hananiah is the commander of Judah's army. Gentlemen . . ."

The three officials bowed, and the prophets returned the respectful gesture.

Hosea glanced at Jonah, hoping the more experienced prophet would begin the conversation. He didn't, and an uncomfortable silence ensued. Hosea noted the advisors' stony expressions, fueling his apprehension. Isaiah, to his credit, remained silent, waiting for whatever prompted Uzziah's meeting to unfold.

"As you know," Uzziah's voice suddenly echoed off the hills, "Israel and Judah have enjoyed peace since Jeroboam and I have ruled our nations, but you may not know at what price. When Jeroboam's abba died and released my abba from a Samaritan prison, no formal treaty was signed, but an informal agreement has been understood."

Hosea sensed Isaiah tense beside him and wondered how much of the privileged political and family information his friend knew.

"I don't actively scout Jeroboam's Israel," Uzziah said, leveling his gaze at Hosea, "and his troops stay out of Judah."

Uzziah glanced at Commander Hananiah, and the man's voice boomed as big as his stature. "But we'd all be fools to turn blind eyes to the weapons and war strategies of neighboring nations."

The king nodded to his scribe, who handed a wax tablet and stylus to his advisor, Maaseiah. The advisor then relayed the writing materials into Jonah's hands.

"I've asked my advisors to attend today's meeting in order to witness your statements," Uzziah said, pointing at the items of exchange.

Jonah looked down at the unmarked tablet and returned an empty stare. "We're not sure what *statements* you'd like us to make."

The commander stepped forward, two long strides that placed him midway between the king and the audience tapestries. "You prophets have spent two full moon cycles in Israel, and we need to know how Jeroboam's troops compare to Judah's. We have a standing army of over three hundred thousand trained soldiers, but I'd still like to know what we'd be up against if Israel attacked us."

At this point, Jeiel stepped forward with a partially unrolled scroll, announcing with delight the things that appeal to scribes. "We have shields, spears, helmets, armor, bows,

and stones for slings. It would be most helpful if we could compile a similar inventory
of Israel's war supplies, including an ac-
counting of chariots, horses, war machines . . ." He looked up from his scroll
and added, "Whatever information you
provide would be helpful."

Hosea sensed Jonah's tension and felt his
own stomach tightening into a knot. Uzziah
was a good and godly king. Did he understand so little of Hosea's calling to Israel?
He must find a way to answer respectfully
and yet remind the king that he and Jonah
had not gone to Israel as spies.

"I would be happy to tell the king everything I witnessed of Israel's military status."
Hosea's earnest tone seemed to relax the
advisors and shed eager delight on Uzziah's
features. "We entered Samaria's gates and
went to the temple, where we saw King
Jeroboam's general, Menahem, standing
next to him at a pagan sacrifice. We then
witnessed a contingent of guards escort a
battered old woman into the temple while
the captain held an infant aloft, marching
toward a brazen altar of Molech. We heard
later that they tossed the infant into the fire,
mirroring the sins of the Canaanite nations
before them."

Uzziah's mouth dropped open, and Hosea

felt a measure of satisfaction that they would see Israel's perversity through Yahweh's eyes. Perhaps then they'd better understand Hosea's role as God's prophet.

He turned to Hananiah, trying to impress on him the importance of righteous military leadership — and God's judgment when it was abused. "My wife, Gomer, endured a brutal beating from one of Jeroboam's top soldiers. She nearly died, but by God's grace she regained the use of her limbs. Our only other contact with Israel's military occurred the night we fled Samaria. Gomer was falsely accused and nearly executed." Hosea eyed each official and finally focused on Judah's regent. "That, King Uzziah, is our complete knowledge of Jeroboam's weapons and war strategies."

The king sat silently, his expression unreadable through the sores that covered his forehead, cheeks, and chin. His advisors, however, returned to the stone-cold stares they'd displayed when the prophets arrived.

Uzziah inhaled deeply, seeming to have pondered the deep mysteries of the earth. "You're telling me that you spent two moon cycles in Israel, but you don't know how many chariots Jeroboam keeps ready for battle in Samaria?"

Hosea turned to Jonah, bewildered, and

watched Isaiah's head drop to his chest. Unfathomable. How could anyone hear stories of child sacrifice and abuse of women yet still be concerned with chariots?

Hosea squeezed the bridge of his nose. "My lord, we know nothing of King Jeroboam's military plans or provisions. I don't know how to say it more plainly."

"How can you know nothing?" Uzziah pushed himself to his feet and winced in pain. "Are you unaware or simply unwilling to help Judah guard against attack? I realize you're both Israelite by birth, but we've welcomed you into our nation with open arms."

"Cousin!" Isaiah jumped to his feet, but before he could say more, Jonah grabbed his arm and struggled to his feet.

"We saw no evidence of any imminent Israelite campaign against Judah or any other nation," Jonah shouted. By this time Hosea had risen and was supporting the old prophet's waist. "Hosea's sole mission was to deliver God's message of judgment, and we —"

Judah's commander stepped forward, hand on his sword hilt, and Hosea laughed in spite of the tension. What was a frail old prophet going to do to a leprous king?

"His so-called mission was to marry a

prostitute!" Uzziah's angry words echoed in the trees. And silence hung like filthy rags.

A cool breeze stirred the leaves, sending a chill down Hosea's spine. The guards and advisors tensed, stepping away from the three men on the audience rugs. The priests fell to their knees and covered their faces. Everyone knew — only Yahweh's presence stirred a chill wind on a sunny desert afternoon.

Speak to the king of Judah, the Lord said to Hosea's spirit.

Hosea glanced at Jonah and Isaiah, who stood beside him, and then turned to King Uzziah, recognizing fear on his features.

"I'm sorry, Hosea," the king said, panic quaking his voice. "I didn't mean to insult you."

"The Lord says, 'Israel's arrogance testifies against them. Israel and Ephraim stumble because of their sins. And Judah stumbles with them. They go with their sheep and cattle to search for the Lord, but they can't find Him. He has left them.' "

Hosea fell silent, Yahweh's message complete.

"No, please." Uzziah appeared stunned, overwhelmed. "It can't be." He turned to the priests, shouting, "Tell him how many bulls I've sacrificed, how faithful I've been to bring my offerings to the temple every day. Tell him! I have given Yahweh *everything*! I have been more faithful than Solomon. I've built fortresses, invented war machines, conquered the Philistines."

The priests remained in their penitent posture, silent before the display of God's presence.

"My lord," Hosea said, "Yahweh did not question your faithfulness. He condemned your arrogance. And because you refuse to acknowledge your sinful pride, the Lord has left you."

Uzziah swallowed hard and fell silent. He stared at his leprous hands and then looked back at the prophets. "How long? How long will Yahweh punish me?"

Hosea felt ill. "The Lord has *left* you, King Uzziah, just as He left Israel. Do you know what that means?" He waited, but the king seemed entranced, studying his hands. Hosea shook his head, uncertain if he was even being heard. "My counsel to you is to humble yourself before Yahweh. Seek Him with all your heart. Perhaps someday He will heal your body after you seek healing for your soul."

Commander Hananiah stepped toward them, glancing first at his king and then at the prophets. He kept his voice low, addressing Hosea with a new level of respect. "King Uzziah is a man of action, my lord. Please be patient with him." Tenderness glistened in his eyes. "He is a good man — and a good friend. He's worked hard to build the nation of Judah."

"That's where you and your king are wrong, Hananiah," Hosea answered gently. "Yahweh will share His glory with no man. It is not Uzziah who has built Judah into a prosperous nation."

"Tell my cousin I'll return this evening to share a few of David's songs." Isaiah patted the commander's shoulder as the three men turned toward camp.

The sound of a sudden crash startled them all. Their eyes were drawn to Judah's king — slid down the door frame into a heap on the floor. No one dared touch him and become unclean. He lay alone, weeping on the threshold of his exile.

16

What should I do with you, Ephraim? What should I do with you, Judah? Your love is like fog in the morning. It disappears as quickly as the morning dew.

Gomer waved good-bye to Yuval, feeling a pang of sadness, watching their shadows stretch long in the dusky glow of sunset. "You're coming back tomorrow, aren't you?" she called out as the woman entered her courtyard gate next door.

"Of course. You and Hosea would starve without me." The twinkle in her eyes was as comforting as the stars on a cloudless night.

Gomer stepped back into her own little courtyard and decided to explore the stable. Sampson had become a fast friend and constantly rubbed against her ankles, his soft, lithe body wrapping around one leg and then the other. "You would make a fine dancer." She leaned over and hoisted the cat into her arms, tucking him under her chin, cuddling him close to her heart.

The stable was a three-sided enclosure, two beams supporting the canopy, open toward the north. "Hello there," she said, reaching over the wooden fence to scratch the donkey behind its large, pointed ears. "Who takes care of you?" Two curious black heads nudged the donkey aside, their long horns curled behind their ears. Bleating loudly, the goats refused to be ignored.

She giggled and offered them some attention while her eyes adjusted to the darkness behind them. The stable was neat and clean. She saw a large, hollowed-out stone container on her right and lifted the lid, finding it full of grain for the animals. She remembered Yuval's recounting of Hosea's extravagant preparations for his harlot wife and wondered if his animals benefited because a woman had arrived.

"You'd better make sure that lid is tight on the grain, or we'll have rodents, and rodents mean snakes."

Gomer jumped as if her toes were on fire. Hosea leaned against one of the beams at the entry.

"I'm sorry," he said. "I didn't mean to

startle you." He walked into the shadow of the canopy, looking weary, almost vulnerable. She wondered what had happened with King Uzziah but didn't want to ask — didn't want to care.

She replaced the lid tightly and kept her head bowed. She felt him watching her. "So will I be expected to feed and tend the animals, or do you have servants for that? I hadn't realized you were the wealthiest prophet this side of Egypt."

He didn't answer, and her curiosity forced her to look at him.

"What makes you think I'm wealthy?" he asked, an infuriating grin replacing his weary expression.

Her heart skipped a beat. "Yuval said you purchased all sorts of supplies in preparation for your new harlot, and a poor man can't afford two goats and a donkey." Sampson wriggled in her arms, and she realized she must have been squeezing him. She eased her grip and tried to hurry past her husband. "Yuval prepared lentil stew for your evening meal."

Hosea grabbed her arm and pulled her to a stop, drawing her close enough to whisper against her blue linen veil. "Who's this?" he asked, reaching over to scratch behind Sampson's ear. His fingers brushed her neck. He kissed her cheek and lingered, waiting for her answer.

She swallowed hard, trying to steady her breathing. "Sampson."

"Why don't you and Sampson wait for me inside, and I'll come in after I take care of the stable animals." He stepped back and tilted her chin up.

She could only nod. No man had ever held this power over her. She hurried away, crossed the small courtyard to the house, and closed the door behind her. Everywhere he'd touched her still tingled.

She hurriedly unwrapped the Asherah she'd hidden under the mattress, stroking her cool, smooth form. "Hear my prayer, Mother of Abundance, giver of life and health. Make me a fruitful vine to bear children for my old age. May I be pleasing to my husband long enough to bring forth an heir." She felt calmed by her prayer — until the iron latch of the front door made her heart race again. She rewrapped the goddess, shoved it back under the mattress, and reached for a clove to suck on. Hosea seemed to like the scent of cloves.

"Gomer?"

Seated on the bed, she waited for him to appear in the doorway. The small window aimed a narrow shaft of light across her body. Dust particles danced in its rays. She heard his footsteps approaching and inhaled a calming breath.

"There you are," he said. His face was shadowed, but she heard pleasure in his voice.

"Are you hungry?" she asked, lying across the bed, patting the space next to her. "Or could you spend a few moments with your wife before you enjoy Yuval's lentil stew?"

She saw him hesitate, standing firm in the doorway. "When I left my wife at midday, she wasn't speaking to me. When I greeted her at the stables, she was cool at best. To what might I attribute this sudden warm welcome?"

Gomer leapt from the bed and stood by the mattress, her cheeks flaming. "Can we never simply enjoy one another's company? Must we always discuss every issue before we reap the benefits of this so-called marriage?"

In slow, measured steps, Hosea closed the distance between them. His face reflected the pain her words had inflicted. "This *so-called* marriage is my life, Gomer. I want to honor both Yahweh and my wife in the way I live it." He placed his hands on her hips and pressed her gently to sit on the edge of the bed. He stood over her, holding her chin. "I don't want to just *enjoy* your company. I want to love you deeply, thoroughly." He leaned over and kissed her. Tenderly at first — then with passion.

She encircled his neck, losing herself in the moment, and tried to lie back on the mattress. But he pulled her arms away and laid them in her lap. "Talk to me, Gomer. Tell me how your heart has been healed from this morning's wounds. I want to know your spirit as well as your body. I never intended to hurt you, and I know Aya didn't either. But friends and family will inadvertently wound each other, and when we do, we must know how to help mend the hurt." His eyes were pleading, sincere.

His well-spoken words almost convinced her she could heal — almost. Never again would she trust anyone with her heart, but she would tell him what he wanted to hear. She'd earned a living making men believe her in Samaria.

"Yuval helped me realize that the whole camp celebrated Yahweh's message to you, and that included our marriage. When she explained that she was once an outcast, it helped me believe that someday I could be accepted as she is now." Gomer almost choked on the lie but trained her eyes to speak for her — changing from sincere to seductive. She licked her lips and saw Hosea's defenses crumble. "Would you like your lentil stew now?" She leaned close, warming his cheek with her cloved breath.

With a slight groan, he swept her into his arms and kissed her passionately. No more talking. No more promises. No more lies.

Asherah, do your work.

Hosea awoke with a start. *Yahweh, please, no!* But his dream had been clear. He must return to Israel, and he must leave today. Dread coiled around his heart. How would he tell Gomer? Would she feel abandoned? With a deep sigh, he turned over, ready to wake her with the difficult news.

But she was gone.

"Gomer?" He scanned their small bedchamber. The ivory comb he'd given her was still on the bedside table, and her extra robe and tunic were folded in the corner. A wave of relief washed over him. "Gomer?" he said a little louder.

"I'm in here," she called from their main room.

He rolled out of bed and donned his robe and tunic. The hard-packed floors were cool on his feet, so he slipped on his sandals and peeked around the corner.

She knelt by the oven, fire lit and fresh

211

bread baking in neat circles on its surface.

"Mmm, smells good." He grabbed a goat-skin rug and laid it next to her, sat down, and pulled her close. He nuzzled her neck, inhaling her scent — better than the warm bread.

"Are you impressed?" she asked, reaching over with her wooden fork to turn three barley loaves, each one a golden brown.

"I am impressed. Yuval must have gotten up early to fix our bread." His barb and chuckle earned him a sharp elbow to the ribs.

"No," she huffed, but then confessed, "she left the dough to rise last night before she left." She started giggling before she could finish. "But I'm baking it!"

He tackled her and buried his beard in her neck, and she dissolved into squeals. Their playful banter was balm to his soul, but the reality of his calling sobered him. She must have sensed a pause and caressed his cheek, then knelt again beside the oven to check the barley bread.

He pulled her back against his chest and rested his chin on her shoulder. "Do you know how much I love you, Gomer?"

She stilled instantly, turning to stone. She rose to her knees, poking at the loaves with the wooden fork. "I don't want to burn the bread."

Startled, he rehearsed his words again, trying to recall what hint he might have given of impending bad news. *How could she know?*

"I thought I'd go to the pottery workshop as soon as you sample Yuval's barley loaves," she said, her shoulders rigid. "I'm not sure when I'll be home. What are your plans?" He heard her voice break.

He reached for her arm, but she pushed him away, keeping her attention on the oven. Had Yahweh somehow told her he was leaving? "I'm going to talk with Jonah after we break our fast. Gomer —"

"Tell the old fish prophet I said, 'Shalom.' He's probably happy to be rid of me."

"He lives next door. I'm guessing you'll see him when you walk to the pottery shop."

She turned on him with the force of a whirlwind, throwing the wooden fork at a vase on the mantle — and missing. "Don't mock me, Hosea! I'm a harlot, not an idiot. You're leaving me, aren't you?"

Shock. Wonder. Pain. Hosea wasn't sure which to feel first or worst. "I need to go away for a while, Gomer. That's all. I'll be back." He searched her stony expression. "How did you know I was going?"

The tears she'd held captive slid down her cheeks, but she revealed no other sign of weakness. Chin held high, she regained her calm. "Men always leave."

"No, Gomer. This is different."

One side of her lips raised in a defiant grin.

"No! Listen to me," he said. "Yahweh came to me in a dream and told me to return to Israel. He didn't tell me the specific message I'm to deliver, just that I'm to leave today." He reached over and placed a hand on her thigh. "Gomer . . ."

She stared at his hand. Silent. Indignant. He removed it, and she lifted a single brow. "Perhaps He's sending you to marry another prostitute."

"No!" he said, resenting her smug expression. "You're being ridiculous! I'm a prophet. It's who I am, who the Lord called me to be. I will occasionally be called away from home. Just like Amos must travel to the markets and festivals to sell goods, I must go wherever God leads me —"

"To sell goods." Her eyes flashed. "And you're very good at it, by the way. You almost had me convinced that I could count on you, that you wouldn't leave me like everyone else in my life —" Her voice broke, and she leapt to her feet. She grabbed her

214

blue veil, wrapped it around her head and shoulders, and swung open the door.

"Gomer, wait! We need to talk."

"Actually, we've talked too long already. Your bread is on fire."

Hosea turned and found his barley loaves smoking and then heard the door slam. "Gomer!" he shouted, hurrying to retrieve the fork and dislodge the charred loaves. He stared at the closed door, waving the smoke away. *Yahweh, what should I do with her?* He reached for a crispy barley loaf and burned his fingers, and then was startled by the undeniable voice of his Elohim.

What should I do with you, Ephraim? What should I do with you, Judah? Your love is like fog in the morning. It disappears as quickly as the morning dew.

Hosea allowed his head to fall back, closed his eyes, and wept. How could the God of all creation describe Gomer's love so precisely? *Because Gomer's love mirrors fickle Israel and Judah, and You understand my frustration, don't You, Yahweh?*

Hosea was overwhelmed by God's presence, humbled anew by the awesome privilege of his calling. *Please, take care of my Gomer.*

Go to Israel. The voice was as clear as Yuval's rooster announcing the new day.

17

HOSEA 6:5–6

That is why I cut you down by sending the prophets. . . . I want your loyalty, not your sacrifices. I want you to know me, not to give me burnt offerings.

Gomer hesitated at her courtyard gate. She glanced at Yuval's house next door and considered spewing her venom about Hosea on the owner's wife. But her new friend had likely never heard such vulgar words or seen a harlot's fury. *I'll never belong with people like Yuval and girls like Aya.* She remembered yesterday's humiliation in the pottery shop, the wide-eyed observation of the pure and innocent girl Isaiah would soon marry. Aya appeared two or three years younger than Gomer, but their true ages were worlds apart.

She pushed through her courtyard gate,

walking past Jonah's house instead, fighting the urge to spit on the ground as she passed. At least with the fish prophet, there was no silk or pearls. He told her plainly that idolaters were doomed for destruction — but he'd said she had a lovely spirit. No man had ever ogled her spirit. Beneath that frightening, curdled skin was a man who could disarm her, expose her. She would stay clear of him for sure.

"You're up early this morning!" Isaiah emerged from the next house in the row. She had no idea he and Amoz lived so close.

She rolled her eyes and walked faster, not able to face another battle.

"Hmm. Grumpy already too." He hurried to catch up. "Poor Hosea. A lifetime of waking up to a surly redhead." Then his smile died. He seemed concerned when she couldn't insult him past the lump in her throat. "What's the matter? Aya told me what she said at the pottery shop yesterday, Gomer. She feels terrible. Are you still mad about that?"

She kept walking, the lump growing, the tears getting harder to swallow.

Isaiah grabbed her shoulder and whirled her to face him. "Stop! Tell me what's going on!"

"Hosea's going back to Israel, and I'm a

harlot in a camp full of righteous bigots." His troubled expression somehow fueled her rage. "Now if you'll excuse me, I'm going to spend the day with your abba. Jealous?"

His face drained of color; his lips fell open but made no sound. She'd gone too far. The pain in his eyes mirrored her own closely guarded wound. Staggering, he backed away from her. "Why so cruel to those trying to help you?"

His words snipped her final thread of control. She felt herself spinning, her legs weakening. Isaiah backed away slowly while the camp around them came to life. She glanced at others going on with their lives. She was exposed, alone. Nothing was familiar. She knew no one, trusted no one. And finally . . . she gave up. She collapsed on the camp's main path, tears coming in torrents, and she cared nothing about the gossip fodder she provided.

She jumped when strong hands helped her stand and then realized Isaiah and Amoz were guiding her toward the pottery shop. She noticed three men unloading a wagon of partially finished pots into the shop. Amoz nodded to them as he walked by, but no one spoke until they ascended the stairs and were tucked away in the loft.

They lowered her onto a stool, resting her back against the wall, while Amoz took his place on a stool behind his potter's wheel. She stared numbly at them for a time, Amoz so much older than his son but just as handsome, with distinguished gray streaks through dark, curly hair.

Isaiah exchanged a quick glance with his abba and then turned his attention on Gomer. "You said Hosea is going to Israel again. I'll talk with him about the details of his mission, but Abba and I want to know how we can help you while Hosea's gone." Again Isaiah glanced at Amoz, almost coaxing him. An extended silence followed, and Isaiah heaved a deep sigh. "I *think* Abba would be happy to have you learn the craft of working clay if you're willing to try."

Gomer's stomach was in knots, and though she was waging her own emotional battle, she was painfully aware of the complex relationship before her. Isaiah's life wasn't the perfection she'd imagined, but neither was Amoz a heartless Philistine. She glanced between abba and son, breathed deeply, and made a decision. "I will stay in Tekoa — at least long enough to learn from a master potter." She glimpsed what seemed like approval in Amoz's eyes. "If you're willing to teach me."

A smile lit his face, making him appear ten years younger. "I'm willing."

"That was almost a wedding dance from my abba," Isaiah said, his own pleasure evident. "Now I must go ask my best friend why he's leaving his bride two days after arriving in their new home."

Hosea trudged the rugged path toward the royal encampment, his body weary, his heart heavy. He'd spent a good portion of the morning packing bread, hard cheese, and figs, hoping Gomer would come back — at least to say good-bye. She didn't.

He'd checked his neighbors' houses, hoping to see his beloved friends before leaving on another mission for Yahweh. Amos was traveling, and Yuval said she hadn't seen Gomer yet this morning. He saw concern on her features but couldn't bring himself to explain. *I'm sure Gomer will inform Yuval of what a terrible husband I am.*

He'd gone in search of encouragement from his friend and mentor, but no one answered when he knocked on Jonah's door. The final blow was Isaiah's absence. He was never awake until well after the rooster crowed, but today he and Amoz were both gone. *Yahweh, will You send me away without any encouragement?*

Hosea emerged into Uzziah's encampment clearing, his prayer answered immediately. Jonah and Micah sat on the king's audience tapestry, deep in conversation. *What are they talking about, and why wasn't I invited?* But his curiosity pricked his conscience, and he chastised himself for thinking everything in camp must revolve around him.

"Shalom the house!" Hosea shouted, and all eyes turned to greet him.

"Unclean! Unclean!" Uzziah shouted. "We've been expecting you."

Commander Hananiah appeared from within Uzziah's house, measuring Hosea as if uncertain whether to reach for his sword or fall to his knees. The chief scribe and the king's advisor followed him with the same hesitation on their faces. Yahweh's presence yesterday seemed to have made a lasting impression.

"Come, Hosea," Jonah said, inviting his student to join him on the tapestry. "I've been telling King Uzziah that you're going back to Israel today."

Hosea gaped. He knew better than to ask how Jonah knew. Of course Yahweh had revealed it. "So what else were you telling King Uzziah that I should know about?" He tousled Micah's hair as he walked to the other side of Jonah and sat down.

"I was explaining that you'll be taking Micah with you on this journey."

Hosea raised both eyebrows and leaned forward to exchange a questioning glance with his young friend. "Oh, really? And what does Micah think about that?"

"I'm ready, Hosea. I can be a great help to you." His eyes were alight with adventure, his joy almost enough to lift the weight of Hosea's heavy heart.

He leaned close and whispered to Jonah, "Did Yahweh also tell you how deeply my wife is hurting because of my quick departure?"

"What's going on?" Isaiah emerged from the copse of fig trees behind them.

Hosea turned, ready to taunt that he'd arrived late for the festival, but the fury brewing on his friend's face stopped him cold. He hurried to his feet and extended his hand to Isaiah, meeting him before he reached the tapestry. "Where were you? I came to your house to tell you I'm going back to Israel, but you weren't there."

"I was comforting your wife!"

Hosea's heart stopped beating. "You were what?" White-hot rage rushed through his veins. Why had Gomer gone to his handsome best friend for *comfort*?

"Abba and I took Gomer to the pottery shop after I found her dazed and sobbing on the main path in camp this morning. Abba has been teaching her about pottery all morning."

Hosea stood speechless. He blinked away his misperception, adjusting to the truth after almost accusing his best friend of the unthinkable.

"Isaiah, Hosea, come sit down." Jonah's calm voice was the anchor in their storm. They exchanged a silent truce and sat on opposite sides of their teacher. Micah had moved to a corner of the rug. Wide-eyed and silent.

Jonah stared straight ahead, directing his words to Uzziah, but in essence addressing everyone in the royal encampment. "The mantle of prophecy has been placed squarely on Hosea's shoulders. I'm not Yahweh's voice for this generation, but I've been given an ear to hear in order to teach my students."

Uzziah nodded but said nothing.

"It is my understanding," Jonah continued, "that you received a scroll from your son Jotham early this morning."

The king's eyes went wide and again he nodded, extending his hand to his chief scribe. Jeiel produced a papyrus scroll, and

Uzziah began reading. "To the honorable son of David and king of Judah, Uzziah, from your faithful son and prince, Jotham. Solitary winds blow through the halls of Yahweh's temple as your fearful Judean subjects have refused to return to the site of your affliction. Your people — and even many of Yahweh's priests — are terrified of Yahweh's wrath and now flock to the pagan shrines on every hill and high place. I await your command and will do your will. May our Lord and Elohim give you wisdom like Solomon, and may He heal and bless your name forever."

Hosea felt as if he might retch. Judeans flocking to worship on high places? Could this day grow darker?

"I've already sent a messenger with my reply," Uzziah was saying. "On the advice of my counselors and Yahweh's high priest, I've commanded that the people of Judah may worship Yahweh at any high place until the Lord's punishment runs its course."

The high priest stepped forward, adding, "We'll assign Yahweh priests to each sacred grove to ensure there's no pagan worship —"

"What? No!" Hosea shouted. "Have you forgotten everything you know about our Elohim?"

The high priest puffed out his chest, exposing the jeweled ephod he wore. "You forget to whom you speak, Prophet."

"And you forget whose nation you serve."

The two exchanged stares while the silence lingered.

Uzziah was the first to speak. "I see no harm in allowing frightened worshipers to offer sacrifices to Yahweh on a hill rather than in a temple."

"You see no harm?" Hosea repeated the words, unable to believe them. How could a son of David forget Yahweh's edict to worship the Lord only in His temple?

But before Hosea resorted to human argument, Yahweh's words filled his spirit. He closed his eyes and spoke from Yahweh's heart. "The Lord says to you, King Uzziah, 'I cut you down by sending the prophets. I killed you with the words from My mouth. My judgments shined on you like light. I want your loyalty, not your sacrifices. I want you to know Me, not to give Me burnt offerings.' "

When Hosea opened his eyes, Uzziah's jaw was set like stone. "It seems you and I are at an impasse, Prophet."

"You and I aren't at an impasse, my lord," he said, rising to his feet. "My role is to deliver Yahweh's messages. I have done so faithfully. You will answer to Yahweh on your decision to let the nation worship at the high places." He stepped closer, drawing as near as the Law allowed. "My advice remains unchanged, King Uzziah. Seek the Lord with all your heart. Seek to know Him. He cares nothing about your sacrifices. He wants your heart."

Without waiting for an answer, he returned to the tapestry and stared down at Isaiah. "My friend, there are two great loves in my life. The first must be Yahweh. The second is Gomer. I'm obeying the first and trusting He'll care for the second."

Isaiah's eyes misted. "I'll watch over her until you return."

A pang of dread pricked Hosea's heart. He knew Isaiah loved Aya, knew he'd never betray their friendship . . . but Gomer was beautiful — so beautiful.

He bent and kissed Jonah's gray head. "Thank you, my friend, for being God's hand on my shoulder. I'll tell you about His faithfulness when we return." The old man nodded but didn't even look up. Hosea saw his shoulders shaking. Why did it feel like a last good-bye?

"Come, Micah." He turned and heard the boy's sandals crunching on the rocky path behind him. "Did Jonah tell you anything else I should know about our journey?"

"He said I should do the cooking or we'll starve."

Hosea chuckled, feeling somehow relieved. *Yahweh's prophet. I'm Yahweh's prophet.* Regardless of his heart's heaviness, Hosea was determined to believe that obedience to the Lord's calling would set all things in order.

A gentle breeze stirred the sycamores and escorted them out of Tekoa.

PART 2

18

HOSEA 5:8, 12

Blow the ram's horn in Gibeah. Blow the trumpet in Ramah. Sound the alarm at Beth Aven, you descendants of Benjamin. . . . I will destroy Ephraim as a moth destroys clothing. I will destroy the nation of Judah as rot destroys wood.

Gomer hugged the ceramic bowl to her chest and wished the gods would strike her dead. How many times could a woman vomit in a single morning? She'd felt this way with her previous pregnancies, but she'd been sickest just prior to Merav's dosage of rue tea. The day after, Gomer had experienced excruciating abdominal pain and bleeding and was delirious for several days. She vaguely recalled Tamir screaming at Merav that if Gomer died, the old midwife would be out on the street. After that,

Merav made all the girls eat pomegranate rinds in the morning and drink water with wild carrot seeds at night.

But Merav was gone, and Asherah had answered Gomer's prayers.

Surely Hosea would be pleased — if he ever returned from Israel. Those in camp had celebrated two new moon festivals without any word from her wandering husband. She and Yuval attended the public feast but excused themselves when the women divided into hens' nests, as Yuval called them. Isaiah's betrothed, Aya, had made a few attempts to apologize for her thoughtless remark at the workshop, but Gomer saw no reason to encourage a friendship that could never last. Aya had her little cluster of friends that she'd known since childhood days.

For some reason, Yuval, the camp's matriarch, seemed above the idle gossip and had taken Gomer under her protective wing. She was so much like Merav. Of course, Yuval was a respectable prophet's wife, not a brothel midwife, but everything about her appearance — even her mannerisms — were so familiar.

Yuval seemed pleased to have a friend too, since Amos was gone so often. Gomer knew the life of traveling merchants, but she'd never tell Yuval that her husband was probably sleeping with harlots in every town he visited. All the traders did it, but Yuval — like all women — undoubtedly thought her husband was different. At least Gomer had no such delusions. She just hoped Hosea had the sense to lie with women from reputable brothels. Lowly street harlots could spread disease or steal his purse — or worse.

Gomer heard the donkey bray and knew Isaiah must be busy with chores in their stable. He'd become one of the bright spots in her tedious days. Yuval still provided cooking lessons when the fig crop allowed her time to do so, and Gomer enjoyed every menial task Amoz taught her at the pottery shop. But her daily lessons with Jonah were unbearable — endless rules from the Law of Moses, numbers and dates and dos and don'ts. No wonder people found it difficult to abide by Yahweh's Law. How did they remember all those details?

She set aside her bowl, sipped a little water, and took another bite of bread. Sampson rubbed against her legs, never too far away. She donned her blue veil, stepping outside to breathe the chilly desert-morning air.

"Shalom, Gomer." The deep, male voice

was balm to her soul.

"Shalom, Isaiah." She spoke as smooth as silk despite her unsettled stomach.

He glanced up, his eyes locking with hers but a moment. He offered an awkward smile and resumed scooping grain into the feed buckets.

Odd. Isaiah's never at a loss for words. She smiled, taking a few steps closer. "Did Uzziah mention I've been visiting him? The priests examine him every seven days, and they keep finding raw flesh in the sores. I know the Law says he's unclean and infectious, but no one else has contracted a rash or skin lesions."

"Uh-huh." His eyes were on his work as he fed the chickens, collected the eggs, and forked hay into the manger.

Something was wrong. "He says your abba Amoz never visits him. Why is that? Is he afraid he'll be infected, or is there some disagreement between them?"

He kept to his work, ignoring her question — or had he decided to ignore *her* completely? She decided to try another subject.

"Amoz is teaching me to wedge the clay — you know, get the air bubbles out and —"

"That's great, Gomer," he said, hanging

the pitchfork between two wooden pegs. "I'll come back before the evening meal to bed down the animals." He lifted his eyes for a moment, barely long enough for her to see . . . was it guilt?

"Isaiah, stop!"

His long strides had carried him halfway to the courtyard gate, but he stilled at her plea. Slowly he turned. "Classes will begin shortly. I should go."

Her stomach rumbled; she steadied her nerves. "Have I done something to upset you?" Tears threatened — again. She seemed to be a never-ending fountain since she was with child.

"No, Gomer. I'm not upset with you." He tried to hold her gaze but looked away.

Silence.

"Tell me!" She stomped her foot, and the tears overflowed.

"Don't cry." Isaiah sighed and combed both hands through his hair, then ambled toward her, arms outstretched as if an embrace would erase her confusion.

"No! Tell me what's wrong." But there was no time for a reply before she emptied her morning meal in the space between them.

Isaiah stopped short of the eruption, his eyes as wide as a camel's.

She felt a measure of satisfaction at his

discomfort, unable to resist a little barb. "Had I known throwing up would have gotten you to look at me, I might have tried it earlier."

"That's not funny!" he said, concern etched on his brow. "Are you sick? Should I get Yuval?"

"I'll feel better in about seven full moons." She watched confusion give way to understanding.

He stepped over the mess and reached out to cradle her elbow — but stopped. He withdrew his hand as if Gomer wore an invisible shield.

"What is *wrong* with you, Isaiah? You're acting as if I'm unclean like . . ." The thought robbed her of breath. "Is that it? You think I've touched Uzziah, and you're unwilling —"

"No. No!" he said before she could finish. "It has nothing to do with Uzziah's leprosy. He's told me you're careful to remain on the audience tapestry when you visit, and your friendship is very important to him. It's not about Uzziah. It's about . . . I can't . . . It's just not . . ."

She watched his cheeks color. "What? Why do you treat me like a leper if you admit I'm not unclean?"

Isaiah searched the windows of her soul

and spoke softly, deliberately. "I am your friend, Gomer. You know that, don't you?"

A cold chill crept up her spine. *I know if you must say it, you plan to test it.* She wanted to say the words, but they lodged in her tightened throat.

"You're a married woman," he said, "and I'm betrothed to Aya. Hosea is my best friend, and though I promised to protect you while he was gone, we must avoid any appearance of wrongdoing."

"Wrongdoing? Have we appeared to do something wrong?"

He squeezed the back of his neck and sighed again. "It's just that Aya is uncomfortable with our friendship —"

"Aya is uncomfortable?" She laughed — joyless, dry, weary. "Well, we wouldn't want Aya or her family or her dozens of friends in camp to feel *uncomfortable* that you've been talking to the town harlot." She turned toward the house before she lost the rest of her breakfast and called over her shoulder, "I'll take care of the stable chores from now on, Isaiah. You need not return."

He caught her arm, spinning her to face him. "It's not just the stable chores. The whole camp is wondering why you visit my cousin Uzziah every day. It seems odd for a beautiful woman — who has no family or provisions of her own — to spend time with a leprous king."

Gomer's breath left her. Gasping, she could barely whisper. "And who else do I have to spend time with?" She twisted away, squaring her shoulders. After two calming breaths, she bored a gaze into his uncaring soul. "Why is it odd that one outcast would find solace in the presence of another outcast, Isaiah?" She saw that her words had hit their mark. "Jonah has taught me your ridiculous laws of *uncleanness,* so I don't touch King Uzziah. But I will not abandon him because a few camp gossips think it *odd* that a harlot has a heart. Go back to your perfect Aya. Tell her you won't be tending Hosea's goats or his wife anymore — *friend.*"

Hosea awoke to the smell of sizzling meat. Sleep slowly gave way to consciousness, and his first thought was the same as it had been for too many days. *Where are we this morning?* He and Micah had traveled all over Israel, visiting every small town and village from Joppa on the northwest coast to Lo-Debar on the border of Aram. The Lord had begun directing them south, and each day Hosea hoped for instruction to go home.

He opened one eye and saw Micah bent

over the fire, holding what appeared to be a small bird on a stick. "What's the occasion?" he said, rolling onto his back, trying to work out the stiffness the cold ground induced.

"It's sort of a long story."

A long story? In the three new moons since leaving Tekoa, Micah had barely spoken three sentences.

Hosea grabbed his blanket and crawled to the fire. He wrapped himself in the woolen warmth, settling beside his young friend. "I think we're far enough from Bethel, out of danger from Israel's troops. We deserve a morning's rest." They'd been relentlessly pursued by Jeroboam's soldiers, run out of every town where they'd proclaimed God's impending judgment. Hosea nodded at their breakfast on the stick. "Can we eat that while you're telling me the long story? We haven't had fresh meat in more than a full moon."

Micah smiled and checked a piece of the quail to be sure it was cooked thoroughly. Fingers dancing on the scorching meat, he picked and prodded to prepare the morning feast. "Aren't you curious how I caught the quail, Master Hosea?" he asked, one eyebrow arched in uncharacteristic mischief.

"Well, now that you mention it . . ." Hosea

chuckled, glancing around their campsite for a makeshift fowler's snare or net. Nothing. He returned his attention to Micah, who seemed bursting to explain. "All right, tell me how you caught the quail."

"Oh, Master Hosea! It was marvelous! I heard Yahweh's voice!" The young man's words gained momentum as they tumbled out. "He called me by name, and at first I thought it was you, but when I looked over, you were still sleeping. When I realized it must be Yahweh, I got up, and He told me to look behind that tree for a quail whose wing had been broken. I found the bird, and He said, 'Kill and eat. You will need strength for your journey back to Judah. You will speak for Me as does My servant Hosea.' So what do you think He meant, Master Hosea?"

Hosea drew a breath, but the boy rattled on. "When do we return to Tekoa? Today? Tonight? Tomorrow? And when do I begin to prophesy? I don't know what to say. How do you know what to say?"

Hosea could only smile, words lodged in his throat. It was a bittersweet moment. The joy and pride he felt now must have been like Jonah's when Hosea had returned from his wilderness fast with the directive to prophesy to Israel. But how would Isaiah take the news? Had he received a call from Yahweh while back in Tekoa? Or would young Micah's calling make Isaiah's impatience that much harder to bear?

Micah looked at him with wide, expectant eyes.

Yahweh, give me wisdom to teach this young man, and give Isaiah grace to accept Your plan for us all!

"The first thing we must do is finish our quail," he said, squeezing Micah's shoulder. "And then we will continue to the three cities Yahweh told us to speak to today. Beth Aven, Ramah, and Gibeah are in perfect order — north to south — for the journey back to Judah."

"But when will *I* get to prophesy?" Micah sounded like a spoiled child, and Hosea remembered his own complaints to Jonah sounding much the same.

"You will prophesy when it breaks your heart, Micah." He pinned the young man with a stare. "You will speak unimaginable pain to real people. They are breaking God's heart. Their leaders are perverting justice, mistreating the poor, and worshiping idols of metal, wood, and stone. When your heart can't bear to proclaim the judgment God has determined for them, then — and only then — are you ready to speak for Yahweh."

Micah's eyes welled with tears. "Do you know what Yahweh has declared for the three cities we'll visit today?"

Hosea breathed deeply and closed his eyes, allowing the Lord's words to fill him. "Sound the alarm in Gibeah, Ramah, and Beth Aven. You descendants of Benjamin won't escape the punishment coming to all of Israel. Ephraim will become a wasteland when the time for punishment comes. I'm telling you the truth — all the tribes of Israel face His wrath. And now judgment begins with the leaders of Judah as well. Judgment for Ephraim will start slow, as a moth destroys clothing. The same for Judah, as rot destroys wood."

When Hosea opened his eyes, tears streamed down Micah's cheeks into the tender fuzz of beard just forming, and he knew he was witnessing the birth of a prophet.

Yuval wound the last long strip of cloth around Gomer's hand, covering the red, swollen blisters with the fig poultice she'd prepared.

"My hands feel as if they're on fire. Why didn't anyone tell me to wear gloves for the fig harvest?"

Her friend's voice was full of compassion.

"Oh, my little Gomer, I'm sorry. I've been so busy preparing for the harvest, I forgot that you wouldn't know fig sap irritates the skin. Everyone else in camp has been through the harvest twice a year for ages." Tears formed on her bottom lashes. "Can you forgive me?"

Gomer's heart was in her throat. She hadn't meant to blame Yuval. The poor woman ran the entire fig operation — everything from planting and pinching to harvesting and processing. "There's nothing to forgive, Yuval. I should have seen the others and noticed. I'm just irritable and nauseous, and now my hands are bandaged and I can't even dress myself." Sampson jumped into her lap and purred. She tried petting him with one of her bandaged stubs. "I can't even care for the cat." Tears began to flow, and she cursed herself. "And why am I still crying all the time? Uhh!" In her frustration, she poked her eye with a bandaged hand and sobbed all the more.

She heard Yuval giggle and glanced in her direction, shocked and a little hurt. "Are you laughing at me?"

"Gomer, my daughter, all pregnant women cry. And when the baby comes, you'll cry some more." She patted her bandaged hands. "Don't worry about Sampson. I'll take care of him when I come over each morning to help you with your robe and tunic."

Gomer could do nothing but shake her head, her throat closed by anger and self-pity. When she could speak, her words were clipped. "I'll manage by myself. I've always gotten by on my own. I refuse to need anyone now."

"Well, I'd like to be needed." A deep voice resonated from the darkened front door.

Hosea!

He must have slipped in while she and Yuval were talking. *How much did you hear?* She wanted to crawl in a hole — or better yet, order him to crawl back to Israel!

19

So Hosea married Gomer. . . . She became pregnant and had a son. Yahweh told Hosea, "Name him Jezreel."

Gomer kept her eyes on the oven's glow but felt Hosea's gaze on her. How could she feel cold when she sat a cubit from the fire?

Yuval rushed to greet Hosea at the door, chattering like a sparrow. "When did you get back? Does Amos know you're home? Oh, the fig harvest is almost finished, and we needed extra help, so your sweet little wife came to our aid, and, well . . . she's never worked with figs before and didn't realize the sap would blister her hands and —"

"Yuval, would you like me to help with the figs tomorrow?" Hosea offered softly. "Perhaps after I've had a chance to rest tonight and take care of my wife?"

A short silence required all of Gomer's resolve to keep her eyes averted.

"Ohh, yes, yes. I need to get home and check on Amos." Yuval hurried over to Gomer and squeezed her shoulders, kissing the top of her head. "I'll check on you tomorrow, child. You and your husband have much to discuss." A wink and a smile, and her friend hurried away.

The door clicked shut, and silence fell like a cold, wet blanket.

Gomer began to tremble. So much time had passed without a word from him, and now he was going to take care of her?

Footsteps drew near.

She began shaking violently, unable to stop the tears. How could she ever trust him? Would he leave every time she needed him? She wrapped her arms around herself, rocking, keening like the mourners when her ima had died.

He knelt behind her. She felt his presence but still didn't dare turn to look. Would he disappear again if she saw him? Would he vanish if she dared hope one more time? The ache in her heart deepened, and she felt his legs scoot around her, his arms enfold her. *Like the rafters of the Bethel temple when we were children.* She closed her eyes and remembered the safety of his arms, and her wailing turned to quiet sobs.

Her head lolled against his chest, and he laid her back into the crook of his elbow. She closed her eyes, still terrified to see the handsome face hovering above her. She felt his breath, warm on her cheek.

"I have missed you, my precious wife. I'm sorry I had to leave you, but I'm home now, and I'll be everything you need me to be while I'm here." He kissed the tears from her cheek.

A thousand thoughts raced through her mind, but only one couldn't wait. She opened her eyes to look at her child's abba. "Hosea, I'm pregnant," she said, scrutinizing his first reaction.

A lazy grin creased his lips. His soft brown eyes danced with delight. "I know."

"You know?" She sat upright, her back straight as a rod. "How do you know?"

He curled one of her copper locks around his finger. "Yahweh told me, and it's going to be a boy."

"Oh! That's not fair! I endure all the retching, but you get all the good news —" Without a moment's warning, Gomer vomited all over her husband. Fortunately, she didn't have much in her stomach. When she finished, they stared at each other wide-eyed.

A slow, satisfied grin stretched across Gomer's lips. "Welcome home, Husband."

"Good Sabbath, my love." Hosea's voice reached into the pleasant half-consciousness of Gomer's first thoughts.

Smiling, she nestled into his warmth. "Mmm, yes it is, because you are here with me." Nearly five full moons had passed since Hosea's return, and their lives had fallen into a comfortable rhythm. Gomer's sickness was forgotten with the joyful flutter of life in her womb, and Hosea — true to his word — had been everything she needed him to be, which included a constant friend and companion.

The morning air was crisp, but she felt him nudge the blanket off her belly. He chuckled when she growled, but she still refused to open her eyes. "We'll break our fast, and then . . ." He traced little circles around the dark, flat place that was once her belly button, seemingly fascinated by her changing body. "And then I think we should invite Amoz to join us for today's visit with King Uzziah."

Gomer's eyes popped open to find Hosea hovering over her. "Amoz hasn't visited Uzziah since he moved to camp. Why today? Has Yahweh spoken to you?"

He tucked a stray copper curl behind her ear. "I haven't heard a direct word from Yahweh, but Uzziah and I have become friends during our daily visits — man-to-man more than prophet-to-king — and I sense a real sadness at the relationship he and Amoz have lost through the years."

Gomer traced her husband's eyebrow and let her hand slide around his jaw onto his lips. He kissed her finger, and she drew him close. After a moment of tenderness, she lay at his side. "Whatever destroyed Uzziah's relationship with Amoz has also come between Isaiah and his abba."

Hosea remained silent for a time, and Gomer wondered if he'd fallen asleep. She glanced over, saw him staring at the ceiling.

"I plan to be an excellent abba." He propped himself up on one elbow and hovered over her. "I will go to Israel whenever Yahweh calls me, but I will *always* come back, Gomer."

Her heart stopped, all blood draining from her face. "Are . . . are you leaving?" It came out in a squeak.

"No! No! I'm just thinking about Isaiah and Amoz —"

"Uhh!" She shoved him away, frustration

and anger seizing her. "Don't ever do that to me again!"

He pulled her to his chest in spite of her protests, holding her tightly, whispering above the loud pounding of her heart. "Isaiah has lived in the same house with his abba all his life, yet they barely speak. I may be called away from my wife and children for long periods of time, but I believe Yahweh will still bless our family, Gomer. I have to trust Him. *We* have to trust Him."

"I can't think about you leaving," she said. "I don't know how I'd survive, Hosea. Yuval is still trying to teach me to cook, and I've never taken care of a baby — Merav tended all the brothel children." She squeezed her eyes shut. Why did she bring up her past when he was thinking of leaving? What if he *did* abandon her? Where could she go now?

"I think we should ask Aya to help you with the baby when he comes."

"No!" Gomer sat up straight as an arrow. "I won't have Maiden Do-Right spying on me and then telling everyone in camp I'm a terrible ima. Why can't Yuval help me?"

"Yuval will be busy with the breba fig harvest."

Panic shot through Gomer. "Will she be here for the birth?"

"Yes, of course. Amos told me she's

already got that birthing contraption at their house, ready to bring it over when you show the first signs of labor. But remember, when fig harvest begins, she's busy from sunrise to well past dark."

Gomer had spent most of her time with Hosea during the past days and wondered how he knew Yuval's schedule better than she. The thought of Aya's pure and polite presence hovering over her every morning set her teeth on edge. "Why can't we ask someone else?"

The tenderness in his expression disarmed her. "Aya wants to be your friend, Gomer. She's apologized a dozen times to you and to me. She could care for the baby and prepare an evening meal, making it possible for you to return to work at the pottery shop after midday — if you still wish to work the clay."

All her bluster, all her anger — gone with his proposal about the workshop. She was still awed that he'd allowed her apprenticeship to continue during the pregnancy. Each morning Hosea taught her lessons from Yahweh's Law and then escorted her to the pottery shop after their midday meal. But working *after* the baby came?

"You'd let Amoz continue to teach me?"

"I see the joy in your eyes when you tell

me what you've learned. Yahweh has called me to prophesy. I feel His pleasure when I obey. Perhaps He's called you to work the clay."

Tears stung her eyes. She wasn't ready to admit Yahweh had any plans for her, nor was she willing to agree to Aya's daily invasion — but she was overwhelmed at the love of her husband. It was more than she had ever dreamed of.

With a quick kiss, she scooted off the bed. "I'm hungry. I'll bring us some goat cheese and bread so we can break our fast in bed." She hurried into the main room, hoping to silence him. "We'll decide about Aya later. We'll invite Amoz to our visit with Uzziah today."

Hosea pulled his outer garment around his ears and began pacing again — fourteen footsteps between his front door and the stable. Gomer had gone into labor just after midday. Her water had broken while at the pottery workshop, and Amoz had run home, carrying Gomer in his arms.

The moon was now well past its midpoint, and the winter winds whipped Hosea's hair as he counted. "One, two, three . . ."

"Aahh!" Gomer screamed. Her shouts had become more frequent but weaker.

"I can't stand this!" Hosea marched toward the door, but Isaiah blocked his path.

"Yuval is taking care of Gomer. I don't think you should go in there."

"But I need to *see* her," Hosea said, empowered by fear. Isaiah was taller and stronger, but he was easily shoved aside.

"The last thing Gomer needs is a frantic husband frightening her." A gentle voice restrained him. Both young men turned and found Amoz offering Hosea his stool. "And the last thing you need is to watch your wife suffer." His voice faltered. "It's an image you can never erase." The potter worked his jaw like his hands worked clay.

Hosea clenched and unclenched his fists, torn between wise counsel and his wife's weakened wails.

"I never knew you were with her in the end." Isaiah's voice was a whisper, his face as gray as the moon above. "Is that why you've never lov—" He stopped, his voice choked.

"I took you from her arms," Amoz said, raising his chin. "And I have loved you both every day of my life."

Hosea watched abba and son stand like pillars in unyielding Years of pain. "I'm sorry, Amoz. I had no idea you were with

Isaiah's ima . . ." He glanced at Isaiah. "I didn't know."

"They'll come for you if Gomer is in danger." Amoz's eyes welled with tears. "Sometimes no news is good news." He stole a glimpse of his son and cleared his throat. "I should get back to the pottery shop and clean up." He turned and hurried from the courtyard.

Hosea sighed and laid his hand on Isaiah's shoulder. "I knew your ima died giving you birth, but I had no idea . . ."

"Now we both know," Isaiah said, his words dripping with venom. He squeezed his eyes shut. "I'm sorry. I'm not angry with you."

Hosea nodded. "Do you want to talk?" Gomer let out another scream, and Hosea fought the urge to claw down the door. "Talk to me, Isaiah. Tell me something to keep me from going in there."

Eyes wide, Isaiah began recounting his story. "My ima's name was Levana. All I know about her, I learned from cousin Uzziah. He said my parents weren't married long, but Abba loved her." He wiped his eyes. "Uzziah said my abba used to laugh. He used to talk more — even sing sometimes — before I was born. Something happened between Abba and Uzziah when we

254

moved here to Tekoa. They've spoken very little, but Abba makes sure I spend a lot of time with my cousin." He wiped his face on his sleeve and laid an arm around Hosea's shoulder. "Come on. Let's walk. I'm done talking for a while."

The front door opened, and Hosea whirled around. Lamplight cast a glow around Yuval, who held a small bundle wrapped in brown wool. "Your wife would like to see you now."

Hosea rushed to the babe, inspecting his downy black hair and pinched face. "He's beautiful." He leaned over to kiss the little one, and Yahweh's voice echoed in his spirit: *Name him Jezreel. You must proclaim throughout Israel that in a little while I will punish Jehu's family for the people they slaughtered at Jezreel. Then I will put an end to the kingdom of Israel. On that day I will break Israel's bows and arrows in the valley of Jezreel.*

Hosea looked up at Yuval, startled. "Did you hear that?"

Brows furrowed, she looked to Isaiah for clarification. "Hear what?"

Isaiah grinned. "I believe our friend has heard from the Lord again." Eyes damp, he said, "I felt a cool breeze but didn't hear His words, my friend."

Hosea patted Isaiah's cheek. "You're right about Yahweh's presence, and I did hear a message." His spirit stirred again, and he waited for another word from the Lord. Nothing specific this time, but a sort of quickening told Hosea that Yahweh had more to impart.

Hosea returned his attention to Isaiah, whose face reflected the joy Hosea felt. *What are You telling me, Yahweh?* He heard no inner voice, felt no breeze, saw no burning bush or fiery chariot like prophets before him had.

He received a thought. An understanding. Isaiah had a role in this calling of Jezreel.

Hosea leaned over to kiss Yuval's cheek and lifted his newborn son from her arms. "Yahweh told me to name the boy Jezreel."

" 'God will sow,' " Isaiah said, nodding his approval. "It's a fine name, rich with meaning."

"The meaning is greater than you realize, my friend." Yuval had already retreated into the house, leaving the two men alone with the infant. "My son's name reflects Yahweh's judgment on the house of Jehu for those they slaughtered in the valley of Jezreel." He saw Isaiah's joy fade and could only imagine Gomer's response to the gruesome symbolism. "I'm to return to Israel with this message of judgment — tomor-row."

Isaiah's face went ashen. "What about Gomer? What about your new son?"

"Don't you think I've asked those questions too?" The words, spoken almost as a reflex, sounded harsher than he intended.

Isaiah's expression softened. "I know you're doing what you believe you must, but are you sure it has to be tomorrow? Perhaps you misunderstood, and Yahweh is *preparing* you for your next mission — later — after you've spent more time with Gomer and Jezreel."

Hosea studied the small form in his arms, memorizing every wrinkle and eyelash illuminated by the torchlight. His heart broke at the thought of leaving his newborn — and his wife.

"I heard Yahweh's voice clearly, Isaiah. I must leave at sunrise." Hesitating, he measured again his understanding of Isaiah's role in this mission. *Yahweh, are You truly calling Isaiah to accompany me to Israel, or is it my own idea?* Hearing no clear answer, he pressed forward with his impression. "I felt a nudge from the Spirit, but it wasn't as definite as the prophecy of judgment. I'd like you to seek the Lord's will and then give me your answer before sunrise."

Isaiah looked puzzled but stood a little taller, seemingly honored to be asked for counsel.

"I realize your marriage to Aya is planned for the next new moon celebration." Hosea cringed at the thought of missing it. "Though Yahweh didn't speak directly, I believe He wants you to accompany me to Israel — and I doubt that we could return in time for your wedding."

The dawning of Hosea's plan settled on Isaiah's features, and all eagerness fled. "You're asking me to miss my own wedding?"

Hosea bit back an angry response in favor of a pointed one. "Yahweh doesn't always choose the most convenient times for His prophets to obey His commands."

Isaiah narrowed his eyes and raised his chin. "You'll have my answer by sunrise."

The baby squirmed and fussed, stealing Hosea's attention. When he glanced up, Isaiah was walking out of his courtyard. "Wait! Isaiah!"

His friend raised his hand and waved. "You were right. If I'm going to be Yahweh's prophet, I must sometimes choose between comfort and obedience." He cast a grin over his shoulder. "Go tell your wife she's amazing. I'll pray about my decision and talk to you at sunrise." He continued out the gate and toward his house.

Hosea felt full, blessed, awed by Yahweh's provision. He was surrounded by dear friends, family of the heart. His firstborn son lay in his arms, and a renewed urgency to see Gomer surged through him.

An urgency equaled only by the dread of her reaction to his departure. *Yahweh, give me wisdom to speak Your message tenderly. Give Gomer ears to hear and eyes to see the deeper meaning of our lives.*

20

LEVITICUS 12:2

When a woman gives birth to a boy, she will be unclean for seven days.

Yuval scurried about, gathering soiled linens and sprinkling scented oils in the dusty corners of the room. Gomer drifted in and out of exhausted slumber, still trying to grasp the truth. Asherah had answered her prayers.

A child. She had borne Hosea a child.

"Say shalom to your ima, Jezreel." Hosea slipped into their bedchamber, nuzzling the bundle in his arms. His eyes glistened as he approached their bed. "He's beautiful, my love. You are amazing."

A sob escaped before she could restrain it. She'd never felt so loved, so treasured.

Hosea placed the babe in Yuval's arms and knelt a cubit from the bed, careful not to touch it — or Gomer. Confusion warred with disappointment. "What's the matter? Why don't you come clos—" Before she finished the question, she remembered the Law and quoted it aloud. " 'When a woman gives birth to a boy, she will be *unclean* for seven days.' "

He seemed pleased that she remembered until she spat the word *unclean.* "Gomer, Yahweh's Law protects women from infection. Men in other nations disrespect their wives and return to their beds too soon, placing them in danger and —"

"I'm too tired for a lesson, Hosea." She turned toward the wall. Sleep. She'd feel better after she slept.

"Gomer, please. We need to talk."

She turned slowly, meeting his gaze and lifting a single brow.

Yuval split the space between them and placed Jezreel on the mattress beside Gomer. "I'll leave you three alone," she said. "There's bread and cheese, olives, and dates on the table in the other room." Pinning Hosea with a stare, she added, "Make sure she eats something and drinks plenty of water. It's your job to tend her until I come back in the morning."

Gomer silently cheered her friend and champion. It felt good to have someone on her side.

Hosea winked and smiled at the old woman. The two were close, and somehow, that too felt good.

Yuval nodded a sleepy good-bye, and the couple waited in silence until the door clicked shut behind her.

"Yahweh told me our son's name," Hosea said. "Jezreel. It means 'God will sow.' "

Gomer cuddled the babe into the crook of her arm, running her finger over the slope of his nose, entranced by the little being she'd just birthed.

And then she realized what Hosea was saying.

"Yahweh spoke to you?" When she lifted her gaze, the eyes that had adored her moments ago now floated in unshed tears.

"Yahweh is going to punish the family of Jehu — King Jeroboam's ancestor — for the people Jehu slaughtered at the valley of Jezreel. Our son's name will forever symbolize God's wrath against Jeroboam and his clan." His tears spilled over, coursing down his cheeks. He reached out as if to touch Jezreel's soft black curls but pulled his hand away. "I leave tomorrow to proclaim Yahweh's message to Israel."

Gomer couldn't breathe. Exhaustion strangled her. Why had she dared to hope?

Why go on living when men always left? But when she gazed at the precious babe beside her, the thought of his future revived her will to fight.

"Look at this innocent child, Hosea. Look at your son." She ripped the blanket away from his tiny body, revealing his perfect toes, his pink skin. "You're going to let Yahweh mark our baby with an abominable name. Then you're going to leave your family to travel through Israel and threaten powerful people who would rather kill you than spit on you?" Tears leapt over her bottom lashes. She was trembling in silence.

Hosea swallowed hard as he choked out the words. "I want to gather you both in my arms and never let you go."

She allowed herself a whimper, her brows lifted, pleading. It was as close to begging as Gomer would allow herself. Let Hosea choose now — this invisible god who demanded a bridegroom to abandon his bride and an abba to abandon his newborn son, or Gomer and Jezreel, a family who could love him here, now, forever.

Hosea lunged toward the bed and cradled both her and Jezreel in his arms, breaking Yahweh's laws of uncleanness.

Sobbing, she choked out the words, "I love you, Hosea. I love you." Relief washed over her like a flood.

He kissed her forehead, her cheeks, and finally her lips. They cried together, cradling Jezreel between them. When Hosea released her, he cupped her face and held her gaze. "I love you with all my heart, Wife." He hesitated a moment — long enough for Gomer to see determination etched in the windows of his soul. "I must obey Yahweh and leave for Israel at sunrise. I will return to you and Jezreel as soon as the Lord allows it."

Gomer felt as if a dagger had been thrust into her chest. "But you made yourself unclean for me . . ."

"I made myself unclean because I believe the essence of Yahweh's Law is to protect, not to punish. It would have been punishment to part without demonstrating my love. I will abide by the Law and wash my robe, making myself clean again by morning."

He leaned in to kiss her again, but she used her remaining strength to push him away. "Get out." Her voice was controlled fury, his expression shocked confusion.

"What? But I don't need to leave until morning."

Something inside her shifted, and she saw the man in her bed like so many others who'd lingered after she'd had her fill of them. She hugged Jezreel close, brushing her lips against his downy head. "I don't need you anymore, Hosea. Now I have someone who will love me — and won't abandon me."

"You look awful," Isaiah said, waiting at Hosea's courtyard gate just before dawn. He picked a piece of straw from Hosea's beard. "Did you sleep in the stable? Ohh, Gomer must have taken the news badly."

Yuval's rooster crowed, giving Hosea a moment to gather his thoughts. "I haven't seen that deadness in her eyes since we found her in Samaria." Cold fear had kept him awake, making his woolen blanket useless against the night chill. He noticed his friend's bulging shoulder bag, and his heart felt lighter. "So, you're coming with me?" A slender ray of hope dawned with morning's light.

"Perhaps my abba and Aya can comfort Gomer. Neither of them was happy about Yahweh's timing either. I can't understand why Aya would get her headpiece in a twist because I *might* be late for our wedding." He bit back a chuckle, and Hosea shoved him, sending him into the scrub bushes along the path.

"And why did your abba protest?" Hosea regretted the question when he saw his friend's expression dim.

"Who knows," he said, whacking his walking stick at the bushes. "Abba has words for everyone but me. I got a grunt and an 'utter foolishness.' I guess I'm supposed to figure out what that means."

"I'm sorry, Isaiah." Hosea let the silence speak the comfort he couldn't express.

They approached King Uzziah's encampment and saw the familiar shadow in the doorway of the rented house.

"Can we stop for a few moments?" Isaiah asked. "He's always been more of an abba to me than my abba Amoz anyway." Not waiting for an answer, Isaiah hurried his pace, and Hosea let him rush ahead.

Though his friend had an earthly abba, he'd had less security and consistency than Hosea had gotten from Jonah. It seemed Isaiah was always rushing from Amoz to Uzziah, yearning for one of them to be that strong and loving abba every boy needs. Unfortunately, neither seemed to embrace the role, and Isaiah had developed a brash outer shell to hide the insecure boy inside.

"Unclean! Unclean!" Uzziah's voice rang out, and Hosea wondered if the king ever slept. His sores continued to worsen, and the priests now examined him as more of a courtesy than a hope that he would return to his throne. Rumors were circulating in camp that Prince Jotham might soon be named coregent in order to squelch doubts of Judah's leadership that might tempt foreign nations to aggression.

"It's better this way, my son." Hosea arrived at the audience tapestry in time to hear Uzziah's words to Isaiah. "Much preferable to spend time away from Aya before you're wed than to leave your new bride —" The king's face grew even paler. "Forgive me, Hosea. I meant no disrespect."

"Before our friendship was strengthened, my lord, I might have been offended." He nodded at the king, and Uzziah returned the gesture. "But I've seen your heart changed by suffering, and somehow I believe you now understand the hardships of my calling."

"I'm learning, Hosea," the king said. "I'm learning that we must hold loosely *all* that Yahweh gives us on this earth. Even our very lives."

Silence.

"You are a good man, King Uzziah." Hosea longed to say more, to command this righteous king to destroy the high places and obey the Law completely. But he'd already spoken Yahweh's words to Uzziah — and even added some of his own nagging. The choice was in the king's hands. "May the Lord bless you and keep you, my lord, until we return and see you again."

Hosea felt Isaiah's hand on his shoulder.

"Come, my friend. The quicker you proclaim Yahweh's message, the sooner I can marry Aya and you can return to your wife and son."

21

LEVITICUS 12:3

The boy must be circumcised when he is eight days old.

Jezreel had been screaming all night, and Gomer's nerves were as frayed as ten-year-old sandals. How dare they mutilate her son? He was only eight days old. She tried to reason with Jonah and the other prophets, explaining that many of the men in Israel no longer adopted the archaic tradition of circumcision. But would they listen to her? *No, I'm just the child's ima!* She'd had no voice in naming him. Why would she have a say in any decision concerning her child?

A knock at the door raised the baby's cries to fevered pitch. She rocked Jezreel in the sling over her shoulder and stomped toward the door. "What!" she shouted, flinging it open.

Yuval jumped, both feet leaving the ground. "Oh dear! I heard him crying through the night. What can I do to help?" She lifted Jezreel out of the sling, bouncing and rocking in a rhythm that his mournful cries soon adopted.

Gomer stretched her aching arms and then covered her ears, exploding at her friend. "You can tell the men who did this that *they* can come over and comfort my baby through the night, feed him, cradle him —" Suddenly her breasts tightened and released a flood of milk. "Ohh! This is humiliating! How can I go anywhere or do anything when every moment is full of feeding a child and changing dirty loincloths?" She wilted, all bluster spent, rivers of tears flowing down her cheeks and breast milk soaking her robe.

Yuval offered a compassionate smile. "Well, it would appear you have an ample supply of milk, so at least the boy isn't hungry." She continued bouncing.

Gomer was not comforted. She felt fat, ugly, and alone. She knew nothing about raising a child, nor did she care to learn. Where was this innate maternal instinct Yuval had promised would come? "I can't do this, Yuval. I just can't." She looked at the door and then at her child. *I'm not fit to raise him. He'd be better off without me.*

"Gomer, look at me." She heard Yuval's voice as if in a dream. "Gomer!"

Startled from her stupor, she met her friend's gaze.

"I will send Aya to help you with Jezreel."

"No! I don't want —"

"Enough!" Yuval's hand went up, stifling both Gomer's words and Jezreel's cries. The old woman continued bouncing and spoke calmly, Jezreel whimpering. "I know you had a rough start with Aya, but she's the oldest of seven children and has helped raise her last three siblings." Yuval pinned her with a hard stare. "Don't look at that door like you plan to flee."

Gomer felt her cheeks burn, ashamed that her thoughts had been written on her face.

"You're going to be all right." Yuval tilted Gomer's chin and met her gaze. "Every new ima struggles with her emotions. It's harder for you because — well, you're trying to do this alone."

The familiar anger bubbled inside her. "I *must* do this alone. I was given no choice."

"We have few choices in life. Make important ones wisely, Daughter." Jezzy's fussing resumed, and Yuval bounced and danced. "The first important choice is to let Aya help you with cooking and caring for Jezreel.

271

The fig harvest is upon us, and I'm not as free to help you."

Gomer clenched her teeth and bit back a reply, moving to the pile of goatskin rugs. She pulled one out and positioned her back against the wall, ready to nurse her babe. "Thank you, Yuval. I'll take him now."

She received the whimpering bundle, inhaling his sweet scent, and Yuval nestled close beside them. "Tell me the real reason you don't want Aya to help you. Is it payment? Because we will see that Aya is compensated until Hosea returns, and then I'm sure his portion of property and income is sufficient to provide for a nursemaid."

"I would never ask you and Amos to pay for my nursemaid," she said, mortified. "And I know nothing about Hosea's holding, but I'm sure Aya would never agree to come since she's so coddled by the old hens in camp. They might peck her to death if she enters the *harlot's* house." She dare not tell Yuval that just days before Jezreel's birth, Hosea nearly begged Gomer to ask for Aya's help.

Yuval smoothed a stray curl off her forehead and tucked it behind her ear — just like Merav used to do. Gomer's throat tightened, but she swallowed down the emotion.

"You are no longer a harlot, Daughter, and I think you've misjudged Aya. It's true that she was raised in camp, so she's well acquainted with the old hens, but she's not one of them." With a gentle pat on her cheek, Yuval groaned and rocked to her knees and finally to her feet. "These old bones don't work like they used to." She scratched Sampson between the ears and walked toward the door.

Gomer released a sigh. "Are you coming back?"

"Amos is leaving for another merchant's trip today. I'll be back after I feed him, and I'll bring Aya with me."

Gomer nodded but remained silent. It was no use arguing. Yuval would have her way.

"Wait!" she shouted before Yuval closed the door. The old woman peeked her head back inside. "Hosea said that if Aya helped me, I would be free to work in the pottery shop again." It was as much a question as a declaration. Had he told anyone else his generous plan?

"If your husband said it, no one in camp can argue with it." The twinkle in Yuval's eyes returned as she pulled the door closed behind her.

The thought of working the clay bolstered her spirits. She whispered to her precious babe, "I love you, Jezzy, but I wasn't made to be an ima."

And then, as if the mother goddess herself spoke from beneath the mattress in her bed-chamber, Gomer knew what she must do. She stroked Jezzy's cheek, watching this miracle of life draw nourishment from her. His little hand wrapped around her finger, and she gasped. How precious he was, an undeniable gift. Could she give up the joy of nursing her child in order to keep him with her forever? A tear made its way down her cheek.

"Hear me, Lady Asherah," she whispered, her heart breaking. "If I sacrifice this time with Jezzy in order to learn the pottery trade, please endow a wet nurse with your life-giving nectar when I bind my breasts to dry the milk." Her heart raced at the plan forming in her mind. "And please, Mother Goddess, help your servant to learn well from the master potter Amoz, so I might earn enough silver to take my son from this prison of Yahweh's prophets."

Gomer's right hand cramped with every quick stroke of the smooth stone across the leather-hard vase. Burnishing pottery at precisely the right stage of dryness ensured the stunning gleam she'd noticed at her first

274

visit to Jerusalem. Amoz had begun trusting her with more intricate tasks as she'd proven her talent with the clay. "You were born for it," he'd told her one day after she'd burnished a vase to a glimmering shine. She smiled at the memory, glancing over her shoulder at the old potter. The man of few words had become quite dear to her.

After five moon cycles in the pottery workshop, she felt more like a real person again. Her figure had returned, causing the shepherds, fig pickers, and carpenters to stop their work and stare — much to the old hens' delight and despair. Delight because it provided endless gossip fodder. Despair because some of those staring were their husbands.

Gomer, however, was interested in only one man. He visited the pottery workshop each evening before sunset — wrapped in a blanket, carried in Aya's arms. Jezzy greeted Amoz and Gomer with a wide, one-toothed grin.

"How's ima's little man?" Gomer asked.

Aya giggled and relinquished her charge. Jezzy's feet kicked, and he squealed with delight during the transfer. Gomer's heart took flight.

"He loves his ima," Amoz said, giving his potter's wheel another kick. Gomer saw his eyes glisten in the torchlight that framed his workspace.

Aya caressed Jezzy's downy black curls and exchanged a caring smile with Gomer. "He's been a little fussy today. I think he's trying to get a second tooth. He's been sucking on this." She fingered a smooth stone with a hole in its middle, tied to his wrist.

Gomer grinned and lifted an eyebrow. "A gift from Savta Yuval?"

Aya nodded. "It came with two days' supply of fig paste for sweetening." She handed Gomer the clay cup with the hollow reed that Jezzy used to drink his breast milk.

Gomer set it aside and kissed Jezzy's nose. "Your savta spoils you, little one!" She held him close, feeling the blessed warmth of this precious gift of life. *Thank you, Mother Goddess, for answering my prayer.*

Aya meandered over to Amoz and knelt beside his kick wheel. "What is this beautiful piece?" she asked, pointing to the amphora he'd been working on all day.

"It's dust and ashes compared to you, sweet girl." The master potter grinned and winked at his soon-to-be daughter-in-law. This girl had cast a spell on both the men in Gomer's life. Jezzy was well cared for and loved, and Amoz spoke more words to Aya

276

in a few moments than he spoke all day.

Gomer had been wrong to label the girl as one of the camp's brood of gossiping, self-righteous hens. In those first days of Aya's service, she had proven somewhat agreeable — even likable — and Gomer had to swallow her pride and apologize.

"It's all right," Aya had said. "I deserved your hate. I should never have spoken of your past that morning at the workshop, but I didn't know what to say to you." Sincerity spilled from her wide eyes. "You're the most beautiful woman I've ever seen."

Yuval had laughed out loud when Gomer relayed the girl's compliment. "Maybe our Aya is more of a conniver than I thought. Are you sure she wasn't fattening you up for a slaughter?"

Gomer grinned at the memory, her heart aching at the thought of Yuval. She wouldn't have survived without her help — or Aya's. It had been several days since she'd seen Yuval. The main fig harvest had begun, and the woman was in constant motion.

"Gomer?" Aya spoke from across the small potter's loft. "Are you all right?"

She wiped a tear. "I'm fine." Gomer waved away her concern and propped Jezzy on her hip. "I always miss Yuval when fig season starts."

"Do you want me to keep Jezzy a little longer tonight?"

"Could you? I'll try to find her at the fig barn when I leave here."

Aya laid a hand on Amoz's shoulder, leaning over to arrest his attention from his work. "Will you be finished in time to share a meal with me, or are you working late tonight?"

He placed both feet on the wheel, slowing its rotation. "I never refuse a meal with my daughter." She leaned down and kissed his cheek. A slow, sweet smile formed on his face — much like the clay forming beneath his hands. Aya walked toward Gomer and Jezzy, opening her arms wide.

The image would be burned into Gomer's mind forever. Open arms. Open heart. Innocence embodied. The love Aya radiated was unfathomable. It was a living, breathing entity that consumed everyone within her reach. It was inviting . . . and terrifying. How could Gomer save enough silver to leave this place if she let herself be loved by Aya and Yuval?

She fairly shoved Jezzy into the girl's arms. "I'll be home as soon as I can."

"Tell Yuval I said shalom!"

Gomer heard Aya's words as she descended the loft stairs, and she waved overhead to acknowledge, not trusting her voice to hide the emotions threatening to drown her. She charged through the curtained door and into the sweltering heat of Tekoa's late summer, keeping her head down and legs churning. She was halfway to the fig barn before she realized, *Will Aya remember Jezzy's clay cup?* Jezzy needed it for his morning and bedtime meals, and Gomer always fed him during those hours. Aya wouldn't think about the cup.

A defeated sigh escaped. She must go back to the workshop. Perhaps Aya and Amoz would be gone by now. The sun kissed the mountains in the west. If she hurried, she could get the clay cup, visit with Yuval, and arrive home before dark.

She quickened her pace and arrived at the pottery shop, surprised to find it dark and empty. She peeked inside and listened for lingering workers. All was quiet — except for a slight glow and a soft humming in the loft.

She tiptoed to the stairs and held her breath, listening.

I know that sound, but it can't be.

She climbed the steps slowly, silently, and reached the top. *Creak!*

Amoz stopped chanting, startled from his crudely built altar to Asherah. "Gomer!

What are you — why did you come back?"
He bolted from his knees to stand in front
of his idols, fear etched on his face.

She pointed at Jezzy's lonesome clay cup.
"I needed to get . . ." But her words faded
into silence. "Does anyone know?"

He set his jaw. "Are you going to tell?"

"I won't tell anyone, Amoz." She watched
his boldness fade.

"Why? You're a prophet's wife."

Gomer sat on the top step, feeling her
knees become as wobbly as her emotions.
Dare she confide in this man — any man —
that she, too, worshiped Asherah? Surely he
had as much to lose as she.

She saw Amoz studying her. "You worship
the mother of abundance too, don't you?"
The realization filled his face with wonder.
She'd never seen him so happy.

Unable to restrain a little giggle, she said,
"Yes, Amoz. How long have you kept *your*
secret?" Wonder, curiosity, amazement —
she had so many questions for a pagan man
who had lived among Yahweh's prophets for
almost twenty years.

"Uzziah knows, but we have vowed to
keep the secret. When they killed my brother
— Uzziah's abba — because he was an
idolater, I threatened to leave Judah and
take Isaiah with me. Uzziah wouldn't hear

of it. He moved Isaiah and me to the prophets' camp." His eyes grew damp. "I've had little to say to Uzziah since. I have little to say about anything."

"Does Isaiah know —"

"No! And don't you dare tell him!"

The venom in his voice surprised her. "I wouldn't, Amoz. I won't."

He dropped his gaze. Silence descended.

"Why didn't you run?" Her voice sounded like a trumpet. "Why not take Isaiah to Egypt or Damascus? Your talent could have provided a profitable living."

He gave a mirthless laugh. "Where can a man escape Yahweh? I may not worship Him as a god, but I cannot deny that Yahweh is powerful. When you and Hosea took me to Uzziah's rented house, I was reminded what happens to those who displease Judah's god."

Gomer swallowed the lump forming in her throat. "Amoz, I want to leave the prophets' camp, and I want to take Jezreel with me."

The fear she'd seen when he'd first glimpsed her returned. "I cannot involve myself in any conspiracy against Yahweh. I have vowed to leave Him alone, and so far He has left me and my son unharmed."

"But what about Aya? What about their children? Don't you want your grandchildren to know the mother goddess?"

His jaw clenched, and he extended his hand to help Gomer to her feet. "I will keep my vow to stay silent. But if your husband drags Isaiah into the altar fires with this prophecy nonsense . . ." His last words were mumbled, and Gomer heard only, "Foolishness . . . utter foolishness." He returned to his altar, nestling the goddess into her hiding place.

Gomer knew their conversation was over. What about her plans to escape with Jezreel? Were they crushed like the pile of shards in which Amoz hid his worship? She descended the stairs, glancing back at the one person in the camp who shared her faith in Asherah. A man too afraid of Yahweh to speak to his own son.

Who was this god of Hosea's? And why did He torment her so?

22

Jeroboam's son Zechariah was king of Israel in Samaria for six months. He did what Yahweh considered evil, as his ancestors had done.

Isaiah nudged a crate full of chickens off a slipshod-stacked wagon, causing a terrible ruckus at Tirzah's city gate. Hosea slipped behind a cart full of tapestries, and Isaiah crouched low beside him. Both prophets passed by two distracted sentries unnoticed. They'd been deep in the heart of Israel for more than seven moon cycles and become extremely unpopular with Jeroboam's troops and city officials.

After witnessing repeated abominations, Isaiah had asked one night by the fire, "Why hasn't Yahweh already brought Israel to its knees?"

Hosea had no answer. He proclaimed Yahweh's message — the judgment of Jezreel — and saw his son's face with each declaration of the name. He declared it in Gibeon, then Mizpah and Timnah. "The Lord told me to name my son Jezreel and has promised to punish Jehu's descendants for the people they slaughtered in that valley. Yahweh will put an end to the kingdom of Israel. On that day He will break Israel's bows and arrows in the valley of Jezreel."

But in every town and village, people laughed, they scoffed. Some even threw stones and rotten food at him. Isaiah's fiery temper had nearly gotten them arrested in two villages.

Why, Lord? Why must we continue to warn these ungrateful people? His baby's newborn cry haunted his dreams. Gomer's empty expression plagued his waking thoughts. Would she be in Tekoa when he returned? Surely Yuval would have convinced her to stay.

"Make way for Israel's general!" A herald stood at Tirzah's well, his voice carrying over the midday market noise. "General Menahem comes to deliver news from King Jeroboam in Samaria!"

Isaiah nodded in the direction of an abandoned wagon where they could hide but still hear and see the general. With a deep sigh, Hosea followed his friend to their hiding place. He'd heard Menahem had been stationed in Tirzah as military governor for the northern region. Perhaps the rumblings of rebellion from the southern hill country of Ephraim had forced King Jeroboam to spread his military power across all of northern Israel.

He and Isaiah crouched behind the overturned wagon, using their bulky collars to hide their faces. It had been over a year since Hosea had seen Menahem at Gomer's trial in Samaria, but they'd come too far to let Menahem arrest them now. A growing number of soldiers surrounded the audience, and Hosea realized they were trapped — no way of escape after proclaiming Yahweh's judgment.

You will remain silent.

Hosea glanced at Isaiah, startled by Yahweh's clear message. "Did you hear it?"

Isaiah was consumed by the commotion at the center of town. "Hear what?" he asked without taking his eyes from Israel's hulking general. "Look at Menahem. He seems different somehow. Older. Weary."

Hosea was still trying to reason why Yahweh would bring them to Tirzah if he wasn't supposed to prophesy when he followed

Isaiah's gaze — and saw Eitan, Menahem's second-in-command. Gomer had pointed him out as the man who had beaten her, and seeing the mountainous man standing in his full leather armor made Hosea's heart race with pent-up fury. How could any man beat a woman and still call himself a man, a soldier even?

Eitan raised his sword above his head, whistling above the crowd noise, and everyone fell silent. With a full bow, he paid homage to Menahem, and Hosea realized Isaiah's observation was correct. Israel's general looked haggard.

Menahem stepped up on the well curb slowly, almost painfully. The battle scars on his face seemed deeper, his brows severely furrowed. "I bring you sad news, people of Israel." He paused, tilting his head heavenward. Was he fighting emotion? "King Jeroboam is dead."

The crowd gasped, shock and confusion rippling like a wave on the sea.

Isaiah gripped Hosea's arm. "The Lord's judgment has begun," he whispered.

Hosea nodded and squeezed his eyes shut. *Thank You, Yahweh, for bringing us to Tirzah to hear it from Menahem himself.*

"How did he die?" someone in the crowd shouted.

Menahem dragged his large paw down the length of his face. "The king died peacefully in his bed."

Peacefully? Hosea's anger stirred. Yahweh's prophecy foretold Jehu's family would be punished, not die peacefully in their beds! He turned a puzzled glance to Isaiah, whose expression mirrored his own confusion.

Eitan lifted his sword again, quieting the people's chatter.

Menahem cleared his throat, his deep voice rumbling. "The king's son Zechariah will succeed his abba and rule Israel with wisdom and power from the gods. As commander of Israel's hosts and as King Jeroboam's friend, let me assure you . . ." He climbed atop the well and unsheathed his sword. Eitan mirrored the warrior's stance and created a wide berth as Menahem shouted his decree. "The line of Jeroboam's descendants will remain unbroken. King Zechariah rules Israel in Samaria!" A deafening cheer arose, and Menahem's arrogance appeared reborn with his sweeping appraisal of those before him. Whatever grief the general felt seemed to fuel his ferocity, and his ferocity seemed to fuel the crowd's depravity.

A timbrel and flute started to play. The

shock of moments ago was overwhelmed by festive music, hopeful celebration, and dancing women. Hosea felt warm arms descend over his shoulders, follow the contours of his chest, and a woman's body press against his back. "Shall we mourn Jeroboam together?" came a whisper with the acrid scent of perfume.

Hosea leapt to his feet, ready to berate her, intending to shove her away. But he froze at the child before him. Twelve, maybe thirteen years old. *Like Gomer had been.* Hosea stumbled backward, catching himself on the wagon. Yahweh's Spirit began to stir, and Hosea's heart was troubled.

"Come on," Isaiah whispered, tugging his arm, weaving through the crowd toward the gates of Tirzah.

Hosea allowed his friend to lead them, hearing Yahweh's voice in a gentle whisper as they continued on the road south toward Judah. *Since the time of Adam, they have rejected My promises. They have been unfaithful.*

The last word resounded in his spirit again and again. *Unfaithful. They've been unfaithful.*

Isaiah begged him to stop at Tiphsah, but Hosea refused. Delirious with anger and fear, he repeated the last few words of the message. "Unfaithful, Isaiah. We must hurry home. They've been unfaithful."

They pressed on through the night, denying themselves sleep, stopping only to fill their water skins at springs along the way. Their food ran out before they reached Ramah, but the two men leaned on each other. Did Isaiah feel it too? Did he realize they must hurry home?

Unfaithful . . . been unfaithful.

Hosea and Isaiah crested a rocky rise and peered down at the small town of Netophah. Then, glancing farther south, Hosea pointed at Tekoa nestled in the second valley. "Almost home."

Lord, give us strength. He was certain Isaiah was praying the same thing after three days with little food or water and virtually no sleep. They should be home before sunset, before Sabbath began. *Yahweh, please let Gomer be there waiting for me.*

Isaiah led them on a narrow stretch of rocky terrain. He stopped abruptly, and Hosea wondered if a viper had darted into their path, but he stilled when Isaiah placed a quieting finger against his lips. "Listen."

Echoes of pagan chanting emerged from a copse of trees ahead. They'd grown accustomed to the sounds while traveling through Israel, but to hear the rhythmic clanging of sistrums and bells in Judah still sounded foreign to Hosea's ears. Drawn like moths to a flame, Hosea and Isaiah left the path, forcing wobbly legs toward the sounds of revelry in a sycamore grove north of Netophah.

The music grew louder, and the sound of laughter and celebration seeped through the thick brush. They pressed to the edge of a circular clearing and crouched beside a boulder, remaining hidden to watch twenty Judean souls betray Yahweh. A high priestess stood beside the seductively carved Asherah pole, receiving treasures from the faithful unfaithful. Beside the pole lay an altar heaped with burning grain and animal portions. A bald priest added sacrifices to the fire.

In the center of the clearing, young priestesses played instruments while worshipers danced, waiting to be called to the tents aligned on the eastern rim of the clearing. Each tent was guarded by two large soldiers. Someone emerged from the third tent — a man, adjusting his belt and robe, smiling. A soldier motioned to one of the men dancing. His dancing stopped, and he eagerly approached the tent to worship Asherah with the waiting priestess.

One word resounded in Hosea's head. *Unfaithful. Unfaithful. Unfaithful.* How would he feel if Gomer waited inside that tent to "accept the worship" of Asherah's male patrons? Not all the women in those tents were priestesses. Some were women fulfilling a vow, girls proving their first act of loyalty to the goddess, or wives paying their husbands' debts to the priests. Judah had become unfaithful to her God as surely as Israel had played the harlot.

Driven by righteous fury, Hosea burst through the thick brush, entering the clearing with a shout. "Nooo!" Isaiah followed close behind, silent but a formidable rear guard.

All music and dancing stopped, every eye fastened on the two intruders.

"You are unfaithful to Yahweh, every one of you!" Hosea ran to the Asherah pole. "This is not your god, Judah!" He glimpsed an alabaster goddess in the hand of a priestess and snatched it from her.

"Wait!" she cried, but Isaiah blocked her path as Hosea crushed the idol between two stones. "No!" The priestess crumpled to the ground, weeping over the dust that remained.

The guards seemed frozen, hands on their swords but unable or unwilling to challenge

Yahweh's fiery prophet. Others in the grove slipped away, averting their eyes.

"Return to Yahweh," Hosea pleaded with them as they left. "Return to His temple in Jerusalem. Present sin offerings, and return to your Elohim."

The weeping priestess raised herself slowly, her face as pale as the alabaster dust now blown by the wind. "What have you done? Surely you've called down a curse on us all."

"What have *I* done? It is you, and those like you, who call down Yahweh's wrath on the nation of Judah." Tears welled in his eyes. The scantily dressed cult prostitutes emerged from their tents, so similar to what Gomer had been not so long ago. These Judean maidens broke God's heart as surely as the girls in Israel had been grieving Him for generations.

Would Judah be lost too?

Suddenly overwhelmed by his fatigue, he stumbled backward into Isaiah's arms. "We must find the strength to deliver one more message, my friend."

Isaiah slid his arm around Hosea's waist, and they leaned on each other. "I know. We must talk to Uzziah — tonight."

Hosea leaned on his friend's shoulder, and

they descended the hill into the king's encampment, finding the priests preparing the Sabbath meal. They rounded the corner of King Uzziah's house, and Hosea watched his eyes light up at the sight of Isaiah. His smile died as they trudged closer.

"Unclean! Unclean!" came the familiar refrain, and royal attendants paused their preparations in search of the visitors the announcement proclaimed. "Welcome home, wandering prophet. What news do you bring from our faithless brothers in the north?" Hosea heard the strain in his voice. He'd grown noticeably weaker during their absence.

Hosea waved to acknowledge the king's greeting but remained silent, saving his strength to deliver Yahweh's message.

As they drew nearer, Isaiah helped Hosea to the audience tapestry and began speaking before the prophet had a chance. "We bring news from Israel, Cousin, but it pales when compared to what we've just witnessed on Judah's soil."

Hosea was startled when Commander Hananiah emerged from the king's house.

Uzziah must have noticed his surprise. "Your return is quite timely. Hananiah has come with news from Jerusalem." Judah's top soldier cleared his throat and issued a warning glance to his king. Uzziah, undaunted by the commander's not-so-subtle suggestion, continued his explanation. "We're planning a coalition of nations — nineteen nations total — so Judah can stand against Assyria's aggression."

"Judah will be destroyed — with or without a coalition — if the people continue to worship on every hill and high place, my lord," Hosea said flatly.

A storm gathered on Commander Hananiah's face, but Uzziah remained calm. "Isaiah said you witnessed something as you journeyed home. What has stirred your passion, Prophet?"

Sitting so close to home, Hosea felt the full weight of his exhaustion. "I ask that you let me speak without interruption, for we are at the end of a long journey and in need of food and rest."

The king nodded. "As you wish, my friend."

"First, I bring news of King Jeroboam's death —"

Uzziah gasped.

"When? How?" Hananiah's deep voice echoed off the surrounding hills.

"Please, as I said, let me speak, and I'll give more details later."

Uzziah hesitated, brows furrowed, but

nodded for Hosea to continue. The commander looked as if his head might burst.

"Thank you. I will tell you that we were present in Tirzah when General Menahem announced the king's death, and Zechariah, Jeroboam's son, has assumed Israel's throne."

Uzziah exchanged a glance with Hananiah, but true to his word, his lips remained tightly sealed.

"We have come from Netophah, where we happened on a secret grove with an altar to Asherah."

Uzziah's expression clouded.

"I smashed an idol and dispersed the worshipers, but unless the high places are destroyed, they'll continue their idolatry, and Judah will fall under the same judgment as Israel."

With icy calm, Uzziah cast an accusing glance at his commander. "Why is there a sacred grove in Netophah?"

Hananiah's cool façade never wavered. "I've assigned as many men as I can spare to scout for pagan altars. I don't have enough soldiers to patrol religious zealots when my primary duty is to protect the nation." His final words were aimed like arrows at Hosea.

"You will have no soldiers — and no nation to protect — if the so-called religious zealots aren't stopped." Hosea shifted his gaze to the king. "Ultimately, King Uzziah, it is not Judah's commander Yahweh holds responsible for the nation's obedience."

The sun was sinking on the horizon, and Hosea knew Uzziah could pronounce the beginning of Sabbath at any moment, ending their meeting.

"You must destroy the high places, Cousin." Isaiah's voice was kind but firm, and Uzziah seemed suddenly overwhelmed.

"You prophets must be reasonable. Yes, some of the high places have become pagan sites, but many Judeans worship Yahweh on the high places because they're too frightened to enter the temple. If I destroy the high places, where will the people worship Yahweh? They're horrified at the Lord's wrath on me! Even my own son Jotham won't enter the temple to sacrifice! Don't you see? If I take away their high places, they'll turn away from the Lord completely!"

"That's a lie!" Isaiah's venom erupted without warning. "Has Hananiah told you that, or has it been whispered to your soul by the false gods that deceive your nation?"

Hosea saw the king's wounded expression and quieted his friend, whispering, "Unless you receive a specific word from the Lord, don't make this your fight, Isaiah. Let your relationship with Uzziah remain unbroken."

The fire in his friend's eyes still burned, but he nodded his understanding and pressed his lips into a thin, straight line.

"*Demonstrate* your love for Yahweh," Hosea said, returning his attention to Judah's king. "*Show* the nation your respect for His holiness, and stop condoning their spiritual adultery by leaving the high places intact."

Uzziah appeared to be wrestling with some unspoken inner turmoil. Hosea quieted his spirit, pleading with Yahweh for more words — different words — that might convince Judah's king to relent.

Unfaithful. Unfaithful. Unfaithful.

Hosea remembered the shrine prostitutes emerging from the tents after they'd heard his shouting. His heart had twisted at the thought of Gomer in such a life. He pushed himself to stand before offering a final plea. "Imagine one of your family members worshiping the goddess Asherah. Imagine how your heart would ache at such betrayal."

The two men leaned on each other and turned toward camp, hearing the quiet sobs of Judah's king welcoming the Sabbath.

23

Hosea 2:8

She doesn't believe that I gave her grain, new wine, and olive oil. I gave her plenty of silver and gold, but she used it to make statues of Baal.

Silence hung heavily between Hosea and Isaiah as they concentrated on their final steps toward home. Dusk settled, they entered the camp's gates, and Isaiah sighed. "Has Yahweh told you what awaits you at home?"

Hosea shook his head, too exhausted — too frightened — to speak. They stopped at Hosea's courtyard gate.

"Do you want me to go in with you?" Isaiah asked.

Hosea nodded, thankful beyond words for a friend like Isaiah. He glanced at the neat row of stone houses. Amos, his northern neighbor, and Jonah, the next home south. Familiar. Unchanged. They passed through Hosea's courtyard gate, and he inhaled deeply. Home. The figs. The desert breeze. Even his small stable. It was good to be home.

Isaiah hesitated at the door, letting Hosea open it when he was ready. A low humming sound rose from the other side, and they exchanged a puzzled glance.

Then Hosea's heart stopped beating.

It was the same chanting they'd heard in Asherah's grove. This time Gomer's voice droned the song. Isaiah must have realized it at the same time. Hosea watched his head fall forward, defeat written in his stance. Exactly what Hosea felt.

"Go home, my friend."

Isaiah looked up, his eyes full of tears. "Are you sure you want to face this alone?"

Gomer's chanting stopped. *She must have heard us.* Hosea's heart beat faster, emotions swirling within. Just as he was ready to beg for Isaiah's help, a chilly breeze lifted the hair from his shoulders, and peace flowed into his spirit. *Yahweh.*

Isaiah recognized the Lord's presence and smiled.

Hosea chuckled. "I'm not alone. I'll know what to say when I see her."

299

Isaiah placed a supportive hand on his shoulder and then was gone. Hosea breathed in God's presence and opened the door.

No one was in the main room, but he noticed several changes. A bucket for Jezreel's soiled loincloths sat by the front door, and several wooden toys littered the floor near a large goatskin. *The baby must be crawling.* The thought sent a pang of regret through him.

He shrugged off his shoulder bag, letting it fall to the floor. "Gomer?"

No answer.

He tiptoed toward their bedchamber, more an effort to avoid the toys than avoid being heard. "Gomer?"

She was seated on their mattress, holding the Asherah in plain view. "I won't hide it anymore." Her eyes sparked with the same challenge that was in her voice. "You need to know the truth, Hosea. I prayed to *Asherah* the night Jezzy was conceived. *Asherah* was hidden under this mattress and blessed our union each night. And it is *Asherah* to whom I will always offer my sacrifices."

Each mention of Asherah was like a dagger to his soul. "Where did you get that? I know you didn't bring it from Samaria."

She shot off the bed like an arrow from a

bow, leaning into him, daring him to object. "I purchased it in Jerusalem — with your silver — after I saw how your god punished a righteous king. *This* was the so-called *gift* I hid in my pocket alongside your dagger in Jerusalem!"

Holy fury kindled inside Hosea. Had anything they'd shared been true? He stepped forward, moving Gomer back. "If you choose to worship a lie, so be it, but you will *not* steal Yahweh's glory and give it to a piece of stone. Look around you, woman. Count the baskets of grain, the skins of wine, the pitchers of oil. It is *not* your pathetic idol that provided your bread and robes and shelter. It. Was. Yahweh!" he thundered. "And yet you take the silver the Lord provided and squander it on this powerless Asherah." Hosea secured her wrist with one hand and snatched the goddess away with the other.

"No!" she screamed. "Give her back to me!"

"If she is god, let her strike me down and jump back into your hand."

Gomer gasped. "How dare you blaspheme the mother godde —"

"How dare you lie to me with every breath." His voice broke. *Unfaithful.* Yahweh's message had been for him and for Judah.

Uzziah had refused to destroy the high places, but Hosea would not make the same mistake. He hurled the Asherah at their bed-chamber's stone wall. The satisfying crash was followed by Gomer's wail. He watched her kneel beside the broken pieces, mourning shattered stone, while his tattered heart bled alone.

"Where is my son?"

No answer.

"Where is Jezreel?" he shouted.

"With Aya," she said without looking up, then returned to her weeping, ignoring him. Would she always hate him? Forever defy his authority as her husband?

Through the anger, Hosea remembered Yahweh's words to Jeroboam. *There is no faithfulness, no love, no acknowledgment of God in the land.*

Hosea sat on the cold, dirt-packed floor and wept — for Israel, for Judah, for Yahweh, for his wife. *Lord, teach me to love as You love.*

Gomer rolled onto her side and felt Sampson's prickly tongue licking her knuckles. She opened one eye, remembering the harsh reality of her new life. Hosea had been back since last Sabbath, and Gomer had chosen to spend her nights on the stack of goat-skins in the main room. Her back ached, but at least she didn't have to face Hosea morning and night. She hardly saw him at all.

She sat up, listening for Jezzy's morning gurgle. All was silent. She slipped on her robe, grabbed a piece of bread and hard cheese, wrapped them in a cloth, and shoved them into her pocket. Her midday meal. She sipped the remainder of last night's goat's milk. On the edge of sour. She stared at the cup of white liquid, considering whether to throw it out or save it for baking.

Then she pondered a similar choice for her rancid existence — give up or salvage it? Oh, how she wished she had Lady Asherah to pray to. Perhaps Amoz could somehow purchase one for her — but could she use Hosea's silver again?

"Good morning." Hosea's gravelly voice startled her, and she sloshed goat's milk all over the table.

She growled and soaked it up with a nearby cloth, refusing to acknowledge his presence.

"I've been home since last Sabbath, Gomer. You must talk to me sometime."

She slammed the cloth down. "Perhaps,

but I will only talk to you when I *must*."
Sighing, she tried to steady her nerves. She
couldn't think when he looked at her that
way.

"Why are you going to the pottery shop
so early this morning?" Hosea had insisted
on maintaining their routine. Jezzy still slept
on a goatskin in the bedchamber. Aya still
cared for him daily. And Gomer still worked
all day at the pottery workshop. "You usually wait until after you've given Jezzy a
fresh cup of milk."

Gomer's mind reeled to think of an excuse. She couldn't tell him she hoped to
find Amoz worshiping Asherah! "Isaiah and
Aya's wedding is less than two moons away,
and Amoz asked me to help finish a special
project he's working on."

Hosea studied her. Could he see the lie
written on her face? "I love you, Gomer."

A knot of emotion hardened into a boulder in her stomach. *Love. What is love?*
"You'll find a clean cup by the wash-basin."
She grabbed her walking stick and fled
before he could say more.

Dawn's light bathed the main path, and
Gomer drew in a deep breath of morning
air. She stirred the dusty path with her walking stick to alert sunbathing vipers of her
presence. Tekoa. She hated it. Why didn't

304

she leave? *Because I have nothing of my own — except Jezzy.* The thought of leaving her son ripped her heart open. But fleeing Tekoa was a ridiculous dream anyway. She was trapped in this marriage as she'd been imprisoned at the brothel — the same hopelessness, different chains. She thought learning a trade would free her, but Amoz had made it clear he wouldn't share profits. Like every other woman's, Gomer's options were few. She needed that new Asherah.

She hurried her pace, noticing three men pulling a wagon full of leather-hard pots through the southern gates near the shop. "Shalom, and good morning," she said, pretending gaiety. All three men were familiar — cave runners for Amoz's drying procedure. She encouraged their hungry stares and slowed her walk, giving them a lingering view. "Has Master Amoz arrived yet?" She joined them beside the wagon, running her fingers along the edge of the rows of clay pots.

The tallest of the workmen stepped forward, exchanging glances with his two friends. "I don't believe Master Amoz is here. We go to the caves at sunrise to retrieve the pots so they're waiting in the shop when he arrives." He stepped closer, just a handbreadth away. He smelled like stale sweat and watered wine, but Gomer didn't recoil. Smiling, he revealed yellowed teeth and kept his voice low. "Aren't you the prophet's wife from Israel?" His eyes roamed her. "The one they say used to be a harlot?"

Gomer glanced left and right, motioning for the tall man to lean closer. "How do you feel about keeping Yahweh's laws?" she asked, brushing his ear with her lips.

"I'm not much of a religious man." He chuckled and remained bent low.

"I need to earn some silver," she whispered, "but I would need to trust a man's discretion before I could revisit my old profession." Blowing on his ear, she added, "Would you or your two friends like to show me the caves where the pottery dries? Perhaps there I could show you my unique skills — for a price?"

The man stood to his full height and swallowed hard. "The lady wants to see the caves where we dry the pottery," he said to his friends. Their brows furrowed in confusion, so he lifted both eyebrows in a not-so-subtle explanation. "You two deliver this wagonload to the shop while the lady and I visit the last cave. Then each of you can take a turn — showing the lady the caves."

His companions glanced at him and then

at Gomer, their eyes wide.

Gomer's heart raced, the familiar rush of excitement, the thrill of the forbidden. She licked her lips slowly. "Before we leave, I must have two things." The men began nodding before she listed her requirements. "You must keep your mouths shut, and I want to see your silver before we go."

Two of them reached into their pockets to produce payment, but the third sounded panicked. "I keep my silver at home."

Gomer stepped over to the nervous little man. "Well, you'd better hurry home before your friend and I return then." She glanced in the direction of Hosea's house. "I'm finished offering my services for free."

24

King Uzziah had a skin disease until the day he died. . . . He lived in a separate house and was barred from Yahweh's temple. His son Jotham was in charge of the royal palace and governed the country.

Aya was beauty defined on her wedding day, and Isaiah couldn't seem to tear his gaze from her. Wedding preparations had taken entirely too long, according to the young groom, but the reward for his wait stood before him in fine white linen and a delicate golden-edged veil. Surrounded by what seemed the entire prophets' camp, the bride and groom stood under their wedding canopy ten cubits from King Uzziah's rented house. Hosea, friend of the bridegroom, read their betrothal agreement:

On this, the eighth day of Chislev, in the city of Tekoa, Isaiah, son of Amoz, enters into this agreement with Aya, daughter of Enoch. Let Isaiah, with the help of heaven, honor, support, and maintain her . . .

Hosea spoke to the audience, but his heart was set on one person alone. Gomer. She stood beside Amoz, her placement an honor, designating her as family. Today was a day for celebration — but she stood like granite. Emotionless. Heartless.

Amoz reached into his robe and passed her a small, cloth-wrapped bundle hidden beneath his giant paw. Perhaps he'd made her a cup or a bowl. Maybe a toy for Jezzy. She shifted Jezzy to one hip and buried the treasure in her robe pocket.

Hosea read the final words on the scroll: "Let this treaty seal Isaiah's vow to marry Aya in no less than one year, when he will claim her as his wife according to the Law of Moses and Israel." Hosea glanced up with a sheepish grin. "I'm thankful the agreement didn't specify *exactly* a year, or I would have had to traipse around Israel without my best friend." Good-natured chuckles rippled through the audience, giving the high priest a few moments to instruct the bride and groom on the next portion of the ceremony.

Hosea rejoined Gomer, Jezzy, and Amoz. He cradled his wife's elbow, leaned close. "May I see the gift Amoz gave you?"

Her head snapped toward him. Was it fear or anger in those hazel eyes? "Can't you wait until your best friend's wedding is finished? It's just a new cup for Jezzy." Her whispered words spewed venom, and she returned her attention to the celebration before he could respond.

If it was a clay cup, why was she trembling? Why so disturbed? Suspicion coiled around his heart like a viper, but then he glimpsed Amoz. Isaiah's abba was a good man. Quiet and rather broken, but what could he give Gomer that would be offensive? Hosea squeezed the tight muscles at the back of his neck and sighed. *Enjoy the celebration.*

"Thank you for joining our family to celebrate Isaiah and Aya's special day." King Uzziah's voice rose, and Hosea watched Amoz tense. When the high priest concluded the service, it was customary for the groom's abba to direct the guests. Evidently not so today. "We have prepared a wedding feast fit for a king!" Uzziah's weak voice rose, and the audience cheered.

Hananiah, who stood beside him, raised his sword in the air, motioning for silence.

"I have an announcement to add to this day's celebrating."

Prince Jotham emerged from the rented house, and every sound stilled. "From this day forward," Uzziah said, "my son Jotham reigns as coregent in Jerusalem!" He tried to shout the ending declaration, working to regain the crowd's vigor. But a slow, forced applause that began with Commander Hananiah was the crowd's only offering. Jotham looked as if he might run back into the house. Isaiah and Aya kept their heads bowed under the wedding canopy.

Amoz cursed under his breath, and Gomer turned to Hosea. "Go talk to Uzziah."

The wedding guests began ambling toward the feasting tables, an uncomfortable pall settling over them. Jezzy leaned toward his father, arms extended, and Hosea's heart melted. His son had grown quite fond of him in the full moon since he'd returned home. He reached for the boy and nuzzled that soft, sweaty place where his neck and shoulder met.

Gomer followed Amoz without looking back.

Hosea felt like a fish swimming upstream, walking toward the king when all others walked away. Hananiah and Jotham remained. Hosea stood beneath the wedding canopy since the audience tapestry had been replaced for the day. "Shalom, my lord," he said to the king, and then nodded silent recognition to the others.

"Isaiah married a beautiful bride." Uzziah seemed eager to keep the conversation light.

Hosea saw no need to. "I'm puzzled at the timing of your announcement, my king."

Uzziah hesitated, and Hosea sensed some inner turmoil. "Will you come closer so we might talk privately, my friend?"

"You know the Law. I cannot."

"Do you love your son, Hosea?" Uzziah's expression was unreadable, and a deep sense of foreboding shadowed Hosea's spirit.

"Of course. As you love Jotham."

"As King Jeroboam undoubtedly loved Zechariah, his son." His eyes nearly pierced Hosea's soul.

Hosea pondered each word, searching for Uzziah's hidden message. Silence hung between them, and Jezzy began to squirm. Hosea bounced and shushed him, kissing his forehead, promising Yuval's candied figs. But the boy wriggled and stiffened, a toddler needing space to roam.

"Jotham," Uzziah said, "would you take Hosea's son to his ima? Hananiah will escort you."

"But Abba, I need to hear what you say to the prophet if I'm going to rule —"

"Please, Jotham. Do as I ask."

Hosea relinquished his son to the new coregent. "He's still a little wobbly on the uneven ground. You'll need to hold his hand."

Jotham's smile was kind. "I have a son of my own about his age. His name is Ahaz — red curls and a temper to match." He laid a hand on Hosea's shoulder. "I'll watch over him." Cautiously, he approached Jezzy. "Hey, little one. Let's go find your ima."

Hananiah followed them, jaw flexing, fists clenched.

When they were safely out of hearing range, Uzziah spoke in low tones. "A king's love can't keep his son safe forever, Hosea."

"Is King Zechariah —"

"Israel's young king still sits on his abba's throne, but my spies in Israel's court say Jeroboam's trusted advisors are plotting to kill Zechariah. His abba's friends, Hosea — men who watched the boy grow up. Zechariah has ruled Israel for only a few Sabbaths." Uzziah's voice faltered. "What about *my* son? *My* advisors?" He rushed on, not waiting for an answer. "I've worked hard to prepare Jotham for the throne. Priests began teaching him the Law when he was a little older than your Jezreel, but now he's afraid to enter the temple because of Yahweh's wrath against *me*." He pinned Hosea with a stare. "Will the Lord's punishment last forever? Will my advisors betray me or my son?" This time he waited, almost daring the prophet to remain silent.

"I wish I knew the answers, my friend."

"Why don't you?" He spat the words — more an accusation than a question. "Plead with Yahweh. Find out His plan. Both you and Amos have prophesied that Israel will be destroyed and taken into exile. When? I need to know if Assyria will move against them now, while Israel's power is divided. Will they come as far south as Judah?"

Hosea shook his head, his own frustration mounting. "It doesn't work that way, Uzziah. If I could shout at the heavens, asking anything I desired, don't you think I'd have a few answers of my own by now?"

More turmoil roiled behind the king's eyes, but he held back. Hosea couldn't define it, but some emotion pressed on Uzziah's shoulders and defeated Judah's once-great king. "If Yahweh's prophets have no answers, how can I hope to save this nation — or my son?"

The king's question slapped Hosea like an offended virgin. "Prophets are mere mortals, and you will never save Judah or your son. But Yahweh has all the answers and has promised to save us all." Uzziah's head fell forward, and Hosea knew his frustration. "We must remain faithful, my friend, and then trust Yahweh to protect those we love most."

"If I didn't know better, I might think you were avoiding me." Yuval eyed Gomer while flattening the barley dough with her hands. "Would you have invited me over if Aya wasn't locked away for her wedding week?"

"Since when do you need an invitation?" Gomer smiled and kissed the woman's cheek, the subtle scent of coriander warming her heart. She'd missed her friend. "You've been traveling with Amos." She paused, considered Yuval's slight frown. "Why is that? You told me you never traveled with Amos. Why start now?"

Gomer pulled over a goatskin rug, plopping Jezzy into her lap. She grabbed a few playthings to keep his hands busy, and Sampson joined them, never far away when she was home. Yuval seemed to be choosing her words carefully, but then an impish grin and true sparkle lit her eyes.

"Can't an old woman enjoy a little adventure?" A little giggle passed between them.

"Amos invited me to join him, and I've been lonely since you're working more at the pottery shop." She halted her bread making and captured Gomer's chin, examining the windows of her soul. "What keeps you so busy at the pottery shop? I've come over as early as sunrise, and you're already gone. What could you be doing that early?"

Gomer pulled away from her grasp and retrieved one of Jezzy's wooden blocks, happy for the distraction. Yuval knew her too well. What if she read the guilt on her face? "I prepare the leather-hard pots for burnishing. It's a technique Amoz has taught me. I take a small, smooth stone and polish the pottery to a shine."

"Mm-hmm." Yuval seemed intent on her barley bread project again, slapping the small, round loaves on the outer surface of the clay oven.

Relieved, Gomer sighed and wound Jezzy's black curls around her finger. She loved Yuval and was thankful for her help, but she had also invited her over to determine if news of her morning "business" had reached the camp's gossip mills. She couldn't come right out and ask if Yuval had heard rumors. Perhaps more talk about the pottery shop would remind her if she'd heard anything.

"Amoz let me throw my first pot on the

kick wheel."

"Oh my!" Yuval looked up from her barley bread, stricken. "I'm not sure I approve of all this throwing and kicking of pottery, dear."

Gomer giggled, and Jezreel clapped his hands. "No, no, Yuval. 'Throwing a pot' means Amoz taught me to take a wet lump of clay and place it on a turning wheel, which you keep spinning by 'kicking' it. And then you mold that lump into a pot by shaping it with wet hands."

"Oh! Well, I can see why my comment sounded so silly." She winked and turned the barley loaves over to brown the other side. "So, you enjoy working the clay? Don't you miss being home with little Jezreel?"

"Of course I miss him, but Aya takes good care of him. And yes, I *really* enjoy my work." Gomer's heart thudded. She loved this dear woman and decided she didn't want to know if Yuval had heard any rumors or suspected the worst of her. "What about you? Do you enjoy your travels with Amos?"

"We have a lovely time, dear. Now, tell me again why you spend so much time at the pottery shop?" She reached for the cooking pot and lentils. "Jezreel is almost a year old, and he needs his ima."

Gomer remained silent, watching her

friend turn the lamb on the spit over the cooking fire. "Aya has been a godsend," she said, swallowing hard. Her stomach rolled, nerves getting the best of her. "I've been home more now that she and Isaiah are married." How could she tell Yuval she'd be gone by spring if her harlotry continued to pay well? Would she take Jezzy with her, or could she leave without him? She'd already saved a handsome sum of silver.

Yuval leaned over the table, holding Gomer's gaze. "I would be happy to resume our cooking lessons, Daughter. As a wife and ima, you should learn to feed your family." Her eyes were full of love, but the rebuke stung.

Gomer didn't want to feed her family. She wanted excitement, adventure. She wanted a man to love her. Was that so terrible? So unfathomable? Her stomach lurched, and she felt as if she might be sick. Her head swam, and she tried to focus on Jezreel and Sampson.

Yuval glanced at her, concern etching her features. "Gomer, you're pale. I'm worried about you. Are you all right?"

Before she could answer, Gomer hoisted Jezreel out of her lap and dove for the nearest bowl. After emptying her stomach, she sat up and met her friend's beaming smile.

"You're pregnant again, aren't you! That's why you invited me over — to tell me the good news!"

Stricken by the possibility, Gomer sorted the thousand thoughts racing through her mind — first and foremost, the names of men she'd lain with and the glaring absence of her husband on that list. This could not be Hosea's child. *Mother Asherah, please no!*

"Have you told Hosea yet?" Yuval had picked up Jezreel and was bouncing him on her hip. "Oh, he'll be so excited!"

"No, Yuval. I haven't told him, and no . . ." She buried her face in her hands. "He won't be excited." How could she tell her one friend of the betrayal? Silence stretched into awkwardness, and when she looked up, she saw tears in Yuval's eyes.

"I love you, my little Gomer, no matter what you've done, but you must tell me the truth. Our friendship deserves the truth."

Gomer's defenses broke under the weight of Yuval's kindness. The woman didn't deserve the awful truth. She didn't deserve to know the countless times Gomer visited the pottery caves — with so many men, she'd stopped asking their names, stopped noticing their faces. The three pottery runners were supposed to be discreet, but their discretion disappeared when they experienced Gomer's unique talents. At the time, she hadn't minded their referrals, since the poorer customers paid less silver, thereby requiring more volume. But she didn't have Merav to feed her pomegranate rinds and wild carrot seeds. In the absence of precautions, her womb had grown fertile.

Merav. Gomer looked into the face that had once reminded her so much of her old friend. Yuval didn't deserve the awful truth; she deserved a pretty lie.

"Hosea is angry that I find such fulfillment at the pottery shop." She paused to formulate the rest of her plan, reaching up to take Yuval's hand. "I don't want to tell him I'm pregnant yet. Will you help me learn to cook and become a better ima before I tell him about the new baby?"

Yuval's eyes glistened with happy tears. "I think you've made a wise decision, Daughter. Your children are young for such a short while, but you can throw and kick pots for the rest of your life." She chuckled, and Gomer smiled with her, issuing a silent prayer to the Asherah hidden under her mattress.

Mother Goddess, give me your feminine charms that I might become enticing to my husband again. For if I cannot tempt him, he will stone me as an adulteress.

25

PROVERBS 6:26

A prostitute's price is only a loaf of bread, but a married woman hunts for your life itself.

The days had grown shorter, and Jonah was growing weaker. "I'm sorry, my son, but I'm too tired to continue today."

Hosea leaned over his bed and kissed his forehead. "Rest a while. Whatever Micah is cooking over there smells wonderful. I may eat your share, Jonah." He glanced at the young prophet, noticing his tear-streaked cheeks, and offered a conciliatory grin. They shared a sorrowful nod — silent understanding that their teacher and friend was failing quickly.

Micah wiped two bowls with a cloth he'd slung over his shoulder. "I've made plenty of vegetable stew. Stay if you'd like." He sniffed, wiping his nose with the same cloth.

Hosea chuckled. "I think I'll go home. Yuval is cooking tonight, and at least I know what goes into her stew."

"What?" Micah feigned offense, this time blowing his nose on the cloth and rousing a grin from Jonah.

Hosea walked out laughing, but sobered as soon as the door clicked shut behind him. *Lord, give me strength to face Gomer again.* His stomach clenched. For two full moons he'd eaten his evening meals while sitting across from his wife in excruciating silence. They both talked to Jezzy but seldom uttered a word to each other. He was waiting — on Gomer to change, on Yahweh to speak, on life to improve.

The sunset reached through the sycamore trees, casting long shadows on the short path between Jonah's house and Hosea's. He extended his walking stick, scattering the dust and slapping scrub bushes to alert any creatures of his presence. A sudden streak of black shot out from his left. The desert cobra had struck and missed, then darted into the underbrush on the opposite side of the path. Hosea was overtaken by a full-bodied shudder.

He quickened his pace and considered asking Yuval if he could borrow a cat to accompany him on excursions. Sampson had eaten twice his weight in lizards and small house snakes. Still, it was a ridiculous thought. He knew a cat couldn't protect him from a cubit-long cobra, but Yuval's furry little creatures might at least warn him if a viper was near.

Hosea arrived home, reached for the door latch, and noted his shaking hand. The snake had rattled him. Or was it Jonah's weakened state? Perhaps both. He opened the door and found Yuval and Gomer laughing and . . . cooking. A sight he hadn't witnessed since before his wife was pregnant.

"Shalom, Hosea!" Yuval's cheery voice welcomed him, and he noticed his wife maintained a tentative smile. "Gomer has learned to make barley bread. Would you like to try some?"

He set aside his walking stick and removed his heavy robe. Jezreel chased the cat in circles, his favorite pastime now that he was walking. "Sure." He reached for the bread offered by his wife. "Thank you."

She brushed his fingers as he took the morsel. Fire raced up his arm. How long had it been since she'd touched him?

"Well, I should get home," Yuval prattled on, clapping flour from her hands. "Amos was supposed to return from Beersheba today. I didn't see him after midday, but perhaps he made it home by now." She wiped her hands on her apron and hugged her student. "Listen, Daughter, you've done very well today. I have confidence that you'll learn quickly. The lentil stew should be ready for tomorrow's midday meal, and the roasted lamb and vegetables should satisfy your hunger tonight."

Hosea lifted an eyebrow, marveling that Gomer would know the first thing about roasted lamb and vegetables. Aya had previously done all the cooking and serving for their family, and he assumed she'd continue after her wedding week was over.

"I've lost track. When will our newlyweds emerge from their wedded bliss?" he asked, throwing out the question to whichever woman felt like answering.

The ladies exchanged knowing glances, and Yuval nodded, seeming to encourage Gomer's answer.

"I've asked Yuval to help me cook. Aya and Isaiah will be starting their own family, and I'll need to take over her duties." Gomer looked at the floor, hands gripped humbly before her.

Suspicion niggled at Hosea's spirit. She had just spoken more civil words than he'd heard since he'd returned from Israel.

Yuval pecked a kiss on Gomer's cheek. "I'll be back tomorrow to help with the stew." Then she hurried out the door, leaving the little family alone in the looming darkness.

"Could you light a few more lamps and prepare the table mat? I'll bring over the lamb and vegetables." Gomer moved toward the cooking fire, and Hosea obeyed, keeping a watchful eye on this stranger in his wife's body.

She'd been gone when he awoke this morning — the same as every morning. What had changed in one day's time to create this meek, obedient wife? He could think of only one thing — Yuval. Hosea knew the older woman held great influence over his wife's emotions. Amos and Yuval had been away on trade journeys a lot recently, so Gomer hadn't spent much time with her friend. Perhaps today Yuval had convinced her that being a wife and ima were her most important calling. *Seems too easy.* He watched her carefully as he placed two goatskins beside their leather table mat and corralled Jezreel on his lap.

"Thank you." She placed the platter of meat and vegetables between the plates and filled a mug of watered wine at each plate.

"Here, I'll take him." Jezreel reached for her, and she swayed in time to a silent tune, cradling the toddler in her arms.

Hosea watched her while he ate and marveled at the way she loved Jezzy. He'd been wrong about her. She did know how to love. His heart seized as her singing washed over him, filling the awkward silence between them.

When he finished his meal, he stood and tried to lift Jezreel from her arms. "Here, I'll take him while you eat."

But she pulled the boy away, shushing Hosea while still humming her lullaby. The child was fast asleep. After a long, meaningful gaze, she said, "I'll go put him in our bed."

Hosca's heart was in his throat as he watched her walk away — the sway of her hips, the glide of her movement across the dirt-packed floor. His head swam. Was it the wine, or was he still in love with his wife? Before he could answer, she reappeared, her eyes sparkling flecks of green, blue, and copper. She removed her veil, and auburn curls floated to her shoulders.

"Are you hungry?" he asked, suddenly as nervous as a new groom. He spooned vegetables onto her plate and felt her arms slide around his waist. Was it nerves or anticipation that made him shudder?

"I must tell you I'm sorry, Hosea," she whispered. He stood and faced her, and she melted into his arms. "I realized after talking with Yuval that I've been selfish and let my desires push aside the needs of our family. Can you forgive me?" She held him as if he was her lifeline — her anchor in a storm of emotions she kept buried in her downturned face.

"Yes, my wife. I forgive you." He kissed the top of her head and worked his way down her forehead, her cheeks, and then found her lips.

"I want to make you happy," she said, seemingly as starved for passion as he felt. "I need you to love me, Hosea. Love me."

Yahweh, have You answered my prayers?

Without waiting for an answer, he allowed his desires to drive him. Yearnings he thought long dead raged until late in the night. She teased him, tempted him, taunted him with the pleasures she had learned in the days of her harlotry. Mad with desire, he gave himself over to her talents. Such a sensuous, amorous wife. He'd been home for eight long Sabbaths, denied the pleasures of the marriage bed because of Gomer's stubborn rebellion. But no more. He thanked Yahweh for the fire she kindled in his soul and then fell asleep, satiated by the throes of ecstasy.

Gomer awoke in time to empty her stomach into the bowl beside her. She wiped her mouth and tensed, feeling Hosea's hand on her back.

"Your cooking wasn't that bad." His sleepy voice sounded amused.

Relieved, she covered her nakedness and leaned over him with a smile. "We'll see. You haven't tried my lentil stew yet."

He reached up and grabbed her, playfully rolling her into his arms. Her heart ached at the tenderness in his eyes. He hadn't treated her so sweetly since before Jezreel was born, since before he left for Israel. Then she remembered — she hadn't given him the chance. His first sight of her upon his return was her sitting in their bedchamber with Asherah in her hand.

"What are you thinking?" He was searching her expression, his brow furrowed.

"I haven't told Amoz about my decision to be a wife and ima first and foremost. I should tell him I can't help at the workshop as often." She pulled away and felt Hosea's disappointment like a wet robe on her shoulders. She donned her tunic, robe, and sandals and moved toward the door as she spoke. "Would you mind if I went to the shop this morning — one last time to let everyone know of my decision?"

"I could go for you," he said, his voice pleading. "I could explain to Amoz."

"No, it's best if I tell him. I have a couple of pots that need burnishing before they're ready for market. Tell Yuval I'll be back to serve the lentil stew at midday." She wrapped her veil around her head and shoulders. She hurried out the door, clicking it shut behind her, and then rushed to the stables. She retched again beside the donkey's stall and wiped her mouth on her sleeve. Hiding her morning sickness from Hosea would be difficult, but she must find a way until at least two Sabbaths passed. By then she could convince him the child was his.

The sun rose over the eastern hills. She'd scheduled a new client this morning at the first cave and didn't want to be late. She kept a watchful eye on the path before her, cursing herself for leaving her walking stick behind. Her thoughts raced with her feet. Perhaps she could maintain her business until the pregnancy became obvious. No one would pay for a pregnant harlot. She'd have to delay her escape until after this second child was born. But one of the pottery shop women had just announced she was with child. Perhaps she could be a wet nurse for the new baby. Gomer would bind her breasts right after delivery and return to harlotry, adding to her already significant savings. The pregnancy would delay her escape; it need not cancel it.

She saw the three cave runners ahead, entering through the southern gates. Each one issued a leering smile, and she hurried past them to her first cave, not far from where the men had retrieved the wagonload of dried pots.

"You're late," said an angry voice from the deep recesses of the cavern. "I shouldn't have to pay when you're late."

The stench of stale sweat and the foulness of the man's breath caused Gomer to run for the path and retch once more. *Men are pigs.* She was in no mood to beg for a meager piece of silver.

"Get back in here." A meaty hand grabbed her waist and lifted her from the earth. He carried her a few steps and then dropped her, untying his belt. Her mind reeled. She saw Israel's captain, Eitan, raining blows on her face and body. Others before him had tried to abuse her, but she'd always carried a dagger. She'd become careless, forgotten this part of harlotry — the brutality, the entitlement men felt when paying for pleasure.

She scrambled to her feet, trying to flee, but he caught her cheekbone with the back of his hand. "We're not finished here." She struggled, but he was too strong. She dared not cry out. Who would help her? Tears streamed down her face as she silently pounded the ground with her fists, cursing her life. By the gods, she would find better men to build a respectable business. She was a harlot, not a whore.

When he finished with her, he tossed her a piece of silver. "Next time, don't be late." And then he was gone.

Anger and shame curled her into a ball, and she wept. Why was she born a woman? Why couldn't she choose her own destiny, love whom she wished, live how *she* determined best?

She crawled to one of the drying racks and pushed herself to her feet. Her left cheek was already puffy, and she tasted blood when running her tongue along every tooth. *No teeth gone. Thank you, Asherah.* She must become more vigilant in her worship and in her precautions.

She tried to resist panic and decided to go to the pottery shop to clean up before going home. Her other customers would be disappointed when she didn't show up, but it couldn't be helped.

The pottery shop was just a short, rugged hike from the cave. She entered through the back, trying to shield her face from the women at their stations. Still, three old gossips stopped their work and dropped their jaws. The shop grew quiet as a tomb. She stood at the bottom of the loft stairs, waiting for Amoz to notice her.

"Gomer, what happened?" He rushed down the stairs, his hands poised beside her as if she were as fragile as his finest vase.

"I fell while walking here." It was an absurd lie, but she couldn't think of anything more plausible. "Could you get a bowl of water and a cloth and meet me behind the shop, under the sycamore?" She walked out the door, not waiting for his answer.

Moments later, Amoz was sitting beside her. The morning chill made their meeting uncomfortable, but it was appropriate for what she was about to do. He lifted the wet cloth to her face, dabbing her bruised cheek, but Gomer stilled his hand. "I'm pregnant, Amoz."

He froze, his hand suspended in her grasp. "I'm sure Hosea is pleased."

She started to tremble and took the cloth from his hand and splashed water onto her face. The shock of it prepared her for whatever reaction Amoz would give. She patted her face dry, lifted her chin, and hardened her heart. "The baby can't be Hosea's."

His gaze turned to stone. "Why are you telling me this?"

"Because all I need are a few Sabbaths to convince Hosea the baby is his. I can hide it until then."

"And how will you hide that?" He pointed to her bruised cheek.

"I'll tell him what I've told you. I fell."

"Your husband is not stupid, Gomer." Crimson crept up his neck, and he spoke between clenched teeth. "Hosea is my friend. What makes you think I'll lie to him when I know you've committed adultery?"

The words pierced her like a dagger. "*Hosea* is your friend? I thought *I* was your friend, Amoz. I've kept your secret and protected you. I *lied* for you."

"I never asked you to lie for me! I've asked you to remain silent."

"Ha! Your whole life is a lie, Amoz! Your son is training to be a Yahweh prophet, but you worship Asherah!"

"Keep your voice down!" He grabbed her head and clamped his hand over her mouth, glancing right and left. She clawed his hand away, and his fury died. He sighed, raking his hands through his hair like Isaiah did so often. "You are my friend, Gomer, but I don't want to —"

"You will lie because you love your son, and you don't want him to hate you more than he already does." She was finished being polite.

"You wouldn't dare."

A slow, wicked smile reopened the cut on her lip. But it reminded her of her goal — survival. "If you wish your idolatry to remain hidden, you will help me convince Hosea this child is his."

26

HOSEA 7:1–2

Whenever I want to heal Israel, all I can see is Ephraim's sin and Samaria's wickedness. . . . They don't realize that I remember all the evil things they've done.

Hosea wanted to believe Gomer. The day she'd gone to the pottery shop to inform Amoz of her wifely decision, she'd returned bruised with some ridiculous story about falling. How was he supposed to protect his wife if she wouldn't tell him who hurt her? He'd asked Amoz about it, and his friend had claimed ignorance, said Gomer had given him the same story. He seemed as frustrated with her as Hosea was.

He watched her now, kneading bread for their evening meal, her expression looking pained. Angry. Beads of sweat formed above her top lip.

"May I help you with anything?" he offered, watching her painted smile appear. She tilted her head, cast an adoring glance at Jezzy. "You're helping by playing with our son."

For almost a full moon cycle, she had cooked, cleaned, and remained at home, venturing out of their courtyard only to visit Yuval. It wasn't like her. When he asked if she was happy at home, she lavished praise on some new recipe Yuval had shown her. She'd returned to his bed, her passion seemingly tempered by the long days of household chores. Dutiful yet distant.

He glanced at Jezzy just in time to see him crawl over to Sampson and put the cat's tail in his mouth. "No, Jezreel. Nasty tail. No, no."

A sudden breeze raced past him. It was Gomer, grabbing her robe on her way outside. "I must get some eggs," she mumbled, slamming the door behind her.

Hosea couldn't stand the pretense any longer. Something was going on with his wife, and he must know — tonight. Lifting Jezreel into his arms, he followed his wife outside . . . and heard her vomiting by the stable. "Are you all right?" He walked toward her, and she turned, looking surprised.

He'd seen his wife's face that pale once before. *She's pregnant!* The realization brought instant joy. Then, just as quickly, pain. *It can't be mine — can it?*

"I didn't want to tell you until I was sure." Again the painted smile, the right side quivering slightly. "We're going to have another baby."

Jezzy leaned toward his ima, silently pleading for her to hold him, but Hosea hugged him tightly to his chest. He studied their son's features — Gomer's nose, his own dark eyes — and then stared at his wife's stomach. *It can't be mine.*

"Say something, Hosea. Aren't you pleased?"

"What have you done?"

"I threw up our midday meal," she said, chuckling, maintaining the pretense. "I think it's pretty obvious, isn't it?" Finally, her smile died in the silence. "I thought you'd be pleased. Another child means another reason for me to stay at home, cook your meals, wash your clothes, feed your children." The defiance returned. This was Gomer. He'd been living with an imposter for so long, he'd almost forgotten the stony heart beneath the lovely form.

"I'm going to take our son to Yuval or Aya. He shouldn't hear what his parents are

338

about to say to one another." Hosea trembled, fighting to control his rage. Leaving the courtyard, he prayed one of the two women he trusted would be at home.

In too few steps, he found himself at Yuval's door, wondering what he could say. *Hello, Yuval. Could you tend to Jezreel while my wife and I discuss the child of adultery in her womb?* Then another thought sliced him. What if she already knew?

"Oh, Hosea!" Yuval opened her door, startled at his presence. "I was just coming to see Gomer." Her usual sunny smile faded when she noticed his countenance. "What's wrong? Is it Gomer? The baby?"

She knew. His world shifted at the realization. How could she have concealed such a sin? "How long have you known?"

A gentle winter rain began to fall, and she stepped back into the house. "Why don't you bring Jezzy inside, and we'll talk."

"Can you keep Jezreel while Gomer and I talk privately?" he asked, stepping over the threshold.

"Of course, but —"

"I need to know how long you've known she's pregnant."

Jezzy reached for Yuval, and she received the bundle into her arms. "Come to Savta Yuval, baby boy."

Hosea covered his face, unable to hold back the tears. This woman's heart was genuine. How could he be angry with her for keeping Gomer's confidence? Still, it was unthinkable that she'd known about the adultery and said nothing.

"How long have you known, Yuval!"

His shout frightened Jezzy, and Yuval comforted him as she talked. "That night when you came home and we were making barley loaves — it was the first time Gomer had shown signs of sickness, so we sort of figured it out together."

Each word of her explanation was like another hole in a sinking ship. Hosea was drowning in despair. Breathless, speechless, he stared at the kindhearted woman before him and realized — she thought the baby was his.

"I thought you'd be pleased," she said finally, reaching up to pat his shoulder. "Is there anything I can do to help?"

His mind reeled. He had no idea what she could do because he had no inkling what *he* was going to do. *Yahweh, give me wisdom.* Who could be the baby's abba? Did Gomer love someone else, or had she resumed her harlotry? As far as Hosea knew, Gomer spent most of her time with three people — Yuval, Aya, and Amoz. *Amoz.*

"Yuval, when Gomer isn't with you, where does she spend her time?"

Frowning, she seemed puzzled by the question. "She's either taking care of Jezzy or at the pottery shop . . ." Yuval suddenly looked as if she'd caught a wave of Hosea's despair. "Hosea, what are you say —"

He stepped forward and kissed her forehead. "Thank you for loving my son." He saw her fresh tears and hugged her tight. "Though you are not my ima or Gomer's by blood, Jezreel is blessed to call you Savta. He'll need a woman of honor to guide him through life." He turned to leave, but she stopped him with a question.

"Do you remember the exact words of Yahweh's first prophecy through you?"

Incredulous, he felt irritation bordering on anger. "Of course. How could you ask that?" But she lifted an eyebrow, silently pressing for his answer. Grudgingly, he spoke the oft-repeated words. "Yahweh said, 'Marry a prostitute.' I know Gomer is a prostitute, Yuval. I shouldn't be surprised by her unfaithfulness. Is that what you're telling me?"

"No, Hosea." Tears now streamed down her cheeks. "What else did Yahweh say?"

In the span of a heartbeat, Hosea heard the call repeated in his spirit: *Marry a prostitute, and take to yourself children of unfaithfulness.* "Did you hear the voice?" he asked Yuval.

"No, my son, but sometimes a woman hears things men do not. I remember hearing you explain Yahweh's prophecy and thinking it impossible for anyone to obey." She swayed with Jezreel, cradling his head to her heart. "Women aren't supposed to comment on Yahweh's Law or His commands — that's up to His prophets and priests — but sometimes a woman sees and hears things that men don't because our mouths are closed." A tender smile now softened her prodding. "Now speak Yahweh's words aloud — *exactly* as you heard them."

A battle raged inside him. He didn't want to speak them because they'd become even more real if Yuval heard them from his lips. He hesitated until his pounding heart was unbearable. "Yahweh said, 'Marry a prostitute, and take to yourself children of unfaithfulness.' " He sighed, realizing God's command to do the unthinkable. "I am to raise this child as my own. Aren't I, Yuval?"

Hosea left Jezzy dozing in Yuval's arms, his heart heavy, his emotions raw at the thought of his wife in another man's arms. He stood in the light drizzle of winter rains, staring into his empty courtyard. Gomer had gone inside.

What should I do now, Yahweh?

He could march into the house and confront his wife, demanding to know every detail. Would she tell him? She'd deceived him since she'd become his wife. Even if she confided every detail, he knew at this point it would be meant to wound him.

No. He would not look to the one who broke his heart to heal it — not when she was still broken.

Jonah. Perhaps he'd heard from Yahweh on Hosea's behalf. The Lord often used his old teacher as a personal mouthpiece.

Hosea knocked on the door, swiping his wet hair out of his face. The rain had soaked him.

"Master Hosea?" Micah answered but slipped outside, closing the door behind him. "Master Jonah is sleeping. He's been especially weak today. Is there something I can help you with?"

Hosea's heart plummeted. "No, Micah. Just take good care of our teacher. Keep him well." He clapped the boy's shoulders and tried to appear the strong, resourceful teacher Micah thought him to be. The young man went inside and closed the door, and Hosea stood alone again, longing for Jonah's wisdom.

Yahweh, please! What do I do now? Amos is traveling. Jonah is ill. It's me. Only me. I don't know what to do, what to say, how to proceed.

Silence. Rain pattered on the rocky path. Distant thunder rolled. Silence again. The camp was quiet. The workday finished. People wandered home.

Hosea walked — and remembered.

The day he and Gomer had heard Amos's prophesy in the Bethel temple. She'd fallen from the rafters, and he'd been so afraid of losing her. He'd begged Abba Beeri to take her with them to Amos's farm, but Diblaim had refused Beeri's offer of an early betrothal agreement. Hosea understood now — it was because Diblaim planned to use Gomer's beauty for his future political gain. *Why, Yahweh? Why allow such horrible things in Gomer's life?* The gentle rain was His answer.

Hosea waved at a passing shepherd who was herding his sheep toward the folds. One of the camp women walked by wearing a new veil — blue, like Gomer's. His heart squeezed in his chest as he remembered the day he'd first seen Gomer in Samaria — in her harlot garb and gold jewelry at Jeroboam's temple, her eyes so full of lust and hate. Later that night, her broken body lying motionless in the brothel, he'd wanted to hold her and never let her go. He thought bringing her here to the prophets' camp would heal her wounds.

His stomach rolled. All he could see now was the unfaithful wife waiting in his home. *Yahweh, I see only her betrayal. The little girl at Bethel, the woman I fell in love with — they've been swallowed up by all the pain this wife of mine has inflicted.*

The rain changed to great sheets, and the wind blew it in waves. Hosea lifted the collar of his robe to shield his face from the stinging drops. He pressed the woolen cloth against his ears and felt the voice speak to his spirit: *Whenever I want to heal Israel, all I can see is Ephraim's sin and Samaria's wickedness. They don't realize that I remember all the evil things they've done. Now their sins surround them. Their sins are in My presence.*

The rain and wind ceased, and Hosea knelt in the mud, anointed by the holy moment. "You know my heart, Yahweh," he whispered in wonder. Head bowed, he worshiped the only One who could have truly ministered to his despair. A wry smile creased his lips as a thought formed. "I'm thankful Jonah was sleeping, Lord."

Strengthened, empowered for the task before him, he stood and realized the pottery workshop was a few camels' lengths ahead. Perhaps he could catch Amoz before he went home.

Hosea started off at a pace that could have won a chariot race but slowed when he considered how to begin the conversation. What should he say? *Shalom, Amoz. Did you sleep with my wife?* The man was old enough to be her abba, but what did it matter? A harlot gave herself to anyone for a price. What was Gomer's price? What had Amoz paid?

He arrived at the shop and, with a weary sigh, drew back the curtain and saw Amoz alone in his potter's loft. He was drizzling water on a new piece, kicking the wheel, concentrating deeply.

Hosea stood at the bottom of the stairs. "Shalom, my friend."

Startled, Amoz shoved his hand into the clay, and the cylindrical vessel became a wobbly glob of mud. The potter gasped, squeezed his eyes shut, and lifted his hands away — too late.

Hosea buried his head in his hands. The meeting had not begun well.

"No matter. Only clay, right?" Amoz's

346

voice seemed overly cheery. He stood and stopped at the water trough to wash his hands. He jogged down the stairs, spry for a man his age. He appraised Hosea's rain-soaked robe and tossed him a towel. "What brings you to my shop?"

"I need to talk about Gomer."

Amoz's concern appeared genuine. "Of course." He guided Hosea to a stool across from the steps, then sat on the bottom stair, waiting quietly.

Hosea's heart felt as if it would pound from his chest. How should he begin? "You've been a good friend to Gomer, Amoz. You accepted her when others excluded her, and you taught her a skill that she enjoys and values."

"She's been a good friend to me." His eyes grew distant. "Her presence beside me at Isaiah's wedding made Uzziah's behavior easier to bear."

The gift Amoz gave Gomer at the wedding. Hosea had nearly forgotten the secret exchange. The timely quickening in his spirit bolstered his confidence. "I must ask you a hard question, Amoz. Is there something you need to tell me about the gift you slipped to Gomer at the wedding?"

The man's face lost all color.

"I know I'm being deceived, and I need

my friend to tell me the truth."

Amoz's breathing grew ragged, and he looked right and left as if fearing harm. "Who told you?" His eyes filled with tears. "We never meant to hurt anyone."

Hosea's heart was in his throat. *It can't be true.*

"Who told you?" Amoz shouted. "Did Uzziah tell you?"

"What? You mean Uzziah knew about this?" *How could he know and not tell me?* "No, your nephew did not tell me."

"Who, then?" His eyes went wide, terror-stricken. "Yahweh? Did Yahweh reveal this to you?"

"No, Amoz."

"Why would Gomer tell you that I worship Asherah? I kept her secret! I never told you about her harlotry! It couldn't have been Gomer."

"Did you say harlotry?" Hosea tried to ask more questions, but Amoz was frantic.

"Please, don't tell Isaiah. He already hates me. I'll stop. I'll —"

Hosea grabbed Amoz's head, locking him eye to eye. "Tell me again what you said about Gomer. Has she returned to harlotry?"

The potter fell silent, eyes wide at the realization. "I thought you knew you were being deceived."

Hosea released the man's head, bowed, and wept. *No, Yahweh. I don't want to know. I'd rather think of her with Amoz — with one man — than with many.*

"I'm sorry." Amoz spoke to Hosea's bowed head. "It seems many have been deceived by more than one deceiver." A deep sigh, and the man of few words spoke again. "I don't deserve forgiveness, but you deserve the truth. I don't know when Gomer began — when men started paying her, but I discovered it the morning she came here beaten. That's when she threatened to reveal my secret if I revealed hers. That's the last time I saw your wife."

Hosea grabbed fistfuls of his hair, unable to listen but needing to hear. "You said Uzziah knows? Does he know about Gomer?"

"I'm not sure who knows about Gomer. You know how gossip spreads in camp." Hosea buried his face in his hands at the thought, and Amoz sighed again. "But Uzziah does know of my idolatry. Isaiah does not — and I'd like to keep it that way."

Hosea shot him a look that could burn stone. "I will not lie to my best friend — or protect a liar."

Tears spilled onto Amoz's cheeks. "I have kept silent all these years to protect us all.

When conspirators killed my brother, Uzziah demanded that I abandon Asherah and move Isaiah to Tekoa. I agreed to remain silent — allow others to teach my son of Yahweh. My silence protects Isaiah *and* Uzziah."

"Your idolatry threatens the nation."

"Yahweh threatens everyone." Amoz spat the words.

Hosea saw a stranger before him, a man who had given up everything — his home, his freedom, even his son — for what? For a piece of stone with carved breasts.

Hosea sat motionless. *What should I do now, Yahweh? Find every Asherah and smash them all?* The prayer brought the shrouded wedding gift to mind. "Did you give my wife an Asherah to replace the one I destroyed?" His voice was controlled, though his chest was pounding.

"Yes."

Hosea's breath left him, as if he'd taken a blow. "Don't ever buy her another."

Amoz nodded his assent and turned away. "What will you do now? Tell Isaiah? Make my idolatry known and endanger my life — Uzziah's life too?"

Hosea's stomach rolled. "I don't know. I'll spend time with Yahweh before making any decisions." He pushed himself to stand, took

350

a few steps, and then paused. "Tell me, Amoz. What about Asherah seems so appealing? Why do both you and my wife refuse Yahweh so vehemently?"

"I've never seen Yahweh do anything kind. I hear only His demands, His rules, His wrath. He is the destroyer of lives, not the healer of broken hearts. At least I find some fleeting pleasure at Asherah's altar."

"Amoz, that's not —"

The potter lifted his hand to silence the prophet. Hosea nodded, turned, and walked away. He wasn't going to convince his friend with a few words when kings and prophets had tried and failed to convert him for years.

Yahweh, will I ever convince my wife?

27

Gomer became pregnant again and had a daughter. Yahweh told Hosea, "Name her Lo Ruhamah [Unloved]. I will no longer love the nation of Israel. I will no longer forgive them."

Gomer sat beside the oven on a soft rug, trying to stave off the winter chill. She couldn't stop trembling. Hosea had stormed out of the courtyard before dusk but still wasn't home. Perhaps he'd abandoned her already — though she couldn't imagine he'd leave her to enjoy his house and wealth. *More likely, he's having a divorce decree written or gathering witnesses to have me stoned.* But even as the thought formed in her heart, she knew it wasn't true. She once thought him too weak to stand against her, but he wasn't weak.

Hosea loved her.

She doubled over, rocking, keening in tortured prayer. *Why? Why does he still love me? Make him stop, Lady Asherah! I can't abide it any longer!* Tekoa's walls weren't the prison she feared most. It was the love of the people surrounding her that threatened to crush her. She could survive beatings, endure betrayals — but the love she'd found in Hosea, Aya, and Yuval threatened to drown her. If she allowed herself to wade into their love too deeply, she'd be left gasping like a fish out of water when they took it away.

People always leave.

A gentle knock and quiet "Gomer?" startled her. She turned her back to the door, but not before she saw Yuval with Jezzy on her hip.

"M' ima!" Little hands patted her, and her baby boy's head rested on her back. He breathed a contented sigh. "M' ima."

His novice pronunciation of her title drew an uncontrolled sob, and she engulfed him, drinking in the scent of candied figs, mud pies, and little-boy sweat. "Thank you, Yuval," she whispered. Could she leave Jezzy? Hosea would never let him go. If she stole the baby, Hosea would enlist Uzziah's whole army to find them.

Yuval sat down beside her, the smell of coriander stirred by the breeze of her presence. "What did Hosea say?" Her expression was so transparent, her emotions so close to the surface.

Gomer turned away, unable to see the truth reflected on the woman's face. Yuval knew she was an adulteress.

"Hosea hasn't been home yet." Tears choked her. "I'm not sure he's coming home."

A hand tugged at her chin, but Gomer jerked away. "No, I can't look at you." Yuval brushed her cheek and tugged her chin again. Gomer relented, allowing those rheumy eyes to bore into her soul.

"I do not condone your sin, Daughter, but I will never stop loving you." She bent and kissed Gomer's forehead.

The door clicked, and both women turned. Hosea entered, followed by Isaiah, Micah, and —

Gomer gasped and stood, clutching Jezzy like a lifeline. "What is Commander Hananiah doing here?" Her voice trembled like the rest of her. Had she been wrong about Hosea's love? Had Lady Asherah answered her prayer?

Yuval slipped a supportive arm around Gomer's waist.

"I've asked all three men here as witnesses," Hosea said, his features stern. "I spent time with Yahweh when I left here, and the message I received affects each one of us in some way." He motioned to the goatskins. "You're all welcome to be seated, though I doubt that what I have to say will feel like a friendly conversation to anyone."

Gomer glanced at the commander. His stature consumed most of the room, his jaw flexing in a quick, impatient rhythm. Isaiah looked furious, the color of a ripe grape, and Micah appeared as if he would burst into tears at any moment.

"If you brought them here to witness a divorce decree — " Gomer began, but Hosea's burning glare silenced her.

"I've brought them here to speak the word of the Lord in their hearing — and in your hearing, Gomer. Yahweh, the Creator of heaven and earth, says, 'Gomer will have a daughter. She is to be named Lo Ruhamah — Unloved. For I will no longer love the nation of Israel. I will no longer forgive them. Yet I will love the descendants of Judah. I will rescue them because I am Yahweh their Elohim. I won't use bows, swords, wars, horses, or horsemen to rescue them.' "

The room fell silent, and Gomer sank down onto a goatskin with Jezzy. *Lo-*

Ruhamah. Unloved. She glanced up into Hosea's cold stare and offered a seething smile. "When the gods wish to punish you, they answer your prayers." She snuggled Jezzy into the bend of her arm and rocked him while Hosea began his explanation to the witnesses.

"Commander Hananiah, you are to inform King Uzziah that Yahweh will have mercy on Judah because of the king's faithful heart. The Lord will rescue Judah, but without military might."

"You prophets have no idea what it takes to —" Hananiah's angry words were cut short, causing Gomer to glance up.

She saw Hosea step closer to the hulking commander, meeting his stare. "Prophets have no need to know military strategy. We need only have ears to hear the Lord."

He turned to Isaiah next, leaving the commander clenching his fists. "I know you're hurt and angry with your abba, my friend." Hosea placed a comforting hand on Isaiah's shoulder, and Gomer's stomach tightened. *He discovered Amoz's Asherah?*

"Now that you know of your abba's idolatry, you can build a relationship on truth."

Isaiah shook his head, clearly struggling to restrain his emotions. "I don't know if I can forgive him. How can I ever trust Uzziah again? They've done nothing but deceive me my whole life."

"They've done much more than deceive you, Isaiah." Hosea's words were kind but firm. "They've loved you, but they made a grave error when they chose deception over truth. Your abba needs to see Yahweh's love, Isaiah, and I believe your forgiveness and this prophecy can demonstrate it." When Isaiah's face showed the confusion Gomer herself felt, Hosea cast a glance at Hananiah and reaffirmed Yahweh's words. "The Lord will rescue Judah without bows, swords, wars, horses, or horsemen. Amoz said he'd never seen Yahweh do anything kind. I don't know how Yahweh will rescue Judah, but I believe He intends to prove His kindness to your abba." He patted his friend's cheek. "Our Elohim cares enough for your abba to do that for him."

Gomer's heart twisted in her chest. *Yahweh cares enough for Amoz, but He hates harlots. He said so. Unloved. No longer forgive . . .* A small whimper escaped, and Yuval tightened her embrace.

Hosea stepped toward Micah, meeting the boy's sad eyes. "Did Jonah already inform you that you'll accompany me to Israel?"

The boy nodded, and Gomer squeezed her eyes shut. *He's leaving again.*

"I'll go now and make sure Jonah knows the full message of God's prophecy." Hosea raised his voice, almost shouting in their small, crowded home. "I speak in the hearing of these witnesses. No one except Yahweh's prophets has authority to impose legal proceedings or pass official judgment on my wife while I'm away." He glared at Hananiah. "Yahweh has spoken, and I trust you will make it clear to my friend the king."

Gomer didn't know whether to feel vindicated or offended. Was she a piece of property to be tossed about?

Before she could decide how she felt, Hosea dismissed the men and turned his attention to Yuval. He knelt before her, eyes softening instantly. "Jezzy will need you more than ever." He hesitated, looking away as if struggling for words. When he returned his gaze, his eyes swam with unshed tears. "Gomer will need your love and care when Lo-Ruhamah is born." Without another word, he pushed himself to his feet and walked toward the door.

"Wait!" Panic seized Gomer. The word escaped before she knew what she'd say next.

Hosea turned, waiting. His eyes so full of anger and hate . . . He'd never looked at her that way before. "I've been waiting,

Gomer." He turned and walked out the door.

She choked back a sob, clutching Jezzy to her chest, rocking him to comfort herself.

"I'm sorry, Daughter." Yuval's voice pierced the silence, and Gomer realized her friend had been rubbing her back, reassuring her through every painful moment.

She would not — could not — give in to her emotions. Jezzy depended on her, and now she knew a daughter grew inside her womb. Gomer painted on a smile, squared her shoulders, and breathed in with forced control. "It's all right, Yuval. I've come to expect it." Her mind wandered to the silver she'd saved. It lay hidden in a small pitcher on the top shelf. "Men always leave."

28

2 KINGS 15:10, 12

Shallum, son of Jabesh, plotted against Zechariah, attacked him at Kabal Am, killed him, and succeeded him as king. . . . It happened exactly as Yahweh had told Jehu: "Four generations of your descendants will sit on the throne of Israel."

Hosea and Micah crouched in the underbrush of the forest, hidden. Five full moons of prophesying judgment in Israel had rendered them criminals. Zechariah had ordered them arrested on sight. But tonight Yahweh's command overruled Israel's king, and the prophets lurked near the king's encampment, close enough to watch the king and his advisors commit abominable acts. Their feasting and womanizing had distracted even the perimeter guards — a blessing and a curse.

"Why do you think they've come to Kabal Am?" Micah rubbed his blistered feet, his passion waning. "Why doesn't Zechariah settle into his abba's throne in Samaria and rule the nation from there?"

Yahweh had appeared to Micah in a dream, giving him nothing more than a sense of urgency to watch the events of King Zechariah's life — and death — unfold. They'd kept a safe distance behind the king's troops for nearly two full moons.

"Zechariah must convince an entire nation of his power to rule. Kabal Am is safely situated north of the rebellious hill country of Ephraim, so General Menahem can provide rear guard. Secondly, this valley holds great significance for his family's royal line." Hosea hesitated, hoping his student would volunteer the rest. "You should have been paying closer attention to your teachers, young prophet."

"Aahhrr . . ." The boy's frustration earned a chuckle and a shush from his teacher.

"When Yahweh destroyed Baal worship the first time in Israel, He raised up the general of Israel's army to kill King Ahab, Jezebel, and their descendants. He also injured the reigning king of Judah, who was visiting his family here at Kabal Am. The general's name was —"

"Jehu!"

"Shh!" Both men ducked lower into the bushes, fearing Micah's zeal had revealed their hiding place. After a chastising glance, Hosea continued in a whisper. "Yes, Jehu slaughtered Ahab's whole clan, and because of his ruthlessness, Yahweh vowed four of his generations would reign on Israel's throne." He squeezed the boy's shoulder. "And who is the end of that fourth generation, Micah?"

"Zechariaaaahhhh." Like the dawn of a new day, his eyes went wide. "And you named your son Jezreel because Yahweh told you that He would punish Jehu's line and break Israel's bows in the valley of Jezreel."

Delighted satisfaction filled Hosea. "And Kabal Am — where we sit watching the last of Jehu's descendants — is located at the mouth of the Jezreel Valley near the *city* of Jezreel!"

Micah's face glowed. "I'm astounded at Yahweh's sovereignty."

"And I'm astounded at men's depravity." Hosea pointed to King Zechariah and the advisors around him. "Look at them, Micah. Some of those men have known the king all his life, and yet one of them will kill him — possibly tonight." The words had barely been spoken when he felt the warmth of

Yahweh's presence fill his whole being.

Micah backed away from him. "Master Hosea, you're burning up."

Hosea began to speak quietly, but with a stream of words not his own. "Those men make their king happy with the wicked things they do. They make each other happy by filling each other with lies. Every one of them commits adultery and thinks nothing of it. They are all like a heated oven, an oven so hot that a baker need not fan its flame to bake bread."

A vision flashed in his memory, and he fell silent. Gomer, kneeling by the oven, baking barley bread. He felt the lust she'd stirred in him that night, the heat of uncontrolled passion matching the heat of the anointing that washed over him now. Words came again, this time silently seared into his being. "On the day of the king's celebration, the officials become drunk from wine, and the king joins his mockers. They all become hot like an oven and then lie in ambush. All night long their anger smolders, but in the morning it becomes a raging fire. They are all as hot as an oven. They consume their judges like a fire. All their kings die in battle, and none of them calls on Yahweh."

Hosea was perspiring, his whole body felt

like a flame. He covered his face and wept. *Gomer.* That night of their passion — Hosea had known something was different. He'd allowed lust to drive him instead of love, and he'd treated his wife like a harlot. *But she is a harlot!* His heart cried out to the God who understood his pain. Why did he still love her? Why couldn't he stop loving her as God had stopped loving Israel?

Micah's hand rested on his shoulder, startling him. "Did you receive another message from the Lord?" he whispered.

Hosea nodded but delayed, considering what — how much — to disclose to his young student. He shrugged off his robe and used it like a towel to wipe away the sweat, then sat in the summer night, covered only by a loincloth. "I believe the advisors will kill Zechariah in the morning." His heart thudded in his chest. Should he ask one so young about the struggle of his heart?

Micah stared at him. "Does Yahweh always visit you that way — with such heat?"

"It's different every time."

They sat in silence then, listening to the revelry in the king's camp, watching as women were passed from one drunken official to the next.

Hosea's stomach rolled. "I want to hate Gomer, Micah." He pointed to one of the harlots. "*That* is what she was — what she has chosen to become again. If Yahweh no longer loves Israel and no longer forgives them, can *I* refuse to love and forgive?"

Micah pulled his knobby knees to his chest and rested his chin on them, brow furrowed in the moonlight. "Can a man's heart be as pure as Yahweh's? Can you refuse to love without sinning? Can you refuse to forgive without becoming bitter?"

It wasn't the answer Hosea wanted. "Hmm." Perhaps the boy had been paying attention in class.

"So, what do we do now?" Micah asked.

"We watch Israel's king die in the morning."

Gomer's hands trembled as she wrapped Rahmy's sling over her shoulder and around her waist. Thank the gods, her daughter had entered the world easier than Jezzy, but Gomer was still a bit weak. Yuval had attended her, of course, and this time Aya helped. Isaiah came later to pronounce the baby's name: Lo-Ruhamah — Unloved.

Gomer leaned down to nuzzle her soft cheek. "But Ima loves you, so we're calling you Rahmy, aren't we, precious one?"

She heard a crash in the other room. "Jezzy, what are you doing?"

No answer. She secured Rahmy's sling and then wrapped her linen veil around her head and shoulders. Was there no end to all a woman must wear? Today was her first day out of the house since the birth, and she thought it more trouble than it was worth, but when the king calls . . .

What could Uzziah want? She was two days from being declared clean by the priests. Perhaps he simply wanted to hold her hand or feel the touch of another who was unclean. She couldn't blame him. The ridiculous ritual had nearly driven her mad in less than two Sabbaths. She couldn't imagine what Uzziah had endured for more than two years. No one else had contracted his skin disease, but raw flesh appeared in his sores with each priestly examination, so he remained in his rented prison outside Amos's farm.

"I thought I had washed more loincloths for Jezzy," she murmured while looking through a pile of clean linens. She hurried into the main room and found her son chasing the cat. Sampson jumped onto the table, knocking over a jar of barley flour.

"Jezzy, leave the cat alone. Come on, we're going to visit King Uzziah." She had no other choice than to take him with her. Yuval had accompanied Amos on another merchant's trip, and Aya refused to come near her for fear she might become unclean and unable to touch her husband. Gomer rolled her eyes, rushing toward the door, and Rahmy began to cry. She couldn't be hungry.

"Uhhhh!"

Jezzy looked up at her, his eyes round. "M' ima?" Then he began to cry.

She knelt down beside him, trying to console. He was such a sensitive little man — a trait he'd inherited from his abba. He wouldn't stop crying, so she grabbed his hand and started walking. "That's enough, Jezreel. No more crying. Quiet!" Her final word ended his sobbing, and gentle sniffing wafted on the wind as they walked the rocky path in the afternoon sun.

King Uzziah awaited them in his open doorway, his son Jotham at his side, and the well-muscled commander stood guard behind them. This was the first she'd seen Jotham since Isaiah's wedding. Her stomach twisted. Did he know about Rahmy's parentage? Was she just another harlot to him, an object of Yahweh's prophecy? Or did he understand the friendship between his abba, Hosea, and her?

She hid a wry grin as she neared the house. Even she wasn't certain she understood the friendship between the three of them.

"Unclean! Unc—" Uzziah's pronouncement was interrupted by Gomer's.

"Unclean! Unclean!" She approached the house, holding Jezzy's hand, and bowed before both of Judah's kings. "It is an honor to see you again, King Uzziah." She ruffled Jezzy's black curls and leaned over to instruct him. "We must bow to our new king as well. It is an honor, King Jotham."

Uzziah offered a warm smile. "It is we who are honored, Gomer, by the service of your husband in Israel."

All blood drained from her face. "Hosea?"

"Jotham, will you take the boy back to camp and play with him within the security of the walls? We don't want any accidents with beasts or vipers." He pointed to one of the small houses in his encampment.

"No, wait." Gomer shielded Jezzy behind her. "My son has touched me, so his uncleanness will make King Jotham unclean as well."

Uzziah reached up and squeezed his son's shoulder, his eyes welling with tears. "Jotham hasn't believed my sores to be infectious for some time, and he has chosen to make the sacrifice of uncleanness to have physical contact with me. When he visits, he understands that he is unclean until evening."

Uzziah's voice broke, and he was unable to go on. Jotham turned to Gomer, his expression so warm she nearly melted. "I would be happy to play with Jezreel."

She stared at him, unable to speak past the lump in her throat. A son who willingly made himself unclean to embrace his abba? "Thank you," she said. The words were barely a whisper. His reply, barely a nod.

He swept Jezreel into the air and caught him above his shoulders. "Whee!"

Jezzy giggled and squealed with delight.

"My little boy likes that too."

Jotham planted him back on the path, and Gomer watched them walk away, feeling a fresh ache of loneliness. When a hand rested on her shoulder, she didn't even mind that it was leprous. She turned and found herself staring instead at the handsome face of Judah's commander.

He nudged her onto the stool he'd placed beside the king. "Please, sit here." The concern on his features suddenly registered, and Gomer looked to Uzziah with a questioning glance.

"We have news from Hosea that you need to hear." The king's voice was forced calm.

"No. I don't want to hear news of Hosea."

She alternated glances between the two men. When they hesitated, she leapt to her feet, cradling Rahmy in the sling. "Hosea wants nothing to do with me, and my life is quite fulfilling without him." She took one step and heard Uzziah's voice.

"Hosea was captured near Kabal Am."

The sun dimmed, and a terrible roar sounded in her head.

"Hananiah! Grab her!"

Gomer felt strong arms embrace her, and then she was weightless. *Rahmy!* In an instant, she clutched the babe around her middle, and the roar inside her head faded.

"I've got you and your little one." A deep voice wrapped around her, and she looked up into caring eyes. She felt small in Hananiah's arms — but safe.

"Get a tapestry," he shouted at a guard. Then, settling her on the rug, he said, "Let's keep you and the little one closer to the floor." His kind smile breached the walls around her heart, and tears began to fall.

Uzziah sat beside her, consoling her as best he could. "I'm sorry. I should have told you about Hosea more delicately."

Hosea. "You said he'd been captured. Where is he now? Is he dea—"

"No, oh no! He's not dead. Hosea was captured in King Zechariah's camp. But he's safe now."

A thousand thoughts raced through Gomer's mind, but one overshadowed them all. *Why do I care when Hosea doesn't love me?* "That's good news, but . . ." She folded her knees beneath her and started to rise.

"The prophecy of Jezreel's name was fulfilled a few nights ago," he said, ignoring her attempt to leave. "King Zechariah, the fourth and last of Jehu's descendants, was killed in a town in the valley of Jezreel. The valley for which Yahweh named your son. And if my spies are accurate — and my spies at Shiloh are always accurate — it happened the night of your daughter's birth." He paused, locking eyes with Gomer.

A cold chill raced up her spine. "So Hosea's god is using *my* children as omens for His amusement?" Anger bubbled up in her maternal soul. "Why do the gods think they can use humans for their sick games?"

Horror stretched across the king's face. "Gomer, no! Yahweh does not play games. He loves His people, and . . ." His protests died into silence.

Her cynical chuckle rumbled low. "You see? Even the righteous Uzziah must admit —"

"I admit nothing." He seemed indignant

at her accusation. "I fell silent because I have only now realized the depth of Yahweh's love."

Her jaw dropped open. How could he see love in death and capture and judgment?

"I started to tell you how Yahweh loves Israel and has warned them repeatedly. And then it occurred to me — He loves Judah and has warned me and my nation as often." He grasped his head covering with oozing hands, seemingly stunned at his slowness of mind. "My arrogance not only caused my suffering but has almost led Judah to destruction."

"No!" she shouted, startling the king, his guards, and her sleeping baby. Rahmy began to cry, but Gomer spoke over the noise. "I will not let you take the blame that Hosea and his god try to place on you. You are a good and righteous man. You don't deserve this illness, and your god made a mistake when He cursed you."

Uzziah gave no thunderous reply. Instead, a slight grin creased his lips. "Yahweh is not like the false gods of Canaan you were told about as a child. He isn't the benign one, El, who watches powerlessly as Baal and Anat squabble with Mot over who gets to send rain. He isn't seduced into submission by his conniving wife, Asherah."

"What?" Gomer had never heard anyone from Judah recite the stories of her gods. "How do you know —"

"How do I know of the Canaanite gods? I choose to worship Yahweh because He is the one true God, Gomer — not because I am ignorant of other choices." He paused a moment, then shook his head as if clearing his thoughts. "I'm sorry. I didn't call you here to give you a lesson on Yahweh. I know how Amoz hates it when I repeat things he's heard a thousand times. I simply wanted to tell you about your husband."

As he began to relate more details about her husband's mission, Gomer was a little disappointed he didn't continue his explanation of Yahweh. She was curious to hear the testimony of a man who had been cursed by a god but remained faithful in spite of it.

"As I was saying, it seems Hosea and Micah were hidden near Zechariah's encampment and discovered by the royal guard in the middle of the night. Micah escaped, but Hosea was bound and taken into custody to await a morning trial. Evidently, before the king and judges awoke to convene court, Shallum, one of King Jeroboam's dearest friends, slipped into Zechariah's tent and murdered him."

Gomer saw the agony on Uzziah's face.

"Did you know King Zechariah?"

"No. I didn't know the young man, but my heart aches at the thought that a dear friend of his abba's could so heartlessly turn against Zechariah. It makes me fear for my own son. I trust all the men on my council, but I'm sure Jeroboam trusted Shallum too."

Gomer stole a glance at Uzziah's commander.

"I've told King Uzziah I am willing to maintain my position as commander or step down. Whichever he feels is most beneficial to young Jotham's reign." He slammed his fist against his leather chest armor. "I am loyal to the king of Judah — unto death."

Gomer nodded and laid her hand on Uzziah's shoulder. He winced. "I'm sorry," she said, starting to pull away, but he steadied her hand there.

"No, please. Don't move it. It's painful, but I need to feel someone's touch once in a while just to remember I'm human." Tears spilled onto his cheeks, traveling over the uneven tracks of the pockmarks. "I trust Hananiah with my life — and with my son's life." He nodded at his commander and received a bow in return. "I pray Judah never faces a conspiracy like the one your husband witnessed. It seems Micah was watching the camp from a distance and

374

rescued Hosea when it fell into chaos. My spies have hidden Hosea and Micah at the old prophets' house in Shiloh — where the ark of the covenant was once housed. If Yahweh can protect His presence there, He can guard Hosea and Micah until it's safe for them to travel again."

Gomer felt a flutter in her chest, hope stirred — and she hated herself for it. "So will they be coming home? Since the prophecy was fulfilled?" She tried to hide her excitement, but it slipped out between her quickened breaths.

Uzziah and Hananiah exchanged an awkward glance. The king studied the rocky ground as if searching for lost words — they were as absent as Gomer's husband.

Her hope died another inglorious death. She removed her hand from his shoulder, straightening her posture and raising her chin. "He's not coming home." It was a statement, no longer a question.

Uzziah shook his head.

She looked down at Rahmy, sound asleep. *Lo-Ruhamah* — *Not Loved.* She and her daughter would always share that bond. Gomer stroked her downy-soft hair, her mind reeling. Anger. Bitterness. Yes, but more than that.

Survival.

What was she doing? Waiting on Hosea to come back and then leave her again? No. She leaned down to kiss Rahmy's head, making her decision — hardening her heart. She would find a wet nurse and bind her breasts right away. Gomer was an old maid by many standards, nearly twenty-one years old. Time was running short to find wealthy men willing to care for her. The sooner she faced the inevitable, the quicker she'd be able to leave. Yuval and Aya would take good care of her children. They loved Jezzy and Rahmy — almost as much as she did.

Standing, she bowed to Uzziah. "Thank you, my lord, for informing me of my husband's condition." She leaned over and kissed his pocked cheek. "And thank you for your kindness — to an unclean harlot."

She had walked a few steps when she heard an imposing voice.

"Gomer, wait."

She stopped, closing her eyes, hoping she need not turn to face the commander's kindness again. *Abuse me. Cheat me. Even hate me, but my heart cannot bear a man's tenderness now.*

He stood behind her. She kept her back turned, trying to master her emotions. "What is it, Commander?"

A moment's hesitation, and then he said,

"If the prophet has left you in need of anything, I can help."

Gomer squeezed her eyes shut, releasing a river of tears. "Thank you, Commander," she said, walking away. She must make herself marketable again — and soon. Perhaps the commander would be her first wealthy customer.

29

2 KINGS 15:14, 16

Then Menahem . . . came from Tirzah to Samaria, attacked Shallum . . . killed him, and succeeded him as king. . . . Then Menahem attacked Tiphsah. . . . Because the city didn't open its gates for him, he attacked it and ripped open all its pregnant women.

Crossing the narrow plain north of the hideaway in Shiloh, Hosea quickened his step. He must reach Tiphsah before Menahem broke through its walls. Judean spies had reported Menahem's rampage after Zechariah's death. The general had been King Jeroboam's most loyal friend and demanded revenge on those responsible for the young king's death. His first mission — to Samaria, to kill the conspirator, King Shallum — was complete within a month of

Zechariah's death.

Menahem's second decision revealed the military genius of a well-experienced general and won him the undying loyalty of his men. He returned to his home in Tirzah and allowed his soldiers to do the same, encouraging them to work their fields and complete the summer harvest. When the olive presses started turning, Menahem's troops reported back to their commanders, barns and bellies full. Now they were thirsty for vengeance on any who opposed their gracious king.

Poor Tiphsah was the first city to lock its gates against King Menahem.

Hosea crested a hill and looked north. Smoke rose in four great columns from the next hilltop. Tiphsah was burning. *Yahweh Elohim! What would You have me do?* He stood frozen, realizing he was too late to save the souls within the city's gates.

His feet moved of their own accord, and a slight breeze lifted the hair from his shoulders. Yahweh whispered to his spirit: *How horrible it will be for these people. They have run away from Me rather than to Me. They must be destroyed because they have rebelled against Me. I want to reclaim them, but they don't pray to Me sincerely. They cry out and make cuts on their bodies while praying for grain and new wine. They have turned against Me though I trained them and made them strong. Yet they don't return to the Most High.*

With every step toward the burning city, Hosea felt Yahweh's sorrow — and His growing wrath. This carnage was prophesied, a declaration of Yahweh, but in response to the acts of men. Menahem's choice to slaughter. Tiphsah's choice to rebel. Israel's choice to worship idols. Everyone had a choice to hear or silence the whisper of Yahweh. These men silenced Him and acted on the evil in their hearts.

Menahem's encampment created a giant yoke around Tiphsah. Crude soldiers' tents dotted the countryside, nothing more than sackcloth lifted by center sticks. No royal goat's-hair dwelling for the king and his advisors. Menahem slept among his men — now a king, forever a soldier.

Hosea walked through the rows of tents, waiting for a guard to stop him, ready to be shackled as he neared the city. But the camp was deserted. *All of them must be looting.*

Hosea approached the city, hearing screams and smelling the unmistakable stench of death — blood, urine, smoke. He paused near one of the war machines that had pummeled the gates. Abandoned. Scarred. Used up. It had served its purpose.

Charred gates hung on broken iron hinges. The screaming continued — screams of terror. *Odd, no grieving wails.* Hosea stood frozen, listening, staring at the broken bodies strewn near the charred gates.

Yahweh commanded, *Press on.*

A few screams remained.

Then only one.

Then silence.

Hosea stepped inside the city, expecting bedlam, finding instead shocked horror. Consuming silence descended like a shroud. Soldiers stood over their savagery, dazed. Swords dripping. Seemingly stunned at the sight before them. Many dropped their swords and fell to their knees. The silence was broken — as broken as the warriors who had committed unspeakable barbarism. No one dared wail. None were worthy to grieve. Only shameful sobs escaped covered faces.

Hosea stepped away from the city wall where he'd been hidden by afternoon shadows and walked resolutely toward the central city well. He was cautiously tiptoeing over death and misery when a war cry erupted behind him.

"In the name of King Jeroboam and King Zechariah, you will die!"

Footsteps ran at him from behind, and

Hosea turned an extended hand toward his attacker. "In the name of Yahweh, you will be silent before me!"

Menahem held his sword in striking position and skidded to a halt a mere camel's length from Hosea's hand.

"King Menahem, return to Yahweh or face destruction," Hosea panted, heart racing. "Israel has chosen kings Yahweh did not approve and princes He did not know. But you are now Israel's king, and you must lead God's people. King Menahem, will you acknowledge Yahweh as Israel's Elohim?"

Menahem's arms trembled from his striking pose. A moment of decision crossed his face, and he lowered his sword. "I remember you," he said, eyes narrowing. "You were the prophet that threatened Jeroboam at the temple sacrifice in Samaria." His expression almost held a measure of amusement. "And you married that harlot."

"That harlot and I have a son named Jezreel — named by Yahweh to foretell Zechariah's assassination in the valley of Jezreel."

"You knew of the conspiracy and didn't send a warning?" All amusement fled, and Menahem adjusted his grip on his sword.

"Yahweh speaks truth to me, but He seldom reveals timing." Hosea stepped forward, now a cubit from the new king's imposing form. He swallowed hard, reminding himself that obedience to the Lord must outweigh fear of man. "Sound the ram's horn, Menahem. Assyria will swoop down on you like an eagle. The people of Israel have rejected Yahweh's promises and rebelled against His teachings."

"We have *not* rejected El!" He closed the gap between them and shrieked in Hosea's face, his fury sudden and unchecked. "You prophets and priests spout your legends while warriors bathe in blood. Look around you, Prophet. A king deals with real life — traitors and rebellions."

"Real life *is* Yahweh, King Menahem." Hosea spoke with a calmness he didn't yet feel. "If you will acknowledge Him, He will give you the wisdom and power to rule. But you must seek Him sincerely."

Menahem's rage grew like a living thing, crimson climbing up his neck and consuming his face. He looked to the heavens, shaking his fist. "I acknowledge You, Elohim! What more do You want from me?" His sword clattered to the ground, and he drew his dagger. "Blood? Do You want more blood?"

Hosea gasped, closing his eyes and bracing himself, certain he would feel the searing slice of the king's blade.

Instead, Menahem's tortured cries continued. "Let mighty Baal arise, the rider of the clouds. Speak on your servant's behalf to the benign one, our El. Protect us from Assyria's eagle god, Nisroch, and bless our grain and new wine."

Hosea opened his eyes to see Israel's king cutting his own arms and legs. "No!" he shouted as others unsheathed their daggers. "No, stop!" He watched in horror, soldiers all around them following their king's example, and Hosea remembered Yahweh's words: *They don't pray to Me sincerely. They cry out and make cuts on their bodies.*

Numbly, Hosea walked away from the frenzied worshipers, his heart twisting in his chest. The whisper of Yahweh's Spirit drew him out of the city. *They have rejected what is good. Now the enemy will persecute them.*

As he was almost to the city gate, a giant shadow fell across Hosea's path. "Keep your distance, Prophet. King Menahem has given me freedom to assess and attack any threat to his throne."

Hosea looked up to meet the menacing grin of Eitan, the soldier he remembered from Samaria — the man who had beaten Gomer nearly to death. "I am no threat, Eitan."

The man raised an eyebrow. "Should I be honored you remembered my name, or should I have you arrested as a spy?"

"Neither. I remember the name of the man who almost killed my wife."

A smirk replaced the curiosity. "Forgive me if I do not remember your wife — or her name." Then pointing to a crumpled mound a camel's length away, he said, "Women are of little concern to me." He shoved Hosea as he walked past him into the bedlam of pagan worship.

When Hosea regained his footing, he focused on the bloody mound Eitan had pointed to with his sword. A pregnant woman whose child had been torn from her womb. *Yahweh, Lord in heaven! How could anyone . . .*

He turned away. *Gomer.* His wife's face, her swollen belly flashed in his mind. The woman on the ground was someone's wife, the child someone's babe. He fell to his hands and knees and retched.

He began to tremble with unanswered questions. Why was he here? What good had his prophecies done? *Yahweh, must I continue to speak to people who refuse to hear?* A sob escaped, and he remained on his knees. Waiting. Was it a coincidence he'd encountered Eitan? Seen the savagery of the maimed woman?

He wiped his face and stood, lifting his voice to heaven. "I haven't heard Your direct command, but I feel You leading me back to Tekoa, Lord." Again he waited. Silence. Closing his eyes, he bowed his head. "I'll move toward home until I hear You tell me differently."

And then he ran.

Gomer rinsed the last clay bowl, dried it with an old cloth, and stacked it with the other dishes on the shelf above the work-table. Her eyelids felt heavy, bones weary. Jezzy and Rahmy had been especially rambunctious tonight, difficult to settle onto their sleeping mat in the bedchamber. Aya didn't run and play with them as much since she was expecting her first little one, but she still loved Gomer's children as if they were her own. And Aya did most of the cooking since Gomer had returned to work at the shop. Amoz had forgiven Gomer's coercive tactics and seemed eager to help her develop her pottery skills.

Life had settled into a comfortable routine again.

It was time to think about leaving.

She emptied her silver out of the small pitcher and counted it again, hoping it had miraculously multiplied. It hadn't.

Unable to imagine life without her children, she'd hoped Amoz might help her start a new life in another city. Her skill at the kick wheel had improved, and she'd thrown her first amphora today. His pride in her work was tempered by her interest in Lachish.

"Have you forgotten what it's like to be a woman alone on the streets?" he'd whispered, glancing left and right to be sure no one overheard. "Don't be a fool, Gomer. You wouldn't make it to the next town without being sold into slavery — you *and* your children. Don't decide something when you're warm and dry that could make you cold and destitute."

When she asked if he'd share sales profits on her pieces, he'd unequivocally refused, saying he didn't want to encourage her nonsense.

She scooped her meager silver pieces back into the pitcher and picked up Sampson. She snuggled into the soft fur, bracing herself against the hard truth. If she was ever going to escape Tekoa, she'd have to resume her harlotry. Yuval's dear face came to mind, and her heart ached. Her friend had been gone a lot recently, traveling with Amos to help with trading, she'd said. But

Yuval was hiding something.

Gomer chuckled quietly. "Yuval is hiding something." The irony didn't escape her. She was planning to leave her friend without a word, and yet she was concerned that Yuval was spending time away with her husband. *Ridiculous, Gomer.*

Perhaps after she and the children left Tekoa and were settled somewhere, she could get word to Yuval. *No. Too dangerous.* Hosea would undoubtedly search for Jezzy. She might need to go to Egypt or Aram in order to escape beyond her husband's reach. *That means more silver.* She squeezed her eyes shut and wiped her weary face, determining to cultivate a wealthier clientele. She didn't have time to see more men.

A knock on the door interrupted her planning. "Who could that be?" she asked the cat. Sampson answered with his normal purr and wiggled out of her arms.

She opened the door and found Hananiah filling the space. "Commander?" Her heart leapt to her throat. "Is it Hosea?"

"I'm here to deliver a message from your husband." He bowed slightly, a hint of a smile. "I'm sorry to disturb you so late. I hope I didn't wake you or the children." His focus was behind her, inspecting her house.

"The children are sleeping. Would you like to come in?"

He stepped over the threshold before her invitation was complete, his shoulders wider than the door, bowing his head to enter. "Hosea sent a message, and I thought you might be anxious to hear from him." His eyes roamed her face as if measuring her reaction. Whatever game he was playing, she was too tired to care.

"Actually, I'm not anxious to hear from him at all, Commander." She went to the worktable and reached for the grinding wheel. *I might as well grind barley for tomorrow's bread if he's going to talk.* She ladled a cup of grain into the furrow, smoothed it with her fingers. "What's the message? Does he want me out of the house before he returns?" She was partly jesting. As long as Hosea let her keep her children, she'd gladly leave. She turned to lay the grinder on the worktable and was startled to see the commander standing so near.

He stepped closer. Loomed over her. Gazed down at her. Hungry.

Her mind reeled. What was he doing here? Did he really have a message from Hosea? Should she be afraid? The kitchen knife on the other side of the table came to mind. "I'm suddenly anxious to hear whatever you

389

have to say, Commander Hananiah." She kept her voice low, seductive.

He stepped to within a handbreadth, leaning over her, whispering, "Your husband has sent word through King Uzziah's spies. He'll be returning before next Sabbath."

Her heart pounded, but she wasn't sure if it was because of Hosea's news or Hananiah's nearness.

The commander traced a line from her shoulder to her fingertips, then bent and kissed her shoulder. His large hand came to rest on her kitchen knife. "You won't need that tonight — or ever — with me, Gomer. Though I have wanted you since the moment I saw you, I will never force myself on you." He placed both hands on her waist, felt the curves of her form. "It's a crime that your husband leaves you alone for so long. Such a fine piece of pottery is worth a high price. I will pay you well if you are willing to be discreet. Tell no one of our visits. I'll come at night, while your children sleep." He bent to kiss her, hesitantly at first, teasing her. He smiled and pulled away, but she captured his face with her hands and kissed him thoroughly.

When was Hosea coming home?

Hosea's heart pounded in his ears, and even

Micah was breathing heavily. They'd pushed themselves hard on the final hike from Bethlehem to Tekoa. Hosea needed to see Gomer, and they both needed to talk with Jonah. The gruesome images of Tiphsah still haunted Hosea. When he'd returned to the hideaway in Shiloh and recounted the atrocities to Micah, they'd gathered their supplies and sent word through Uzziah's spies of their imminent return home.

"What's the first thing you'll do when you get home?" Micah asked, picking up speed on the way down a rocky incline.

A wash of sadness paused Hosea's answer.

The young man looked back. "I'm sorry, Hosea. I wasn't thinking."

"It's hard to plan when I don't know what or who awaits me." He'd considered the possibility that Gomer would be gone — even that she would have taken the children. "But I'm trying hard to trust that I'm not too late here as well." That terrible feeling of helplessness revisited him. If he'd gotten to Tiphsah a little sooner, could he have stopped the carnage?

Micah waited for him on the trail at the crest of the next hill. Almost as tall as Hosea, the young man settled his hand on his teacher's shoulder. "An eerily white old man once told me that Yahweh's timing is perfect, and we should never live in a state of regret for things we cannot control."

The comment earned a smile and lightened Hosea's heart. "What old coot told you that?" Both chuckled and hurried toward camp, eager to see their old teacher. *Lord, let him be alive.*

Jogging now that the camp was in sight, Micah pointed at the small stone structures situated north of Amos's walled compound. "Should we stop and report to King Uzziah before we go home?"

Hosea was huffing, feeling older than his twenty-four years. "I say we shout a promise to return after we say hello to our households." Micah laughed, and Hosea added, "He can send his guards to collect us if he feels it's a matter of national security."

The jovial mood helped dull Hosea's angst, but once he was inside the camp's gate, emotion overwhelmed him. They passed Amos's house and then hesitated at Hosea's courtyard gate. Micah patted his shoulder and stopped at Jonah's gate next door. They shared a glance, nodded, and stepped into their unknown circumstances.

Hosea noted the stable — clean and neatly kept, the animals calm and peaceful. The sun had begun its descent over the western hills. *Hmm. Isaiah did the chores early.*

He stopped at the front door, his heart pounding in his chest. He reached for the latch three times before finally pushing it open. Jezzy was toddling after the cat, and a baby was swaddled on the worktable. Gomer looked up. Her hands stilled, full of barley dough.

"Hosea?"

She was the most beautiful woman he'd ever seen. His breathing grew more ragged, his knees suddenly weak. He leaned on his walking stick, stumbling to a goatskin rug.

"Are you hurt?" Gomer grabbed the baby and laid her on the rug beside him, then lifted his chin to search his face. "Are you hurt?" she asked again.

He stared into her beautiful hazel eyes with flecks of green, gold, and brown. Tears choked him. "You're safe." It was all he could think of to say. Somewhere in his soul, he had feared she'd be maimed or beaten — or gone.

"Hosea, are you all right?" She reached out to brush his beard with her fingers. "What happened? What's wrong with you?"

"Ima?" Jezzy came to her for comfort, laying his head on her chest.

Hosea's heart fluttered. Their son adored her, it was clear. He choked back sobs, his words garbled amid the emotions that tore at his heart and strangled his voice. "Tiph-sah . . . families . . . Eitan said . . ."

Fear etched her features as she stroked his cheeks. "I can't understand what you're saying, Hosea."

He shook his head, fell silent. How could he tell her he'd been too late? He glimpsed the baby girl on the rug beside him and whispered, "Lo-Ruhamah."

"Rahmy." Gomer's voice grew cold.

Defeated, he let his head fall forward. "I can't fight with you now, Gomer." Hesitating, he pleaded, "Please be the little girl at Bethel. Be my Gomer." He closed his eyes, spent.

She held Jezzy in one arm and slid her other arm around his shoulders, rocking them both. "You're home, Hosea. Rest now. You're home." Her strength soaked into him, reviving, restoring.

He lost track of time, but when Jezzy's tummy rumbled, Gomer sat him on Hosea's lap. "I need to fix our meal."

Hosea halted her and reached for the swaddled bundle beside him. "May I hold Rahmy while you cook?"

She hesitated, glancing between Hosea and Jezzy, seemingly cautious to trust him with her newest treasure. She nodded once but kept a watchful eye on all three. Hosea lifted the little bundle into his arms, studying her pink cheeks, wrinkled fingers, tiny nose. "She's beautiful, Gomer." Tears came again, this time grateful offerings to the One who plants the seeds of love. *Thank You, Yahweh, for this baby — for changing my heart to call her Rahmy, not Lo-Ruhamah.*

He lay down on the goatskin rug, placing the babe on his chest. Jezzy resumed his pursuit of Sampson, too wiggly to cuddle for long. Throughout the night, Hosea marveled at Gomer's tenderness toward the children, the richness with which she loved them.

"Tell your abba good night," she said, holding Jezzy's hand, guiding him toward Hosea. He received the sweet kiss from his son's rosebud lips and listened to Gomer sing a bedtime tune. *Yahweh, thank You for bringing me home.*

"Hosea." His wife stood over him in the dim light of a single oil lamp. She reached down, inviting him. "I'm no longer the girl from Bethel." Her eyes were filled with compassion. "I can't bear to see you in torment. Let me comfort you."

He stared at her hand, breathless. *Yahweh, is this right?* What about his realization that he'd taken his wife in lust rather than love?

Could he love her tonight? Did he still love her?

Her hand fell to her side, pain fleeting in her eyes before she squared her shoulders and turned toward their bedchamber — alone.

His silence had hurt her, and his heart broke. *Yes, Yahweh, I love her.* His heart pounded. "Wait."

"I've *been* waiting, Hosea." The words stung, aimed to wound as he'd wounded her before he left for Israel. Silence filled the space between them. She extended her hand once more, lifting a single eyebrow — her last invitation.

He stood on shaky legs and followed her into their bedchamber. *I love you, Gomer. I cannot stop loving you.*

30

AMOS 5:27

I will send you into exile beyond Damascus, says Yahweh, whose name is Elohe Tsebaoth [God of Armies].

Gomer woke to an empty bed. *Why am I surprised?* She moved through her morning routine, trying to push Hosea out of her mind — and every corner of her heart. "Ouch!" She nicked her thumb with the knife while slicing the melon for Jezzy's breakfast.

"Ima, ouchy!"

"Yes, lovey. Eat." She shoved the meager offering in front of her son and lifted a squalling Rahmy into her arms. "Shh, baby. Ima's here. Your wet nurse will be here any moment." Where was that fat, lazy cow? Jezzy's wet nurse had let her milk dry, so Gomer had hired a new woman — far less responsible but the only one agreeable to nurse the *harlot's child.*

The morning sun streamed in through the window. She'd slept late, and she wanted to get to the pottery shop before Hosea decided to come back — if he came back. Maybe he'd already gone back to Israel. Or was he staying home this time? Would Yahweh call him away again? What did last night mean?

Nothing. Last night meant nothing. She was taking the children and leaving Tekoa as soon as —

"Good morning." The deep voice startled her. Hosea grinned as he clicked the door shut behind him. "I thought I'd let you sleep while I tended to the stable." He tousled Jezzy's curly hair and lifted Rahmy from her arms — as if she were his own.

Heart racing, she wasn't sure what to say, what to expect. Was he staying? How could she earn enough silver to leave Tekoa if Hananiah couldn't come at night? Did she even want to leave if Hosea promised to stay?

"What would you like to eat?" It was the safest question she could think of.

"I already ate some bread and cheese. I'm on my way to see Jonah and Uzziah. Have you heard how Jonah's been feeling lately?"

She kept her hands busy, packing her mid-day meal, straightening Jezzy's toys. "I haven't heard. Jonah and I don't exactly celebrate new moons together." She met Hosea's chuckle with a wry grin.

"Well, I suppose I can understand that," he said. "Micah and I need to report to Uzziah after I see Jonah. I'm sure the king and his commander will want to know what we saw at Tiphsah . . ." His words trailed off as his eyes grew distant.

"Hosea?"

Deep sadness prefaced his words. "I saw Eitan."

The mere name made her shudder. "Where did you see him?"

"It doesn't matter. What matters is Mena-hem is now Israel's king, and Eitan is his general. They've committed unspeakable acts of savagery against fellow Israelites, and I believe Yahweh's judgment is imminent."

She tried to sound uninterested, aloof. "What does this mean for you?" Fighting tears, she refused to ask, *What does it mean for us?*

"I don't know," he said, averting his gaze. "I need to speak with Jonah and King Uzziah . . ." He paused, hugged Rahmy a little tighter. "And then find out what Yahweh wants me to do next."

She closed her eyes against the pain. *What Yahweh wants him to do next.* Nothing had changed. Hosea hadn't come home to stay, he'd come home to refresh himself for another mission.

"I'll prepare your travel bag." She turned away, stuffing hard cheese and bread in a pack, wrapping herself in the shroud of indifference that kept her sane.

At least when Hosea left this time, Hananiah would hold her at night. The commander had been kind, brought her gifts — and he'd visited every night since delivering Hosea's message last week. Dependable as the sun and moon.

The door clicked, and she looked up, finding Rahmy nestled on the goatskin and Jezzy eating his melon. *Hosea always leaves.*

She allowed a single tear to fall down her cheek. Just one tear. *I must have Yuval bring back pomegranates from her next market journey with Amos.* Hopefully, her friend wouldn't realize the fruit was a measure of birth control. If Gomer was to start entertaining men again, she'd need to employ some of Merav's midwife tricks, or she'd end up with a third child.

Hosea's visit to Tekoa had been too short but life giving — because death now had a face. The impact of the lives lost at Tiphsah didn't sink into his soul until he saw Gomer with Jezzy and Rahmy. Families just like theirs were living in Israel — doing chores, preparing meals, playing with children — all without an inkling of Yahweh's coming wrath. Amos had prophesied exile twenty years ago, and now Assyria and Aram were poised at Israel's borders. Hosea and Micah felt Yahweh's urgency as never before, proclaiming Yahweh's truth to all of Israel during the spring, summer, and fall.

"Are you sure Amos said he would meet us here?" Micah asked for the third time, standing in the doorway of the old prophets' hideaway in Shiloh. "Does he even know how to find this place?" The sun was sinking fast over the western horizon, and they'd wasted the whole day waiting on their friend.

"You saw the scroll Uzziah's spy gave me in Ephraim yesterday." Hosea heard an exaggerated sigh. "Amos has traveled from Damascus to Egypt. He's a merchant *and* a prophet. Of course he knows how to find this place." He chuckled, expecting their usual friendly banter.

"What's so funny?" Micah shouted, fear glistening on his brow. "Do you enjoy being chased out of Gilgal with pitchforks and scythes? We offered those people life, and they wanted to butcher us rather than listen to Yahweh!"

The tension had been harder on his young friend than he'd realized. They'd been declaring Yahweh's message in Israelite towns and villages since last year's spring thaw. By summer, mounting persecution kept them off the trade routes, restricting their travel to the hills and shepherds' trails. Hunted by Israelite soldiers and hated by pagan worshipers, they'd found themselves relying on Yahweh's protection for every breath.

Hosea rose from his comfortable bench and joined Micah at the door, settling his arm around the boy's shoulder. "True prophets are seldom popular, my friend. We speak Yahweh's truth no matter the consequences, and it's up to the Lord to protect us." He squeezed his shoulder, trying to impart peace with a light heart. "Like He did at Gilgal when He made us run faster than those farmers."

Micah offered a begrudging grin, but both men froze when they heard rustling in the brush near the doorway.

"Those are the faces we've longed to see since leaving Hazor two days ago!" Amos emerged with Yuval on his arm, greeting them as if they were all back home in Tekoa.

"Yuval? Why did you bring Yuval here?" Hosea hurried to meet his friends, noticing the old woman's weary gait. He circled her waist, and she leaned into his support. "Gomer told me Yuval had begun traveling with you, Amos, but she didn't know why."

"It wasn't my idea!" she protested. "My old feet would much rather stay on Tekoan soil."

Amos wrapped his arm around Micah's shoulders, chatting as they climbed the few steps into the safe house. "We've got some news that you're not going to like."

They settled the weary travelers on the stone bench and removed their sandals, readying a warm bowl of water to wash their blistered feet.

Micah began washing, and Hosea read the tension on his friends' faces. "Since when do you care what I like," he said, nudging Amos's sturdy arm. The man had been a shepherd, farmer, and tradesman his whole life. Though he was twice Hosea's age, he was still as solid as a rock.

Amos inhaled deeply, gathered Yuval under his arm, and began his explanation. "Though we are brother prophets, Hosea, at times like these, you must remember that I am Judean and serve King Uzziah as my sovereign."

Dread twisted Hosea's stomach. "Uzziah is my friend too, Amos."

"Exactly. Uzziah is my *king* first, my friend second."

Hosea nodded, acknowledging the distinction — though as predicted, he didn't like where the topic was going.

"When you and Jonah returned from your first journey to Israel without any military knowledge, King Uzziah enlisted my aid to begin carrying messages to his Judean spies throughout Israel. I suppose the idea of using a prophet hadn't occurred to him until you two had traveled so thoroughly unscathed."

"Unscathed? Is that what he called it? Unscathed?"

"Please, Hosea. I know both you and Gomer endured much while you were in Samaria. But Yahweh is bringing about His judgment on a whole nation — many nations, in fact — and I must ask you to look beyond what Yahweh is doing in *your* life to His larger plan. In the strictest sense of military strategy, you were unscathed."

Duly chastised, Hosea felt his irritation fade. "I'm sorry, Amos. Go on." But when he glimpsed Yuval's pained features, his defenses stirred again. "Why did Uzziah involve Yuval? She's never traveled on your merchant trips before. Why now?"

"On one of my journeys into Bethel, I was recognized by a man who had seen me prophesy twenty years ago in the temple there. He aroused the city's anger, and I was driven out. Fearful that my identity might jeopardize my effectiveness, Uzziah asked if Yuval would be willing to accompany me in order to appear more benign as an old merchant couple." He leaned over to kiss the top of her veiled head. "I must admit, I've enjoyed having her with me — though it's been hard on her."

The tears she'd held in check spilled down her cheeks. "I was doing quite well until yesterday, don't you think, my love?"

Amos hugged her tightly, and she buried her face in his barreled chest. "I think you were stronger yesterday than a thousand Assyrian soldiers, my wife."

"Assyrian soldiers?" Hosea's heart skipped a beat. "Amos." He pinned the man with a stare. "Assyrian soldiers?"

Amos closed his eyes, dread evident in his weary sigh. "We'd made it as far north as Hazor and heard of Aramean raiding parties, so we decided not to risk traveling farther to Damascus. We'd walked a half day south when the ground began to shake beneath our feet."

Yuval looked up then, seemingly overtaken by the memory and compelled to do the telling. "We saw a farmhouse in the distance and ran for shelter. The thunder beneath our feet intensified. Horses — many horses — and fast approaching. We reached the house and found a young couple with three children. They rushed us to a dried-up well, begging us to be lowered down with their children and keep them safe and quiet while they dealt with the invaders. We agreed. There was fighting above us. Metal against metal. Men screaming, dying. We remained hidden until the only sound was a woman's keening." Yuval's words tumbled out in a wave of grief, and Amos held her, letting her tears wet his dusty robe.

Hosea and Micah sat speechless.

"When I was certain the danger had passed," Amos said finally, "I pulled us up by the pulley rope. Yuval distracted the children while the young widow and I washed their abba's body." Amos dropped his head, shaking away the memory. Almost too quiet to be heard, he whispered, "They were Assyrian soldiers. The widow said they'd boasted of annihilating an Aramean raiding party in Hazor." He looked up then, eyes full of tears. "She said they vowed to violate every woman in Israel and Judah unless our kings paid tribute to the new king of Assyria."

Hosea shot a questioning glance at his teacher. "I didn't know Assyria had a new king."

Amos nodded. "It's the reason Uzziah's been sending Yuval and me on trade journeys to Tyre, Syria, and Aram — in hopes of forming a coalition against Assyria's rising new king."

"Uzziah mentioned the coalition, but I had no idea Assyria's campaign had already begun."

Amos nodded sadly. "Their new king is much like Menahem — he began as Assyria's ruthless general. However, unlike Menahem, King Pul has ascended to the throne through a bloody civil war, and his thirst for blood continues."

Hosea felt a cold chill race up his spine. "The Assyrian soldiers you encountered — how can they already be this close to Israel?"

"They were mere scouts, but they've already begun assaults in Aram."

The news was like cold water in Hosea's face. "Are they headed to Judah?"

Amos nodded again, confirming Hosea's worst fears. "King Uzziah believes Judah is Pul's first target because Uzziah is the strongest leader — even though he's ruling from the house near my farm."

"Does King Pul know Uzziah has leprosy? Does young Jotham know he's inheriting his abba's fight?"

"We're not sure if or how much Assyria's king knows of Uzziah's illness, but yes, Jotham knows, and he's terrified." He reached into his pocket and produced a scroll with Uzziah's wax seal. "This is the last scroll, intended for Menahem. He's the last king we must convince to join Uzziah's coalition against Assyria. But he's the most important because he's the last buffer between Judah and the other nations."

Hosea exchanged a wary glance with Micah, and the young prophet returned a single nod. "Micah and I will take the scroll to Samaria. You shouldn't take Yuval any-where near Menahem. He's a loose wheel, ready to fall off the cart and take all of Israel over the cliff with him."

"I'm not afraid, child." Yuval's expression was tired but peaceful. Hosea had no doubt that she trusted Amos and Yahweh with her life.

He patted her hand, assuring her of his respect. "Well, I'm afraid for you, my friend. I want my children to grow up knowing their savta." He turned his gaze to his friend and mentor. "Take your wife home, my friend. Report to King Uzziah the Assyrian troop activity south of Hazor. Micah and I will return to Tekoa after we've delivered the scroll in Samaria."

Amos hesitated and then leaned over to kiss his wife again. "I think your plan is a wise one, but I have one request."

"Anything, my friend." Hosea extended his hand and locked forearms, sealing the oath.

"Pray for our friend Jonah. When I return to Tekoa and tell him that the Ninevites to whom he preached Yahweh's repentance have resurged to world power, he may struggle with regret — as would any man."

Hosea squeezed his eyes shut. *Jonah.* He was the teacher of wisdom to Yahweh's prophets, but Amos — also a patriarch among them — realized every man struggles with God when world events defy understanding. "I will pray."

Micah laid his hand on their arms. "*We* will pray — and then we will be home to greet him ourselves."

31

HOSEA 1:8–9; 1:11–2:1

After Gomer had weaned Lo Ruhamah, she became pregnant again and had a son. Yahweh said, "Name him Lo Ammi [Not My People]. You are no longer my people, and I am no longer your Ehyeh [I AM]. . . . The day of Jezreel will be a great day. So call your brothers Ammi [My People], and call your sisters Ruhamah [Loved]."

Hosea and Micah sat on the audience tapestry, staring at the shadow of a king they once knew. "We're sorry for the delay in our return, King Uzziah, but as I hope your spies reported, Micah and I were forced to remain hidden at Shiloh after our brief encounter with Menahem in Samaria." Hosea noted the angry stare from Commander Hananiah and wondered if Uzziah shared his obvious disdain.

"I'm just glad you're safe, my friend." The king's voice was thready and weak. Kind eyes peeked out between heavy bandages. "Amos told me you and Micah volunteered to deliver the scroll. You faced great danger from the Israelites and from Menahem. I'm grateful." He paused. Swallowed with difficulty and nodded at Micah. "Judah thanks you." His words and actions were deliberate, appearing to take their toll.

Hosea dreaded adding to the king's pain with the news he had to give. "The Lord ushered us safely into Menahem's throne room, though I've been threatened with death if I enter Menahem's presence again. However, the worst of it, my friend, was that neither King Menahem nor General Eitan would commit Israel's participation in the coalition."

Uzziah exchanged a wary glance with his commander. "We've received reports that Israel has already begun sending tribute to Assyria to secure aid against Aram's harassment. The Arameans have long been a thorn in Israel's side —"

"But if Menahem thinks King Pul will be a protective big brother," Hananiah interrupted, "he's deceived himself!"

Hosea gasped at the audacity of a soldier

to interrupt his king, but Uzziah spiraled into a fit of coughing before any of them could react to the breach in protocol.

Hananiah hovered over him. "Call the physician," he shouted at one of his guards, then turned a blazing gaze on Hosea. "The king grows weary. You've told us nothing we don't already know." He motioned again to his guards, and this time several of them ringed the tapestry around Hosea and Micah. "The king will summon you if he requires further information. You both may leave."

"Wait . . . Don't leave . . ." Uzziah's coughing grew worse, and Hosea was torn. He wanted to stay and help his friend, but Hananiah was obviously in control. Hosea had sensed the commander's contempt from the beginning, but never the sheer hatred that burned in his eyes now.

He refused to be cowed and remembered Hananiah's true grievance against him. "Have I offended you in a new way, Commander, or are you still angry that Yahweh transcends your shield and sword — that the Lord's promise to rescue Judah without military involvement remains?"

An ominous grin added to his spite. "Go home to your wife, Prophet. I've heard she's a lonely woman, in need of a man's touch."

The words hit their mark, and Hosea sprang to his feet, trembling with rage.

Micah restrained him, whispering, "Come with me now, Master Hosea. You can return when the commander goes back to Jerusalem. Talk with King Uzziah alone." Micah tugged him toward camp. "Surely Judah's commander doesn't *live* in Tekoa. You'll have your chance to make a formal complaint when he leaves."

Gomer stood before the long, polished bronze mirror in her bedchamber, admiring the elegant linen robe and veil. How had she ever lived without Hananiah? In less than a year, he'd brought her back to life, making her feel loved, desired, hopeful again. Though her pregnant form looked more like a camel than a gazelle, Hananiah still came to her every night, his passion unchecked. If anything, her maternal qualities seemed to endear her more to the rugged soldier who held her heart. She twirled in a delighted circle, watching the lightweight blue linen flutter around her. The exquisite color and cloth did much to mask her sins.

A wicked grin creased her lips. But who could prove her sins? Hosea's fleeting visit and instant passion had given the perfect alibi for her swollen belly. Whenever Tekoa's gossips began counting moon cycles, she mentioned her husband's well-timed visit and silenced Yahweh's priests and prophets as well.

Yuval hadn't been so easy to fool.

Her friend and self-proclaimed ima had challenged Gomer's rosy cheeks and rounding middle. "You're happy about more than making pottery," she'd grumbled one evening while helping Gomer prepare their meal.

She tried to keep the conversation light, saying, "I'm very *good* at making pottery."

But Yuval's instincts were impeccable, and she recognized Gomer's jest as a flippant confession. The disappointment in her eyes hurt more than a thousand gossips' tales. "I love you, Daughter," she said. "*I'm* good at that."

Their visits had become less frequent since then. Yuval traveled a lot with Amos, even brought Gomer a gift from the markets now and then.

Gomer smoothed the soft cloth over her middle and spoke to her reflection. "Too bad she forgot the pomegranate and carrot seeds." She giggled, patting her tummy. "I will love you, little one, because you are Hananiah's." She was certain of it. Perhaps after the baby was born, Hananiah would talk with Uzziah about taking her from Hosea. It was a dream, of course, but Judah's commander was a man who took what he wanted. She'd witnessed that first-hand.

Though he was kind to her and showered her with gifts from Jerusalem's market — spices, perfume, linen, and even a gold anklet with bells — he was still a soldier. She placed his newest gift, a gold band, around her arm above the elbow. It hid the bruises well. He hadn't meant to handle her roughly. She had been slow to retrieve his leather armor last night. He'd said he was sorry.

She twirled again, listening to the sound of the bells on her ankle. Oh, how she loved the sound of bells. Finally. Someone loved her. Hananiah had never actually said the words, but a woman could tell these things.

Was she in love with him?

She thought of Isaiah and Aya, remembering the tenderness of their words and touch. Their love radiated like the warmth of the sun, and Gomer thanked the gods that her children were warmed by it. They spent each day in Aya's care while Gomer worked at the shop, and when evening came, even Gomer allowed herself a glimpse of this loving family by sharing the evening meal. Tonight Isaiah and Aya had asked to keep the children overnight — to give Gomer an evening of rest.

Hananiah would enjoy a night without the children.

She turned from the mirror and began tidying the bedchamber. Jezzy's wooden blocks seemed to multiply daily, and Rahmy had acquired three new wool-stuffed balls. Aya spoiled the little princess.

"Gomer?" A deep voice resonated from the front room, sending a pang of fear through her. Darkness hadn't fallen. Hananiah never visited before dark. He'd said they needed to be discreet. The gossips had rumored him as a customer, but he'd denied it, justifying his visits by claiming he delivered official messages from Hosea.

"Gomer?" The voice drew nearer. It wasn't Hananiah.

Her heart was in her throat, choking away any sound.

Hosea appeared in the doorway.

"Wha . . . I . . . whe . . ." Hosea breathed half words, his heart at first rejoicing, then horrified. His eyes traveled the length of the woman in his bedchamber. She was dressed in fine linen. He smelled her perfume, saw her kohl-rimmed eyes. And he knew.

"How could you?" Rage coursed through him. He clenched his fists and moved toward her, backing her up as he advanced. "You would have died in Samaria, but I rescued you from Tamir's brothel. I brought you here, gave you a home." His throat tightened, but he choked out the words. "I loved you, Gomer."

"Love?" she spat in his face. "You once questioned me about love, making me feel as if I was the one who didn't know its meaning. Well, it's you who needs the lesson, Hosea. You thought because you bought me a veil to wear in public, I was yours to command. But I am not yours. I will never be yours. I —" She grasped her swollen belly and doubled over, reaching for the mattress to steady her.

He stood in the instant silence, still panting with fury. What should he do? They had much to discuss, but she was in no condition at the moment.

"Hosea, go get Yuval." Before he could respond, she crumpled to the floor and muffled a groan into the mattress. Not knowing what to do, he hovered over her and grasped her shoulders for support. When she was able to lift her face out of the mattress, she shrugged off his hands.

"Go! Leave me alone, and get Yuval."

She wasn't going to like what he was about to say. He knelt in front of her and spoke calmly. "I just knocked on their door. One of the shepherds told me Amos and Yuval are away on a trade journey."

He watched a sudden transition — panic turned to resignation. "Leave, Hosea. I'll do this alone."

"Do you want me to get Aya?"

She rested her forehead on the mattress and shook her head, her unspoken message clear. She'd felt abandoned all her life. Tonight would be no different.

"You're not alone, my wife."

She laughed then, meeting his gaze, the hatred in her eyes staggering. "Your words mean nothing. I've been alone all my li—". Her words were cut off by a gasp, and again she buried her face in the mattress, stifling a cry.

A sudden gush of fluid wet the packed dirt beneath her, and Hosea wished with his whole being that Yuval hadn't gone with Amos on this trip. "What should I do? What can I do to help?"

She offered no answers, seemingly distracted by sheer survival. Cursing the gods and every man she'd ever known, Gomer panted through the contractions in relentless succession. "I don't know what's happening. The other two births weren't like this." Fear laced her tone, and her eyes darted from Hosea to the bed and then to her stomach. "If I die, tell Jezreel and Rahmy I love them. Please don't tell them what I was. Tell them I was a good ima. Please, Hosea." Her pleading was interrupted by the cool breeze of Yahweh's presence. It blew through their bedchamber and lifted Gomer's copper curls from her shoulder. Fear was replaced by terror. "What was *that*?"

"That was the Lord." Hosea chuckled, caressing her cheek. "He's come to anoint the moment."

"He's come to kill my baby," she said, looking resigned and suddenly humbled. "I suppose I deserve it, but my baby is innocent, Hosea. Can't you reason with Him? Beg Him for the child's life? Please . . ." Another contraction tore at her, causing her to cry out.

Hosea held her, letting her lean into him. "Yahweh isn't here to kill anyone." He whispered constant reassurance as she fought the pain, uncertain what she heard or if she heard anything he said. Hosea sat beside the bed, locking his shoulder against hers, his back feeling as if it would break.

419

"Gomer, this can't be the best position for you to endure labor. Doesn't Yuval have some sort of contraption for women to use while birthing?"

A hint of a smile creased her lips. "It's called a birthing stool, and I have no idea who used it last or where it is. But if you'd help me squat with my back against the wall, I'd be in the same position as the birthing stool."

Relief washed over him. Finally, a task to accomplish! Hosea lifted her into his arms — even heavy with child, she weighed little more than two sacks of grain.

But before he could position her against the wall, she cried, "Wait!" Another contraction gripped her. She buried her head in his neck, and the scent of cloves overwhelmed him. His heart twisted in his chest. *Yahweh, how can I love her still? After all she's done to hurt me, how can I still —*

The gentle voice of Yahweh's Spirit echoed inside Hosea: *You will name him Lo-Ammi — Not My People — for the Israelites are no longer My people and I am no longer their Ehyeh — no longer their I Am. But a day is coming when the people of Israel and Judah will be reunited and become so numerous, they'll not be able to be counted. I will sow My people, and they'll grow in the land of their liv-*

ing God. Great will be the day of Jezreel, and in the place where it was said Lo-Ruhamah — Not Loved — I will call them Ruhamah, and where they were called Lo-Ammi — Not My People — I will call them Ammi.

"Hosea, did you hear me?"

He realized Gomer had spoken to him but didn't know what she'd said.

"You can put me down — oh, not yet, not yet . . ." Another contraction seized her, and she held her breath against the pain. When it lasted longer than her breath could sustain, she gasped for more air. Finally released from the pain, she lost all color. "I'm dizzy, Hosea. Don't put me down. I think I'm going to faint."

"Well, you've got to breathe, Gomer!" His frustrated observation came out with more venom than he intended.

"And what makes you the expert on childbirth?" she shot back. "In your vast experience, have all the women you've helped breathed their way to healthy — aaahhhh!"

"Breathe!" he shouted at her, startling her into obedience. "That's it. Breathe, Gomer." Yahweh's cool breeze blew on them again, and this time she inhaled deeply of His refreshing. The contraction ebbed, and she melted into Hosea's arms, exhausted. He kissed her forehead and whispered, "Are you ready to sit by the wall?"

She nodded, and he placed her feet on the floor, back against the wall. Hosea assessed the awkward position and dared amend the solution, lifting her slightly and perching behind her. He settled her between his legs, laying her back against his chest.

"Rest your arms on my thighs," he said. "It will keep you elevated without requiring as much strength from your legs." He leaned around to kiss her cheek. "All right. I'm here. Yahweh is here. You will have a healthy baby boy tonight."

She lolled her head against his shoulder. "A boy?"

"Mm-hmm." He brushed the copper curls from her sweaty forehead.

The cool breeze flowed with the next contraction, helping her breathe through the pain. On and on it went through the night.

You are so beautiful, my Gomer, so strong and full of life. "Beautiful, you're beautiful . . . you're doing a beautiful job. Keep breathing."

After one especially long contraction, her head lolled against his chest. Had she fainted? Fear nipped at the edges of his heart. He strummed the fingers on her limp

422

hand as he'd done when they were children. At first he thought she hadn't noticed, but then he heard a quiet sniff and saw tears mixed with sweat running down her cheeks.

Her face scrunched, and he thought another contraction would overtake her.

No. A sob instead. "Thank you for not hating me, Hosea." The tender moment passed when she groaned, "Ohhhhh, I've got to push!"

In less time than a hike from Jerusalem to Tekoa, Hosea witnessed the most beautiful sight on earth: Gomer giving birth in Yahweh's presence.

With her final push, the baby slipped onto the goatskin and Hosea hugged the woman he'd loved all his life. "He's beautiful, Gomer."

"How can you stand to look at him? Or me." Her voice was weak, but the emptiness was more than fatigue.

He left his place behind her, hurrying to find a blanket to wrap Lo-Ammi. For the moment, he must ignore his wife's comment and rub the child with salt — he knew at least that much about newborns.

As he lifted the babe into a blanket, he was startled to see Gomer have another contraction. "Are you having twins?" He was near panic. Yahweh had only told him of one child!

She shook her head, the contraction making it impossible to explain. He watched the miracle of afterbirth being delivered, amazed by Gomer's unruffled knowledge of these womanly things. She gave him direction on how to rub the boy with salt — he'd done it wrong — how to dispose of the afterbirth, what herbs to pack into her womb. Never had he imagined such a world existed, this culture of women. He was astounded, astonished, awed.

When finally their tasks were complete and Gomer was settled with the babe at her breast, he sat on the mattress beside her. "Do you remember Yahweh's presence during the birth?" She didn't respond. Didn't flinch. "You asked how I could look at you, how I could look at your baby. Yahweh has commanded that we name your son Lo-Ammi — Not My People." He watched pain and rebellion replace her indifference. "But it was the second part of His message that gives me hope that we'll be a family again, Gomer. All of us."

Her head shot up, eyes full of fire. "You name my son 'Not My People' and then expect to claim us as your family? I shouldn't be surprised. It's how you've always treated me. You promise friendship, marriage, family — and then you leave, Hosea. You always leave." She turned her face away, closing her eyes — and evidently her heart.

If he were sitting in her place, wouldn't he think the same thing? *Yahweh, how can I tell her of Your promises when they seem so far away, so impossible? I can trust You because I've seen You prove faithful, but Gomer has been hurt and abandoned again and again — sometimes because of my obedience to You.* He sat beside her in silence, unsure if he should tell her the rest of Yahweh's message. What if sharing the truth pushed her farther from the true God?

In the stillness, Yahweh again spoke to Hosea's spirit: *When Israel was a child, I loved him, and I called my son out of Egypt. The more I called them, the farther they went away. They sacrificed to other gods — the Baals — and they burned incense to idols. I was the one who took them by the hand and taught them to walk. But they didn't realize that I led them with cords of human kindness, with ropes of love. I removed the yokes from their necks. I bent down and fed them.*

Hosea realized that in this too, Gomer was like Israel. Yahweh had been leading her, revealing Himself, since she was a child, but she refused to see Him. She'd interpreted

His restraints of kindness as a yoke of rules.

"Gomer," he said haltingly, "I know it seems to you as though I've done nothing but abandon you, and you may believe Yahweh is some vindictive judge."

"Leave me alone, Hosea," she said, turning toward the wall and swaddling the baby beside her.

"I may leave you alone for a day, a Sabbath, even many cycles of the moon, but you are my wife forever. And you are Yahweh's child for eternity. He will never leave you alone, Gomer. He is with you even when I am not." His declaration was met with silence, and he wondered if she'd fallen asleep after her all-night delivery.

Determined to be obedient, he whispered Yahweh's words to the baby beside his ima. "Your name is Lo-Ammi — Not My People — but a day is coming when the people of Israel and Judah will be reunited and become numerous. The living God will sow His people — Jezreel — and great will be that day when Jezzy unites this family. And though your sister was named Lo-Ruhamah — Not Loved — we will call her Ruhamah, and though you are named Lo-Ammi, little one, we will call you Ammi."

Gomer pretended to be asleep, held her

breath until she felt Hosea kiss her forehead and leave their bedchamber. Quiet sobs racked her exhausted body at the words he'd spoken over her new son. How could he show her such kindness? How could he seem to love children of unfaithfulness — Rahmy, who was certainly born of another man's seed, and now Ammi, who by the chiseled, rugged features of his little face, was clearly Hananiah's child?

One thought terrified her more than any other. *Yahweh is real.* She couldn't deny it any longer. She'd felt the cool breeze of His presence on a stifling summer night — *inside* her house. Yes, Hosea's god was real, and He seemed intent on making her life miserable. Perhaps when she was strong again, she could escape to Asherah's grove and ask a priestess for wisdom. How does one evade a god?

Turning her face into the lamb's-wool pillow, she released her confused sobs. Sleep. She needed sleep. She must think with a clear mind to find a way of escape from Hosea and his god.

32

Remember your Creator before the silver cord is snapped, the golden bowl is broken, the pitcher is smashed near the spring.

Hosea peeked around the corner of their bedchamber doorway, watching his wife's shoulders shake while she sobbed into her lamb's-wool headrest. Surely he had married the most stubborn woman alive, just as Yahweh had chosen Israel — the most stiffnecked people on earth. He longed to curl up beside her and comfort her, but she'd made her feelings clear. She didn't trust him to keep his promises, and no amount of words would change her mind. Only time could heal their wounds.

Exhaustion threatened to consume him, but he needed to see Jonah and check on

Jezzy and Rahmy. He grabbed his walking stick, stepped into dawn's first glow, and passed the well-fed animals in his stable. *Thank you for Isaiah, Yahweh, who tends my stables and oversees the camp.* Uzziah had sent word that Amos's farm and the prophets' camp were thriving under Isaiah's watchful eye. Though the young man hadn't yet heard Yahweh's personal call, he'd filled the void of leadership when Amos was called away and Jonah fell ill.

Hosea pushed open his courtyard gate and noticed a cluster of people outside Jonah's house. "Unclean! Unclean!" he shouted, gaining everyone's attention. "I helped Gomer deliver the baby last night, so I'll be cautious not to touch anyone." He ambled toward the crowd, arriving at the door as Amos emerged.

"What are you doing home?" Hosea's question died when he saw the grief on Amos's face. "No." Tears choked him. "Get out of the way. I want to see Jonah."

Amos placed a steadying hand on his shoulder. "He's gone, Hosea. I was coming to tell you. I arrived just a few moments ago myself. Micah awoke this morning and found him . . . peaceful."

Wails from the gathered crowd split the dawn's peaceful silence. Clothing ripped.

Dust flew from the hands of men who mourned the great prophet, falling on their heads and peppering their beards.

Micah emerged from the house, his face twisting when he saw Hosea. He ran into his arms, weeping. "Master Hosea, our great teacher is gone — Jonah is gone."

They held each other until Hosea felt a hand on his shoulder. Isaiah. They welcomed him into their circle of grief. *Yahweh, how will we learn to prophesy without our teacher?*

Hosea heard Amos shouting instructions over the mourners. "I need volunteers to anoint the body. We must do it quickly because of the heat."

Hosea interrupted Amos's recruiting. "I'll wash him. I'm already unclean. I helped Gomer deliver her child last night."

Micah stepped forward. "And I'm unclean because I already touched my master's dead body to check for breathing or a heartbeat this morning."

"And I've touched them," Isaiah said, shrugging his shoulders. "We'll wash and anoint the body together." He laid his arms over Hosea's and Micah's shoulders, uniting them in their grim honor.

Amos nodded his approval and turned to dismiss the other volunteers. Hosea heard garbled rumbles from the dispersing crowd while Amos herded them onto the main path and then joined the three younger men inside. "I've sent one of the shepherds to get spices and ointment from Yuval." Hosea was glad to hear it because, like the birth, he'd sounded more confident than he felt to complete this women's task.

Amos was quite capable, however, and they were soon working together like a well-tuned harp, each string strummed in perfect rhythm. In the silent reverence of their last act of love for Jonah, Hosea spoke the question that weighed heaviest on his heart. "Who will teach the prophets if the Lord calls me back to Israel?"

Amos dipped a long piece of cloth in myrrh, continuing his quiet ministrations. "Isaiah speaks with great wisdom, though he has not yet received his prophetic call. And I teach occasionally, when I'm not traveling — though you know I've never been eloquent like the great prophets of old." He paused, seemingly deep in thought, and Hosea pondered Amos's self-doubt — or was it simply a fact? The burly shepherd hadn't set out to become a prophet, nor was he the son of a prophet. He had been faithful when Yahweh gave him a message for King Jeroboam fifteen years ago but hadn't spoken for the Lord since.

Amos set aside the burial cloths and waited for Hosea to meet his gaze. "When you are called to Israel, my son, the Lord will provide for our students here. But make no mistake. The mantle of teaching has been passed to you. You are Yahweh's prophet for this time."

The words felt like an avalanche on Hosea's shoulders. "But who will teach me?" His voice sounded small, like Jezzy's, and tears blurred his vision. His soul was assaulted with regrets from his past, doubts of the present, and fear for the future. *Too much, Yahweh. I can't withstand it.* Sobs overtook him, and he leaned over the body of his mentor, crying out, "I've been faithful to Yahweh. When will Yahweh be faithful to me?"

The words came from someplace deep within him, shocking him into silence. He'd never expressed — even to himself — the magnitude of his loss and frustration. He kept his head buried. What more was there to say?

"Look at me, Hosea."

Ashamed, he couldn't meet Amos's gaze. But this man was an honored teacher and friend like Jonah. Hosea must obey. He must listen — and learn.

Hosea stood and faced him, seeing no judgment, only love, on Amos's features.

"You have made great sacrifices to serve Yahweh, it is true. But never forget the Lord's plan reaches beyond this moment. We fight for Yahweh's victory, which is far greater than our temporary struggles." He cradled Hosea's cheek with his giant, calloused hand. "Men — and women — will fail you, but Yahweh will be your teacher." Amos patted Hosea's cheek, cleared his throat, and began coating bandages with balm and spices again. Hosea noticed him swipe a pesky tear and considered for the first time how difficult Jonah's death must be for Amos.

A weary sigh escaped as he let Amos's words sink into his soul. Three prophets stood with him. Young and old — fighting different battles for the one true God. They must all let Yahweh teach them.

"Jezreel, stop chasing the cat!" Gomer couldn't hear anything Yuval was saying over the ruckus of her three children. "Jezreel, if Sampson bites off your hand, don't come crying to me. Rahmy, don't touch Ima's vase —"

Crash!

The burnished Egyptian amphora shattered on the packed dirt floor, and Gomer stood frozen, staring at the pieces. Ammi must have sensed her tension, hugged close in his sling, and he began his newborn wail — which instigated Rahmy's fearful cry. She knew she'd get a swat for breaking Ima's favorite vase. Jezzy sat beside Sampson, gathered his four-legged friend into his arms, and began sobbing — because of his tender heart.

Gomer braced her hands on the worktable and expelled a long sigh, letting a few tears of her own escape. "I can't do this, Yuval."

A gnarled, wrinkled hand stroked her arm. "You are doing it, Daughter. You're a wonderful ima."

How could she tell her beloved friend she didn't *want* to do this? She didn't want to spend her days locked up in this house, smelling like soiled loincloths and baby vomit. Tomorrow she and Hosea would travel to Jerusalem for her purification at the temple. Finally, she'd be allowed to leave the house. She thought it ridiculous to make such a fuss over the third child when she hadn't been purified according to the Law with either of the others, but Hosea had been adamant. Since he was home, they would follow the Law. Which meant she'd been cooped up inside since Ammi's birth.

It had been a long thirty-two days — made longer by Hananiah's absence. He hadn't even tried to see her.

Yuval gathered Jezzy and Rahmy in her arms while Gomer picked up the broken pottery. Jezzy pulled at the gray tufts of hair peeking from Yuval's veil and asked, "Why do you and Saba Amos go 'way? Why does Abba go 'way too?"

Yuval rubbed their noses together, making the answer to Jezzy's question seem almost happy. "Sometimes big people must go away to do important things for Yahweh and help keep us safe. Saba and Savta do important work for Yahweh, and your abba is a prophet. Do you know what that means, Jezzy?"

"It means," Gomer interrupted, "we never know when your abba will be home and when he will leave us."

Yuval's eyes snapped in her direction, and the hurt Gomer saw pierced her own heart. "It's true that a prophet never knows when or where Yahweh will call him," she said softly to Jezzy, "but we know Yahweh's ways are right, so those who follow Him can walk in peace — if they choose to."

Gomer threw the broken pieces of clay into the basket set aside for trash, lifted Jezzy from Yuval's arms, and planted him firmly on the floor. "Jezzy, take your sister into Ima's bedchamber. It's time for your midday nap." She held Yuval's gaze. It was time for a private talk with her old friend.

"But Ima, I not sleepy."

"Jezreel!" Heat rose on Gomer's neck. She tried to calm herself, not wanting Yuval to see the kind of ima she'd become. Her patience with Jezzy and Rahmy had dwindled to bare tolerance — and she hated herself for it. She placed a guiding hand on Jezzy's curly head and set Rahmy on the floor beside him. "Take your sister."

"C'mon, Rahmy." He grasped her hand and slogged into the other room.

Gomer returned her attention to Yuval and found the woman glaring at her. She walked over, sat on a rug beside her, and waited for the reprimand. She didn't wait long.

"You cannot teach them your disdain for Yahweh. Not only will Hosea forbid it, I forbid it." She lifted her chin and seemed to be awaiting a heated reply. There would be none.

"I have a question for you, Yuval." The surprise and relief on her friend's face gave Gomer permission to continue. "What did you mean when you told Jezzy that you and Amos do important work for Yahweh? When I asked you before why you started traveling

436

with Amos, you told me you were lonely and wanted the adventure. I think you've been deceiving me, Yuval."

Her friend glanced at Ammi, swaddled in the sling. "I've been deceiving you?"

Gomer's heart skipped a beat. Did Yuval know about Hananiah? They'd been so careful. Gomer knew she suspected her harlotry, but had she somehow discovered Hananiah was the boy's abba? Did she dare confide in her friend?

"It seems our missions for King Uzziah are finished." Yuval stared at her hands. "I suppose I can finally tell you."

"Missions?" Gomer decided Hananiah could wait until later. "What are you talking about, *missions*?"

"Amos began carrying messages for Judean spies in Israel soon after Hosea brought you to live in Tekoa. When he was recognized on a mission, I began traveling with him to provide a more plausible ruse." She lifted misty eyes, offering a weak smile. "An old merchant and his wife draw less attention — especially when traveling to the northern nations to propose Uzziah's coalition against Assyria."

"Coalition? Assyria? Yuval, you're a fig picker, the wife of a shepherd-merchant from Tekoa. Why would King Uzziah send you and Amos on *missions*?" She rubbed her weary face. This was too much information for a sleep-deprived woman. "Please. I don't care about kings and messages and coalitions. Are you going to leave me like everyone else?"

Yuval reached for Gomer's hand, squeezing her love into it. "I learned something very important while traveling with Amos, Daughter, something you need to hear. The messages of a prophet — the words of your husband and mine — affect the decisions of kings. The decisions of kings determine not just the course of nations but also the life and death of individuals in those countries. If we become so enamored with our own little world that we disregard the nations, we are no better than those who focus on nations and ruthlessly disregard human life."

Yuval's eyes were deep wells of sadness, different from the innocence Gomer had seen her first night in Tekoa. What depths of horror had changed her so deeply? "Yuval, you're frightening me. Why are you telling me this?"

"You speak of being abandoned, Gomer, and I know you've experienced crushing losses in your life. But Hosea didn't leave you. He's teaching his students a few buildings away. I traveled a few times, but I'm holding your hands here and now. But everyone leaves us, Gomer, because we're all dust. Only Yahweh will never abandon you."

"No!" She ripped her hand from Yuval's grasp. "I won't listen to any more nonsense about Yahweh. I wish He *would* abandon me. I wish He'd leave me alone! I just want to live in peace with a man who loves me like Hana—" Her tantrum was cut short by the blunder.

Yuval's tenderness never wavered. "King Uzziah ordered Hananiah back to Jerusalem the day after Ammi was born — to counsel young King Jotham in decisions regarding the coalition. Though King Uzziah built Judah's towers, reinforced the gates, and prepared an army, it must be his son who leads Judah into war if Assyria's King Pul invades."

Gomer contemplated what Yuval said, but everything past the news of Hananiah resounded like a second shout after an echo. *Hananiah didn't abandon me! He was ordered back to Jerusalem!* Her heart leapt with joy, but she should at least acknowledge poor King Jotham's predicament. He was so young to face such a daunting task.

"I see only relief on your face, and it

troubles me. There's no sorrow for sin, no compassion for others, not even a glimmer of fear or curiosity to learn more about the changing world around you." Yuval's appraisal stripped Gomer's heart bare.

"You didn't give me a chance to respond." It was a pathetic answer, and Yuval's silent challenge stirred her defenses. "What do you want me to say? Should I wail and moan because Assyria might someday attack Jerusalem? Why is it so terrible to be relieved that Hananiah didn't abandon me?"

"It is your definition of *abandoned* that breaks my heart, little Gomer."

Yuval reached for her walking stick and pushed herself to her feet, and Gomer's heart plummeted. Her friend had finally given up on her. But to her shock and relief, the old woman pressed the stick into the dirt floor and drew a circle around herself.

When she finished, she looked up, a tender smile on her face. "I'm going to teach you what abandoned *doesn't* mean, Daughter. You have drawn a circle around yourself — a very small circle. As long as everyone stays in your little circle, you believe they are with you. However, if someone steps outside of it, even for a moment, you feel abandoned and label that one a betrayer."

440

"I do not!" Gomer's indignation waned as the truth nibbled the edges of her heart.

Yuval raised a single eyebrow, silently awaiting permission to continue.

"You can keep going — since you've already scarred my floor with your drawing."

The old woman tried to hide a wry smile. "Remember what I said before about the danger of becoming too focused on your own little circle — to the exclusion of the world around you. That great big world, where prophets and kings and nations are making all those decisions, can swallow you without warning. Those whom you accuse of abandoning you have stepped into a bigger circle — a circle you've chosen to ignore. Hosea has not abandoned you. Yahweh has not abandoned you. They are working in the wider world around you."

Gomer blinked and nodded. All this talk of circles was confusing. What had happened to her no-nonsense, practical, fig-picking friend? The world would continue on its course with or without Gomer's intervention or concern. In the meantime, she would hold tightly to the one thing that had given her hope since Ammi's birth. Hananiah hadn't left of his own choice. He'd been ordered to leave Tekoa. And now he was in . . .

Jerusalem.

I'm going to Jerusalem tomorrow!

33

HOSEA 8:14

The people of Israel have built palaces,
and they have forgotten their maker. The
people of Judah have built many fortified
cities. [Yahweh] will send a fire on their
cities and burn down their palaces.

Hosea and Gomer stood atop the hillside
across the Kidron Valley. "Look," he said,
pointing at Yahweh's temple. "It's like a
gleaming jewel, and the city walls are like a
crown."

Gomer smiled in response — really smiled
— with a grin that reached her eyes.

He turned and hurried down the hill. His
wife would no doubt keep the pace, maintaining the renewed vigor she'd shown since
early this morning. She'd awakened before
dawn, rattling around in the main room,
packing for their journey. He hadn't seen

her this happy since before Jezzy was born. Her days of uncleanness and seclusion had been difficult. She needed activity and people like olive trees needed sun, soil, and rain, and this trip to Jerusalem seemed to blow a fresh breeze of life into her.

Hosea looked up, shaded his eyes, and measured the sun's position. "It's past midday. We've made good time."

He glanced behind him and saw that Gomer was following closely but didn't answer. She'd seemed lighthearted throughout their journey — though not especially talkative. The joy of the olive harvest anointed their travel, and each time they rested for little Ammi to nurse, Gomer chatted with a local farmer and invariably convinced him to shake an olive tree. She would then dance in circles, palms upturned, catching the falling fruit like raindrops. The farmers were so entertained, they made a gift of the olives Gomer captured. Hosea chuckled at the memory and stopped to catch his breath.

"What are you laughing about?" Gomer caught up and issued an annoyed glance.

He produced a few olives from his pocket as a peace offering. "I was wondering how you could still be so enamored with olive tree shaking after living on Amos's farm for three years."

Her brow furrowed, and Hosea feared he would catch her all-too-familiar wrath, but a wry smile tugged at a corner of her lips instead. "It's the only time I can dance without drawing scorn."

The revelation stole Hosea's breath — and broke his heart. She'd undoubtedly intended the remark as humorous, but it revealed a yearning for her old life. Had she wished she could dance this morning when they'd passed Amos's hired hands shaking the camp's olive trees? *My wife will never be free to dance and catch olives in the prophets' camp.* In Tekoa, Gomer would always be Hosea's wife, the harlot.

"Come on. We'll need to hurry home after your purification to help press the olives." He resumed his downhill march, unwilling to dwell on the realities of their future when today was about the joy of Ammi's life. "Amos said some of the shepherds weren't able to help with the olive processing this year because the drought was sending them deeper into the wilderness for water." He planted his toes into the dusty ground, steadying his descent toward the Kidron Valley. "Let's cut across here. We'll take a shortcut to the northern entrance of the city."

"Hosea, slow down! I'm afraid I'll fall."

He looked back and watched his petite wife picking her way down the steep grade, cradling the precious bundle in the sling wrapped over her shoulder and around her waist. Her eyes were intent on the rocky terrain, and a deep scowl etched her brow. *What am I thinking?* Gomer wasn't an experienced traveler like Micah — or even Jonah. He'd let his mind wander instead of tending to his wife.

He charged back up the hill. "Here, let me help you." Before she could protest, he circled her waist, practically lifting her off her feet.

"Hosea, be careful! I'm unsteady with Ammi in this sling!" Her feet slipped as she said the words, and he swept her into his arms, baby and all. A little giggle escaped her — the first he'd heard in many moon cycles. She cradled Ammi in the sling with one arm, clinging to Hosea's neck with the other.

"I won't let you fall, Gomer." He nuzzled her neck. "Don't let go, and I promise — I won't let you fall."

Her smile died. The amiable moment faded, and a flash of despair appeared before she hid her face in his chest. "Who will choose the lamb for my offering?"

446

His heart ached each time she refused his tender emotions. Yuval said Gomer was always more volatile after childbirth, but Hosea had sensed a stronger storm brewing during her uncleanness. Today had been better, but he would honor her current attempt at avoidance. "Since it's after midday, the temple supply of lambs may be picked over, but we'll talk with the high priest. Perhaps he'll do us the honor of choosing our lamb."

He walked the rest of the way in silence, the feel of her in his arms enough to satisfy him for now. He would need to confront her moods if she didn't change soon, however. Her indifference toward him was tolerable; her impatience with Jezzy and Rahmy was not.

Gasping, Gomer pointed to something on Jerusalem's northern tower. "Hosea, look!"

He stopped on the main road into the city, other travelers flowing around him. Some sort of large contraption perched atop each tower on every corner of Jerusalem's wall. "I've never seen anything like those, Gomer. They look like some type of war machines."

"You can put me down now." She ignored Hosea's observation, wriggled out of his arms, and started walking toward the gate.

"Gomer, wait!" She looked startled, then

annoyed, when he straightened her blue linen veil to cover her hair properly before they entered the city. The veil's edges were fraying, and it showed a few small tears. "Perhaps we should visit the market while we're here and buy you a new veil."

She averted her gaze and rejoined the bustling crowd. "Perhaps."

Hosea rushed to her, careful not to become separated by the sea of people entering Jerusalem's Sheep Gate.

Because they arrived at the rear of Yahweh's temple, Hosea didn't notice its shoddy appearance until they rounded its southwest corner. The great pillars, Jakin and Boaz, looked soiled, the lily and pomegranate ornamentation caked with dirt. He reached for Gomer's hand, pulled her from the rushing crowd, and stepped toward the animal corrals. One lamb awaited purchase, and the pen was in desperate need of repair.

"I hope *that* one is without blemish." Gomer's tone dripped with sarcasm, but anger sparked in Hosea's heart.

"There isn't even a priest here to take our silver for the offering," he said to no one in particular. Incredulous, he issued another general plea. "How can Yahweh's people worship without a priest to make the sacrifice?"

His anger now burning like a red-hot flame, Hosea turned in a full circle, seeing no one but travelers hurrying away from the temple. None in this city seemed concerned about their God. The wind blew through the empty temple court.

"Where have the faithful gone?" he screamed, stopping every passerby where they stood. "How can Yahweh's temple stand empty when the high places in Judah are swarming with worshipers?"

"Hosea, please." Gomer placed a quieting hand on his arm. "People are staring."

"Staring?" He gaped at her, breathless. Could she really have no grasp of what consumed his heart, his life? Did she think that *staring* was the worst persecution he had faced while they'd been separated all this time? He drew breath to begin his deriding but was stopped by a familiar voice.

"Hosea, I'm sure this is a shock to you." The high priest stood before him, worn, weary. "If you'll follow me to the palace, we can talk on the way. I'll try to explain what's happened in Judah while you've been prophesying in Israel." The sadness in the priest's countenance tempered Hosea's anger, and Gomer issued a silent nudge. "Please, Hosea," the high priest begged. "Please listen."

Hosea's heart thundered in his chest. *Yahweh, give me wisdom.* He refused to be cowed by Gomer's embarrassment or the high priest's shame, but if Yahweh wished him to prophesy at the palace, this could be the way He was providing entry. "All right. We'll go to the palace, but I've brought my wife for her purification ceremony. Our son — the baby is thirty-three days old, and we've come to fulfill the Law."

He winced at his verbal pause. Ammi wasn't his son, but Yahweh was giving him a love for the boy similar to his love that had grown for little Rahmy. He glanced over his shoulder at Gomer. She had fallen in step behind them, her head bowed, whispering to Ammi. She momentarily glanced at Hosea but seemed more interested in the city sights.

Gomer could barely contain her delight. The gods must be smiling on her today. Her greatest obstacle to finding Hananiah — getting into the palace — had been overcome without a word on her part. "You're going to meet your abba," she whispered to Ammi.

They hurried through Jerusalem's streets, Gomer feigning indifference with every sidelong glance. In truth, she was studying every landmark, having realized she'd need to maneuver the city after she escaped from Hosea. She'd made her decision on their journey this morning — when she danced. Tekoa was behind her. Forever. Isaiah and Aya would love her children as their own, adding them to their growing family. She and Hananiah could begin their lives here in Jerusalem with Ammi.

She etched into her mind every street and building, combining what she saw with reports she'd heard from traveling merchants. They said every city was alike: the outer wall followed the shape of the central street's contour, wealthy homes perched on the highest elevations since refuse of every kind flowed downhill, and wells or natural springs lay at the center of town. She'd heard Jerusalem was unique because the Gihon spring was positioned southwest of the city, near the Water Gate.

But Jerusalem was unique in many ways.

Legends abounded of underground tunnels stretching to Jericho, heavenly beings hovering over the temple site, and a dozen more stories she believed less as she lived more. However, to be safe, she would purchase another Asherah with the silver she'd saved from her harlotry. Thank the gods she'd decided to bring it. She hadn't been certain she'd leave Hosea today — until she danced, until she felt free again.

Not far from the temple, they arrived at a wide set of marble steps. Exquisite white pillars lined an outer portico, each pillar intricately engraved with pomegranates, grapes, and palms. She'd heard of Solomon's architecture. The seven years spent building Yahweh's temple were surpassed in time and splendor by the thirteen-year project of his personal palace.

Her worn leather sandals slapped the mosaic entry, but the sound was swallowed up when the doors of the crowded Cedar Hall were opened.

Hananiah. He stood behind King Jotham, eyes scanning the room.

She gasped, and Hosea gathered her into a protective embrace, steering her through the crowd in front of them. "Quite different than King Jeroboam's ivory palace, isn't it?" He had to lean down and shout to be heard. King Jotham was between rulings. She held Ammi tightly to her chest as wall-to-wall people pressed for position.

The high priest led Hosea and Gomer forward, blocking her view of the king — and his commander — while the steward announced the next case. "Ezra, son of Benyamin, brings charges against Berechiah, his neighbor."

Gomer recognized the palace official Maaseiah from Uzziah's rented house. He now stood on King Jotham's right hand, and the chief scribe, Jeiel, scribbled furiously as a line of other scribes alternately rested and wrote according to their system of record keeping. Hananiah looked over the crowd. *He must not have seen me yet,* Gomer thought.

Jotham struck his scepter on the floor, creating a loud *pop.* "Your neighbor will pay restitution for the animal. The Law of Moses is clear on the matter."

Jotham sounded so regal. Gomer smiled, feeling a sense of pride on Uzziah's behalf — then sadness that he'd never see his son reigning so capably.

The crowd resumed its nondescript roar, and Gomer kept her eyes focused on the commander. Still no recognition.

"Hosea, my friend! And Gomer! I see you have a new little one." The king's greeting hushed the hall instantly, and Gomer felt like a prize on display.

Hosea cradled her elbow, and she felt his hand tremble. Was it anger or nerves that made her husband quake?

"King Jotham, we thank you for the welcome." He bowed, and Gomer did likewise.

"We came to offer the sacrifice for Gomer's purification, but we couldn't bear the condition of Yahweh's temple."

We? Did he say "we"? With all her heart, Gomer wished to run and hide. Anything to spare her the embarrassment of what she knew he was about to say. She glanced at Hananiah again, but his eyes seemed to burn a hole through Hosea.

"We saw many fortifications as we approached Jerusalem today. Your abba built towers on the corners of Jerusalem's wall, and we noticed your addition of some type of war machines."

Hananiah whispered something to the king. Jotham nodded, and Hananiah's bass voice resounded in the silent courtroom. "Those 'war machines,' as you call them, can shoot a cluster of arrows in a single motion and hurl large stones at an army pummeling our wall. King Jotham graciously gave me leave to share these details — though make no mistake, Judah's war strategy is no concern of an Israelite prophet."

Hosea glared at the king, ignoring the commander completely. "It is not war strategy that will save or destroy Judah, King Jotham. Yahweh says, 'The people of Israel have built palaces, and they have forgotten their Maker. The people of Judah have built many fortified cities. Yahweh will send a fire on their cities and burn down their palaces.' "

"It sounds like a threat, my lord." Hananiah had taken two steps before Jotham's scepter blocked his path.

"It is no threat. It is a promise." Jotham's words were calm. Resigned. "I hear you, Prophet, and I believe I understand Yahweh's message. We will spend more energy and resources to repair Yahweh's temple and reinstate the daily offerings, and spend less time on military preparations."

Hosea bowed, but Gomer was suspicious. The king seemed to concede too easily. Hananiah, however, looked as if he was ready to burst.

"One more thing," Jotham added, "before you take your lovely wife back to Tekoa."

For the first time, Gomer noticed a small boy seated on the other side of the scribe, Jeiel.

"Come here, Ahaz," Jotham said to the little one who was watching with wide eyes. He ran across the dais and crawled into the king's lap, a miniature crown perched amid a riot of red curls.

Jotham kissed the boy's head and returned his attention to Hosea. "This is my son, Ahaz. I have not taken him to Yahweh's temple since his saba's curse, nor will *I* ever darken the temple doorway — because I want my son to grow up with his abba seated on Judah's throne, not wasting away on a farm in Tekoa."

Gomer couldn't swallow the lump in her throat. Finally, a Yahweh follower who seemed to understand her fear, her doubts, about this capricious god.

Hosea stepped forward, his anger seemingly spent. He knelt and bowed while speaking. "I believe your heart is pure, King Jotham, but I must warn you as I warned your abba. Destroy the high places and return to Yahweh's temple to worship. King Uzziah was not cursed by some random act of bitterness by a fickle deity. Your abba has been disciplined by a loving God and is a better man for it." He raised his head, pointing to little Ahaz. "I'd rather your son have an abba learning of Yahweh's love in a rented house than growing up as a captive, exiled in a foreign land. Yahweh has warned you and will not tolerate Judah's blatant disobedience."

Gomer covered her mouth to stifle a gasp. Had Hosea just threatened a child?

King Jotham's face was unreadable parchment. Emotionless. "Use caution, Prophet. You are welcome here because I have extended hospitality, against the better judgment of some of my officials." After a deep breath, Jotham continued. "I will order the temple repairs and reinstate the daily offerings, but I will *not* compel those who are frightened of Yahweh's presence to abandon the high places. Judeans must have a safe place to worship Him, and each one must choose where he or she worships."

Hosea pinned him with a stare. "You are making a grave error, my lord."

"And you are no longer welcome in my courtroom." Jotham nodded to the guards behind them.

Gomer's heart raced as the guards moved to escort them out. This was her only chance to speak to Hananiah. "No!" she said, fighting the rough hands that grabbed her. Her cry startled Ammi, and he let out a wail. She fumbled in the sling to remove him, desperate to show him to his true abba. But the guards pushed and shoved them. She fought, keeping Ammi clutched to her chest yet still trying to untangle him from the sling. Even Hosea seemed to be pushing her.

"Stop! Let me show him the child!" she screamed.

"Gomer, you can take care of Ammi outside." Hosea's voice was muffled in the confusion.

She finally broke free and lifted Ammi from his sling, presenting him like a shiny piece of silver. "See how he looks like his abba —"

"Take that madwoman back to Tekoa." The guards sneered, shoving Hosea into the palace entry. They'd been discarded outside like waste.

Hosea stood, lifting stormy eyes to meet her gaze. "Ammi looks like his abba?"

34

ISAIAH 49:15

Can a woman forget her nursing child? . . .
Although mothers may forget, I will not
forget you.

Lo-Ammi — Not My People. The baby's
name resounded in Hosea's mind and
boiled his blood. "What makes you think
Ammi is Hananiah's child? You're a harlot,
Gomer!" His voice echoed against the
marble palace entry; people stopped and
stared. "He could belong to any number of
nameless, faceless men!"

Her neck and face flamed crimson, but
she stood as erect as the pillars around
them. "Hananiah was the only man in my
bed while you were away, and he *loves* me,
Hosea." She spat the word like an indict-
ment. "Something you only talk about."

He grabbed her arm, moving them away

from the gathering crowd. "If he loves you, where is he? Why isn't he begging to be your child's abba?" The hesitation on her features invited his scorn. "Hananiah doesn't love you. He's just —"

"Go back to Tekoa," came a gruff bass voice. "Both of you."

Hosea turned to face the imposing frame of Judah's commander and four armed guards.

"You're causing a disturbance on palace property, and I'd hate to arrest a prophet with his wife and — her illegitimate son."

"He's your son!" Gomer screamed, tears coursing down her cheeks. Hananiah raised his hand to strike her, but Hosea leapt in front of her.

The commander grinned. "I wouldn't hit a woman," he said, then glanced side to side. "In broad daylight." His guards laughed uproariously.

Hosea trembled with rage but felt helpless to defend Gomer. She denied his love and refused to be his wife. "We'll leave."

He turned to collect Gomer and be on their way but found her firm as granite, shoulders straight, jaw set. "I'm not leaving," she said, staring at Hananiah and then at Hosea. Before he could question her, she placed Ammi in Hosea's arms and started down the steps.

Hananiah and Hosea stood dumbstruck. The first to gather his wits, Hosea charged after her. "What do you mean you're not leaving? What about our children? What about Ammi?"

She kept walking, and soon Hananiah flanked her other side. "You *will* leave Jerusalem, Gomer." He motioned to his four guards, who blocked her progress and brought the whole caravan to a halt. "Neither you nor your husband are welcome in Jerusalem. You will go back to Tekoa —"

"My husband will go back to Tekoa, and he can take *your* son with him, but I am staying in Jerusalem. I'll find a potter to hire me, and I'll earn a living here in the city." Tears gathered on her lower lashes, and she turned to Hosea. "I can't go back. I can't. I wasn't created to be a wife and ima. I'm a harlot, like you said. It's what I'm good at."

Hananiah grabbed her arm, lifting her off her feet. "I said you're not staying in Jerusalem. I don't care if you go back to Tekoa or travel to Egypt." He cast her aside, and Hosea watched her heart shatter in the gold flecks of her eyes.

She turned and ran down the remaining palace steps, out of the royal courtyard. "Gomer, wait!" Hosea stood rooted to the marble, Ammi whimpering in his arms.

"He does have my nose." Hananiah smirked. A crushing hand landed on Hosea's shoulder. "If you leave now, you should reach Tekoa by sunset." He strutted back into the palace, his guards shoving and laughing like bullies who'd beaten a weakling.

Hosea looked at the babe in his arms, wondering how he could satisfy the hungry cries. *Yahweh, give me strength to love when everything in me wants to hate.* A resolute step, and then another. Hosea would visit the high priest. Perhaps he'd know of a wet nurse in the city. *But I must return to Tekoa tonight.* He couldn't face his future alone.

Gomer pressed through the crowded Jerusalem market, blinded by tears. Whom would Hosea find to nurse her baby? Did he know anyone in Jerusalem? Surely he'd go to the temple, and the high priest could guide him to a wet nurse. The baby's cries echoed in her memory, torturing her as she passed countless merchants' booths. She covered her ears against the phantom sound, drawing stares from puzzled shoppers. Maybe she was a madwoman, like the guard said. Only a madwoman would leave her baby in the street and two more children at home.

She stumbled in the street, and a dusty young boy steadied her. "Mistress, are you all right? Do you need water from the spring?"

His wide eyes were so innocent. He didn't know he'd touched a filthy harlot. "A spring?"

"Yes, mistress." He pointed south, down a sloping street. "Do you want me to show you?"

"No, no," she said, backing away from him, fearing her vileness might somehow corrupt his goodness. "Thank you."

The sun was past midday. The spring would be deserted, a good time to draw water without facing the righteous women of Jerusalem. She'd refresh herself and then find a merchant who might help her leave the city.

Or perhaps I could wait until tonight, find Hananiah, and remind him of all we've meant to each other? How could he have been so cruel? He'd seemed like another person, someone she didn't even recognize. Perhaps he'd been put off by her appearance. Her figure hadn't returned to normal yet, but she'd regain her shape once she bound her breasts and skipped a few meals.

"Shalom, lovely lady." A smooth bass voice sent a chill up her spine, and a finger traced a line from her wrist to shoulder.

Without thinking, she turned and slapped the stranger who'd crept up behind her.

His reflexes were equally quick. He grabbed her wrists, shoved her out of the street, and pinned her against a wall behind the booths, covering her mouth. "You aren't being very friendly." She glanced in every direction but saw no means of escape. "If I remove my hand, can I trust you not to scream?"

She nodded, buying a few more moments to think of an escape. "What's your name?" she asked, desperate to slow his attack.

"Does it matter? It seems to me you've done this before." He placed his hand at her throat, squeezed, and then kissed her roughly.

She couldn't breathe and began to fight. "Please. Please!" His hand remained on her throat but loosened enough that she could speak. If she could distract him . . . "Tell me why you think I've done this before," she said, trying to keep the shame from her voice. He laughed and waved her off, as if the answer was too obvious to dignify by voicing it. When he moved in for another kiss, she turned her head. "Tell me. Tell me why you picked me."

His hand held her face like a vice, and he

leaned closer, his leering eyes now unavoidable. "Everything about you screams 'harlot.' You're alone, visiting the spring at midday without a water jug. The way you walk. The way you —"

Suddenly, the man was gone, lying on the ground. Stunned, Gomer stood shaking, staring into Hananiah's eyes. His guards were pummeling her attacker while Judah's hulking commander towered over her.

"You came for me!" She threw her arms around his neck, but he pushed her away. Stumbling back, she felt as if he'd struck her. The hatred in his eyes lingered.

He stepped closer, letting his hands roam the length of her, and then ripped away the pouch of silver she'd been saving for years. "I want my silver back," he said, disgust lacing his tone. "You can find your own way out of Jerusalem." He threw the bag to his guards, and they celebrated like children with a new toy. "Consider that payment for rescuing you."

"But that's all I have. How can I —"

"I don't care how you get out of Jerusalem, but your husband has already left. He's on his way back to Tekoa with that child."

Her heart skipped a beat at the mention of Ammi. "You didn't hurt him, did you? Ammi's all right?"

"Don't even act like you care." Hananiah began to tremble, his fists clenching and unclenching. She could see his rage boiling.

"Please. Let me explain. I —"

He lifted his hand, and she winced, expecting the blow — usually a white-hot burst of pain on the cheekbone. Instead, she heard a low, seething growl. "I need no explanation. You have shown what kind of woman you are." He spit in her face and then stepped aside, pointing at the man who'd attacked her, lying unconscious.

Gomer's fear settled into resignation, like the final few olives falling from a tree shaken bare of its fruit. She thought her dance meant freedom — but it was her final folly.

"Get out of Jerusalem, harlot. Your husband has left the city and is returning to Tekoa tonight. I doubt that he'll have you — I wouldn't — but you could try to catch up with him. Or I can recommend a brothel to house you overnight."

Gomer swallowed hard and glanced at the guards, hoping for a glimmer of mercy. They turned their backs, folding their arms across Judean breastplates.

"My guards are loyal to me alone, Gomer. How do you think I found you so quickly? I'll take you to a brothel if you like. Otherwise . . ." He kicked the man on the ground.

"Otherwise, you'll run into more like this one."

She nodded, staring at her sandals.

"Hurry up. My wife is expecting me home for the evening meal." Hananiah shared a laugh with his friends, and Gomer's humiliation was forged into white-hot rage.

She bit back a reply that would question his wife's intelligence and earn the black eye she'd anticipated. Instead, she followed him obediently, noticing that the merchants' observations held true. *All refuse drains downhill.* They passed drunkards and brothels, proving the theory accurate of people as well as waste.

At the end of the street stood two multi-leveled structures. One was undoubtedly their destination, where women leaned against the door frames and called to passersby. The second looked to be a warehouse, and a gentle breeze revealed the perfumer's shop. Even in her misery, she smiled at the irony. She'd wished for perfume while in Tekoa, having to settle instead for the pathetic scent of cloves — until Hananiah had given her a small vial of nard. She'd left it behind with the rest of her belongings. Perhaps someday she'd wear perfume again — if she could get back the hard-earned silver Hananiah had stolen.

"Miriam! I've brought a harlot for your herd — but she stays only one night." Hananiah pressed his way through the fawning women blocking the door.

They eyed Gomer but were distracted by the guards, who waited outside for their commander. One of the girls teased, "Come in, boys. We can light twice the flame *she* stirs in you. She's old enough to be our ima."

"Ha!" Unbelievable that this *child* would call her old.

"Here she is." Hananiah reappeared at the door with a curvaceous woman a bit older than Gomer. "She stays tonight only. Do you understand?"

Miriam appeared annoyed, and Gomer wondered if she'd kick her out as soon as the commander left. A man's interference in a harlot's world was a breach of unwritten law.

"Come on," the woman said flatly. "I'll show you to our common room. Private chambers are reserved for business. You'll have a mattress of your own in a roomful of girls."

"She'd be more comfortable in a roomful of men." Hananiah laughed and elbowed one of his guards. Without a parting glance or a coarse good-bye, Judah's commander walked away.

If Gomer had been a warrior, she would have sunk a dagger between his shoulder blades. But she was a woman. Powerless. Friendless. Worthless.

"Did you love him?"

She gasped, startled as much by the intimate question as by the woman who asked it. Every harlot knew love wasn't part of their business.

Miriam's lips were pressed into a seething, thin line. "He's played most of us in Jerusalem. Gives us gifts, makes us feel like we're the love of his life. But at the end of the day, he goes home to his wealthy wife in their mansion on the hill."

"Why doesn't someone stop him?"

"Stop him?" Miriam choked out a mirthless laugh. "Who can stop him?"

"Get me a bottle of perfume, and tell me where his wealthy wife waits in this mansion." Gomer had nothing left to lose. "I'll show you who can stop him."

"What if I've been wrong all this time, Isaiah?" Hosea sat huddled in his friend's home, trembling on a late summer night, exhausted after his grueling journey home alone with Ammi. "What if I heard Yahweh's prophecies and interpreted them the way I wanted to hear them — that our family would one day be united? What if Yahweh's intention was for me to literally stop loving Gomer, to stop forgiving her?"

Aya offered him a cup of watered wine, and he thanked her with a nod. She squeezed his shoulder, tears streaming down her face. "I'll take Jezzy and Rahmy for a walk. Ammi's finally asleep." Hosea had hired a wet nurse in Jerusalem at the recommendation of the high priest, but the baby had gone hungry for the remainder of the half-day journey and then required a Tekoan wet nurse and Aya's comfort to rest.

Isaiah grabbed his wife's hand and kissed it before she walked away. "Don't wear yourself out." She smiled at his concern.

Hosea's heart shattered into smaller pieces. *Why, Yahweh? Why couldn't Gomer receive and give that kind of love?*

"I don't know if you've interpreted Yahweh's message correctly," Isaiah said, touching his shoulder, drawing him back. "But I know you've been faithful, my friend, and that's what Yahweh asks of us. He doesn't ask us to understand."

"But I want to understand!" The frustration emerged with a sob.

Isaiah's eyes closed tight. "And I want to be a prophet." A sigh, and then he opened his eyes, focusing again on his friend. "But we don't always know the Lord's plan."

"I'm sorry," Hosea said, dragging his hands through his hair, "but how can it be the Lord's plan for an ima to turn her back on her children — on a nursing child? You saw her love them, Isaiah. Can she really forget them? Forget us?"

"I don't know the answers, Hosea, but I know Yahweh never turns His back on us, never forgets us. I've watched Abba Amoz open his heart when Aya speaks of Yahweh's love. He wouldn't hear it from Uzziah — or from me — but Yahweh keeps placing people in Abba's life to speak the truth." His eyes welled with tears. "Yahweh will not forget Gomer, even if Gomer forgets her friends, her husband — and her children."

35

HOSEA 2:5

Their mother acted like a prostitute . . .
[and] did shameful things. She said, "I'll
chase after my lovers."

Gomer covered her head with the drab,
brown sackcloth she'd borrowed from Miriam and approached the guard at Hananiah's mansion gate. Dusk cast long shadows
across Jerusalem's northern streets, and she
prayed none of the guards would recognize
her from today's palace visit.

"You there, what do you want?" A large
soldier with full armor stood on the opposite side of iron bars, holding his spear at
the ready.

"I've come with Lord Hananiah's gift for
his wife. I'm sorry I'm late, but the perfumer
mixed this blend for the commander's lady."
She sensed his hesitation but then heard

the click of an iron latch and the door creak open.

He thrust out his grimy hand. "I'll take it to the commander. He and his wife are eating their evening meal and do not wish to be disturbed."

She lifted her eyes, offering her most beguiling smile. "The perfumer asked that I deliver the gift myself. I won't linger, but I believe the commander would be pleased to have this aroma grace his lady's wrist." She lifted the sleeve of her robe, exposing her wrist for the soldier to sniff. "Perhaps I can find a way to show my gratitude after I complete my task. Can you tell me where the commander and his wife are enjoying their evening meal?"

He gazed, starry-eyed and speechless, proving her ploy's success, then pointed toward a two-story home at the top of a winding, uphill path.

Gomer's heart thudded like a herd of horses while her feet kept a slow, silent pace. She rounded the corner and ascended the structure's outer stairs to the roof. Hearing raised voices, she realized Hananiah and his wife weren't "enjoying" their private meal after all. She crouched on the top step, hidden by an enormous clay planter, and listened to the lovers' quarrel.

"How dare you lie to me!" The woman's hysterical sob was followed by the crashing sound of broken pottery. "Amalya saw you in the market today and followed you to a brothel. You said you'd never visit a brothel again, Hananiah. You promised!"

"Shoshana, I wasn't visiting the brothel. I rescued a harlot from an abusive customer today, and my guards and I escorted her home. Did Amalya include *that* in her busybody report?"

"Don't you dare blame Amalya. She's a good friend, trying to protect me from your lies. As surely as the Lord lives, Hananiah, if you hurt me again, my abba will go to King Jotham and have you stripped of your duties. You are Judah's commander because Uncle Zechariah — blessed be his soul by the Judge of the earth — was King Uzziah's best friend, and Abba bought your position."

"I'm Judah's commander because I've earned it, Shoshana!"

"Excuse me." Gomer rose from her hiding place and faced the couple in awkward silence. "I tried to interrupt earlier but wasn't heard."

Hananiah ground out his words between clenched teeth. "What are you doing in my home?"

"I've come to thank you and bring your wife this perfume."

She stepped toward Shoshana, but Hananiah stepped between them. "Get out."

"Hananiah, don't be rude." His wife nudged him out of the way and accepted the alabaster flask. "Thank you. Would you like to sit down?"

"No, she doesn't want to sit down. Shoshana, do you know who this is?"

Before his wife could guess, Gomer accepted the lady's invitation, resting on a cushioned couch beside her. "I'm the harlot your husband rescued today. A man took advantage of me, thinking that because I'm a harlot, I have no feelings. Some think they can take what they want without asking." She turned to Hananiah, her smile so warm it could've melted the snow on Mount Hermon. "But your husband took me home to my brothel madam — her name is Miriam. When Miriam saw that I was safe under Commander Hananiah's protection, we both agreed there's no need to ever leave Jerusalem."

"Oh, were you thinking of leaving?"

Gomer mustered a few tears and turned away. She mustn't overact, but Shoshana seemed to be convinced so far. "My family abandoned me some time ago, and I wasn't certain what to do or where to go." She glanced at Shoshana, smiling through tears. "It's nice to see Commander Hananiah has your love and your abba's support. A family can make or break a man."

Feeling vindicated, Gomer rose from the cushioned bench and dried her eyes. "I don't want to intrude any further on your evening."

"Well, thank you for the perfume, um . . . ," Shoshana stuttered, lifting a questioning brow. "I'm sorry, I didn't get your name."

Hananiah stood between them, creating a visual barrier between his two worlds. "Her name isn't important, my love. It's not as if you two will ever meet at a social gathering." He turned Gomer toward the stairs and placed a firm hand at the small of her back, encouraging a quick exit. "I'm going to walk the harlot to our gate to be sure a guard escorts her home. I'll be back in a moment."

"Good-bye, Shoshana," Gomer called over her shoulder. "Enjoy your perfume."

When they reached the last step, the commander spun her around. "What do you think you're doing?"

"I'm surviving, Hananiah. It's what I do. You're lucky I'm in a forgiving mood, or Shoshana's abba would be visiting King

Jotham as we speak."

His fingers dug into her arm. "Don't cross swords with me, woman. You will die."

"I'll stay on my side of Jerusalem. You stay on yours." She twisted out of his grasp and walked toward the anxious guard at the gate.

He was watching for her return and stepped into her path. "Have you considered how you'll thank me for helping you?"

She stepped around him and smiled at his disappointment, relishing the singular power she held over men. "Wait one moon cycle, and then find me at Miriam's brothel." She waved without looking back. "Bring your friends. And bring your silver."

Gomer inhaled the cool night air, her mind spinning with the preparations necessary by the next moon cycle if she hoped to accept customers. Binding her breasts would dry up her milk, and she'd eat once a day to get rid of the extra bulges. The brothel owner would be relieved at her meager portions.

The reality of Gomer's poverty overwhelmed her. With nothing but the clothes on her back, how could she compete with the youthful harlots half her age? Perhaps Gomer's little visit to the commander would win enough favor with Miriam to garner an advance on wages. Gomer would need some tools for her trade — cosmetics, perfume, jewelry, a new robe. But all that was window dressing.

She cradled her breasts to relieve the pressure of Ammi's absence and allowed her emotions a controlled escape. Just into her twenty-second year now, she'd born two children before she left Samaria and three more in Tekoa. Her body wasn't the lithe, firm treasure it had once been. Though she knew her beauty remained, she was equally certain the younger harlots held greater appeal. *I will find other ways to distinguish myself.*

Jezzy's dark curls and Rahmy's sweet smile flashed in her mind. "No!" she sobbed, quickening her pace. She wouldn't — she couldn't — dwell on the past. Her life had changed today, for better or worse, and she couldn't change what she'd done. From this moment on, she was Gomer, harlot of Jerusalem.

Hosea sat on his goatskin rug, leaning against the wall beside the oven, trying to chase away winter's dampness — and the chilling memories that assaulted him. It had been over a year, and Gomer still stared back at him from every corner of their home. He'd asked Aya to dispose of his

478

wife's robes, combs, and personal items —
many of which must have been gifts from
her lovers — as soon as he returned from
Jerusalem.

But what about the daily reminders of
their lives?

How could he replace the window that
had cast dawn's glow on her copper curls?
Should he break every bowl she'd touched,
every plate on which she'd served their
meals? And what about the most painful
reminders of all — the three precious jewels
that lay beside him each night and greeted
him with smiles each morning?

"Good morning, Abba," Jezzy would say
so properly. He had Hosea's dark curls,
Gomer's hazel eyes.

They were now his children. Isaiah and
Aya had offered to take them permanently,
adding to their own growing family. But
somehow loving Gomer's children justified
hating her. At least that was how it began.
Bitterness had nearly consumed him in
those early days. He could never have
survived without these three innocent beings full of love and forgiveness. He and the
children were happier and healthier without
Gomer. He could say that now without bitterness. It was the truth.

Hosea wiped his face, drying his seemingly endless fountain of tears. Yuval would be arriving with his little ones any moment. She'd been a rock of support, even when Amos fell ill in the sheep pasture a few Sabbaths past. Since then, Hosea had been the lone instructor training the camp's would-be prophets. Their eyes sparked with zeal each time they discovered a new mystery of Yahweh.

What about my zeal, Lord? Will I ever hear Your voice again? The questions he'd asked Isaiah still echoed in his empty heart. *Did I misunderstand You, Yahweh? Did I hear what I wanted to hear?* He'd been so certain of what he'd heard. Yahweh had been so present, so palpable. He'd thought they'd be a family. He thought Jezzy would unite them somehow. Instead, Jezzy, Rahmy, and Ammi would forever live with the crushing reality — they'd been abandoned by their ima.

Abandoned. Gomer's favorite accusation. *Yahweh, have You abandoned me?*

He hadn't felt God's presence or heard His voice since Gomer left. Micah was receiving regular messages from Yahweh now, powerful prophecies that were written on clay tablets and transferred to scrolls. He was anxious to speak to Israel's and Judah's kings, but Hosea advised against it, warning of the tenuous political environment.

Or do I hesitate to send him because You've chosen him instead of me?

Hosea's cheeks burned at the silent admission of petty jealousy. But it was more than envy, it was a practical question. How could Hosea teach prophets when he wasn't sure he could discern God's voice for himself?

He rolled onto his stomach, planting his face into the curly goatskin rug. "Please, Elohim! Hear my prayer! Speak. Your servant is listening!" Racking sobs shook him, but heaven remained silent. His sorrow swirled into despair, and despair turned rancid in his gut. "If You will not speak, then at least direct me toward a purpose, a mission — a task!"

Hosea's heart began to pound violently. An indescribable heaviness overtook his limbs and chest, pressing him to the floor. Was it a heightened sensation of angst? Perhaps. But this was somehow different. "Yahweh, is this You?" He squeaked out the words and finished in prayer. *I much prefer the warmth of Your presence or the cool breeze when You're about to speak.*

Nothing. No reply. Simply more of this crushing heaviness, growing more unbearable by the moment.

He buried his face in the rug. "Yahweh, help me. What's happening?" Hosea stilled, closed his eyes, waited.

No words, but an overwhelming sense of a hand covering his whole body. Shielding. Protecting. Pressing him into the floor. *Change.*

There had been no voice, but somehow Hosea knew. His life changed the day Gomer left, and he must change too. Whether he traveled to Israel or stayed in Tekoa for the rest of his days, Yahweh's presence must be enough. Whether Hosea felt it or not. Whether Yahweh *spoke* or not. Could he serve Yahweh without words, without a task — only submission?

"Shalom, dear." Yuval's cheerful voice accompanied the creak of the door. "Oh my! Are you all right?"

"Did you fall down, Abba?" Jezzy hurried over, his hand patting Hosea's cheek gently.

"Abba was praying to Yahweh," he said, scooping his son into his arms and rolling him over for a playful hug.

"Is it Gomer?" Yuval's voice was panicked. "Did you receive word from Jerusalem?"

Hosea looked up, finding fear on Yuval's features. The familiar feeling of betrayal stirred, but he tamped it down, remembering Yuval's tender care when he'd returned from Jerusalem with Ammi in his arms. She'd told him about the conversation she and Gomer had on that last day before leaving for Jerusalem. Guilt nearly consumed her. Hosea wished she'd warned him of Gomer's unrest, but he ended up consoling instead of chastising.

"No, I've had no word from Jerusalem." He grinned at this dear woman, her heart too big for a single chest. "But I received word from a little higher up."

She squeezed Ammi closer to her heart and danced in a circle, holding little Rahmy's hand. "Your abba's been talking with Yahweh, Yahweh, Yahweh. Your abba's been talking with Yahweh today, today, today." Her impromptu song and dance inspired Hosea and Jezzy to join the loop, celebrating outwardly what Hosea felt inwardly.

He broke the joyful chain, swinging Jezzy into his arms. "Have the children eaten, or should I slice up some bread and cheese?"

Yuval began unpacking all the items she'd stashed with Ammi in the sling around her shoulder and waist — bread, figs, cucumbers, cheese. "I've packed all you need right here." She looked up, eyes glistening. "I'll tell Amos you've heard from the Lord. Will you be returning to Israel with a message?"

Hosea felt his cheeks flame. Was he embarrassed that he had no prophetic message? It was a sure sign he'd let pride slip in unnoticed. "Tell Amos I was given no specific message to prophesy. My highest calling is to submit to Yahweh in whatever needs done." He picked up Ammi, kissing his rosy cheek. "Right now, I serve Yahweh in camp."

■ ■ ■ ■

PART 3

■ ■ ■ ■

36

HOSEA 9:11–12

Ephraim's glory will fly away. . . . There will be no more pregnancies, births, or babies. Even if they bring up children, I will take those children away before they grow up.

"Breathe!" Gomer shouted. The girl had gone white as stone, laboring to deliver her first child. "You're dizzy because you're holding your breath. Now breathe through the pain!" Hosea's advice during Ammi's birth nearly four years ago had made Gomer one of the foremost midwives among Jerusalem's harlots. If this girl had been a member of Miriam's household, Gomer would have fed her pomegranate rinds and wild carrot tea months ago, sparing her the heartache of carrying this baby to term.

"I have to puuuushh . . ." She bore down

487

without coaching.

Gomer had learned much during the past four years of midwifery. At the top of the list? A woman's body — left to its own design — would signal its needs and fulfill them naturally if possible. The other things Gomer learned provided *unnatural* solutions to women's foolish choices.

"I see the baby's head. A few more pushes, and you'll greet this child in person!" She had to give the girl hope, but she refused to fill her thoughts with candied figs when an anxious brothel madam waited to whisk the baby away to the highest bidder. "Here it comes. Here it comes!"

With one final *whoosh,* a little boy entered his cold, harsh reality. Gomer had locked the door of her heart and swallowed the key — except in these moments. Fighting tears, she wiped the baby clean and rubbed him with salt as he wailed that first newborn cry.

"Let me see him," the new ima whispered, her exhaustion all too familiar.

Gomer remained silent, hurrying through the prescribed tasks. "You'll feel another contraction soon, and I'll help you deliver the afterbirth."

"What? Oh —" The girl, surprised yet efficient, resumed her laboring for a few short moments.

The final task complete, Gomer shouted to the women waiting beyond the curtain, "We're finished in here."

Two women entered. The first Gomer recognized as the girl's madam, owner of a competing brothel a few houses north. The second was Miriam.

"We'll need compensation for the use of a room and my midwife." Miriam extended her hand.

"Fine." The girl's madam dropped her silver pieces into the proffered hand and snatched the infant from Gomer's arms. "I'll make five times that on the child."

"No!" the new ima screamed, watching her child being carried away. She leapt off the birthing stool and tried to follow, but her legs wouldn't hold her. Miriam and Gomer caught the girl as she fainted, a rush of her blood flooding the wood-planked floor.

"Help me get her to the straw mattress, Miriam." Gomer grabbed her herbs and poured some boiling water into a mug over a spoonful of broken leaves, stems, and stalks. She stirred its contents, blew the steamy liquid, and coaxed the girl to drink. Delirious, she drank and tried to speak but lost consciousness again.

"What are you doing?" Miriam said,

panicked. "She's bleeding to death and you're giving her rue tea? Are you trying to kill her?"

Gomer rolled her eyes. Her friend could be so dramatic sometimes. "No. Rue tightens the abdominal muscles and stops the bleeding."

She felt Miriam staring. "How do you know all this? I worked as a street harlot for years and then inherited this place from my dear old madam — but I don't have half your knowledge of herbs and midwifery."

Gomer's heart squeezed in her chest. *Merav.* Even in death, she gave her life. "I had a friend in my first brothel, the midwife there, who taught me about herbs and keeping a man's seed from taking root." She glanced up to meet her friend's gaze. "I also know from personal experience. I've given birth to five children and survived one rue-induced drop, so I know a little about what this girl's going through."

Miriam's eyes welled with tears. "You left five children to come to Jerusalem?"

"I left three children with loving people who will give them a better life. My first two children were taken from me — as that baby was taken from her."

"Taken?" A weak voice interrupted their conversation, and Gomer checked the straw

490

mattress. The bloodstain had stopped spreading. The girl opened bleary eyes. "Where's my baby?"

Gomer swallowed hard, replacing the impenetrable armor around her heart. "You are alive. You survived. That's what's important. You'll have more children someday, but if you're smart, you'll never allow this to happen again — until you marry a wealthy old merchant with a house on a hill." The girl turned her face away, but Gomer couldn't let her deny reality. "Do you understand? If you remain a harlot, don't let yourself become pregnant!"

The girl nodded, her eyes swimming in unshed tears, and Gomer felt her cheeks burn with shame. Who was she to shout such commands? She'd maintained an empty womb in Jerusalem because of Miriam's willingness to supply pomegranates and wild carrot seed for the girls, but without the provision of a kind madam, this girl had no chance to survive. She lifted an eyebrow at Miriam, a silent plea.

Miriam rolled her eyes and sighed. "I have space for one more girl in my house." A spark lit the girl's eyes. "If you promise to work hard, bring in at least two clients a night, I'll take you in. And Gomer can help you remain childless."

"Yes! Oh, yes. Thank you." The girl reached for Miriam's hand, but the madam turned and left without a word. The girl undoubtedly thought it was because she was harsh and uncaring — as was intended. Gomer knew a madam couldn't reveal her heart any more than a midwife could share her soul.

"Gomer, wake up."

The haze of deep sleep cleared slowly.

"Gomer, Commander Hananiah is down-stairs. He says he must see you right away."

Miriam's mention of Hananiah's name brought Gomer to her feet and out of her chamber door in one swift motion. She fol-lowed her madam downstairs, riddling her with questions. "Did he say what's wrong? Is he alone or did he bring guards? Does he have a message or a scroll? You know I can't read."

"He said that he must see you right away. When I told him you see a few select clients, he became outraged and said he hadn't come to sleep with you, only to talk with you."

Momentary relief was replaced with fear. What could they possibly have to talk about? Unless he had word from Tekoa . . .

Her foot reached the last step, and she

saw the terrified expression of Judah's commander. Her heart stopped. "Hananiah, what is it?"

He glanced at Miriam and back at Gomer. "I must speak with you alone."

The madam touched her friend's elbow and leaned close. "Do you need me to call the house guards? I believe all four of them could restrain the commander if it came to that."

Gomer patted her hand, touched by her concern. "No. I'll be fine. Commander, you may come to my private chamber upstairs." He appeared shocked, embarrassed. "Don't worry." She grinned. "What was it someone once said? 'I'll never force myself on you.' " She caught a glimpse of his fury before leading him upstairs. Neither spoke until they entered her chamber, where she lit an oil lamp. The room was small but seemed even smaller with his mountainous form consuming it. "So, Commander, what brings you to my home in the middle of the night?"

His jaw muscles danced, and he swayed from one foot to the other, looking more like a nervous groom than a confident soldier. "I've heard you're the best midwife in Jerusalem." He paused. "There's a girl." Another pause. "She's pregnant."

Gomer's mind began to spin. He'd come

to secure her midwife services for a pregnant girl? "And who is this pregnant girl, Commander?"

"Does it matter?" He spat the words, more like a threat than a question.

"She obviously matters very much if you've sought out the best midwife in Jerusalem."

He sighed deeply and folded his arms across his leather breastplate — the first signs of defeat. "She is the daughter of a royal advisor, and she's carrying my child."

In that moment, Gomer was thankful she'd had four years to harden her heart and perfect her indifference. It gave her the strength to conduct business rather than melt into tears. "How far along is she?"

He looked at her as if she'd asked for directions to the moon.

"How many months since she's experienced her womanly flow of blood?"

"Well, how would I know that?"

She wasn't sure whether to laugh or slap him. "What is it you're asking me to do, Commander?"

"We want to be rid of it."

Now she was certain she wanted to slap him. "Is the girl as anxious to 'be rid of it' as you seem to be?"

His eyes narrowed. "She's waiting outside

with a guard. Why don't you ask her your-self?"

"I'll speak with her only after you've settled on a price with Miriam. She negoti-ates the fees for my services, and I'm guess-ing this will cost you plenty."

She started toward the door, but Hana-niah grabbed her shoulders. "You were right before when you said this girl matters. She matters very much to me — personally and politically. Don't think you can harm her and take your revenge on me. If anything should happen to her, I'll charge you as a criminal, and you'll endure the harshest penalties conceived in Judah's kingdom."

Gomer twisted out of his grip and stopped at her doorway. "Your threats don't frighten me, Hananiah. I know who holds true power in your household. Now, do you want to talk with Miriam or not?"

He followed her downstairs like a lamb to the slaughter. Certain Miriam would require an exorbitant fee, Gomer hid a satisfied smile. She'd done dozens of rue-induced drops on the harlots in Jerusalem. Could nobility's wombs be different? She would begin preparing the delivery room while Hananiah and Miriam worked out the details. By this time tomorrow night, their brothel would be richer, and Gomer would've won another victory over Judah's commander. She must remember to plant a kiss on Lady Asherah's bronze head before she offered rue tea to the advisor's daughter.

"At least she's stopped screaming." Miriam's pale face and sweat-stained robe testified to the lengthy vigil she'd kept beside the advisor's daughter.

Gomer could only stare. Horror. Disbelief. How could this be happening? "She's dying, Miriam."

"What? No! She can't be!" Panic seemed to set in, and she began shaking the girl's shoulders. "Breathe! Isn't that what you always tell them, Gomer? Breathe!"

"It's too late for that." She pushed Miriam away, cradling the girl onto the straw mattress. "Let her last moments be peaceful ones."

They sat in silence, listening to the whisper of breath escaping the young girl's blue lips. Finally, a long exhale.

Miriam lifted terrified eyes to Gomer. "What do we do?"

A girl poked her head through the curtain. "I don't hear any more screaming. Should I send word to the commander that he can come to collect her now?"

"No!" they shouted as one.

Miriam took the lead. "Get out. We must clean her up before any message is sent. Do you hear me? No message until I give the order."

The girl backed out penitently.

"We have two choices." Gomer spoke quietly, ensuring they wouldn't be overheard. "I can go to King Jotham with the truth and hope for his mercy."

"King Jotham would never believe the word of a street harlot over his commander!"

Gomer shook her head, donning a wry smile.

"How can you smile at a time like this?"

"I forget you know almost nothing about my past. King Jotham is an old friend. I showed kindness to his abba Uzziah after he was struck with leprosy."

Miriam stared blankly. "And you're just mentioning this now?" She shook her head, seeming to dislodge all she'd just heard. "I don't care if you're Jotham's ima, he's not likely to overlook a murder charge — and that's what Hananiah will call this — when it involves the daughter of one of his advisors."

Gomer knew she was right, and the tears she'd held back breached the stronghold. "That leaves us with choice number two. I

497

slip out of Jerusalem now, and you delay the news of the girl's death as long as possible." She reached for Miriam's hand and squeezed it as tears streamed down both their faces. "When Hananiah discovers you've let me escape, he'll try to close you down."

Miriam nodded, swiped at her tears, and exhaled deeply. "He may try, but he'll have a lot of explaining to do if he admits to bringing the girl here himself. I'm sure we can reach an agreement on discretion when it comes to disclosing *all* the facts publicly." Miriam squared her shoulders and leveled her gaze. "He still has a wife and father-in-law to please."

A sob escaped before Gomer could bridle it. She turned away quickly, covering her face, trying to rebuild her emotional wall. When she returned her attention to the girl, Miriam had already begun washing the body.

"Thank you, my friend. I'll never forget you."

Without looking up, Miriam said simply, "Go."

37

HOSEA 2:2

Plead with your mother; plead with her.
She no longer acts like my wife. She no
longer treats me like her husband.

Gomer leaned hard on a walking stick she'd
fashioned from an old branch somewhere
between Jerusalem and Bethlehem. Her feet
were blistered and bleeding, the beaded
sandals not intended for an all-day hike to
Tekoa. Hananiah's girl had died just before
dawn, which allowed Gomer to slip from
Jerusalem unnoticed — with only the
clothes on her back. Her heavy cosmetics
and perfume announced her profession, but
she'd staved off advances with the dagger
concealed in the sheath above her right
knee. The long slit in her robe made the
blade as accessible as her legs. The slit and
the dagger — necessary tools of trade for

any harlot these days.

She'd passed through Bethlehem long before midday, so she guessed she'd arrive in Tekoa during the midday meal. Gomer crested the last rocky rise before entering the camp, paused, and scanned the width and breadth of the valley she'd once called home. Amos's renowned dwarf sheep grazed on the foothills below. Yuval's fig trees were between harvests, their bright green foliage massaged by early summer sunshine. The olive grove waved a silver and green shalom as she hurried down the hill toward Uzziah's rented house. He would be her first plea for mercy — perhaps her only chance.

"Unclean! Uncl— Gomer?" The shock on his face must have mirrored her own. Bandages shrouded living bones that were once the great King Uzziah. He was a whisper of the king she'd first met, sitting on a fresh straw mat in his doorway.

"Shalom, my friend." Her suffering suddenly paled in light of the pain on the king's face.

"I would love to embrace you, but I dare not make you unclean."

She laughed through her tears. "You can look at my appearance and worry about making *me* unclean? You are perhaps the most gracious man on earth, King Uzziah."

A sparkle in his eyes showed a smile, though his face was covered. "I must confess, I hesitate to touch anyone anymore. The pain is too great." Tears wet the bandages on his cheeks. "What trouble brings you to Tekoa unannounced, Gomer?"

The disease had not impaired his instincts. "I come seeking mercy, my king." She paused, wondering where to begin.

"Does this involve Commander Hananiah?"

A niggling fear began eating at the edges of her heart. "Yes, my lord, how did you know?"

"When Hosea arrived home from Jerusalem with baby Ammi nearly four years ago, he told me of the child's abba. I know my commander, and though he is an impeccable soldier, he is a flawed man. And he is now my son's military commander. So before you speak, I must warn you. I cannot — I will not — overturn any judgment my son has made regarding Hananiah."

"But King Jotham hasn't made any judgment yet — I don't think." It was the truth, at least when she'd left Jerusalem this morning.

"Gomer." Her name on his lips broke her heart. It was the voice of a loving abba — an abba she'd never known.

She bowed her head and let the tears fall. "Yes, my lord."

"Go to Hosea. Only Yahweh can overturn the laws of Judah. Hananiah is a powerful man, and I am dying. My son rules Judah with strength and wisdom, but he must choose to fight the political battles that will strengthen his reign." He fell silent, and Gomer knew he waited for her to look at him. Defiance kept her head bowed, but at last respect lifted her gaze. "Yahweh is the only one who can help you now. Let Him."

"Like He's helped you?" The words tasted bitter on her tongue, and she regretted them as soon as they left her lips. But how could Uzziah defend a god who tortured him like this? She stood, and Uzziah looked away. "I'm sorry, my lord. I will do as you say. I'll lay my case before Hosea and see if he might help." She longed to embrace Uzziah, to stay with him — however many days he had left. But this would be the first place Hananiah would look for her.

"Hosea should be with his students. He's taken over all the teaching and become camp administrator since Amos fell ill."

"What?" Gomer's heart leapt to her throat. "Amos? Is Yuval . . ."

Uzziah's eyes smiled. "Yuval is still Yuval. We can all be thankful for that."

502

She swallowed another lump in her throat, bid him good-bye, and stepped onto the path toward camp. They were the hardest steps she'd ever taken.

An excited buzz filled the room, and Hosea let the anticipation build. Micah had completed his first Sabbath-to-Sabbath wilderness fast and returned this morning with news of a clear message from Yahweh.

When Hosea had rejoiced with him, asking to hear the Lord's words, he'd seemed unsettled, saddened. "Yahweh instructed me to speak only to the group of prophets, Master Hosea. I'm sorry. I can't reveal it to you alone."

Though Hosea had grown content in his role as teacher, the words still stung. Yahweh had chosen another — as Gomer had chosen others. Had he failed them both?

Hosea set aside his personal brooding, assembled the students, and coached himself to be content — no matter what Yahweh's message revealed. "All right, Micah. We're all anxious to hear what Yahweh has spoken to your heart." He nodded, signaling the boy who'd long been his student to speak as a seasoned young prophet.

"Master Hosea, may I first share something you said to me the morning after I heard Yahweh's first calling?"

Hosea smiled, granting permission.

"You said I wasn't ready to prophesy until the words broke my heart — as the messages broke Yahweh's heart." His face twisted with emotion; he wiped instant tears from his eyes. "What I'm about to say breaks my heart, Master Hosea . . ."

Hosea's stomach knotted, dread pulling it tighter and twisting.

"Yahweh says, 'I will turn Samaria into a pile of rubble, a place for planting vineyards. I will roll its stones down into a valley and expose its foundations. All its idols will be smashed to pieces. All its wages for being a prostit—' " Micah faltered, bowing his head.

And Hosea realized he'd stopped because Yahweh's reference to Israel's prostitution was too similar to Hosea's life experience, too personal to espouse as a general call to holiness. "You must speak the prophecy, Micah, no matter who is listening. A prophet must declare Yahweh's words in every audience, in any forum."

Micah lifted his head, eyes closed, and proclaimed through tears, " 'All Samaria's wages for being a prostitute will be burned. All its statues will be turned into a pile of rubble. Samaria collected its wages for being a prostitute. That money will again pay

504

for prostitutes. I will mourn and cry because of this. I will walk around barefoot and naked. I will cry like a jackal and mourn like an ostrich. Samaria's wounds are incurable . . .' "

Hosea's heart leapt to his throat. *Incurable . . . Samaria's wounds are incurable . . .*

Micah continued the message, but Hosea heard Yahweh's fresh revelation. Gomer's wounds were incurable. It was time to mourn her as if she were dead. Stop looking back for lessons. Stop questioning Yahweh's plan. Gomer would never recover from her life of prostitution, as Israel would never recover from her idolatry. He must release any lingering shred of hope.

Micah's words echoed in the periphery of his thoughts. "Shave your head in mourning for the children you love . . ."

"Hosea, I'm sorry to interrupt." Yuval stood in the doorway, eyes red-rimmed and swollen. The room inhaled a collective gasp.

"Is it Amos?" Hosea's heart couldn't beat until he heard her answer.

"No, Amos is well."

"The children?"

"Please, Hosea." She fought tears. "Come outside. I must speak with you in private."

"Is Aya all right?" Isaiah stood among the students.

Hosea grasped his shoulders. "If it concerns Aya or the children, I'll send word for you." The two locked eyes, a silent pact.

Hosea exited the building, shielding his eyes from the midday sun. Yuval led him to a large boulder beneath a sycamore, where his children waited with a woman.

No! It can't be!

Gomer held Ammi propped on her hip. Jezzy and Rahmy clung to her legs.

"Get away from them!" He ran at her, grabbing Ammi away, breaking Jezzy's and Rahmy's grasp. He guided his older children into Yuval's care and placed the toddler in her arms. "What do you want?" he asked, standing as a barrier between the harlot and his children. Her copper curls cascaded over her shoulders, tangled and dusty. The malachite on her eyelids was faded, the kohl around them smudged by tears.

"I come seeking mercy, Hosea." She stood like granite, as cold and heartless as ever, her chin lifted in defiance even as she asked for the unthinkable.

"*You* seek mercy?"

Yuval nudged him aside, pleading. "Hosea, she's been falsely accused."

Incredulous, he stared at the old woman. "You're asking mercy for *Gomer*? What about her children, Yuval? *My* children.

Don't *they* deserve mercy?"

He snatched Ammi from Yuval's arms and grabbed Jezreel, standing a camel's length from Gomer. The heady scent of perfume overpowered him. "Plead with your ima, Jezzy. Ask her for mercy, Ammi." The youngest whimpered in his arms.

"Hosea!" Yuval said, taking Ammi from him. "That's enough."

Rahmy hugged Hosea's leg, and he cradled her head, whispering, "Tell your ima to stop being a prostitute. Tell her to give up the lovers that are more important than you."

"Please, stop!" The granite statue cracked, and a single tear fell down Gomer's cheek. "Don't speak to me this way in front of our children."

"Our children? You can't call them that when you no longer act like my wife. I should strip you as naked as the day you were born. You come back in some sort of mess, thinking you might as well return to your husband because he's always there to pick up the pieces when you shatter the lives of those around you."

Yuval laid her hand on his arm. "Hosea, will you just listen to her? She's not asking to come back. She's asking for protection against a wrong that's been done her."

"There's always a 'wrong that's been done her,' Yuval. Don't you understand? It's never her fault, and as long as she refuses to acknowledge that Yahweh is Elohim, she is dead to me."

Yahweh's words echoed in his spirit: *Mourn her as if she were dead . . . She will never recover from her prostitution, as Israel will never recover from her idolatry.*

His heart twisted in his chest. He knew what he must do. "Go to Israel, Gomer."

She looked at him, startled, and wiped her tears. "Why?"

"Because both you and Israel have an incurable lust for sin. Israel will value her prostitutes until Assyria crushes Samaria to rubble. I don't know when it'll happen, but I know Yahweh has given up on Israel — and I've given up on you."

"Good," she said, raising her chin. "You were a fool to ever love a harlot." With the hardness he'd first glimpsed in Jeroboam's temple, she turned and walked away.

"Hosea, you can't let her go." Yuval's near panic stirred the older children's weeping. "She has no provisions, no silver. She'll never make it to Israel. She'll die in the wilderness."

He sat on the ground with Ammi and called the other two into his arms. Hosea quieted them against his chest, nodding in Gomer's direction. "She has rejected Yahweh and her family. You can do whatever you must, but she is dead to us, Yuval."

38

Hosea 8:9–10

The people of Israel went to Assyria. . . .
Even though they sold themselves among
the nations, I will gather them now.

Gomer stormed through Hosea's courtyard
gate, nearly breaking it off its hinges. She
heard the chickens clucking and noticed
he'd added a cow to his stable. Maybe he
was finally letting go of some of that silver
he'd stashed away. He never spent a shekel
on gifts for his wife — when she was alive.
She is dead to me, he'd said. Well, he was
about to discover that dead people steal
valuables in very real shoulder bags.

She burst through the door, tripping over
Sampson. He screeched and scampered
away but danced around her legs when he
realized who'd come home. She lifted him
into her arms, enjoying his soft purring. "At

least someone is happy to see me."

"Can you blame them, Daughter?" Yuval's voice startled her. The old woman walked past her, removed a travel bag from its peg on the wall, and collected a few silver pieces from Hosea's money pouch. "Start wrapping cheese and bread. You'll need as much as you can carry to get to Israel through the wilderness."

Gomer held Sampson, paralyzed by confusion. "The wilderness? Wait. Are you helping me steal from Hosea?"

"He said to do what I must. And you must go through the wilderness if you hope to avoid Hananiah's wrath and Israel's troops."

Gomer set aside the cat and helped Yuval wrap food at the worktable. When the pack was full, Yuval stared at her. "Hananiah will have guards posted on Judah's main roads. He's a dangerous man, but now he's lethal because you've shamed him. So you must stay off the trading paths, but you mustn't travel too closely to the Salt Sea. Its water is tainted, so you'll need to find oases or slip into small villages at night."

"But how will I know where to go if I don't follow a path?"

"All those journeys with Amos taught me a thing or two about traveling, and I'm going to give you a quick lesson. You're going north, so keep the sun on your right in the morning, at your back all day, and on your left in the evening. The desert is unforgiving — unspeakably hot during the day and deathly cold at night. You must find shelter for the most extreme temperatures during the day. Any kind of shelter will do — a boulder, a scrub bush, a cave. But if you choose a cave, throw rocks inside before you enter to alert any wild beasts."

Panic rose within her. "I can't travel alone in the wilderness! I barely made it to Tekoa from Jerusalem. I have no idea how to protect myself against lions, bears, jackals — and what about the snakes?"

"Wild beasts are the least of your worries, Daughter. Keep a fire lit at night, and they'll keep their distance. Vipers are the only poisonous snakes, and desert cobras are the most lethal, but snakes in general will flee unless you step on them or they feel threatened. It's the soldiers you need to fear."

"Soldiers? Hananiah has no influence outside of Judah. Once I get into Israel, I won't have to worry about soldiers. I can travel on main roads again, right?"

The question shattered Yuval's instructive countenance and propelled her into a fierce embrace. "King Uzziah has received word that Israel's military is on high alert. Assyria has begun a siege against Arpad in the north, and they're pressing hard against Damascus on Israel's east side. Tensions are high. Menahem's soldiers have orders to attack first, ask questions later." The words tumbled out as if she had to speak them before she lost heart. "You are no safer on the roads of Israel than in Judah. I will pray for your wisdom to survive."

Yuval's instructions assaulted Gomer's mind and joined Hosea's words like a clashing cymbal. *Israel will value her prostitutes until Assyria crushes Samaria to rubble.* It seemed the terrible irony of her life had come to this. "I will return to Israel — and die like the harlot I was at first."

Yuval released her and then held her shoulders, staring hard. "You don't have to return to harlotry, Daughter. Find a way to survive until you reach a city in Israel, and perhaps Yahweh will open a door for you to work in a pottery workshop."

She brushed Yuval's cheek. "Perhaps the sky will rain silver, and a handsome king will walk out of my dreams and carry me away to a faraway, peaceful land." She hoisted the bag onto her shoulder, smiling sadly at her optimistic friend. "I wish the world was as kind as you are." She grabbed a water skin on her way to the door.

"Gomer, wait." Yuval untied her belt, removed her outer robe, and slipped off her sandals. "You'll have a better chance at finding work with a potter if you don't wear that." She removed Gomer's shoulder bag and untied her belt, then replaced the harlotry garb with her own woolen robe.

Fresh tears stung Gomer's eyes. "So you would give me the robe off your back, my friend? What more can you give me but your lifeblood, eh?" She hugged her and wept.

"Yahweh is my lifeblood, Daughter, and He can renew your life too — if you let Him." Gomer released her and started to protest, but Yuval placed a finger on her lips. "I know it seems impossible, but the answer is so simple — not easy, no. But simple. If you would only believe."

Gomer leaned down and kissed her feather-soft cheek. A fleeting vision of her old friend Merav invaded her thoughts. Why had the gods played such a cruel trick — placing the same face and the same kind heart in separate bodies — haunting Gomer with the memory of a friend taken too soon, and another she must now leave behind? "Wanting it to be true doesn't make it so, Yuval. If that were the case, you'd be my ima, and I'd have a husband who loves me."

■ ■ ■ ■

The scorching sun seared Gomer's already blistered face. She lifted the water skin to her lips once more. Sucked on it. As dry as the dusty hills around her. She hadn't tasted water for three days. Why couldn't Hananiah have brought his royal princess for a rue drop in the springtime? At least then she could have fled for her life when the wadis flowed with mountain thaw.

Gomer sat in the shade of a lonely scrub bush, shuffling through her travel bag for her last piece of bread. Moldy. How long had she wandered in the wilderness? What did it matter? No one would find her body anyway. The jackals would pick her bones clean. A pack of them had circled her campfire every night since . . . well, for a long time.

She checked the sun over her shoulder. It hadn't moved. Yuval would be proud of her. She'd remembered the old woman's instructions. *Keep the sun at your back all day.* How had her face become so blistered with the sun at her back?

She must be somewhere in Israel by now. She had counted six days before her mind grew muddled.

A faint sound in the distance clattered like a cymbal falling to the floor. Not a wilderness sound. A people sound. She listened harder. Her heart pounded. It was a soldier sound.

Many soldiers.

She'd lay her head on this bag and rest a moment. Should she find the soldiers? Would they help her or kill her?

A sudden splash of water revived her. "What?" She sat up, her head swimming. The sound of men's laughter surrounded her.

"Well, she's alive after all." A large soldier nudged her ribs with his sandal. "You got a name?"

Gomer shielded her eyes, trying to judge by his armor if he was Judean or Israelite. He stood in the sun's glare. She couldn't tell.

He kicked her this time, and she curled into a ball, gasping. "I said, you got a name?"

"Yes. I'm Gomer."

"Gomer, eh?" He crouched beside her. "Complete."

She furrowed her brow, unsure what he intended.

"Your name. Gomer. It means *complete*." He stood and announced to the rest of his

516

troop, "She looks like a *complete* mess to me, but maybe our girls can clean her up and make her useful."

"Wait." Her voice sounded more like a croak. Her tongue swollen and sticking to the roof of her mouth. "Where am I?"

"You're in Israel, Complete. And you've just been acquired by Pekah, one of King Menahem's officials, to serve General Eitan's royal guard." He turned and began shouting orders; a whole band of people scurried at his command. "You two, load her into that cart. She doesn't look like she can walk with the rest of the harlots yet. You, Atarah, as soon as she can walk and dress, I want her serving with the rest of the women. How many did we lose at the last town?"

Through a haze of confusion, Gomer watched this woman named Atarah give a trembling report to Pekah. "Two women died from dysentery at the last town, my lord."

"Well, maybe Complete over there can do the work of two women when you get her healed up." He grabbed her throat and pulled her face to within a handbreadth of his own. "We can't stop moving, Atarah. General Eitan has ordered us to Arpad, and we must arrive in time to observe Assyria's pillage tactics. If you make me late, I will practice what I learn on you. Do you understand?"

Atarah nodded but made no sound. Pekah shoved her away, turned, and pressed on — shouting orders again to the men under his command.

Gomer felt herself being lifted, gasping at the sharp pain in her side where the officer's sandal had left its mark. The name *Eitan* floated through her consciousness like a familiar spirit in a recurring nightmare.

The woman Atarah leaned over and whispered, "If you have a god, Gomer Complete, pray that it kills you now. That would be the most merciful fate for a harlot in Israel these days."

Gomer laid her head back and let the jostling cart shake her into darkness. Her last thought — regret that she'd kept the jackals away.

Hosea hurried to Uzziah's rented house, wondering what could be so urgent that the king would call him away from his students at midday. He'd noticed Isaiah's absence from class and prayed Aya was all right. She was expecting their second child, but it was too early for her to deliver.

He emerged from the sycamores, entering

518

the clearing where Uzziah's camp had become a small village. "Unclean, unclean" was now little more than a whisper.

Isaiah stood beside his cousin near the audience tapestry, arms folded over his chest. Hosea sensed the tension immediately. "I came as quickly as I could, my lord. What's happened?"

Uzziah's eyes, visible between the bandages, remained alert — but today they radiated fear. "We received word during the early rains that the Assyrians continue to press their campaign west. They've seemed content to let raiding parties harass most towns, except for Arpad. The siege ended recently — Arpad has fallen."

"Arpad is more than a full moon's march north of Samaria. Isn't it good news that Assyria is moving away from us?"

"If it were anyone except King Pul, we might rejoice that he'd conquered a fortress so far north, but Assyria won't be satisfied until they rule the earth. When victory over Arpad was imminent, King Pul summoned the coalition kings I had been trying to rally. He *requested* their presence for the final phase of his conquest. Menahem and his royal guard obeyed King Pul's summons and began their way north with a reported tribute of 75,000 pounds of silver."

Hosea squeezed his eyes shut and expelled a long, defeated breath. "That's not good news."

"It gets worse. Reports are flooding in of Pul's intimidation tactics, displaying Assyria's barbaric torture practices on Arpad's citizens in the days after the conquest. They're waiting until all the coalition nations arrive with their tributes to finish Arpad's king and his advisors. If Menahem and the other kings pay their tribute to Pul, my dream of a coalition dies, Hosea. That silver will finance the Assyrian war machine's march across the earth — and into Judah."

Hosea felt as if the ground had shifted beneath his feet. "If the coalition is already gathered at Arpad, how am I to help, my lord?"

"Indeed!" Isaiah's eyes flashed, his outburst startling Hosea. "There's no reason for Hosea to risk his life."

"Risk my life, King Uzziah?" Hosea glanced from one friend to the other. "What exactly are you asking of me?"

"I'm asking you — *Judah* is asking you — to travel to Arpad and reason with King Menahem before he pays tribute to Assyria. One man on a camel can reach Arpad in fifteen days, and my spies tell me the Assyrians' torture is planned to last until the new moon."

"But even if I reached Arpad in time, what could I do —"

"The size of the gathered coalition armies is substantial. It's a risk, Hosea, but if you can convince Menahem to stand against King Pul, perhaps the others will join the resistance."

Hosea saw Isaiah's eyes flutter closed. His friend was obviously frustrated but resigned to Uzziah's desperate request.

"What does King Jotham think of the idea? I don't see Commander Hananiah ready to charge in as my rear guard." Hosea's stomach twisted at the mention of Ammi's abba. The commander had stormed into Tekoa the evening after Gomer left and searched every corner of the camp. In a rage, he'd damaged property and shouted threats. King Uzziah had ordered that he be forcibly removed, but to Hosea's knowledge, he'd never been disciplined for his actions — nor had Gomer been found.

"Commander Hananiah has been relieved of his command."

"What?" Hosea and Isaiah spoke in concert.

Before Uzziah could answer, a cool breeze stirred the sycamore fig trees above them.

Isaiah gasped. "It's Yahweh, isn't it?" He stared into the trees as if he might see the physical presence of Elohim.

Hosea was both awed and delighted. The Lord's manifest presence was like a familiar tune on a favorite harp. "Yes, my friend. It's Yahweh." He closed his eyes and let the voice wash over him. *The people of Israel went to Assyria. They were like wild donkeys wandering off alone. The people of Ephraim sold themselves to their lovers. Even though they sold themselves among the nations, I will gather them now. They will suffer for a while under the burdens of kings and princes.*

The words stopped. The breeze calmed. Hosea opened his eyes and found both his friends staring.

"Your face is as red as Gomer's hair." Isaiah's eyes sparkled, and he was seemingly delighted by his observation.

Gomer. Why would he mention Gomer at a time like this? "Let's concentrate on the message from Yahweh. I believe He wants me to deliver it to King Menahem personally."

"Thank you, Hosea." Uzziah's eyes expressed both gratitude and sorrow. "I can't send troops with you. Jotham believes their presence might draw King Pul's attention and bring a premature invasion. And Judah

522

has no general. Commander Hananiah was relieved of his command because . . . well, his character was revealed through the death of another young girl who suffered similar circumstances as those Gomer described to Yuval."

Hosea's heart squeezed in his chest. Why did they have to say her name? Why couldn't they leave Gomer to herself and focus on Yahweh and the mission before them? "I don't want troops, my lord. Remember," he said, following his own advice, "Yahweh has promised to rescue Judah without bows, swords, wars, horses, or horsemen. Perhaps it means He'll use a simple prophet." He tried to smile.

Uzziah nodded, seemingly overcome with emotion, exhaustion, or both. Isaiah laid his arm around Hosea's shoulders and bid his cousin farewell.

The two men walked back to camp, and Isaiah was quiet, almost brooding.

"Trust Yahweh, my friend," Hosea said, hoping to relieve his friend's fears. "I have no doubt He's called me to Arpad. He'll shelter me beneath His wing."

Isaiah stopped, his eyes filled with unshed tears. "When you heard Yahweh's message, I saw Gomer's face."

The words assaulted him, stole his breath.

Isaiah steadied him with a hand on his shoulder. "You will see her in Arpad."

39

HOSEA 13:15–16

Yahweh's scorching wind will come from the east. . . . Their springs will run dry, and their wells will dry up. . . . Their children will be smashed to death, and their pregnant women will be ripped open.

General Eitan leaned back on the stack of pillows Gomer had arranged as she handed him a polished brass mirror. "You'll stay in my tent again tonight," he said, reaching for her wrist instead of the shiny metal. "I don't mind sharing you with my officers, but I don't want Menahem to catch a glimpse of you." He squeezed harder, digging her silver wristband into her flesh. "Do you understand me?"

She winced but forced a smile. "I've had our good King Menahem. I have no desire to leave your tent."

"Ha!" He released her wrist but grabbed the back of her neck, pulling her into a quick, harsh kiss. "You're good for my ego," he said, taking the mirror. "Now shave my cheeks and trim my beard. I can't meet King Pul looking like an uncivilized pagan."

Gomer leaned forward, suspending his dagger near his throat. The blade caught a glint of torchlight, and he captured her wrist again. "Cut me, and I'll bury you with Arpad's citizens."

She pulled away from his grasp. "Lie back. You sound like an old woman. I'm not going to cut you." Gomer feigned anger to hide fear, willing her hand to stop shaking.

A wicked smile moved his cheek under the blade, nearly causing her to nick him. "That's why you're my harlot. You've got fire in your blood."

More like ice in my veins. Roiling hatred kept Gomer alive. She hated the gods, hated the other women in camp, hated the barbaric Assyrians — at least what she'd seen from a distance. But most of all, she hated this man lounging under the scraping of his dagger. Eitan, the brutal soldier from Samaria who had beaten her, was now her master. He owned her. Fate was almost as cruel as Eitan.

"What will you do while I attend Pul's

feast tonight with Menahem?" His hands violated her while he talked. How was she supposed to shave his cheeks when he kept moving?

"Your men brought back two antelopes from their hunt today. The other girls never get all the meat off the hides. I'll stretch the hides and go down to the stream to wash a few clothes."

He raised his head from the cushions, a dangerous glint in his eyes. "Did I not make myself clear? I said you will stay *in my tent* tonight."

"But there are only ten women to serve a hundred of your soldiers. If I stay in the tent, how will the others dress the game, prepare the feast, wash the clothes, *and* entertain Menahem and his men?"

He snatched the blade from her hand and hurled it at the center tent post, sinking it into the wood. "Your task is to obey your lord!"

His temper was hot and quick, but she dare not show fear. Any sign of weakness was an invitation for heightened abuse.

She leapt to her feet, her frustration real. "I'll never finish shaving you if you keep interrupting!" She'd made it halfway to the tent post when an iron grip snared her waist and dragged her back to the cushions.

"Mmm. Fire in your blood." His leering gaze made her skin crawl, the look in his eye all too familiar. The other women in camp envied her, hated her for monopolizing the handsome young general. She wished he would take them instead.

She struggled, and he laughed at her futile attempts. Exhausted, she finally gave up, her bruises from last night still tender and aching. "Do what you must, but be quick about it." She turned her face away, sighing. "You don't want to have one shaven cheek for your first meeting with Assyria's king."

He laughed and burrowed in her neck. She feigned pleasure, pondering what she might do with the two new antelope hides.

Hosea left Tekoa the day after his meeting with Uzziah, nudged by the urgency of Yahweh's call and harassed by Isaiah's troubling prophecy. *You will see her in Arpad.* Why had the Lord told Isaiah and not him? And why must he *ever* see Gomer again?

He traveled hard on the first leg of his journey, pressing the Bactrian camel from Uzziah's stable too hard. It went lame just north of Hazor. Hosea traded with a wily Aramean merchant, securing a fine young dromedary with one blind eye. The beast galloped for the next fifteen days over every kind of terrain, following the wide swath of death and destruction Assyria had left in its wake across the lands north of Israel. On the sixteenth night of his journey, Hosea slept on the outskirts of Aleppo, a small town just a morning's ride south of Arpad. He'd spent the chilly night among merchants who had supplied the soldiers during the yearlong siege. Now their coffers were full from the visiting troops of nations called to witness King Pul's final — and cruelest — forms of torture.

His camel lumbered north on the road to Arpad, and he searched the sea of soldiers for Israel's army standard. The smell of death assaulted him. He looked to the right and left, checking the soldiers' camps for burning bodies. Nothing. He turned in the sedan atop his camel, checking the wind's direction for the source of the acrid smell. When he reached the top of a rise, the beast stopped of its own accord. Its feet sank into the soil, softened by winter rains and fresh blood. Hosea followed the slope of the hill, looking toward the vanquished city.

"Elohim, no. Please no." The whispered prayer ascended, and he leaned over to empty his stomach. He'd never seen anything so gruesome.

Arpad lay nestled in a valley, the surrounding area crimson with its citizens' blood. Giant wooden stakes, as tall as the city wall, were planted around the perimeter like flowers in a garden. Impaled bodies, some still writhing, formed the grisly petals on each stem. How could any human do this to another?

Assyria's so-called mental warfare had become legendary. If a king foolishly refused to pay tribute and become Pul's vassal, Assyria marched on the city to overtake it. If the king dared close his city gates, King Pul instituted a siege. No water or food in or out, and Assyria maintained constant attacks on the gates and wall. The fiercest trained soldiers alive used the most advanced war machines on earth. Reports were consistent from Jerusalem to Aleppo. Assyria was unstoppable.

Arpad had lasted a year before their gates were breached. When Assyrian soldiers finally flooded the streets of the beleaguered city, starving people were tortured as Arpad's king and its officials helplessly observed. King Pul lingered in his grisly display day after day, saving the worst torture for the city's king and his officials. Hosea had learned during his overnight stay in Aleppo that the entertainment at tonight's feast would be the death of Arpad's king. The guest list was royalty — all the kings of Uzziah's failed coalition. King Pul would give a final, vivid display of his victory, leaving them quaking in their sandals, too frightened to ever refuse tribute as the king of Arpad had done.

"Are you here to deliver Israel's standard?" a soldier in Israelite armor demanded, grabbing the bridle of Hosea's camel.

"Excuse me?"

"You! I see by the weave of your robe and blanket that you're Hebrew. King Menahem has been waiting all day for the Israelite standard to display at tonight's banquet. Your head is on a platter if something's happened to it."

Hosea's heart was in his throat. Yahweh had just provided a guide to Menahem's camp. "No, I don't have the standard, but I bring a message to the king."

The soldier's eyes narrowed. "Sure you do. And I'm the king's twin brother."

He turned to walk away, but Hosea stopped him with an extended scroll. "Look! It bears the seal of King Uzziah from Judah. I'm telling you, I have a message. Now take me to Menahem."

A moment of decision flashed in the

soldier's eyes. "Give me your reins."

Hosea tossed him the camel's lead and prayed as the surly guard led him off the road and deep into one of the camps. The familiar scents of Israelite-spiced foods dulled the death scent. Soldiers lounged by campfires, and a few women scurried between tents. A stream rushed through the backside of the encampment, and Hosea thought he caught a glimpse of auburn hair bent over rocks on the shoreline.

Yahweh, is it Gomer? His heart thundered. *She is dead to me. Why do I care?* But he nearly fell from his sedan, twisting to see behind him as the guide rounded a tent corner and halted at a large, black goat's-hair tent. He'd never know who had been at the river.

"Get off the camel, but wait outside. I'll tell the general we've got a visitor, and he can decide what to do with you." The man disappeared inside the fine tent. Not as elegant as some but far above the sackcloth and sticks Menahem had used while pillaging Tiphsah.

Hosea tapped the camel's shoulder and swayed with the beast as it knelt. Heart pounding, he shuddered at the mention of the general — undoubtedly Eitan. *Yahweh, protect me.* His feet had just touched the ground when he heard the familiar growl of Israel's top soldier.

"I thought King Menahem made himself clear during your last visit to Samaria."

Hosea turned, standing nose to chest with the hulking general. He lifted his chin, finding Eitan smiling down at him.

"You're a dead man, Prophet."

"I would suggest you wait to kill me *after* I deliver Uzziah's message." He held up the sealed scroll.

Eitan snatched it from his hand. "The last scroll nearly got you killed. Why should I let you live to deliver this one?"

"Because part of the message isn't in the scroll." Hosea tapped his forehead. "It's in here."

Eitan raised one eyebrow and began walking. Hosea followed, assuming they were moving in Menahem's direction. "We've learned some exceptional torture strategies while here in Arpad, Prophet. Perhaps we can practice on you after your message has been delivered." The general chuckled, clearly amused at his own wit. Hosea swallowed the lump in his throat, thankful he'd already emptied his stomach.

They arrived at a second black tent, equal in size but with armed guards on each corner. Eitan swept aside the tent flap, exposing a darkened interior, the aroma of incense wafting out from within.

Hosea hesitated, two guards eyeing him like Sampson looked at rodents.

"Come!" a gruff voice shouted from within the tent.

Hosea entered the dark sanctum of the man who'd promised to kill him the next time they met. He took three steps inside, stopped, and bowed, allowing his eyes to adjust before proceeding farther. He lingered in the respectful bow, looking right and left. Eight men surrounded the king, all but one wearing armor. Hosea assumed he was a scribe since he held Uzziah's scroll unfurled.

"King Uzziah asks that I refuse to pay tribute and says I should reinstate the coalition." Menahem stared at him dangerously, then chuckled. And then he laughed, nearly bursting a neck vein, so unbridled was his folly. The others ventured nervous chuckles until the king's humor faded. "So, tell me, Prophet. Why would you risk your life to bring a message that is as ridiculous as the vomit on your beard?"

A little embarrassed at his appearance, Hosea wiped his chin. "I also bring a verbal message." He paused, the only acknowledgment a slow nod from the king. "A message from Yahweh."

"Tread carefully, Prophet," Menahem said. "You are still breathing because I remain in good humor."

Hosea moved a few steps closer, and General Eitan stepped between them, lifting one side of a dangerous smile and fingering his dagger. Hosea swallowed hard, praying as he spoke. "Yahweh says to you, King Menahem, 'The people of Israel went to Assyria. They were like wild donkeys wandering off alone. The people of Ephraim sold themselves to their lovers. Even though they sold themselves among the nations, I will gather them now. They will suffer for a while under the burdens of kings and princes.' " Hosea fell silent, holding his breath, waiting for the king's command — life or death.

"I don't understand." Menahem's voice was as unreadable as his expression. "Is Yahweh for us or against us?"

"You have foolishly aligned yourself with Assyria, but Yahweh has promised you a few more years of reprieve from destruction. They will be years of suffering under foreign kings and princes — but at least you still have a kingdom, King Menahem."

Hosea was certain the next words would be his death sentence. Instead, the king grinned. "I think your god is losing his grip on reality, because the other gods are smiling on us. Rains are coming in season, orchards and fields produce record crops. Our cisterns are full and our storehouses are overflowing. Peace with Assyria means increased trade with tributary nations and greater access to the coastal ports of Tyre, Sidon, and Byblos. Israel has never been stronger, Prophet."

Hosea drew a breath to repeat a separate prophecy Yahweh had given him earlier. He'd rehearsed it again and again, preparing for this moment. But a mighty wind swept through the black tent, snuffing out every torch except one. The guards drew their swords, and Eitan threw himself in front of Menahem — as if flesh and blood could stop the wind.

Hosea stood silently, allowing the Lord to speak for Himself.

The scribe sat poised with stylus hovered over his clay tablet, trembling. His wide eyes stared at the king for instruction. How does one record the breath of God?

"Speak, Prophet." Menahem's voice was a growl. "I am not a fool. I know when a god is real. But before you speak on His behalf, make sure you remind Him that *you* will feel Eitan's sword if His words displease me." The king's threat had little venom when he was shaking.

A new message swirled in Hosea's spirit. Similar but more personal for Israel's ruthless king. "This is Yahweh's final word to King Menahem of Israel: 'Yahweh's scorching wind will come from the east. It will blow out of the desert. Your springs and wells will dry up. The wind will destroy every precious thing in your storehouses. The people of Samaria are guilty as charged because you rebelled against your Elohim. You will be killed in war, your children smashed to death, your pregnant women ripped open —' "

"I will rip you open, Prophet!" Eitan advanced, dagger raised.

"Stop!" The single word from Menahem halted Israel's top soldier. "The prophet is offended at our siege tactics from Tiphsah. But he will complete this prophecy, and then *I* will decide his fate, General."

Eitan lowered his weapon and stepped back, seething.

Hosea expelled the breath he'd been holding and returned his attention to Menahem — keeping a watchful eye on the general who was hungry for his blood. "Yahweh has given you a final chance at repentance, King Menahem. Return to Yahweh and say,

'Forgive all our sins, and kindly receive us.' Confess that Assyria cannot save you. Agree not to ride on horses in battle. Never again say that the things your hands have made are your gods. Love orphans and the poor." Hosea's heart pounded more violently than when Eitan had charged him with the dagger. Yahweh's mercy had never been so bold. "Though you have repeatedly sinned against Him, insulted and maligned Him, Yahweh's love for Israel remains stronger than His anger. Choose Yahweh, King Menahem. Without Him, you face certain destruction. He is offering life — for you and your nation."

The silence stretched into eternity, the implications of God's mercy reeling in Hosea's mind. Could Israel be saved after generations of apostasy? Hadn't Yahweh declared them incurable? What if a single king — one faithful decision — led to the revival of a nation? Excitement coursed through his veins. Could even Gomer be saved?

"I will consider it." Menahem's words sent a wave of shock through the darkened tent.

"My lord?" Eitan's question was interrupted by the king's command.

"Have one of your guards escort the prophet to an empty tent. He'll spend the night in camp, and I'll make my decision in the morning after I've had time to think."

Hosea noted a silent exchange between the king and his general before Eitan obeyed, giving orders to the escort.

When Hosea bowed to exit, Menahem warned, "Make sure you remain in your tent this evening. The general and I will be in the valley, attending King Pul's feast near the city. We can't guarantee your safety if you go wandering around camp."

His stomach clenched at the realization. Wouldn't Menahem offer his tribute tonight at the feast? He studied the near glee on Menahem's face. *You have no intention of repenting or setting me free.* Whatever the king had planned, it did not bode well for Hosea — or Judah.

"I have no desire to wander," Hosea said. "I go wherever Yahweh directs me." He bowed to the king and then followed two guards — to who knew where.

40

HOSEA 9:7–8

They think that prophets are fools and that spiritual people are crazy. . . . And they are very hostile. Prophets are Elohim's watchmen over Ephraim. Yet, traps are set on every prophet's path.

"Remember," Eitan said as he sharpened his dagger, "you are to remain in this tent all night. The other harlots will transport food for the banquet, and the guard assigned to the prophet will address his needs." When Gomer remained silent, he halted his dagger on the long leather strap and issued a dangerous stare. "Do you understand?"

"I understand." Everything within her wanted to run to the prophet's tent. Was it Hosea? Eitan had returned from Menahem's tent in good humor, boasting about a

Yahweh prophet on whom they'd practice Pul's torture tactics after tonight's banquet.

"I want all my armor polished by the time I return." He stood over her, threatening with his nearness. Israel's general was as meticulous in his appearance as he was lethal in battle.

Her hands trembled, sloshing some precious oil into the dust while trying to rub it into the leather breastplate. "Don't I always polish your armor perfectly?" He grabbed her arm, kissed her roughly, and stormed out of the tent.

She spit the taste of him from her lips and peered out of the tent, careful not to be seen if he should look over his shoulder. Other officers joined Eitan in their dress armor, primped and polished, whistling an eerie Assyrian tune used during ritual sacrifices and torture ceremonies. Though Eitan had made Gomer attend one ghastly event, her weak stomach proved more than her master cared to endure. Even from a distance, she heard the trilling of the *chalil* mingled with the shrieks and groans of dying men, women, and children. The tune would forever haunt her.

A shiver worked its way through Gomer's body as she watched the line of harlots follow Israel's elite soldiers out of camp. Each woman carried food in baskets on her head and over both arms. Two women transported a char-broiled antelope, suspended on double poles resting on their shoulders. Assyria's king had magnanimously invited the visiting kings and their officers to tonight's feast, making it clear that their gifts of gold and silver should be accompanied by enough food for the meal. Pul would provide the ghastly entertainment.

She stepped away from the tent flap, tugging her woolen robe around her neck and reaching for a blanket. Winter's chill was in the air, but it was more than Arpad's cold that sent a shiver down her spine. "What if it *is* Hosea in that tent, waiting to die?"

Her whisper was met with the familiar dark silence. She wrapped herself in the blanket and considered the single torch in the dark tent. Such a tiny light. Such consuming darkness. She stared at the flame and then closed her eyes. *I still see it.* The imprint of the flame still cast its glow on her mind's eye. A slow, satisfied smile creased her lips, splitting a wound from yesterday's beating. In that moment she knew two things: Hosea was the prophet Eitan had mentioned, and she must try to help him. "If I warn Hosea and he escapes, perhaps I will have left a little light in the world — even after Eitan kills me." And she knew without a doubt her master *would* kill her.

Her decision made, she pawed through Eitan's pile of weapons and found a dagger much like the one she'd carried while she prostituted herself in Jerusalem — lightweight with an iron blade and bone handle. She found a suitable sheath and strapped it above her right knee. She gathered a few food items on a tray to make her ploy believable but hid a travel bag under her robe. Then she charged out of the tent, in a hurry and on a mission, appearing as authoritative as possible in harlots' garb.

She walked along the first row of tents, trying to spy a guarded shelter. Her perusal of the second row of tents revealed nothing but slovenly soldiers lounging by their fires. She marched past, turning down the next row.

"You there. Stop!"

Her heart raced as her feet froze.

A soldier approached from behind, grabbing her shoulder and whirling her around to face him. "Aren't you General Eitan's woman? Why aren't you with the rest of the harlots at the feast?"

She painted on a smile and reached up to trace the line of his beard around his lips.

"Which question would you like me to answer first?"

He stared at her, dumbfounded.

Giggling, she teased him further. "I'm Eitan's woman, but he shares me with his officers. How long before you become an officer, hmm?"

"I, um . . . well, I . . ."

"Eitan instructed me to feed the prophet under guard," she said, "but in his haste to leave for King Pul's feast, he neglected to tell me in which tent the prophet was staying. Can you escort me to the prophet's tent?" A demure tilt of the head, a few coy blinks, and the soldier was potter's clay in Gomer's hands.

"Of course. Follow me."

He led her a few tents south and then stopped beside an unremarkable shelter guarded by a single soldier. Her escort whispered something to the man, who then stood aside without hesitation. "Go right in. He's been praying aloud to his god since he arrived. It's very annoying."

You're telling me? A deep breath, and Gomer straightened her robe. She looked at her dirty fingernails and calloused hands, wondering what Hosea would think when he saw her. *It doesn't matter what he thinks. All that matters is that he lives.* The realization bolstered her courage, and she stepped inside the tent.

"Yahweh Adonay, I will follow You into life and into death. I will worship You in want and in plenty. I will —" Hosea smelled her perfume before he opened his eyes and saw her. "Gomer." Her name escaped on a whisper, his throat tightening against any further utterance. He stood to meet the wife he'd exiled, remembering Isaiah's prediction.

She, too, seemed silenced by their past. Her chin trembled, her lips pressed into a thin, pale line. She was bony and bruised, had cuts on her lip and above her cheekbone. Her hair was uncovered, the lustrous copper curls dulled by dust and tangles.

Righteous fury rose within him. "Who has done this —"

She lowered her voice. "Please, Hosea. There's no time. Eitan said he and Menahem were keeping you here overnight in order to torture you after tonight's banquet. You must escape now." She knelt, removed the travel bag from her robe, and wrapped the food on the tray for his journey.

"Wait," he said, grasping her shoulder, kneeling beside her. She was trembling. "Eitan? You've gone back to Eitan?" Anger warred with pity. How could she choose to endure such abuse?

Their eyes met. He saw momentary fury, but the spark was doused with immediate despair. "I did not go back to him, Hosea. A troop of soldiers found me in the wilderness, and the gods have continued their sick games with my life." She wiped an errant tear and glanced over her shoulder, whispering, "Now take this food and ride as fast and far as you can. I don't think Eitan will break camp to pursue you, but he might send a small detachment. Stay off the trade routes and get back to Judah." She brushed stray curls from his forehead. "Don't ever come near Menahem or Eitan again, Hosea. They will kill you."

He held her gaze — and for the first time in years, she didn't turn away. The golden flecks were swallowed up by weary brown, but compassion seemed to have replaced the bitterness. "I'm Yahweh's prophet, a watchman over Israel and ready to die for the Lord if I must." He touched her cheek, but she startled like a frightened colt. "But why are you risking your life to save me, Gomer? Eitan will kill you if he finds out you've helped me."

She laughed mirthlessly and stood, holding out the travel bag. "I'm already dead to you. Remember?"

Hosea stood and took the bag, his cheeks warming. "Yes. I remember."

"Well, I was dead inside long before you and your god declared it. Tonight, when I realized Eitan planned to kill you, I thought by helping you live, my death will have at least meant something."

The words pierced Hosea's soul. "So if I escape, Eitan will *know* it was you who helped me? Why didn't you bribe the guards or sneak in here unnoticed?"

A slow, sad grin spread across her face. "I have nothing to bribe the guards with, Hosea, and I've never been good at going unnoticed."

"I can't leave you here," he whispered. "I won't."

"What do you mean, you won't? You must leave!"

Hosea clamped one hand over her mouth and the other behind her head, drawing her close. "Shh, the guards will hear you." The travel bag fell to the ground, and she melted against his chest. Hosea cradled her and felt her silent tears soak through his robe. What had they done to his wife that could make her choose sacrifice over survival? *Yahweh, what am I to do now?*

Gomer pushed him away and wiped her

face with her sleeve, creating great smudges of dirt from cheek to chin. "I can't go with you, Hosea. I'm a harlot. Even your god said I'd always be a harlot."

He wanted to argue, wanted nothing more than to take her back to Judah and love her. *Please, Yahweh. Is she truly incurable?*

The torchlight danced with a gentle chill wind. Gomer stood still as a statue. Hosea closed his eyes, drinking in the familiar voice in his spirit: *I will cure them of their unfaithfulness. I will love them freely. I will no longer be angry with them.*

Hosea gasped and buried his face in his hands, relief washing over him. *Thank You, my Lord, Adonay Elohim.*

Yahweh's breeze swept from the tent, swirling Gomer's robe around her legs, causing her to whimper. "What now? Will your god kill me before Eitan has a chance?"

Hosea gathered her into his arms. "No. No. I'm not sure what Eitan will do, but you will live. Yahweh has promised it."

She pulled away from him, renewed wariness on her expression. "Don't be a fool, Hosea. I've disobeyed Eitan, and the guard outside is a witness against me. I won't live to see the dawn."

The weight of her sacrifice crushed him again, but a gentle reminder warmed his heart. *You will see her in Arpad.* He grinned at Isaiah's prophetic good-bye in spite of the danger.

"How can you smile at a time like this?"

"Because I'm trying to imagine how I'll confess to Isaiah he was right and I was wrong." Her brow furrowed in the confusion he'd hoped for. "Yahweh told Isaiah you'd be here, but I said Yahweh wouldn't concern Himself with our marriage when Assyria threatened the whole world." He reached for her hand and cradled it palm up. "Yahweh knew you'd be here, Gomer. Though I'm not always with you, He is." Then he strummed her fingers like he'd done when they were children.

She bowed her head, hair cascading like a copper veil, hiding her face. After a few sniffs, she wiped a dirty sleeve across her eyes and nose. She grabbed the travel bag and held it out to him as if he hadn't spoken at all. "I'll distract the guards while you walk your camel out of camp. If you look like you know what you're doing, no one will take notice. The moment you reach the road, get on the beast and go as fast as it'll carry you."

Hosea looked down once more into those hazel eyes he'd once known and loved. "Thank you, Gomer. I —"

549

"Come on. You're wasting time." She turned and fled the tent, leaving Hosea with a lump in his throat and a hole in his heart.

41

HOSEA 10:11–12

Ephraim is like a trained calf that loves to thresh grain. I will put a yoke on its beautiful neck. . . . Jacob must break up . . . new ground. Plant righteousness, and harvest the fruit that your loyalty will produce for me.

Gomer lay on her tapestry in Eitan's tent, waiting for the general's return. She'd wet the fleece headrest with her tears, hoping — even praying to every god but one — that Hosea made it out of camp without being spotted. She'd leave it to Hosea to pray to Yahweh, since that particular god seemed especially cross with harlots in general and with her in particular.

How could Hosea say Yahweh was with her when every day held new torture? What kind of god allowed this kind of pain? *What*

*kind of woman rebels this brazenly and sur-
vives?* She pushed the troublesome
thoughts aside.

"What do you mean he's not in his tent?"
Eitan's raised voice split the night air. "How
can a prophet and his camel disappear from
an Israelite camp? Bring me his guard!" The
tent flap flew open, the force of his fury rattling the structure. Gomer sat up, watching
him light the torch on the post. "Pour me
some wine!"

She scurried from her tapestry to obey his
command, hands trembling as she reached
for the wineskin on the peg. She poured the
wine, missing the wooden goblet, but Eitan
was pacing and didn't notice. *Thank the
gods.* "Your wine, my lord." She held out
the goblet with a shaky hand.

The terrified guard entered, escorted by
two officers, and immediately fell to his
knees. "I am your faithful warrior, General.
I obeyed your order to escort the harlot
back to your tent, and when I returned, the
prophet and his camel were gone."

Gomer exhaled the breath she'd been
holding. *Well, at least it was quick. Perhaps
the execution will be as merciful.*

Eitan turned his dangerous smile on her
but spoke to the guard. "So, my harlot lured
you from your post so the prophet could

escape?"

"No . . . um, well, I didn't think . . . um . . ." Gomer noted the guard's sinking expression.

"Ha!" Eitan clapped his hands in a mighty slap, causing everyone to jump. "It seems my harlot has outsmarted you." He waved at his officers. "Kill him." They dragged the guard out, screaming. Eitan focused on Gomer, a glint of wicked delight in his eyes. "Why would you risk your life for a Yahweh prophet from Judah?"

He was still smiling. Perhaps she would earn only a beating if she played the sassy harlot. "I'd rather not explain."

His smile died, and she knew she'd miscalculated. He covered the space between them in two strides and grabbed her hair, laying his dagger against her throat. "Satisfy my curiosity."

"He's my husband." She felt a trickle of warm blood run down her neck and marveled at the sharpness of his blade. Perhaps death would come quickly.

Eitan released her and let his hands fall limp at his sides. He stared blankly. "Your husband?"

She watched a war rage in the windows of his soul. Why had those words disturbed him so? "Yes, I was running away from him when one of your officers found me in the wilderness on their way to Arpad."

"Ahhhh!" Eitan hurled his dagger at the center post, and Gomer felt a simultaneous blow to her cheek. A burst of light exploded, and stars decorated the tent's interior. "No! You cannot be joined to the prophet!"

He reached for her, and she tried to crawl away. "Why? Tell me why you're so angry!"

He grabbed her arms, lifting her feet off the floor, and ground out the words in her face. "Menahem has forbidden me to lay a hand on the prophet or anything that belongs to him. I was ordered to release him in the morning and let him ride out on his cursed camel unharmed. Now I can't even kill you because if the king discovers you're the prophet's wife, it will be my head on a platter." He threw her against a corner post. She felt a rib break but dared not scream. He'd turned to go, and she didn't want to give him reason to return.

She melted into a heap, unsure what to feel. Relief? Fear? Victory?

"You will leave in the morning." Startled, she looked up to find Eitan watching her from the tent opening, a sinister grin making his anger all the more frightening. "I'll obey my king, and you'll wish I had killed you."

■ ■ ■ ■

Samaria's ivory palace taunted her in the distance. The last time Gomer had seen the gleaming limestone structure, she'd glimpsed its ivory and ebony furnishings. Granted, she'd been on trial before King Jeroboam, but even that seemed preferable to the shackles now chewing her ankles and wrists.

Eitan was right. Killing her would have been more merciful than the forty-two-day trek she'd endured during the dead of winter with the Aramean slave trader. The slaves wore leather covers over their sandals to protect their feet from ice and snow, but they wore only woolen robes as protection against the icy winter winds. Gomer remembered the glaring heat of her Judean wilderness wandering and decided that numbing cold was worse than blinding sun. By the time they crossed into Israelite territory, the climate had grown milder, and their feet had worn through the leather.

"New slaves, prime flesh coming through." The vile little Aramean cleared a wide path leading up Samaria's hill. He'd stopped north of Shechem to strip the ten remaining slaves of their woolen robes, forcing both men and women into the frigid spring water. It was both refreshing and excruciating on their raw wounds. They would enter the city naked but clean. "Keep moving," he shouted, using his whip on one of the men he especially despised.

The journey from Arpad began with twenty slaves — twelve women, eight men. Seven men remained, three women. When someone slowed the pace, the trader severed that slave's hand and foot, leaving them behind to die. The remaining slaves were left to drag the empty shackle — sufficient motivation to keep their legs churning on slippery terrain.

Gomer mustered her strength and lifted her head, approaching Samaria's gates. She was shivering and wondered if it was because of her empty stomach or the light drizzle. She'd eaten only scraps after the trader and his three underlings ate their fill. Her curiosity stole her full attention, causing her to gawk like a visiting farm girl at Samaria's city gate. It looked as worn as she felt, its fine metals tarnished and exposed wood rotting. She looked east, hoping to glimpse Asherah's grove, her onetime haven. But the path was overgrown and unkempt. The boughs of the lush poplars and terebinths now dipped as low as Gomer's spirits.

Merchants' gossip was rife with tales of the oppressive tribute Assyria demanded from "cooperative" nations. She'd been confused at the difference between a vassal and a cooperative nation. Now she understood. Only the words were different. The effects were the same – written in Samaria's decay.

The chain of slaves entered the city, and Gomer glanced down the hill, longing to pound the gates of her old brothel. Tamir's wicked face flashed in her memory, and the fleeting desire was replaced with disgust. How pathetic her life had become when even her old madam would be a welcome sight.

"Stay together, or I'll cut off whoever's lagging." The hateful little Aramean snapped his whip again, and Gomer squeezed close to the man in front of her. Whatever modesty she'd preserved before this experience — which wasn't much — had been lost somewhere between Arpad and Samaria. Onlookers taunted them as they passed. Some threw rocks and sticks. Others shouted obscenities. Gomer wished they'd throw food, though she doubted she could catch it with her wrists shackled and bloody.

The chain of captives trudged up a narrow alley, and Gomer's panic began to rise.

Where was the trader leading them? The tombs were the only thing north of the city. She knew there was a slave market in Samaria but had never seen it.

Then she smelled it, and it smelled like her.

Filth. Excrement. Slaves. She heard the moaning of tortured souls and knew why they'd placed the market beside the tombs. *Why go on living when life is living death?*

"Form a line so the slave master can inspect you." The Aramean snapped his whip again, and Gomer jumped, lining up shoulder to shoulder with men on both sides. "Look at this one," he said to the slave master. "She's a mess now, but she was General Eitan's personal harlot."

Gomer willed herself to stop trembling and focused on a nondescript cloud in the sky, allowing the man to inspect her from head to toe. "She was once beautiful, I'm sure, but she's been ridden hard like an old mare. The men who buy my slaves are looking for the sleekest, finest fillies in the kingdom."

Gomer emptied herself of all that was human, becoming the thing men desire. She lifted her hand to his cheek, taking with it the shackled hand of the slave beside her. "Do you have any idea what a woman of

558

pleasure learns from so many teachers?" She nestled her face in his sweaty neck, whispering, "Give me the chance to prove myself to a customer. I will not disappoint him — or you." She gagged on the words and for the first time was thankful her stomach was empty. She stepped back into line, noted the glazed look in the slave master's eyes, and knew he'd be her advocate.

"Loose her shackles. I'll redeem her." A stately older gentleman stepped out of the shadows. He offered slow, steady applause. "That was an impressive performance."

She inclined her head, a regal bow.

"I can see why Eitan favored you."

"He didn't favor me. I was his alone." She lifted an eyebrow. "Do you know the general personally?"

The slave master dislodged the pins from her wrist shackles and removed them. The relief was overwhelming. She closed her eyes and blew cool breath on the raw, chafed flesh, lingering in the momentary respite.

Her eyes shot open, and her panic returned. A potential employer stood waiting. Had her delay angered him?

He was staring, an unknown emotion fueling a pleasant smile. "I've met General Eitan and King Menahem. I know them well enough to stay out of their way and keep my treasury locked."

Gomer felt her ankle shackles fall to the ground, and she nearly fell with them. Free. She'd never fathomed the richness of the word until this moment. She returned her gaze to the intriguing nobleman, also realizing she would never be free again. She bowed deeply. "How may I serve you, my lord?"

The man counted five pieces of silver into the slave master's hand and then hoisted her into his arms. "First, I will serve you."

Embarrassed more by her weakness than her nakedness, she pushed resistant hands against his chest. "Please, my lord, I can walk."

He stopped, and she leaned forward, thinking he would set her feet on the ground. Instead, he crushed her to his chest. "Stop struggling." His voice was firm but not angry. She froze, ceasing all movement, afraid he would take her back to the market. But he resumed his stride and repeated more gently, "You can stop struggling now."

The kindness of his tone pierced her, and she fought emotions she thought long dead. She laid her head against his chest, deciding to obey his command, hiding her tears.

He slowed when they reached an ornate wooden cart. Four wheels, almost as tall as

Gomer, bore hammered gold on their spokes. A stack of tapestries lined the cart bed, and when he hoisted her onto them, she sank into the softness as though it were a cloud. "Let's cover you up," he said, unfurling a heavy blanket over her. "You must be freezing, and we need not parade you again —"

"No, wait!" As the fine weave floated onto her travel-worn, bloody body, she thought of the beautiful things she was soiling. "I'm unclean." King Uzziah's familiar word rang in her memory. *Unclean! Unclean!* A knot of emotion choked off any further argument.

The man leaned over the cart rail, kissed his finger, and transferred it to her forehead. "Everything in this wagon can be washed clean, little one. Including you."

He unwound the reins from a hitching post, adeptly stepped on a spoke, and then swung onto the driver's bench. Gomer marveled at the older man's strength and agility. She guessed him the same age as Amos and Yuval — in fact, his features and demeanor reminded her of Yuval. She relaxed into the tapestries, resting her arm over her eyes. *Will I see a resemblance to Yuval in everyone who treats me kindly?*

Her new master slapped the reins, prodding the single ox that was yoked to his cart.

He leaned back and explained, "Most people think me a bit unconventional, using an ox to pull my cart in the city, but Samaria's hills tire a donkey or mule. I'm a merchant, and Sampson here helps me transport my goods with steadier footing on muddy streets."

Sampson. The name of Gomer's cat in Tekoa. Anger replaced her weepy disposition. If the gods were playing tricks, she refused to be their game piece. No more sentimental journeys about Uzziah or Yuval or a stupid cat. "Excuse me, my lord, but would you mind giving me your name?" Exhaustion tore at her, but she might as well begin her work now. But if he said his name was Hosea, she would throw herself beneath the ox's hooves.

He turned on his seat, a glowing smile revealing brilliant white teeth. He was quite handsome for an older man. "I am Ezri, little one. Forgive me for not introducing myself sooner." He seemed pleased that she'd initiated. "And what is your name?"

"Gomer. My name is Gomer. It means *complete*." She was suddenly thankful for the Israelite officer who'd found her in the wilderness and his trivial knowledge of names.

"Complete," he said, returning his attention to the road ahead. "Well, Gomer, I believe it suits the plans I have for you. My wife died three moon cycles ago, and I keep a few servants in my home. I think you'll make my household complete."

Gomer pondered the revelation, realizing that Ezri would have been one of the wealthy merchants in Samaria while she lived in Tamir's brothel. Had he been one of her customers whom she'd failed to recognize? "My lord, I used to live in Samaria — in a house owned by Tamir. Are you familiar with her business?"

She heard him sigh. "I know of Tamir's brothel. In fact, the woman who owned the brothel before Tamir was a family friend of mine. But I never required a harlot's service. I remained loyal to my wife for the thirty-two years we were married." He cast a grin over his shoulder. "I'm sure you and I have never met."

She noticed a slight dimple in his right cheek, above his manicured, gray beard. "But you realize who I am — *what* I am?"

"As I said before, most people think me unconventional, Gomer. I yoke an ox to my cart in the city, and I purchase a young harlot to be my companion in my old age." He shrugged his shoulder and chuckled. "I

guess we're both plowing new ground,
aren't we?"

42

ISAIAH 6:1

In the year King Uzziah died, I saw Adonay sitting on a high and lofty throne. The bottom of his robe filled the temple.

King Uzziah's burial processional stretched from Jerusalem's southernmost gate through the valley of Hinnom and up the hill toward En Rogel. It seemed all of Judah had gathered to mourn their leprous king.

Hosea noticed Isaiah swipe at both eyes, and his heart broke. Uzziah's death had hit his friend hard, the king's role as second abba felt all the more keenly with the loss.

"Was your abba Amoz able to speak with Uzziah before the end?" Hosea's voice was hushed.

Isaiah had chosen to walk among the prophets rather than join the royal household at the head of the processional. Honoring Amoz's wishes, Isaiah and Uzziah agreed to keep silent about his idolatry under the condition that his worship cease. Many of the younger prophets had no reason to notice the strained familial relationship.

"Abba visited Uzziah the day before his death, but I wasn't invited. They spoke privately. When he returned home, his countenance was brighter, so I assume he and cousin Uzziah made their peace." Isaiah glanced at Hosea, smiling through tears. "I believe Aya has softened Abba's heart in many ways while he's lived in our home." They trudged in silence through the muck of Hinnom, the acrid smoke of lingering fires irritating already weepy eyes. "Yesterday, when I emptied our waste containers on the dump pile, I saw broken pieces of an idol, Hosea. I believe it was Abba's Asherah." His features were a mix of joy and fear. "What if he's made all this progress, opened his heart — and then my prophecy today turns Abba away again? I don't know how I could go on, knowing I'd embittered him at the moment he started to believe . . ."

Hosea halted Isaiah with a hand on his shoulder, allowing other prophets to pass them on the march toward the burial field. "Are you sure of your call, Isaiah? Did you hear Yahweh's voice?"

"You know I did."

"Do you believe the Lord called you to speak His message here, today, at King Uzziah's burial?"

Isaiah glanced toward the front of the processional, where King Jotham rode his white donkey and the royal household followed at a respectful distance, Amoz and Aya among them. Hosea and Isaiah would join them for the ceremony, at Jotham's request, but Isaiah's features seemed a battlefield of warring emotions. Finally, resolve took control. "Yahweh's temple remains in ruins. My cousin Jotham has made no attempt to steer the people back to Yahweh's presence. We're standing in the cursed valley of Hinnom, where pagan sacrifices still burn, and the men mourning Uzziah will soon pass by the high place at En Rogel. In what better place, and to what better audience, could I declare Yahweh's message?" Shoulders square, chin raised, Isaiah said, "Yes. Today is the day I am to speak for Yahweh, my friend. I must trust Him to continue His work in Abba's heart."

Hosea laid his arm around Isaiah's shoulders, and the two men resumed their steady gait. "Since Uzziah was denied burial in the royal tombs, maybe Jotham will feel comforted that Yahweh spoke through a prophet at his abba's grave."

"We can hope for that," Isaiah said with a dubious tone and lifted brow.

When the processional began congregating in the field owned by David's descendants, Isaiah leaned close to Hosea. "I'm terrified. I'd rather hide here with the prophets or stand unnoticed near Abba and Aya — mourning Uzziah with the rest of Judah." Hosea drew a breath to encourage him, but Isaiah's determination spoke first. "But I *will* be obedient, my friend. The fire inside me won't be quenched until I speak Yahweh's message."

Hosea patted his shoulder, following Isaiah through the crowd to take their place among the royal household, as Jotham had requested. "Trust Yahweh to lead you," Hosea whispered as they trudged through the knee-high grass.

Will you be obedient, Hosea? Do you trust Me to lead you? The voice was a mere whisper in his spirit, no cool breeze, no fire in his body.

Perhaps he'd imagined it. He continued following Isaiah, hurrying toward the front of the processional.

But before they reached the royal party, Hosea again heard the gentle sound of Yahweh's call: *Show your love to her again.*

568

"What?" He stopped midstride, and Isaiah turned around, looking puzzled.

"Are you all right?" he shouted from a few paces ahead.

"I'll be fine. Go ahead." Isaiah resumed his frenzied pace, but Hosea slowed to a determined march. "What do You mean, 'Show your love to her'?" he whispered.

Buy her back. The voice spoke on a gentle breeze this time.

Fear. Anger. Anticipation. Frustration. He felt them all as he hurried to catch up. It had been almost four years since Gomer had helped him escape from Arpad. He'd rebuilt his life in Tekoa. The children were well adjusted and content, spending their days with Aya and Yuval, their evenings at home with him. How could Yahweh ask him to disrupt *their* lives again? Ammi wouldn't even remember the ima who had abandoned him. *Why bring her back now, Yahweh?*

No answer.

He kept walking in a haze of disillusion, murmuring the reasons he'd surely misunderstood Yahweh's call. Finally, he arrived at the burial site, a projection of rocks in which a natural cave would be sealed with a large boulder. Hosea took his place between Isaiah and his abba Amoz.

Ready to begin his benediction, the high

priest raised the sacred Nehushtan, the bronze snake Moses had crafted in the wilderness to heal those bitten by vipers. But instead of the droning voice of the old priest, Isaiah's resonant tone carried on the breeze. "King Jotham, you know that I loved your abba deeply, and that my love for Judah flows from David's royal blood — the same as yours."

Jotham's single nod gave tentative permission to continue.

"I've been given a message from Yahweh for Judah. May I speak?" He bowed humbly, awaiting his cousin's approval.

"Abba, no!" Prince Ahaz shouted, wagging his knobby arm. "Tell him no, Abba. He shouldn't be allowed to speak at my saba's burial." The boy, very near Jezreel's age, already displayed the arrogant entitlement of royalty.

"Ahaz." Jotham placed a quieting hand on his son's shoulder, returning his attention to Isaiah. "I'm always willing to hear Yahweh's message. Speak, Isaiah."

Hosea watched a silent exchange between Jotham and Isaiah before the first-time prophet closed his eyes and opened his mouth. "I saw Adonay sitting on a high and lofty throne. The bottom of His robe filled His temple. Angels were standing above

Him. Each had six wings. With two they covered their faces, with two they covered their feet, and with two they flew. They called to each other and said, 'Holy, holy, holy is Yahweh Tsebaoth! The whole earth is filled with His glory.' Their voices shook the foundation of the doorposts, and the temple filled with smoke."

"Isaiah," King Jotham interrupted, "did the temple in your vision appear to be the same as Yahweh's temple here in Jerusalem?"

"Yes, my lord — except it was well maintained and gleaming with heavenly light."

The king furrowed his brow, clearly displeased at the reminder of the temple's neglect. "Proceed."

"So I said, 'Oh no! I'm doomed. Every word that passes through my lips is sinful. I live among people with sinful lips. I have seen Yahweh Tsebaoth!'

"Then one of the angels flew to me. In his hand was a burning coal that he had taken from the altar with tongs. He touched my mouth with it and said, 'This has touched your lips. Your guilt has been taken away, and your sin has been forgiven.'

"Then I heard the voice of Adonay, saying, 'Whom will I send? Who will go for us?'

"I said, 'Here I am. Send me!' "

The gathering had fallen silent, caught up in the heavenly scene of Isaiah's vision. Hosea, too, imagined himself in the very throne room of God, cleansed by holy fire, offering himself anew. What an incredible rendering of God's power and mercy working in concert. Yahweh's majesty — so infinite that only the bottom of His robe fit inside the once-grand temple in their golden city. Yet the purpose of His holy fire was always to cleanse, not to destroy.

Hosea fell to his knees, burying his face in his hands. *Send me! Yahweh, send me! I will show my love to Gomer and buy her back. I will obey You, though I am a man of unclean lips among a people of unclean lips. Cleanse us, Adonay, and send me.*

King Jotham's voice interrupted Hosea's holy moment. "Can you interpret your vision for us, Isaiah? Tell us what you believe Yahweh intends me to do with such a vague vision."

Hosea lifted his face from behind trembling hands, dumbstruck. *Vague vision?* He expected to see disappointment on Isaiah's face — the same disillusionment he was feeling. Instead, a confident glow lit his friend's expression.

"Yahweh said to me, 'Go and tell these people: No matter how closely you listen, you'll never understand. No matter how closely you look, you'll never see.' King Jotham, you have been warned repeatedly to destroy the high places and return to Yahweh's temple to worship. Until you become obedient to your current revelation, no further understanding will be given."

And with those words still heavy on Hosea's heart, Isaiah held out his hand to Aya, who willingly joined him. "Let's go home," he said.

"Wait!" Amoz stood like a deer caught in a hunter's bow sight, looking first at Jotham and then at Isaiah. The battle of his heart raged on his features. "Your abba was a good man," he said to the young king. "Yahweh's power didn't destroy him. The suffering made him stronger in the end."

Still seeming to struggle with words left unspoken, Amoz's eyes rested on Aya. His features softened, the battle won. "I've wasted years being angry and frightened." He returned his attention to Jotham and added, "Don't make my mistakes. Don't let your sins hurt your son."

Jotham made no reply, simply watched as the prophets followed Isaiah and his family away from the burial site. The gathered crowd remained silent. Hosea heard only the sound of Amoz's weeping — and Isaiah's comforting whisper as he walked arm in arm with his abba.

Hosea sat at Amos's bedside, staring into the stormy features of his friend and teacher. The patriarch prophet had been bedfast for years, but he was no less headstrong than when he tended flocks. "You will not bring that harlot back into this camp!"

"Will you defy Yahweh's command and force me to live as a liar before my students?" Hosea matched his tone. "I teach my classes that they must obey whatever the Lord speaks to them — whenever, wherever, and to whomever they're called to prophesy."

"But what about your children?" Yuval's whisper assaulted him from behind, and he turned to find her waiting with a cup of watered wine. "They're finally settled, and what if something happens to you when you try to find Gomer? They've already lost one parent."

He declined the drink, wishing he could take both the cup and the sadness from her. She set the wine aside and knelt at her husband's shoulder, stroking his brow.

"I'd rather be bitten by a viper than bring Gomer back into the children's lives — or mine — but I must obey Yahweh's command. The Lord said to buy her back and show her my love again." He squeezed Amos's hand and released a frustrated sigh. "But first I must find her. Yahweh has been silent since we returned from Uzziah's burial. I have no idea where to look."

Hosea glimpsed the silent exchange between his friends. Yuval began picking at a seam, and Amos folded and smoothed his blankets — repeatedly. The silence screamed conspiracy.

"What are you two hiding?"

Yuval raised one eyebrow, insisting Amos bear the explanation. "Gomer is in Samaria," the old prophet whispered. "The Lord woke me last night and told me."

"And you're just now mentioning it?" Hosea shouted, standing so quickly his stool toppled over.

"Sit down, young man!" Yuval's eyes flashed, and she pointed at the errant stool.

Duly chastised, Hosea took a deep breath and regained his calm. "What else did the Lord say?" he asked, settling onto the stool beside his teacher and facing Yuval.

Amos's expression resembled a child's pout. Glancing here and there, he seemed perturbed at the forced confession. "Yahweh said nothing else, but I remain in contact with Judean spies, and they tell me that Samaria is a boiling pot ready to spill out destruction."

"I know the danger, but at least I no longer have to fear the two men trying to kill me." Hosea had felt a measure of relief when he'd heard of Menahem's death, but when his son King Pekahiah replaced Eitan with a new commander named Pekah, Israel churned in turmoil.

Amos's eyes misted, his jaw flexed. "The danger reaches beyond personal matters, my son. Jotham is sending Judean spies to stir the pot, supporting a coup in Ephraim while Menahem's son is still vulnerable in Samaria."

Hosea paused, considering the complication of imminent war within Israel. "I hadn't heard that."

"You must travel through the wilderness and stay at the safe house in Shiloh," Amos said, finally seemingly resigned to Hosea's decision. "As far as we know, it remains a haven for Judean spies."

"But you won't know it's not safe until it's not safe!" Yuval's argument was more emotion than reason, but her tears held more sway than a thousand facts.

"If Yahweh revealed that Gomer is in Samaria" — Hosea reached for Yuval's hand, cradling the weathered, wrinkled treasure

— "don't you suppose He'll protect me on this journey?"

He watched thoughts form behind her eyes. Fear turned to questions, and her questions birthed something new. "I'm going with you!" she gasped, seemingly as surprised as the men.

"Oh, Yuval." Hosea readied his immediate objection. "I don't think —"

"Absolutely not! I forbid it!" Amos's shout instigated a coughing spell. "You'll stay . . . right there . . . on that rug," he said, pointing to the curly goatskin beside him.

Yuval waited for Amos's coughing to still, and Hosea watched quietly, his cheeks flushed with holy fire. He sensed Yahweh calling Yuval to accompany him, but he dared not interfere in matters of husband and wife.

As Amos's cough abated, his brow remained furrowed, and Yuval kissed the furrow away. Rather than address her husband, however, she turned to Hosea. "Have you considered Gomer's reaction to your arrival? From your report at Arpad, she's determined to remain a harlot. Though Yahweh commanded you to show *your* love and buy her back, He didn't say she'd gladly return to Tekoa with you." Her cloudy eyes bore through his soul, and confusion settled like a rock in his stomach.

"But Yahweh promised at Arpad that He would 'cure them of their unfaithfulness.' " Hosea wondered if he'd mistaken both Yahweh's and Yuval's messages. "I thought you wanted to come with me."

"I want you to think as Gomer might think — consider Yahweh as one who doesn't know and believe His words." She squeezed Hosea's hand and spoke the hard truth. "The Lord said Israel was an incurable harlot and that he'd given up on Gomer. But now He tells you to buy her back. Gomer might see these as inconsistencies and capricious ranting from a distant god, but we know Yahweh to be true and faultless in His ways." She hesitated, searching the windows of his soul. "So what's the answer, Hosea? How can Yahweh say He's given up on a woman He commands you to buy back?"

His throat was too tight to speak. He had no answer. Yahweh had always been his unwavering Rock, his constant in life's storms. When Hosea questioned the Lord, it was from a position of belief, not opposition. And why hadn't he considered the possibility of another rejection from Gomer? Yahweh's calling had been so clear, so adamant. Was he naive or ignorant, or both?

Suddenly yearning to know Yuval's thoughts, he patted her hand. "What was it you once told me? Women hear more because their mouths are closed when men speak."

"Well I don't know if I said it, but it certainly deserves saying." A little giggle, and then she continued. "Hosea, my son, Yahweh feels each peak of our emotion, knows every event in a single glimpse. There is no progress in the eternal, only being. Every word that proceeds from the mouth of Elohim is truth. It is beyond human reasoning to arrange it on a timeline."

Hosea swallowed, his mouth dry, his heart full. He glanced at Amos and saw a wry smile on his teacher's face. "Why isn't she teaching the prophets?"

The old man patted his wife's hand. "She's my personal tutor."

Hosea's heart melted at the love he saw between them. Comfortable. Raw. Real.

"I'm going to Samaria with you," Yuval asserted again, shattering the peaceful moment.

"No you're not, woman!" Amos's amiable humor disappeared.

Yuval took her place on the rug beside her husband — the one he'd indicated in his rant. "Amos, my love, look into my eyes."

When he refused, she leaned over, placing her sweet, round face before him. "Look at me and tell me you don't feel the Spirit nudging your heart. You know I'm supposed to go with the boy." She stroked his brow again. "You only shout at me when you're frightened."

Hosea watched a single tear slide from the corner of Amos's eye. "What if Yahweh takes you from me?"

"Yahweh will protect us, my love." Yuval turned to Hosea, her calm seeming to permeate the room. "Gomer has always listened to me. From the moment we met, she associated me with an old friend of hers called Merav. I believe you'll have a better chance of convincing her to return home if I'm with you."

Hosea nodded. "Thank you, Yuval. Perhaps we should make our journey appear to be a business venture. I'll meet you at dawn and gather the newly shorn wool and some of last year's woven cloth. We'll pose as an ima and son in Samaria's market."

She winked. "Not much of a stretch for us, is it, dear?"

Hosea bent to place a kiss on Amos's forehead. "I'll bring her home safely, my friend. Trust me."

Amos grabbed Hosea's hand and squeezed

it with surprising strength. "I'm trusting someone much greater to bring you both back safely. And if Gomer returns — Yahweh will help me welcome her as well."

43

HOSEA 3:1

Then Yahweh told me, "Love your wife
again, even though she is loved by others
and has committed adultery. Love her as
I, Yahweh, love the Israelites."

Ezri sat on a cushion by his ivory inlaid
table, the last piece of fine furniture he
owned. "Twenty-one, twenty-two, twenty-
three." He lifted a defeated gaze to Gomer.

"Is it enough?" she asked, knowing the
answer but needing to hear it anyway. King
Menahem's decision to pay tribute to Assyria had saved Israel from immediate invasion, but it was bleeding the country dry.
When he'd died in his sleep after a ten-year
reign, his son, King Pekahiah, inherited an
empty palace treasury. Each year, when the
Assyrians raised the price of tribute, Pekahiah passed on the burden to Israel's

wealthy merchants. Now the merchants' coffers were as empty as the palace.

"No, it's not enough." He reached for his wineskin, but it was empty — the second he'd drained today, and it was barely past midday.

"Maybe if you saved the silver you spent on wine, you wouldn't have to sell your property to meet the king's demands."

"Maybe if I sell *you,* I'll have enough to pay the king and buy more wine!" He slammed his fist on the table, upsetting his neatly stacked piles of silver.

Gomer turned away so he wouldn't see her fear. He'd never beaten her. In fact, they'd never even exchanged a cross word until a few moon cycles ago. His drinking had increased as his silver dwindled, and the gentle man she'd known had grown irritable. Gomer knew the signs. The beatings would begin soon. She probably deserved it.

"I'm sorry I shouted." His hands glided around her waist, and he nuzzled his favorite place on her neck. "You know I love you, Gomer."

"I know. You're tired. Perhaps you should rest." He was the only man — besides Hosea — to tell her he loved her. If she hadn't decided men incapable of it, she might have believed him. Whatever his faults — and he had very few — Ezri had been kind. More like an abba than a husband, he'd showered her with gifts in the beginning. Offering him occasional pleasure had seemed fair since he made her mistress over three house servants. But the others had been sold along with most of the furniture, jewelry, and Gomer's wardrobe. Only the two of them remained. Ezri spent most of his time apologizing and the rest of his time resting.

At least she was warm and well fed.

A knock on the door interrupted his drunken attempt at passion. He staggered as she pulled away from his grasp. Serious pounding began before Gomer reached the entrance.

"Open up in the name of King Pekahiah!"

She gasped, turning to Ezri for direction. He shrugged, too bleary-eyed from wine to be of any real help.

She opened the door but slipped through a narrow crack, closing it behind her while Ezri remained mute inside. "How may I serve you gentlemen?"

Two soldiers in full leather armor stood, spears at the ready. "We've been ordered to collect the merchant Ezri's tribute or secure whatever valuables he owns."

"My master is resting." She brazenly examined each soldier from the top of his helmet to the tips of his sandals. "He's elderly and quite exhausted after strenuous midday activity." She licked her lips and leaned against the door, hoping they'd take the bait.

The soldiers exchanged wicked grins. "Perhaps we should seize you to fulfill Ezri's obligation."

She curled her finger, beckoning them closer, keeping her voice low. "Why don't you come back tomorrow at this time, and I'll be waiting. It will give me a chance to gather some valuables and make sure my master is sleeping soundly."

A moment of decision passed between them, and the taller soldier brushed her cheek. "Tomorrow, then."

She waited until they rounded the corner of the next house before slipping back through the door.

Ezri stood like a statue, his expression stricken. "You would steal from me and leave while I slept?"

"No!" She stomped her foot, frustration mounting. "Think about it, Ezri. I knew you could hear me, and besides — what is left for me to steal?"

His hurt turned to shame. "What are we

going to do, Gomer? I've failed you — just like I fail everyone. I couldn't find a physician to heal my wife. I didn't protect my sisters years ago. Maybe this is all a curse from the gods." He gathered her into his arms, weeping the slobbering tears of wine-saturated grief. "Perhaps if I sell you to one of my friends, I can keep you out of the slave market. At least then I could choose who . . . who . . ." Sobs shook his aging frame. "I'm sorry . . . so sorry."

"Stop apologizing!" She shoved him back, grasping his shoulders and shaking him. "Think, Ezri! Think. Is there somewhere else we can go? Do you have merchant friends in another city or country who might help us?"

His head lolled in spite of her efforts. "No, Gomer. I built my life here in Samaria with my wife. I paid a trusted steward to travel for me while I stayed home and ran the business."

She released her grip, letting him crumple to his favorite pillow. The loyalty that had made him a wonderful husband now made him a frustrating fugitive.

Another knock on the door caused them both to gasp and stare. "What do we do now?" he whispered.

Gomer gazed into the wide, frightened

586

eyes of the man who had redeemed her from death four years ago. She brushed his cheek and leaned down to kiss him as she walked toward the door. "*We* do nothing, my sweet Ezri. You have done enough. The soldiers were willing to settle for me a few moments ago. We'll hope they'll leave you in peace if I go willingly."

A second knock. *At least they're not shouting again for the neighbors to hear their threats.*

She opened the door, beginning her answer before she glimpsed her visitors. "I'll go if you promise not to —"

Shocked but familiar faces stared back.

She gasped. "Hosea? Yuval?"

Hosea was utterly dumbstruck by Gomer's beauty. Her hair cascaded over her shoulders, spun silk against a seagreen robe. If Yuval hadn't nudged him, he might have stood there gawking.

She reached for Gomer's hand. "Well, I'm glad to hear you're willing to come with us. We're here to take you home, Daughter."

"No, wait." Confusion warred with panic on Gomer's features. "I thought you were the soldiers. They came . . . I mean . . . how did you find me?"

"The same way I found you in Arpad,"

Hosea said, his heart pounding. "Yahweh. We knew you were in Samaria, and then we asked at the market about a beautiful copper-haired woman. You weren't hard to find."

"I can't leave. I'm a slave. I —"

Hosea placed a hand on the door to be sure she wouldn't slam it shut. "I know. Yahweh told me that too. Please, if you'll let us come in, I'd like to explain."

"Who is it, Gomer?" A distinguished older man stepped into the doorway, the smell of wine wafting with him. His face lost all color when he saw Yuval. "Merav, is that you?"

"What did you call her, Ezri?" Gomer touched his cheek as if he were a fragile amphora.

The old gentleman couldn't tear his eyes from Yuval. "Merav, is it really you after all these years?"

Yuval's face was the color of whitewashed stone. Hosea laid his arm around her shoulders, glancing right and left down the row of houses. "Gomer, please. May we come in?"

She nodded, opening the door wide. The man, Ezri, seemed to awaken from his stupor — or sober from his wine. "I'm sorry I have no couch to offer you," he said, "but please make yourselves comfortable on the cushions around the table. Gomer, get our guests some wine."

"No, I don't want wine," Yuval said, uncharacteristically curt. "I want to know who this Merav is and how both of you knew her." Hosea watched her soften as the two confused residents fumbled for their own explanations.

"How could you know Merav?" Gomer asked Ezri. "You said you never visited the harlots at Tamir's brothel."

"Merav was *not* a harlot!" he shouted, but just as suddenly his features grew stricken. "Was she? Is that what happened to her?"

Hosea felt Yuval trembling beneath his protective wing as she watched the story unfold. *Yahweh, give me wisdom to know when to speak, to listen, to retreat, and to assert Your will.* He waited, listening as Gomer and her master sorted out the details of a mystery too incredible to be coincidental.

"Merav was the midwife at Tamir's brothel. She helped raise me when I was taken there as a child of twelve. She was like an ima to me, but she was killed at Jeroboam's first child sacrifice. She was trying to save the infant from death." Tears spilled down Gomer's cheeks, and Hosea marveled at the tenderness in her voice. "How did you know her, Ezri? What did you mean when you asked what had happened to her?"

The old man brushed Gomer's cheek and then smoothed a stray copper curl behind her ear. He treated her so tenderly, not like a slave at all, but as a friend. Hosea watched with wonder — and envy. He couldn't dare think of all they'd shared, their bond evident and sincere.

The gentleman turned to Yuval, including her in his explanation. "My abba was a wealthy man and married into my ima's wealthy family. When he fell in love with one of our house slaves, my ima tolerated the indiscretion until he began showing favor to the slave's children. The serving maid bore him twin girls — Merav and Yuval — and they became very dear to me."

Gomer gasped, and Hosea gripped Yuval's shoulders as her knees gave way. He glimpsed a pillow on the floor and guided her toward it. Gomer supported her waist and sat beside her.

Yuval kept her tearful gaze on Ezri. "Go on."

He swallowed hard. "When I was twelve years old — the age of manhood — my ima ordered that the twins be sold. I pleaded with Abba not to do it, but he wouldn't relent. Ima's family was influential, and such a scandal could have ruined my abba's business."

Hosea knelt beside Yuval, expecting her to need comfort but finding instead a tear-streaked face full of wonder. "My Yahweh knew all along," she said. "So, Master Ezri, how old were your sisters — I mean, how old were *we* when we were sold?"

The old man winced. "You and Merav were about five years old." Ezri's eyes were kind, seeming to search for some recognition. "Do you remember anything about your past?"

"Very little. In fact, it's as if my life is a blank parchment before my journey to Tekoa. I don't remember any family at all. Isn't that strange?" She leaned into Gomer's embrace, her tears flowing unchecked, quiet sobs shaking her shoulders. "I would've liked having a brother and sister."

Ezri knelt before her. "Perhaps I could fill in a few details, and you might remember. Abba often brought me to the servants' quarters to play with you girls while he visited your ima. I always brought candied figs for you and Merav — hidden in the pocket of my robe, they were always covered in lint, but you loved them anyway."

Yuval chuckled. "Perhaps that's why my life feels most fulfilled when I'm tending figs." But the spark suddenly dimmed in her eyes. "I know I was sold and sent to Judah, but what happened to Merav? You seemed surprised at Gomer's report." She pinned Ezri with a stare. "What is the last memory you have of our sister?"

He squeezed his eyes shut before answering, the effort seemingly painful. "When Abba returned from the slave market on my twelfth birthday, I demanded to know what had become of you both. He said a kind Judean farmer purchased you and would be taking you to Tekoa. However, Merav would remain in Samaria with a reputable midwife to learn the trade. I had hoped someday to find Merav and help her, perhaps rescue her if she found herself in dire straits. But . . ."

"But what?" Gomer said. "Did you ever see Merav again?"

Ezri lowered his head as if a heavy mantle of emotion weighed him down. "My wife was still childless after ten years of marriage, so I sought out Merav, who had become the most esteemed midwife in Samaria. She attended even the births of the king's officials, so I trusted her when she prescribed a tonic to make my wife's womb fertile."

He lifted his gaze, his jaw flexing. Hosea tried to read the man's expression. It had changed from obvious pain and regret to . . . Was he angry?

"My wife suffered unspeakable pain for three days. Severe cramping and hemorrhaging. We nearly lost her. Merav never practiced midwifery among the nobles again — and my wife never experienced another womanly red flow."

Hosea heard Yuval gasp. "Surely Merav didn't harm your wife on purpose?"

"No!" Gomer shouted before Ezri could answer. "Merav would *never* have done such a thing. How can you even —"

He lifted his hand, silencing Gomer's objections. "Merav came to me a year later, vowing that the primrose tonic she'd used must have been tainted by a competing midwife. I gave her a bag of silver and told her I never wanted to see her again. I heard later she purchased a brothel with my silver." He looked at Gomer. "It was the brothel that later became Tamir's."

The silence throbbed with emotion.

"I see," Yuval finally said, pain evident in her voice.

Hosea turned to Gomer, seeing a granite expression replace the tenderness he'd glimpsed moments ago. "Well, I don't see," she said flatly, aiming an accusing stare at her master. "Why didn't you believe Merav and help her clear her name so she could continue her business among the royals? And how did she end up as Tamir's midwife — hardly better than a servant in a brothel she once owned?"

"I don't know," he said simply, meeting her fury with resolute defeat. "I confess I was weak and would do many things differently if I could do them over."

Hosea almost pitied this man who seemed beaten by his circumstances and untroubled by the venom in a slave's tone. Was he weak, as he said, or had he used the strength of others to hide his base character?

"Come here, little one." Ezri pulled a pillow toward him and directed Gomer to it. She seemed hesitant at first, but at his prompting, she nestled close. He wrapped one arm possessively around her waist — like it belonged there — and Hosea watched her soften like the clay on Amoz's wheel.

Everything inside him screamed, *Get your hands off my wife!* But before he opened his mouth, a gentle voice whispered to his spirit: *Love your wife again, even though she is loved by others and has committed adultery. Love her as I, Yahweh, love the Israelites, even though they have turned to other gods and love to eat raisin cakes.*

Hosea measured this man to whom Gomer offered more than a slave's obedience.

"I was ruled by the chains of wealth and the whims of my family." Ezri spoke to the women, drawing them with tender charm. Though he was older, his handsome features had undoubtedly won him favor in both business and personal dealings. "I couldn't risk displeasing my abba with the social scandal of defending a tainted woman. My wife was so devastated when the potion stripped away all hope of childbearing that I couldn't bring myself to confess Merav as my sister. Years passed, and my parents died. Soon the secret was easier to keep than to tell." He focused pitiful eyes on Yuval. "I was loyal to my wife in every way until the day she died. But I had hoped that if Merav remained in Samaria, she would hear of my wife's death and come searching for me. I suppose that's why I thought you might be her."

Gomer reached up and brushed his cheek. "So the last you knew of Merav was her purchase of the brothel?"

"Yes, my treasure. Many years ago, I heard from a merchant friend that the brothel Merav once owned was now managed by a woman named Tamir. I assumed — I hoped — Merav had earned enough silver to retire at leisure or move to another town."

Gomer glanced at Yuval and then held Ezri's gaze. "Merav had a kind heart like her brother. I don't know how Tamir acquired ownership of the brothel, but Merav was the heart and soul that kept the girls alive — gave us hope." She gathered Ezri's and Yuval's hands in her own, linking the siblings through her. "I have known all three of you, and I can assure you — the same caring heart has dwelt inside you all."

Hosea wasn't convinced Ezri's heart would prove caring if he was pushed to sacrifice, and the awkward smile on Yuval's face suggested she wasn't sure of his character either. Hosea cleared his throat loudly, signaling the end of the hard-earned tender moment. Gomer tossed him a disapproving glance, but Yuval scooted closer to Hosea, seeming to need his tender care.

He turned to his host and offered a friendly smile. "Ezri, I believe we're the only ones in the room who haven't been introduced. I'm Hosea." He waited until the man nodded and smiled. "I'm Gomer's husband."

44

2 KINGS 15:23–25

In [Uzziah's] fiftieth year as king of Judah, Menahem's son Pekahiah began to rule. Pekahiah was king of Israel for two years. He did what Yahweh considered evil. . . . His officer Pekah, son of Remaliah, plotted against him. With 50 men from Gilead, Pekah attacked Pekahiah . . . in the fortress of the royal palace in Samaria. Pekah killed him and succeeded him as king.

Ezri's charming smile disappeared — as expected. "When you forfeited your wife, you lost a treasure greater than twin sisters."

The sharp reply confirmed Hosea's suspicions. The kind old merchant was a warrior.

Hosea released Yuval and squared his shoulders. "I've come to buy back my wife. When Yahweh, the one true God of Israel, called me to become his prophet years ago, His first command was that I make Gomer my wife. He has commanded me to reclaim her and show her my love."

The room fell silent, battle lines drawn — Yuval at Hosea's side, Gomer beside Ezri.

"I don't know you or your god," Ezri said, his chin beginning to quake, "but I have loved Gomer well for four years. If not for the king's tribute demands, I would never sell her to you or anyone else."

Gomer's face lost all color, but she remained silent, stoic. She stared blankly at a spot on the wall behind Hosea, her breathing as ragged as the hem of her robe. Was she upset about leaving this man — or returning home with Hosea?

"Perhaps your timing is divine," Ezri continued. "She is my greatest treasure, Prophet. If you intend to buy her, you will pay dearly."

The thought of haggling for his wife riled Hosea. "I bring twenty-three ounces of silver and ten bushels of barley — a slave's wage."

Ezri scoffed. "She would bring twice that at the slave market."

At the mention of the slave market, Gomer began to tremble. "Hosea, please." She closed her eyes, releasing streams of tears down her cheeks. "King Pekahiah has demanded tribute from all the merchants. Ezri needs —"

The old man shushed her, covering her hand with his on her thigh. "Quiet, now. I would never send you back to the market, but a merchant always bluffs." He lifted her hand, kissed it, and returned his attention to Hosea. "I accept your offer, though she is worth more than any worldly wealth. You were a fool to let her go the first time. Don't make the same mistake again. Now, where's my silver and barley?"

Before Hosea could explain that Micah was waiting outside the gates with payment, distant screams erupted outside, arresting their attention. Hosea tried to speak over the commotion, to conclude their business before the merchant could change his mind. "My messenger is waiting for a red sash to be display —"

"Long live King Pekah!" Shouting interrupted Hosea's negotiations, filtering up from the street through Ezri's open balcony.

"Death to Pekahiah and his men!" Blood-curdling screams followed the death call.

Ezri struggled to his feet and raced to the balcony. Hosea and the women followed closely behind. One glimpse over the railing revealed the bloody beginnings of a coup.

Soldiers in full armor and on horseback were pouring in through the city gates, while startled palace guards in light leather breastplates rushed into the streets like lambs to the slaughter.

"By the gods, it was true!" Ezri shouted over the din while Gomer shielded Yuval's eyes from the carnage below.

"Let's get the women back into the house!" Hosea shouted, herding them inside. He looked for something with which he might block the door. Chaos bred looting, and it would begin soon. For the first time he noticed the utter starkness of the home — a single low table and a few cushions were the only furniture. Ezri had nothing left to steal.

"Gomer, get some wine." Ezri barked the order, hands trembling. They returned to their pillows, and Gomer poured each of them a small glass of wine — watered considerably. Hosea gave his wife an approving glance. Ezri needed no further impediment if they hoped to escape Samaria alive today.

"When you saw the soldiers ride in through the gate," Hosea said, trying to calm the badly shaken merchant, "you said, 'It was true.' What did you mean? Any news you've heard might aid our escape."

Ezri didn't answer right away, seemingly dazed. Gomer tried prying away his wine glass, but he grasped the cup like a lifeline, offering a weak grin. "Rumors began circulating almost a year ago that General Pekah was raising a rebellion in Gilead. Menahem's son wasn't a warrior like his abba and had been coddled his whole life. He'd let his advisors make most of his decisions." The merchant met Hosea's gaze. "And now it seems General Pekah has decided to become king."

Yuval gasped and startled everyone. "What about Micah? Oh, Hosea, is he safe outside the city?" Tears matched her panic, and Gomer scooted closer to comfort her.

"I know a little bit about soldiers," she whispered, "and my guess is that Micah is safer outside the city than inside these walls." She stared at the two men, lifting her brows to gain their support, while Yuval buried her head in Gomer's shoulder. "Isn't that right, Hosea? Ezri? Micah is safe, isn't he?"

Hosea had already considered Micah and believed he was safer outside the gates — but Gomer's compassion warmed him. "Absolutely. Micah is a bright young man and Yahweh's prophet. The Lord will protect him — as He'll protect us." He held Gomer's gaze as he said the words and felt Yahweh's nudge. Not a voice, just a prod. It was time to press his claim with Ezri.

"Micah is my messenger, waiting for a signal to bring payment to whatever house displays this red sash from its balcony." Hosea produced the linen. "He'll deliver the agreed price. Yuval and I will leave Samaria with Gomer immediately."

The women gasped, but the merchant laughed in utter disbelief. "You can't seriously consider leaving while blood flows ankle-deep outside my door!" Ezri leveled his gaze at Hosea. "You realize I'm no longer in urgent need of funds. Pekah will spend many moon cycles cleaning up his political mess before he worries about enforcing tribute payments from his merchants. I no longer have to sell Gomer."

"You no longer have to sell Gomer *now,*" Hosea amended. "There's a difference, Ezri, and we both know it. You're a merchant, and you're trying to drive up the price. I understand. But I'm a prophet, and Yahweh's offer stands firm."

The old man expelled a deep breath. "I don't want to let her go."

Hosea squeezed his eyes shut. "I know how you feel."

"So what do we do, Prophet?"

Hosea sighed, quieting himself. *Yahweh, I felt your nudge to press him for an answer. Now what?* A breeze stirred, and Hosea held his breath, expecting the acrid scent of battle rising from the street. Instead, he smelled the distinct aroma of cloves — and felt peace flow through him.

"A breeze in the heat of summer? Pekah must be blessed by the gods." Ezri started to rise, undoubtedly to peer over the balcony again.

Hosea laid a steadying hand on his arm. "Sit down, Ezri. That breeze you felt has nothing to do with your false gods. It was Yahweh's presence."

The old man grinned, glancing first at Gomer and then at Yuval. "I don't believe in all that magical nonsense, Prophet."

Gomer closed her eyes, her head falling forward. She knew, and Hosea's heart took flight. The wind blew again, the scent of cloves stronger this time.

Ezri's face lost all color, and Hosea chuckled inwardly. "Well, that 'magical nonsense,' as you call Him, has displayed Himself this time with a distinct scent. Can you tell me what you smell?"

"Cloves." Ezri swallowed hard.

"Does the scent mean anything to you?" Hosea glanced at Gomer and saw her swallow something. This time he and Yuval both chuckled.

"Yes. Gomer always has cloves in her mouth — at least since I can no longer afford to buy her perfume."

"So you understand that Yahweh wants to talk about Gomer?"

He nodded, but Gomer kept her head bowed.

"Are you willing to hear my full interpretation of Yahweh's wind and the cloves?"

Another nod from Ezri. His vocabulary seemed severely depleted after Yahweh had arrived.

"Yahweh's care extends to those He brings into our lives, and it seems He's gone to great lengths to show you His mercy through Yuval's reappearance in your life. I believe Yahweh is offering you salvation, my friend, no matter what your past decisions have been. If you embrace Him today, He will save you from Israel's false gods *and* political woes."

Ezri's brow was deeply furrowed. "How could embracing a new god save me from the death and treachery of Pekah's reign?"

"I believe Yahweh would have you return with us to Tekoa."

Gomer's head snapped to attention, eyes flashing. Was it anger? Confusion? Desperation? Hosea couldn't tell, and Ezri didn't notice.

"Why would you take me with you? I have nothing but the few pieces of silver you see on that table." He pointed a trembling finger at the disheveled stacks.

"I invite you to a new life, to worship and serve Yahweh alone. Yuval's husband Amos owns a successful farm, and I'm sure we can find a way for you to earn your keep." Hosea glanced at Yuval, who nodded her approval. "And you'll have my payment for Gomer," he added, "because though I offer you Yahweh's salvation, I do *not* offer my wife. She belongs to me as surely as Israel belongs to Yahweh." Hosea extended his hand in pledge. "Are we agreed?"

Ezri hesitated. "Does Gomer get to choose? What if she doesn't want to become your wife again?"

Hosea had been so focused on Ezri, he'd lost sight of his wife. He glimpsed her tears and knew he'd somehow hurt her — again.

Gomer felt like a trinket in the market, every fault and flaw exposed. But no. A trinket was treasured and displayed proudly. Gomer was a harlot, a slave, a *wife* — merely a woman to be bought and used and cast aside.

Angry tears burned her eyes and tightened her throat. *If Ezri had any courage, we could stay in Samaria — together.* But even as the thought formed, she knew it wouldn't last. Within a few full moons, Ezri would likely be begging bread or dead, and she'd be left at the mercy of a new king's soldiers. A shiver worked through her. *I can't serve another master like Eitan.*

"Gomer." Hosea's voice interrupted her thoughts, and she found him watching her — his eyes penetrating her soul. "Yahweh told me to buy you back and to love you again."

"No!" she shouted on a sob. "You have no right to say you love me. If you want to buy me — fine. Become my master. But don't pretend you love me, Hosea." Any control she had was lost in her final plea. "You owe me that. Don't pretend to love me."

He wiped both hands down his face, his eyes weepy and red when he looked at her again. "I've never pretended anything with you, Gomer. I've told you the truth from the beginning, and I'll do the same now." He paused, seeming to await her permission to continue. She nodded, and he sighed as if embarking on a long journey. "I intend to pay your master in order to buy you back — as Yahweh commanded. It is a command

I obey willingly, gladly, because whether you believe it or not — I do love you. Yahweh has filled my heart with love for you." He took another breath, staring at the ceiling, fighting emotion. "I want you to return to Tekoa with me, but you must come home with a new heart. You must never again worship or even mention the names of other gods, not in my presence or when I'm away."

Her heart ached. "When you're away." It was the wedge that had split their hearts in two.

"I am Yahweh's prophet, Gomer. I was called away, and you were called to wait for my return, but you refused to wait. You betrayed my love as Israel betrayed Yahweh."

"I was called to wait?" she shouted. "I'm tired of waiting for Yahweh! He betrays *me* every time He takes away the people I love. He took away my ima and then you. He takes it all — everything I have!" The last words came out in sobs, spoken into her hands.

She felt Ezri's arms around her, heard his gentle voice. "Life is all about waiting, little Gomer, and those we love are unavoidably taken away — some prematurely, others by age and death." He grasped both her shoulders firmly, forcing her to meet his gaze. "Life is also about choices. I will not leave my home or the gods I've known since I was a child. You may stay with me if you like, but your hus — Hosea is right. Within a few months, I will need to sell you to pay tribute to Pekah. You're the only treasure I own, my love."

Gomer stared at a stranger. Ezri had cleaned her wounds, reawakened her humanity, and vowed his love. But she was still his slave. Love meant nothing. She turned to Hosea.

And he was there, kneeling before her. His eyes deep pools of . . .

"Please, Gomer. It's time to make your choice. Will you return to Tekoa as my wife?"

He cupped her cheek, and the warmth of his touch weakened her defenses. She couldn't think. The anticipation on the three faces overwhelmed her.

"No," she said, hearing a collective gasp. "I will return as your slave, *Master* Hosea."

Hosea dropped his hand and his head. When he spoke, she heard a mixture of mischief and resolve. "Then we will wait for each other, you and I." He looked up then, meeting her gaze again. "You won't offer yourself to any other man, and I will wait to offer myself to you until Yahweh has won your allegiance." Smiling, he leaned forward and kissed her forehead.

Ezri cleared his throat. "It sounds as if the fighting is moving away from my courtyard gate, uphill toward the palace. If you're going to signal your messenger, now's the time, Prophet." He stood abruptly and walked to the balcony, leaving Gomer to her new master.

Her heart nearly beat out of her chest. Was it from Hosea's kiss? Or was it because they must escape through Samaria's battle zone?

45

HOSEA 2:19–20

Israel, I will make you my wife forever. I will be honest and faithful to you. I will show you my love and compassion. I will be true to you, my wife. Then you will know Yahweh.

Gomer listened to Yuval's slow, rhythmic breathing. The poor woman was exhausted after fleeing Ezri's home this afternoon. Micah's agile build and quick thinking had made their escape possible. He'd arrived with Ezri's payment when the fighting moved into the palace, and then practically carried Yuval when her weary body could run no farther. Once outside Samaria's gates, Micah led them to where he'd hidden the remaining wool and cloth that hadn't sold in the market. After trading the goods for traveling provisions, they joined the swarm of people fleeing toward Judah on the trade routes. North of Shechem, they took to the hill country, avoiding Israelite and Judean scouts on heightened alert.

Gomer gazed up at the half moon, trying to recount the number of times she'd slept in the open wilderness. Yuval snorted, stirred, and turned over. Grinning, Gomer tucked a gray strand of hair behind her friend's ear.

"Yuval?" she whispered. The woman didn't stir. *Thank the go* — She cut short her thought, remembering Hosea's instructions not to mention the gods of her youth. Did that mean she couldn't *think* their names either? She'd been hoping to talk with Hosea during their journey, but he'd seemed too deep in thought to be interrupted with her questions.

She rose quietly and took a large stick from their fire. The makeshift torch would protect her from stalking beasts — though it ruined the element of surprise she'd hoped for when approaching Hosea. She emerged from the rocks and scrub that sheltered her and Yuval, finding Hosea seated by a second fire, Micah snoring on his blanket nearby.

Hosea looked up. The firelight danced in his eyes, casting shadows across his handsome face. She thought of Ezri, his feeble declarations of love. Hananiah's deception. Eitan's cruelty.

Hosea's eyes consumed her, almost drowning her with desire — but not physical desire alone. More. So much more. No other man had ever looked at her that way, and a terrible thought pierced her. *What if he has truly loved me all this time — and I've wasted it?* Her knees felt like water skins, but she commanded her legs to carry her. She stopped a few paces from the fire, inclining her head toward another outcropping of rocks a few cubits east of them.

Hosea lifted both eyebrows and grinned, questioning. He looked like the ten-year-old boy she'd coaxed into trouble.

Her heart twisted. He wasn't ten. She wasn't that girl anymore.

His smile died, as did her playfulness, and he met her where she stood. His hand covered hers on the torch, and he leaned down to whisper, "Is Yuval all right?" His other arm enfolded her. She could barely breathe, feeling his hand sliding to the small of her back. He looked into her eyes, searching, waiting for her answer.

Still breathless, Gomer could only nod and point the torch in the direction she intended him to follow. She gave herself a mental shake. *You're being ridiculous. It's Hosea. Talk to him.* The personal coaxing faded like the moon behind a cloud when they sat on a large boulder and he scooted close for warmth.

He nestled her in the bend of his arm, and they relaxed against the perfect stone backrest. "So, what's on your mind?" he said, peering at the stars, seemingly oblivious to her desires.

"I have a few questions about our . . . relationship."

He nodded but didn't speak.

"Could you explain what you meant when you said I must wait for you?" Her cheeks flushed like a virgin bride, and she rushed on, trying to sound as though he were simply another master and she his slave. "My other masters expected me to perform the customary household duties, but I also visited their beds regularly. I was just wondering . . ."

"Gomer." He uncoiled his arm and sat up, then bowed over his knees. He hesitated.

It was excruciating.

"Well, I don't want to force you into anything so horrible." She pushed herself off the rock, trying to run, but he seized her hand — and then grabbed her waist. He pulled her onto his lap, holding her like a child. "You're not running away this time."

He leaned over her, and she leaned up to kiss him, needing the assurance of his desire.

He turned his face and laid his cheek against hers. "I don't want you to call me 'Master.'" She felt the dampness of his tears between their faces. "I want you to call me 'Husband' and worship my God with your whole heart. When you can do those things willingly, then I will enjoy you as my wife as never before." He dried his eyes on his shoulder and spoke as if taking a vow. "I will not treat you as a harlot or a bed slave. I love you too much for that."

"But you said I was an incurable harlot, dead to you."

He searched the windows of her soul. "Were it not for God's mercy, we would all be incurable. And haven't you felt dead inside for quite some time?"

She felt her familiar stony defenses rise. "I have been walking death for as long as I can remember. It's how I survive." She scooted off his lap onto the rock, sitting beside him.

He leaned over and brushed the tears from her cheeks. "The living God longs to give you life, Gomer. He loves you."

His words were like a swig of vinegar to a thirsty soul. Gomer had almost been fooled again, lulled into Hosea's false hope. She

614

straightened her stooped shoulders and sniffed back tears. "Yahweh hates me — or haven't you listened to your own prophecies? He plans to destroy Israel because of their *harlotry.* I'm a harlot. Surely you see the connection."

He grabbed her face between his hands and shook her. "Stop it!" he shouted in a whisper. "Stop saying that. You're not a harlot — or at least you don't have to be if you choose differently. I paid your bride-price years ago. Why do you refuse to see yourself as a bride?" He waited, staring into her eyes, but she couldn't speak past her strangling shame. She turned away, but he pressed her still. "What makes you believe Yahweh hates you? Give me proof, and I'll declare His love."

Gomer, emotions still reeling at the thought of being a bride, struggled to express the reasons she'd accused Yahweh all these years. "What about my childhood? Abba sold me to Asherah's grove, and then I was abandoned to a brothel. How could a loving god —"

"What about my childhood?" Hosea countered. "My ima died in childbirth — like yours — and Abba died two years after we arrived in Tekoa."

"But you had Jonah and Amos and Yuval.

My abba *sold* me. Priests betrayed me. Men used me. Women reviled me."

"And Yahweh sent me to Samaria to love you." His single argument stopped her cold. After a span of a few heartbeats, he added, "Then you betrayed me, Gomer, as Israel betrayed Yahweh. And I was called to publicly expose my broken heart." A tear slid down his cheek and hid in his curly beard.

Gomer had no answer. Her fear was confirmed. Hosea loved her — and she'd wasted it. Tears erupted from some deep, dark place within her. Old, stagnant tears, held captive through years of denial and abuse. She escaped into a hazy cloud of grief, unaware of her surroundings. Moments of lucidness revealed her lying in Hosea's arms, weeping long into the night. His embrace was . . . well, indescribable. Never had a man caressed her so little and yet touched her so deeply. This love was so strange, so different than any she'd known.

And then another realization. She'd felt this love from Aya and Yuval. Could it really be Yahweh's love?

Sometime before dawn, he returned her to where Yuval slept. She felt exhausted and still confused — but better. Hosea was a good man, a good friend. Would he look at her with disgust after sunrise? He'd seen the inner workings of her brokenness. No one could love her after that.

She cringed at the thought of her repeated betrayals and felt the old stones pile up around her heart. *He says he loves me now, but when we get back to camp, he'll be embarrassed when the old gossips start talking. He'll leave me again. He'll abandon me. Who could blame him?*

She watched Yuval sleep, and a new peace broke through the wall around her heart. "If I can believe Yahweh doesn't hate me, maybe I can learn to love as you love, my friend." Tears choked off more words. *And perhaps in giving love, I'll learn to receive love.*

Since they'd left Jerusalem at midday, Hosea had spent every step wondering what his wife was thinking. He'd taken her to appear before King Jotham to defend her against Commander Hananiah's accusations of murdering the pregnant girl. She was quickly acquitted, since Hananiah had been relieved of his duties for a similar scandal. Jotham had been aloof, and Hosea noticed the temple remained in disrepair. *Yahweh, have mercy on the man and on Your people Judah.*

Micah had led them most of the way home. Gomer supported Yuval over the rugged terrain, and Hosea provided rear guard to protect from stalking beasts or bandits. With every step toward Tekoa, his wife had grown more distant. Now, on this deserted road south of Bethlehem, Hosea wished he could take Gomer in his arms and reassure her. Her wilderness tears the first night had created a foundation for renewed friendship, but each day of their three-day hike seemed to push Gomer further into a pensive shell. She was at ease with Yuval, but as long as his wife confided in someone else, she would never fully rely on him.

A black streak shot across the path in front of him. "Viper!" he shouted.

The women shrieked, and Micah came charging back, stick poised to attack it.

"Wait." Hosea stayed the youth's hand, watching the snake's unnatural behavior. "It didn't try to bite me, and it's not darting away." The desert cobra writhed beside the path but didn't coil to strike. Its actions seemed impeded, slowed. And then it stopped moving altogether, lying limp in the desert sun.

Micah nudged it with his stick, and Gomer shouted, "Don't wake it up!"

Hosea chuckled. "I don't think desert cobras take a nap on a path with four humans watching." He received a glare but dulled it with a wink.

A chill wind blew, and he tilted his face to the sun, ready to receive Yahweh's message: *You must win her back. Lead her into the desert and speak tenderly to her. I will make the valley of disaster a door of hope. Then she will respond as she did when she was young. On that day she will call Me herish — her husband. On that day I will make an arrangement with the wild animals, the birds, and the animals that crawl on the ground so people can live safely.*

The wind lifted to the skies and left the desert still.

Hosea opened his eyes and found three faces waiting expectantly. Micah and Yuval smiling. Gomer — a surprisingly blank parchment. "What did He say about me this time?" she asked, the usual venom gone.

At least she hadn't assumed Yahweh wanted to kill her, like the other times she'd felt His presence. "It seems Yahweh believes I should court you, win your heart."

Yuval did a little hop and unsuccessfully stifled a squeal. Micah laughed aloud.

A wry smile creased his wife's lips. "It's a trick. It's never as simple as it seems with you or your God."

He nodded, conceding her instincts. "I am to take you into the desert — and leave you there. I will return every day with food and provisions."

Gomer's face lost all color, and Yuval's celebrating ceased.

"Yahweh will never leave you," Hosea said, pointing to the viper. "He showed us the viper as part of His promise. He said, 'I will make an arrangement with the wild animals, the birds, and the animals that crawl on the ground.' He will protect you. *I* will protect you."

"No! This is insane!" Gomer turned to Yuval and then to Micah — even his features were frozen in shock. "What if you don't come back for me? What if Yahweh calls you away to prophesy while I'm in the desert, and you forget about me? What then? You always leave, Hosea." Tears began to fall. "You always leave me."

He rushed at her, grabbing her wrist. She flinched and balled her fist, trying to pull away. But he held firm. "Relax your hand," he said. When she glared her defiance, he shook her wrist. "Relax it, I said!"

Her stubbornness faded to confusion, but she finally obeyed.

He turned her palm up, stroking it once — and then strummed her fingers like a harp. "Sometimes I have to leave, Gomer, but I always come back. I will always come back for you. Do you hear me?"

She pulled her hand away to cover a sob, but she didn't recoil from him. Hosea saw wonder in his wife's eyes, a spark of something new.

"You must trust me, Gomer — enough to remain in the wilderness alone. There I will make you my wife forever. I will be honest and faithful to you. I will show you my love and compassion. I will be true to you, my wife. Then you will know Yahweh."

"I will go with you into the wilderness, Hosea." She took a step toward him, sealing her vow. "But I will die if you break my heart again."

He brushed her cheek but remained silent. *If you only knew how many times I've thought that same thing.*

46

HOSEA 2:21–22

"On that day I will answer your prayers," declares Yahweh. . . . "The earth will produce grain, new wine, and olive oil. You will produce many crops, Jezreel."

"You'll be all right, Daughter." It was the third time Yuval had assured her, and Gomer was beginning to think her friend was the one who needed consoling. "Remember, Hosea said he'd visit you every day, which means he'll choose a place less than a morning's walk from the camp, right?" She glanced at Hosea. "You're going to choose a place close to camp, aren't you?"

Hosea kissed her cheek. "Yuval, we need to go before we lose more daylight. I don't know where Yahweh will lead us, but we know we can trust Him." He lifted chastising brows. "Don't *we*?"

"Of course we trust Yahweh." She waved away the question. "It's *you* who must get things right."

Yuval's lighthearted dig lifted the boulder-sized weight of fear from Gomer's chest. Her long, frightening days of wilderness wandering and prowling jackals still plagued her dreams. Yuval hugged her for the fourth time. "You'll be all right."

"Yuval." Hosea's patience had worn thin. "Micah is waiting."

Her eyes grew weepy. "I love you both. Be careful." She hugged Hosea and turned to catch up to the young man at the top of the hill. "I'm coming, I'm coming."

Hosea looked at Gomer, offered his hand. "Are you ready?"

Her heart pounded, and the boulder rolled back onto her chest. "I'm trying to be ready." Hesitantly, she placed her hand in his, and he kissed it before cradling it to his heart.

They left the road and began wandering east into the wilderness, her fear growing with every step. She glanced at Hosea and found a contented expression fixed on his face.

"How can you be so calm?" she asked, thoroughly confounded. "Do you know where you're taking me?"

"No." He kept walking, maintaining that silly grin.

"And another thing. Have you given a moment's thought to how our children will feel about me?"

He kissed her hand again and stopped walking. "I've thought of a lot of things, and I want to talk about all of them, but we don't have to decide everything this moment. We simply have to walk in the direction Yahweh leads us." He kissed her lightly and then combed his fingers through her hair. "Shall we walk some more?"

She was breathless again. This time it wasn't a boulder on her chest. It was this man who pricked her heart. Nodding, she leaned into him, trying — for the first time ever — to let someone else worry about her tomorrow.

"Hosea, it was reckless and cruel. What were you thinking? To leave your wife in the wilderness without weapons to defend herself or any kind of supplies if something should prevent you from providing? It's irresponsible! Unconscionable!"

Hosea released an exhausted sigh. He'd returned just after nightfall from a four-day excursion to deliver Gomer to her wilderness cave. All in all, a successful journey.

They'd remained chaste as Yahweh had commanded — a miracle on the order of Moses's parting the Red Sea. But he'd walked over a half day's journey from her cave to the camp, which meant he'd need to leave before dawn to deliver her supplies and return by nightfall. The commitment to see her every day and supply her needs would be no small endeavor.

"Amos, my friend, I'm not the only one who saw the viper. Micah and Yuval —"

"Don't you dare try to shift blame for a decision you made! If you're going to be the leading prophet in this camp, you're going to have to —"

"Amos, enough!" Hosea shouted at his teacher, causing both Amos and Yuval to gasp. "I'm sorry, but you're not listening to me. I started to say that Micah and Yuval saw Yahweh's signs as clearly as I did. There was no doubt that I was to lead Gomer into the wilderness to woo her. If you have issues with Yahweh's methods, yell at Him."

Yuval laid her hand on Hosea's shoulder and spoke quietly to her husband. "I felt the wind of Yahweh's presence when Hosea received the message of Gomer's wooing, dear. I think we know the son of our hearts well enough to believe he knows Yahweh's voice."

The old curmudgeon's voice settled to a growl. "But what are you going to tell your children, Hosea? When Yuval returned without you, they were terrified. We assured them you were coming back but told them nothing of Gomer. How are you going to explain you're hiding their ima in a cave?"

Hosea pressed his thumbs into his eyes, counting to ten before speaking. "I'll tell them their ima is coming back, but she must learn of Yahweh before she can love them as she wants to love them. It's the truth, Amos. I'll tell them the truth."

The old man pressed his lips into a thin, hard line. "It's your version of the truth. What if Gomer flees? What if you return to the cave one day and she's gone?"

"Then I'll obey Yahweh's next command." He slapped his knees, pushing himself to his feet. "I'm going to gather my children and thank Isaiah and Aya for being such wonderful caregivers."

"The children miss you," Yuval said. "They'll be glad to see you."

Hosea's arms ached to hold them. He bent to kiss his teacher's forehead and whispered, "I'm sorry I shouted."

Amos grabbed his hand as he was rising. "I'm sorry I made you shout to be heard."

Hosea slipped out the door and through

their courtyard, then onto the main path toward his neighbor's house. He passed his own courtyard first, and the dark, deserted house called him to rest, but he resisted.

Moonlight through sycamore boughs cast jagged shadows across what used to be Jonah's house, now Micah's. Times changed. People changed. He thought of Jonah weakening unto death and Micah's youthful, lithe frame. Life was an endless cycle of adjustments, some easier than others.

He pushed through the next courtyard gate, knocked, and opened the front door. "Shalom the house!"

"Abba, you came back!" Rahmy, his little princess, skittered across the room to greet him, arms upraised.

He hoisted her into his arms and buried his beard in her neck amid giggles and squeals. "Abba always comes back," he said, pondering the similarities between his daughter and his wife. Rahmy's bright red hair framed her face in ringlets, and she constantly challenged Aya's authority. But she was perhaps the most compassionate of his children, nurturing her brothers and loving each one for who he was.

Ammi approached, his fists pummeling alternating punches on Hosea's right thigh.

"Greetings, my little soldier, and who are we fighting today?" Hosea asked. Ammi was a born warrior — Hananiah would have been proud had he not been such an arrogant fool.

"I'm killing Philistines," he declared proudly, "like King Uzziah!"

"There will be no killing in this house!" Aya chastised from where she stood at the worktable, kneading tomorrow's barley bread. A smile and wink told Hosea her words were a familiar refrain. "How are you, my friend?" she asked, pushing a stray lock of hair off her forehead as she continued her task. A swaddled infant lay on the table beside her, fussing.

"I would say I'm tired, but after seeing what you must do each day — I'd be ashamed to admit it."

They both chuckled. She nodded in Isaiah's direction, where he sat near the oven with Jezzy tucked beneath a protective arm while their own toddling son played quietly with wooden blocks. Hosea planted Rahmy on the floor, and her little brother immediately considered her a Philistine. War began, and Aya became the commander.

"Where's Saba Amoz this evening?" Hosea asked Isaiah, trying for a casual conversation before engaging his sulking son.

"Would you like to tell your abba where Saba Amoz is, Jezzy?" Isaiah coaxed. A silent head shake was the only answer. "Well, Saba Amoz is where you might imagine him to be."

"The pottery shop," Hosea said with a smile. He folded his legs and sat beside Jezreel. "So is that why you're sad? Do you miss Saba Amoz?"

He lifted round, tear-filled eyes. "He's not really my saba, you know."

Hosea exchanged a glance with Isaiah. "Yes, I know, but we've talked about this. Amoz, Isaiah, and Aya love you the same as if they were family of our blood. And so do Saba Amos and Savta Yuval."

Giant droplets fell onto the boy's cheeks. "Some of the shepherd boys made fun of me today." He buried his head in Isaiah's chest.

"They said Jezzy is like a tree with no roots because his abba is always gone and he has no ima." Isaiah must have seen the effect of the words on Hosea. He placed a steadying hand on his shoulder. "Children can be cruel. We must use these moments to teach Jezzy where his roots should be planted."

Hosea knew he was right, but everything inside him wanted to find those shepherd boys and take a rod to them — and to their parents. For surely children didn't create such a finely crafted image. A tree with no roots, indeed.

"Come here, Jezzy."

His son flew into his arms, choking him with a hug. "I love you, Abba. I don't care what they say. You're my root."

He held him tightly, whispering, "I love you so much, Jezreel." The boy spent his tears and then sat between the two men. "You'll be a man soon, so I believe it's time you knew some things about your ima and me."

"Hosea!" Aya's caution came from behind him.

Hosea lifted his hand to silence her and continued. "Your ima *may* come home to us."

"What?" Jezzy bounced on the rug between them, his smile instant. "She's coming home?"

Hosea laid a quieting hand on his son's knee. "Jezreel, you're not a little child. You must listen with your intellect, not your emotion."

Jezzy looked befuddled. "Listen with my what? I thought I listened with my ears."

Isaiah tried to hide a smile but failed miserably.

"You must listen to my words — all of them — and not let your heart get in the way. I said your ima *may* come back, meaning she *might.* If she can hear Yahweh speak to her heart."

All joy fled Jezzy's face. "Ima doesn't like Yahweh. I don't remember much about her, but I remember the day you said she rejected Yahweh." He looked at Isaiah and then back to Hosea. "I believe Yahweh is good and His ways are right, but I've never heard Him speak. How can Ima hear Him when she has rejected Him?"

Hosea swallowed the lump in his throat. "We pray, Jezzy."

"I've been praying, Abba, but I don't think Yahweh hears me. I only hear silence when I pray."

Isaiah wiped his hand down the length of his face, raised his eyebrows, and stared at Hosea as if to say, *Answer that, teacher of prophets!*

Hosea wished Yuval was in the room. *What do I say, Lord?*

As his prayer ascended, Yahweh's gentle wind blew through the house, stirring the flames on each lamp.

"Abba, it's windy in the house!" Jezzy's eyes were as round as Aya's cooking pot.

On that day I will answer your prayers, Yahweh declared. *I will speak to the sky, and it will speak to the earth, and the earth will produce grain, new wine, and olive oil. You will produce many crops, Jezreel. I will plant My people in the land. Those who are not loved I will call My loved ones. Those who are not My people I will call My people. Then they will say, "You are our Elohim!"*

Hosea looked at the others, expecting them to have heard.

But Jezzy began to cry and scooted toward Isaiah, fear etched on his face. Isaiah gathered him close. "I think your abba just heard Yahweh's voice, but we all felt the wind of His presence."

Hosea held out his hands, inviting his son closer. After only a moment's hesitation, Jezzy snuggled in, still trembling. "Yahweh speaks to each person in a different way," Hosea explained, "and even in different ways to a single person. Our Elohim is so big and creative, He can think of lots of ways to talk to us. That was Him! A breeze in the house!"

Jezzy sat up, eyes sparkling now. "That was amazing!" He wriggled from his abba's grasp and sat between the men again.

"Yahweh revealed Himself to your ima several times. Once when Ammi was born, and a few other times."

"Did He come to Ima when I was born?"

Hosea's heart broke. Someday he would tell his son the full story of his name and the prophecy's meaning. Not today. "No, but Yahweh spoke of you just now. Would you like to know what He said?"

He nodded, enthralled, no longer seeming afraid. "Yes! Can you still remember?"

Hosea chuckled. "I do remember! Yahweh gives His prophets the ability to hear and remember His words exactly. But first I must ask you a question. Do you know what work you'd like to do when you become a man?"

The boy glanced at Isaiah, silently questioning.

"Tell your abba," Isaiah coaxed.

Jezzy kept his head bowed, peeking out from a fringe of curly bangs. "I told Isaiah yesterday, but I was afraid you'd be disappointed. I want to be a farmer like Saba Amos, working the soil and tending the groves."

Hosea barely held back tears. "I'm not disappointed at all, and I think you'll realize Yahweh hears your prayers when you hear His message about you: 'On that day I will answer your prayers,' Yahweh declared. 'I will speak to the sky, and it will speak to the earth, and the earth will produce grain, new

633

wine, and olive oil. You will produce many crops, Jezreel. I will plant My people in the land.' "

"Yahweh said that about me?" The boy's eyes filled with wonder.

Hosea tousled his curly, black hair. "Yes, He did. So tell those mean shepherd boys that you have roots, Jezreel, and pray for your ima. Yahweh will answer your prayers. She's coming home someday."

47

But now, Yahweh, you are our Ab. We are the clay, and you are our potter. We are the work of your hands. . . . Don't remember our sin forever.

Gomer sat staring at the clay vessels lined up on the natural shelf in her cave. One for each day she'd been in this wretched hole in the mountain — seven. Eight, actually. Yesterday had been the Sabbath, so Hosea hadn't come. He'd brought enough provisions to last through his day of rest. *When will I get to rest from this monotonous boredom?*

She hadn't even counted the first four days, when they'd wandered to find the "right" cave, waiting on Yahweh's approval. When the fickle deity had finally made up His mind, Hosea had gone back to Tekoa

635

and left her to spend the longest night of her life in the cold, dark cavern. No dagger. No food. A single blanket and water skin. When Hosea returned the next day, the sun was overhead, and she was overwrought.

"Where have you been?" she shouted through tears. "I thought you weren't coming! I can't do this, Hosea. I'm leaving. Give me whatever supplies you've brought. I'll make my way west, toward the Great Sea, and you'll never have to see me again."

He gathered her into his arms and held her as she cried. That's when Sampson emerged from Hosea's shoulder pack, licked her hand, and scared her. She jumped back and almost fell over the nearby cliff.

The little beast purred in her arms, and she was thankful for his companionship — though even he was becoming bored in this ridiculous cave. They'd left the cave yesterday to do some exploring, but Yahweh's wind stirred the desert dust, chasing them back inside. What was she? His prisoner?

The silent accusation pricked her heart. She'd done nothing but accuse Yahweh all her life. What if Hosea was right? What if human choices — hers and others — had been the source of her wounds, and Yahweh had been her protector, not the instigator of all wrongs?

"Shalom the cave!" Hosea chuckled, thinking his amended greeting witty.

Gomer thought it annoying, but she was thankful to hear any human voice. She stood, waiting for his strong silhouette in the cave entrance.

"Good morning, my love." His gentle voice squeezed her heart, but she couldn't let go of her anger.

"Is it still morning? I thought it was evening. I was afraid I'd have to eat Sampson."

He entered the cave with slow, deliberate steps. Five oil lamps illuminated his handsome features. His robe, wet with perspiration, clung to his well-muscled form, and his hair hung in wet ringlets around his face. This was her Hosea, all of him, every sight and smell and sound of him.

She realized it then — she loved him. In spite of the annoyances, in spite of their past failures — with all her heart, she loved him.

He stopped a camel's length from her, and she ached to hold him. "I've brought another clay vessel for your collection." He opened his pack, withdrawing the supplies first. Bread, cheese, olives, and dates. "Amoz said he'd teach you how to make this type of pitcher when you return to camp — if you'd like to learn." He pulled

637

out a burnished water pitcher the height of a woman's forearm, as slender as a gourd.

She gasped. "It's lovely." Then, suspicion rising, she glanced at the simple clay pieces lined up on her shelf — two bowls, two plates, a jug, and two cups. "Why are you giving me such a fine piece today?"

He sighed, shoulders slumped. "How do you do that?"

"Do what?"

"Know when I have bad news."

She grabbed the pitcher from his hands and stalked over to the shelf to set it with the rest of her collection. "I assume you have bad news, and I haven't been surprised yet."

The silence told her she'd hurt him. She squeezed her eyes shut. Why must her tongue be so sharp?

"I can't stay long today. It's fig harvest, and Yuval relies on my help since Amos is bedfast." She heard him sigh again. "I'm sorry, but I'll be back tomorrow."

Gomer whirled around, and he stepped back, looking startled. "Yuval relies on you? Israel relies on you? What about me, Hosea? When can I rely on you?"

She grabbed the new burnished pitcher and hurled it at his head. He ducked, and the vessel crashed against the cave wall, breaking into a dozen pieces. She gasped, hands over her mouth. "What have I done?"

Hosea said nothing, simply bowed and began picking up the pieces while Gomer stood in humiliated silence.

When he'd placed all the pieces in his shoulder pack, he kissed her forehead. "I'll ask Amoz if I can bring you a project to keep you busy. It seems you have some pent-up energy to expend."

She nodded, holding back her sobs until he disappeared outside the cave, and then melted to the floor. How could she have been so foolish? She imagined Amoz sitting at the kick wheel, his steady hands gliding up the sides of that pitcher, shaping the clay into submissive beauty. Now it was beyond repair.

A gentle wind lifted the hair from her shoulders. *I am the potter. You are the clay. You have been broken.*

"I know! I know!" she screamed. "And shards are worthless! Aaahhhh!" She shrieked like a madwoman, slamming her fists into her lap, spending her anger, her energy, her soul.

Lying against the cave wall, she could only whisper now, "If I'm broken, why don't You leave me alone? Why do You still work with broken shards?"

Silence. No voice. No wind.

Gomer closed her eyes, but even in the darkness, she realized — she was not alone. Her question had not been why Yahweh left, but why He still worked. Though Yahweh remained silent, she knew He had not abandoned her. Just as Hosea had gone back to camp and she knew he would return tomorrow. Yahweh was as real to her in that moment as Hosea.

She opened her eyes and stared at the clay vessels on the shelf — bowls, plates, cups — and she laughed. Actually laughed. The Asherah she'd hidden beneath her mattress was as dead and worthless as those clay dishes. How could she have been so blind? When had Asherah stirred the wind? When had the mother goddess saved her from danger? Had a pagan ritual ever filled her with the peace she felt in this moment?

"You are the one true God." It was a whisper that resounded like a shout.

Fresh tears wet her cheeks, this time tears of joy. Sampson emerged from beneath a cushion, where he'd been hiding from her wrath. He curled into her lap, his presence adding to her peace. Her heartbeat slowed, her breathing deepened. Sleep wrapped her like a warm blanket on a cool night.

■ ■ ■ ■

Hosea returned to camp and went straight to the pottery shop to request a burnishing project for Gomer. How could she hear Yahweh speak when she was completely overwrought?

"Amoz, my friend," he said, sprinting up the loft stairs, "how many pots can you give me for Gomer to work on in that cave?"

Isaiah sat across from his abba while Amoz hunched over his kick wheel, wetting the piece of clay, pulling at its sides to build its height. The potter continued in silence while Isaiah exposed his friend's heart. "Why would you distract Gomer with pottery when the Lord has placed her in a cave to remove her from all distractions?"

Hosea was glad the shop was empty. Keeping Gomer's return from the camp gossips had been difficult. "I can't stand it, Isaiah. She's terrified in that cave, and though I know Yahweh has promised to protect her, I lay in bed at night, praying for her, thinking about her, missing her."

"And so you've decided to rescue her from Yahweh's plan." Isaiah crossed his arms over his chest.

"I'm not *rescuing* her. I'm . . . I'm . . ."

641

Isaiah lifted one eyebrow and waited.

"She's bored, but she hasn't yet experienced Yahweh at a deep level — in a way that changes her perspective on life and love and the world around her. So what's the harm in giving her something to do while she waits?"

"What if giving her a distraction is like bandaging an infected wound?"

Amoz removed his hands from the clay and lifted a single eyebrow, looking remarkably like his son. "I experienced Yahweh through years of living with Isaiah and Aya, seeing Him lived out in their lives. Do you expect Gomer to shed a harlot's skin like a desert cobra, becoming a quiet, submissive wife?" He chuckled. "I think she may be in that cave forever."

Isaiah's eyes were as round as his abba's kick wheel, glancing first at Hosea and then at his suddenly eloquent abba. "I think that's more than you've ever said in a single conversation." He chuckled, and his abba offered a wry grin. "And you raise a good point." Then he asked Hosea, "What changes do you expect? How will you know when she's ready to come home?"

Hosea watched the potter return to his project. "Uh, I don't know. I just know it hasn't happened yet."

Amoz pointed a sloppy hand to a drying rack nearby. "Give her one of those pots to burnish and one of those smooth stones over there. It won't take a full day, but it'll give her a purpose." He looked up again. "What did she think of the pitcher?"

Hosea squinted, having dreaded this moment all the way home. "She loved it — right up to the moment she threw it at me."

"What?" Amoz dragged his feet, slowing the wheel, all traces of good humor halting with it. "What did you do to make her angry?"

"Why is it my fault?" Hosea feigned offense. "She's the one who threw the vase."

"It was a pitcher."

"Regardless — I was wondering . . . ," Hosea stammered, hesitant now that Amoz seemed perturbed. He pulled the broken pieces from his pack. "Is there a way you could fix it?"

Amoz studied the broken shards, and a spark of excitement lit his eyes. "Maybe we could do it," he whispered.

"So, that's a yes? You can fix the vas — I mean the pitcher?"

"Hosea, I think we can fix the workshop!" He exchanged a glance with Isaiah.

"What's wrong with the workshop?" Hosea asked, surprised at the concern he saw on both men's faces.

Amoz sobered and peeked over the loft railing, ensuring they were alone. "Since Isaiah's prophecy at Uzziah's burial, the palace has discontinued its pottery orders. At first I thought it merely a family squabble — Jotham holding a grudge — but when even sales in Jerusalem's market dwindled to half, I realized it was persecution from many in Judah for my son's message from Yahweh."

Anger sparked in Hosea's gut. "I had no idea King Jotham was leading the people away from the Lord."

"Jotham remains obedient to the Lord's commands," Isaiah added quickly. "He's as faithful as his abba Uzziah, with the same unfortunate weakness — he still refuses to tear down the high places." His features grew dark. "And I've heard rumors that Prince Ahaz is becoming more outspoken in his rebellion against Yahweh worship. He will most likely remain obedient as long as Jotham reigns, but we must prepare for a day when Ahaz takes the throne."

"You two can discuss Judah's political woes another time," Amoz said, waving away their concerns. "Right now we must focus on how to keep this shop producing pottery even though we have few markets that sell what we produce." Pointing a clay-covered finger at Hosea, he added, "And I believe your wife's tantrum may have provided our answer."

Hosea studied the shards and then glimpsed Amoz's satisfied smile. "You think a broken pitcher will help the shop's trading struggle?"

The potter offered a confident nod. "When I owned the kiln in Lachish, my fiercest competitor had started experimenting with a new bonding process to mend broken pottery. By boiling a mixture of animal blood, tree sap, and egg whites, he glued the pieces together, let them dry, and then refired the vessel with a short, intense blast of heat. The results left the restored vessel sturdy, though not waterproof, and the residual scarring of the cracks added a new dimension to its beauty."

Hosea's heart began to race as Amoz described the process, and Yahweh's warmth surged through him.

"I think we could create a unique business of restoring broken vessels. I've never heard of another craftsman doing it, and perhaps we could establish a new trade in Jerusalem."

"Yes, Amoz, yes." Hosea was overwhelmed again by the wonder of Yahweh's plan and provision. He stood to go.

"Wait, Hosea!" Amoz pointed to the row of leather-hardened pots waiting for burnishing. "Don't forget to take a pot and burnishing stone to Gomer. I'm sorry I couldn't be more helpful."

Hosea returned and held out his hand. Amoz lifted his brows and showed him both hands full of muddy clay. When Hosea persisted, Amoz laughed and locked wrists with his friend — mud and all.

"You have been more helpful than you can imagine," Hosea said. "Yahweh has used you mightily tonight." He left a shocked and happy Amoz to ponder his words.

"Where are you going?" Isaiah shouted as he hurried out the door.

"To check on Amos and help Yuval with the figs. Then I'll gather my children and thank your wife." He turned before disappearing through the curtained door. "I must make all my visits now because when my wife returns home, you won't see us for many moons!"

He left to the sound of his friends' joyful laughter.

Let her come home soon, Yahweh. Soon.

Gomer stared at the sputtering flame of the last glowing lamp, her heart pounding.

Hosea had forgotten to bring more oil today. He was home by now, enjoying a relaxing evening with the children. Or perhaps they were visiting Yuval and Amos. Maybe they'd shared their meal with Amoz, Isaiah, and Aya.

The flame flickered — and died. Utter darkness. Thick. Heavy. Stealing her breath.

"Yahweh, help me!" she screamed, the echo bouncing off the walls all around her. *Help me, help me, help me.* She listened to the silence, felt Sampson cuddled next to her, counted his steady heartbeat. One, two, three, four . . . He began to purr. Her breathing slowed.

I am here.

It wasn't a voice. It was an understanding. A mere thought, perhaps.

You are Mine.

It was more than a thought — Gomer knew it was Yahweh's Spirit speaking to her inner being. How did she know? She gasped, breaking the silence. She had no idea how she knew. But she was certain of it.

She closed her eyes, saw the same darkness. So she opened them again and spoke aloud. "Why didn't You save me from the pain?"

Silence.

"Why did You call Hosea to abandon me

after Jezzy was born?"

Abandon you?

Her heart twisted within her, and she remembered Yuval's rebuke for Gomer's frivolous use of the word. "I always come back," Hosea had told her repeatedly. And he was right. He always found her.

"But why did You let Hosea forget the oil for my lamps?" It was a silly complaint, but while she was asking, she might as well know. Peace settled over her, the darkness suddenly like a glorious pillow stuffed with the softest of wool.

And that was her answer. Only in utter darkness could she hear His quietest voice.

"I still don't like the darkness," she said, moving her hand across the cold, stone floor. She found her blanket and lamb's-wool pillow, lay down, and stroked Sampson's soft fur. "But I *do* like hearing Your voice." She closed her eyes, and in what seemed like a moment, she woke to birdsong and the glimmer of dawn's new day. "Thank You, Yahweh, for the darkness — and the light."

48

HOSEA 14:5, 8

I will be like dew to the people of Israel. . . .
The people of Ephraim will have nothing
more to do with idols. I will answer them
and take care of them.

Hosea woke to his son's face in the moon-light. "Jezzy?"

"Abba, I want to see Ima." He nestled into bed beside Hosea. "She needs us — now." The other children were asleep on their mattresses in the adjoining room he'd added.

Hosea gathered him into his arms, thoughts racing. Gomer had seemed more peaceful since the broken pitcher incident but refused to share whatever changes were occurring in her heart. He couldn't let her back into the children's lives until her heart was open to Yahweh.

"What makes you think Ima needs us now?"

"I had a dream. She was in a cave, praying Yahweh would bring her family back." He began to tremble. "We need to wake up Rahmy and Ammi and go find her. Is she lost, Abba? Is she out there with the lions and desert cobras?"

Hosea hugged his son to his chest. Awed. Overwhelmed. His heart raced. *Yahweh, is Gomer really in danger, or did You make this dream vivid to speak indelibly to my son?*

No wind. No voice. But an overwhelming sense of peace and a reminder of Yahweh's promise. *I will make an arrangement with the wild animals . . .*

"I believe Ima is safe, Jezzy, but I believe Yahweh spoke to you in your dream."

He was still trembling. "I'd rather have the wind like you get." Hosea kissed the top of his head. "Yes, I like the wind too, but we don't get to choose the way Yahweh speaks." He felt his son nod in understanding. "Ima has been living in a cave for two Sabbaths, but Yahweh has kept her safe, protecting her from all the beasts and birds and snakes."

Jezzy bolted upright on the mattress. "All alone — in a cave?" Hosea watched his tenderhearted boy wilt. "Is she afraid, Abba?

We must go to her now!" His concern turned to weeping, and Hosea gathered him into his arms once more.

"Jezreel, listen to me," he said sternly. "If Yahweh can speak to you in a dream, can He not also place a hedge of protection around your ima in a cave?"

Jezzy quieted some.

"I've been taking her provisions every day, and Sampson the cat has been with her too."

"I wondered where he'd gone."

Hosea grinned in the darkness. Oh, the blessed innocence of a child.

"Jezzy, I'm going to tell you a story about your name and the names of your brother and sister. Since Yahweh has spoken to you, I believe it's time you became aware of His plan for our family."

He sat up, wiped his nose on his sleeve. "Okay, Abba. I'm ready."

His wide, brown eyes captured the moonlight, and Hosea wished he could capture the moment to share with Gomer. She'd be so proud of their son. "Jezreel, your name means —"

"I know. My name means 'God sows.' " The boy clapped his hand over his mouth. "Sorry, Abba. Aya says I interrupt too much."

Hosea chuckled. "It's good to listen to

Aya. Yes, Son, your name means 'God sows,' and we know now that Yahweh has called you to be a farmer. But your name also has special meaning for our family because we've been chosen to tell the story of Yahweh's love for the descendants of Jacob — the house of Israel. Like us, Israel and Judah have been separated, and like with Ima and me, the love relationship between Yahweh and His beloved nation has been difficult. But on the night of Ammi's birth, Yahweh promised that the people of Judah and Israel would be gathered together and would grow in the land — because the day of Jezreel would be a great day."

Jezzy gasped. "The day of *Jezreel.* That's me!" Then his brow furrowed. "Was Yahweh *really* talking about me?"

Hosea wrestled him until the blanket was in a knot, and then they both lay side by side, spent. "You'll have to ask Yuval what Yahweh meant about Israel and Judah being gathered together," Hosea said, chuckling. "She seems to have a better grasp on some of those things than Saba Amos and me, but I can tell you this." He turned on his side, facing Jezreel, and brushed the stray curls off his forehead, noticing a fleck of gold in his moonlit eyes. "As soon as your brother and sister wake up, we're going to bring your ima home — because this day of Jezreel is great!"

Gomer lined up the six burnished pots in a row. Hosea had brought one every day since she'd thrown her tantrum — and the clay pitcher. She picked up a flint and made another mark on the wall, counting the days in this cave. Fifteen. Yesterday was the Sabbath, and she had been alone all day — alone with Yahweh. It had been wonderful.

Memories of the day refreshed her, and she lifted Sampson into her arms, dancing to the heavenly melody in her heart. Unbidden, Jezreel's face appeared in her mind, halting her feet, stopping her heart song. Then Rahmy's likeness. Then Ammi's. Regret pierced her, seeking to rob her joy. The children lingered in her heart a lot these days. *Yahweh, teach me to live beyond my failure — to establish Your strong tower on the rubble of my past.*

She set down the cat and picked up a vase and smooth stone. It was already burnished to a gleaming shine, but she began buffing it again, the activity helping to distract her. Stubborn tears clogged her throat and blurred her vision. How was she supposed to work if she couldn't see? The urge to throw the vase swept over her, but she remembered the shards from the broken pitcher that Hosea had taken back to Amoz. She'd destroyed hours of painstaking labor in a moment of temper. How childish she'd been.

What did Jezzy look like now? Hosea said his head would reach her chin. And Rahmy? She'd had red hair when Gomer last saw her. Had it darkened or remained like hers? And baby Ammi. A sob escaped. He was no longer a baby, but he probably didn't remember her. The old bitterness tried to strangle her, but she considered the caring people who had raised her children, taught them, loved them while she traipsed off to Israel. She thought of Yuval — her selfless sacrifices. And Isaiah and Aya — they'd loved her children as if they were their own.

And the thought of Hosea's unconditional love for Rahmy and Ammi crumbled her last walls of defense. How could a man, knowing those children were conceived in adultery, love them as if they were born of tender passion shared with a faithful wife? If Hosea ever allowed her out of this cave, she must be very cautious with those children not to destroy the masterpiece of love others had so painstakingly crafted over time.

"Gomer?" Hosea appeared, his form

silhouetted in the cave opening. "What's wrong? You're crying. Are you hurt?" Panic washed over his handsome features. He rushed to her and braced her head, wiping her tears with his thumbs as he searched her face.

"No, no. I'm fine. The children . . ." She wanted to tell him everything but couldn't find the words. How could she express the unfathomable restoration of her broken heart — the unspeakable mercy of a God who seeks to rebuild, not destroy? Would Hosea believe her? Or would he think she was trying to manipulate her way out of this cave?

He kissed her gently and gazed into her soul. "Our children will be blessed of the Lord, as Israel will be someday. Yahweh promises, 'I will be like dew to the people of Israel. They will blossom like flowers. They will be firmly rooted like cedars from Lebanon.' " His eyes filled with tears. "All those times you felt as if I'd abandoned you . . ."

She silenced him with a kiss, and his eyes remained closed as she spoke. "I abandoned you long before you abandoned me." She swallowed hard, realizing it for the first time. "I never gave you a chance to love me because I couldn't risk that you'd choose not to."

He opened his eyes then, studying her expression. "Come with me." He led her to a large rock not far from her cave's entrance and helped her to the top, then took his seat beside her. They fell silent, looking across a large chasm.

He focused ahead, his whisper bordering on reverence. "I've seen changes in you — peace where there was anger, hope where despair had always dwelt." He reached for her hand but still stared at the cavern-dotted mountain. "Would you be willing to share the changes in your heart?"

She squeezed her eyes closed and felt the warming rays of the sun. Yahweh had prepared her for this moment. Overwhelmed by the extravagance of Yahweh's care, she felt His presence as surely as the rock upon which they sat. "After I broke Amoz's beautiful pitcher, I realized how very broken I was. During the days that followed, Yahweh began to warm my heart with little signs of His presence — until one night, He consumed me in the darkness."

Hosea's brow furrowed, concern etched on his features. "Yahweh doesn't consume with darkness, Gomer."

She met his concern with a slight chuckle.

"I hope you listen to Yahweh better than you listened to me!" Her hand rested on his cheek. "I didn't say Yahweh consumed *with* darkness. I said He consumed me *in* the darkness. And there's a difference, Husband." She let her thumb brush his lips. "He searched and found me in the darkness — and there consumed me — because I was too frightened to walk into His light."

Hosea lifted her hand and kissed her palm, letting his tears flow into sobs. "Yes. Yes, my love. That sounds like Yahweh."

She pulled his beard toward her, kissing him soundly, longingly — sweetly. He left his eyes closed when she finished the kiss. "I know now what Yahweh sounds like," she said, "even when He's silent."

A slow, satisfied smile creased the lips of the man she'd loved all her life. "Would you like to hear what Yahweh said to me this morning?" he asked. She nodded, and his face took on an ethereal glow. " 'The people of Ephraim will have nothing more to do with idols. I will answer them and take care of them. I am like a growing pine tree. Their fruit comes from me.' "

She feigned a pout. "So Yahweh had already told you that He'd changed my heart. Will I ever be able to surprise you?"

"You surprise me every time I look at you.

I marvel that the Lord returned you to me." He cupped her face, brushing her cheek, tears spilling over his own dark lashes. "And now I will surprise you."

She tilted her head, wondering, but before she could question, she heard the most beautiful sound in the world.

"Ima?"

She gasped. She cried. She trembled. All in a single moment. Her babies stood in a line — each one having grown so much in her absence. Rahmy clutched her big brother's right arm. Ammi, a precocious spark in his eyes, flanked his brother's left. And Jezzy stood like a temple pillar, holding the refurbished pitcher she'd ruined days ago.

Jezzy stepped forward, spokesman for the group. "Saba Amoz said I had to bring this pitcher and said not to drop it." He furrowed his brow and shook his head. "It looks like someone already dropped it and tried to fix it, but it wasn't me."

She laughed through her tears and watched Hosea approach their children. He lifted the pitcher from Jezzy's arms and then whispered something, causing all three to look at Gomer shyly.

Jezzy took another step forward. "We've come to take you home, Ima — if you want to."

Gomer covered her mouth, unable to speak without sobbing. She nodded, barely able to say, "I want to come home very much."

She opened her arms, and Jezzy ran to her, encircling her waist, squeezing as if he'd never let her go. "Oh, Jezzy." She kissed the top of his head, which indeed reached her chin as Hosea had predicted. "You're so tall! What has Aya been feeding you?" She heard his muffled giggle rise from his unrelenting hug.

Hosea came closer, holding Ammi's hand, while Rahmy gazed up with wonder at her ima. "Your hair's just like mine."

Gomer cuddled the other two children in her arms with Jezzy, enjoying the nearness of the family Yahweh had restored.

Hosea leaned in to kiss her cheek. "Jezzy woke me in the night after a dream. The Lord showed him an image of you on your knees in the cave, praying."

Gomer's heart nearly burst. Indeed, she'd been awakened in the night by something lurking outside the cave. She'd heard Sampson hiss when something tried to enter the cave. Whatever Sampson sensed had turned and left, but Gomer was shaken. "Thank you, Jezreel, for listening to Yahweh," she whispered into his curly, dark hair — so much like his abba's. "Does Yahweh often speak to you in dreams?"

A quiet sniff, and then a long swipe of his nose along his forearm. Gomer grinned. "No. It was the first time, but Abba says Yahweh told him on the night of Ammi's birth that I was going to reunite our family, so I guess it was about time for Yahweh to do *something*."

Hosea and Gomer chuckled, exchanging a proud moment, witnessing their son's growing faith. "Would you like to tell Ima about her other surprise?"

"I have another surprise?" Gomer gasped, thrilled with the excuse to hold her older children at arm's length — get a better look at them. "I don't think anything could top this one."

"Saba Amoz has a whole bunch of broken pots at his workshop, waiting for you to fix them." Jezreel shrugged his shoulder. "I don't know why he and Abba are so excited about it. I always get in trouble when I break one of Aya's pots."

Gomer hugged her adorable son again. "Well, I think they're excited about *fixing* those broken pots, lovey. Hopefully, Saba Amoz will teach me how to fix them and make them useful again." She looked up then, holding her husband's gaze. "If Yahweh can take a life as broken as mine and restore it, perhaps there's a way to redeem other broken vessels. I'd like to spend the rest of my life trying."

EPILOGUE

2 CHRONICLES 29:1, 3 NIV

Hezekiah was twenty-five years old when he became king. . . . In the first month of the first year of his reign, he opened the doors of the temple of the LORD and repaired them.

"Ima, why are you still working?" Jezzy rushed into the pottery shop and up the loft stairs. Gomer remained bent over her workbench, trying to find an odd-shaped shard. "Isaiah and Abba are giving King Hezekiah a tour of the farm. They're almost here."

She kept her attention on her work, getting a little frustrated at the missing piece of her latest project. "Good! We'll give them all aprons and put them to work. Isaiah doesn't get to loaf just because Prince Hezekiah became king and named him foreign ambassador."

"Ima, don't be difficult."

A grin stole her thunder. She loved teasing her all-too-serious son. So much like Hosea, he'd grown into a wonderful husband and abba, giving her chubby grandbabies and tending the prophets' camp during the years of King Ahaz's persecution. When King Jotham had died at such an early age, he'd left his rebellious son Ahaz to reign at just twenty years old. The fiery redheaded prince had become a dangerous, idolatrous king, leading Judah into the bowels of pagan practice — child sacrifice. King Jotham's mild aversion to Yahweh's temple had become a burning hatred in his son, and King Ahaz showed his contempt by erecting an Assyrian altar where Yahweh's most sacred presence once dwelt.

"So this is the house of broken vessels." A deep, resonant voice filtered from the entrance below.

"Ima, they're here," Jezzy whispered through clenched teeth.

"Well, show them up, lovey." She winked, and he rolled his eyes — and then gave her a smile.

Jezreel walked down the steps with regal grace. "Welcome, King Hezekiah, to my ima's workshop." She watched him bow and felt the same pride she'd known since he was a babe. He had kept Yuval's fig trees producing and Amos's dwarf sheep profitable, and even harvested enough from their groves to provide olive oil and wine for the families in camp. It was enough. And it was a miracle — after all the prophets had endured at the evil hand of Ahaz.

"My son flatters me." She stood and looked over the loft railing, catching her first glimpse of Judah's young king. "This will always be Amoz's workshop." She inspected Isaiah's new royal robes, nodding a respectful bow at her longtime friend. "Welcome, King Hezekiah and Minister Isaiah. Shalom, Husband."

Hosea bowed and winked.

"Shalom, Gomer." Isaiah's voice seemed weak and reedy. He and Hosea shared the teaching responsibilities, but Isaiah traveled between the palace and the camp to fulfill his new role as Judah's foreign minister. She'd ask Aya how he was faring. "Have you found that missing piece yet?" He chuckled, and she shot him a wry grin. "I'll send Aya to help you."

"Greetings to the mistress potter." The boyish sparkle in King Hezekiah's eyes told Gomer she liked him already. "Should I come up, or will you come down?"

"If you come up, I'll put you to work."

Everyone laughed, and she considered making good her threat. With his stout build, she could put a shovel in his hand and he could stoke the kiln fire. "I'll come down," she said, descending the stairs, admiring his ivory-white, gold-trimmed robe.

Hosea extended his hand, calling her to his side. She obeyed gladly, assuming her cozy spot under his arm. "We've been showing our new king the prophets' camp — what's left of it," he said.

"I've told your husband that I admire his and Isaiah's courage. Their continued teaching will be an important part of Judah's rebuilding process." Hezekiah's voice seemed both kind and sincere. "And your specialized pottery is known world round, Gomer. It's a symbol of what our nation can become. I'm committed to refurbishing and purifying Yahweh's temple — since Abba stripped all its gold and replaced Yahweh's altar with that Assyrian abomination."

Gomer left her husband's sheltering wing to retrieve her favorite restored vase. "This was one of the first pieces Isaiah's abba helped me refurbish. Are you familiar with the process, King Hezekiah?"

"No, but I'm interested to learn."

She smiled, always happy to share the secrets of restoration. "We boil the bonding agent and glue the pieces together, then apply a thin glaze to seal the cracks. The glaze leaves the faint shadow of brokenness." She captured his gaze, the emotions as fresh as they'd been the moment she first heard Yahweh's voice. "This vase is restored, useful again. It can't hold water, but it can store grain or become a lovely doorstop." She chuckled at the thought.

"Judah may never be what it was in the days of David or Solomon," Hosea said. He loved to tell this part. "But if you let Yahweh restore your nation, He'll make it useful in eternity's plan." She watched the young king soak up Hosea's words like fresh cotton. "A wise old prophet once told me that when we're fighting for eternal victories, we mustn't be defeated by temporary struggles. If you prove faithful, King Hezekiah, your abba's idolatry becomes merely a temporary struggle."

Hezekiah's expression grew wistful. "I wish I'd known the other great prophets. Elijah, Elisha, Jonah, and Amos. And Isaiah tells me Saba Uzziah was a faithful king before his leprosy — and became a better man after. I never heard those stories from Saba Jotham or Abba Ahaz. I was filled with terrifying images of Yahweh's fierce wrath and then forced to watch terrible pagan rituals — things no child should see." Isaiah placed a hand on the young king's shoulder. "We can always look back with regret on things in our past. My abba Amoz wasted half his life worshiping idols but discovered Yahweh's heart through the faithful life of my wife and our family. Though I lost years with Abba because of his bitterness and regret, I watched him embrace Yahweh before he closed his eyes in death."

Gomer offered her precious vase to the young king.

"Oh, I can't take this," he said. "I can see it's very special to you."

"It is special, but I want you to have it and remember. We're all broken vessels, King Hezekiah. Redemption comes when we submit to Yahweh's hands and are mended by His mercy. Only then can we be filled with His love and be poured out on the broken lives around us."

The king grasped her hand and lifted it to his lips. "I believe you're right, Gomer. We all carry Yahweh's love in broken vessels."

AUTHOR'S NOTE

Mark Twain said, "Truth is stranger than fiction, but it is because fiction is obliged to stick to possibilities. Truth isn't."

Perhaps this is the single reason the Bible is so unbelievable — because it is completely true. Could there ever be a more preposterous story than Hosea and Gomer — a man who forgives his harlot wife again and again and again? Yet it is true of the prophet God called hundreds of years ago to live a life that mirrored the Lord's own love for beloved, harlot Israel. But the story isn't just about Israel, is it? It's our story too.

Even though we believe that the Old Testament story of Gomer and Hosea is true, how can you or I put our faith in such an unfathomable God? Why trust a God whose wrath seems harsh?

Because His love is beyond extravagant.

When people find out I write biblical fiction, the first question I'm asked is, "How much is based on Scripture, and how much is fiction?" I try to break the story down into three parts. The starting point is always the absolute truth of Scripture. If you find anything in the story that disagrees with God's Word, I assure you it was an oversight, not intentional disregard. The book of Hosea, however, is tricky in this respect. In his commentary *The Books of Amos and Hosea,* Harry Mowvley explains that the number of footnotes in the English-version Bible translations should give the reader an indication of the difficulty translators encountered while interpreting the original manuscripts. Different translations of Hosea's Scriptures sometimes portray different messages.*

That being said, I read both the New International Version and New King James Version in the early days of pondering this story. After beginning extensive research on the Canaanite pantheon of gods and the deception both Israel and Judah succumbed to because of the false concepts of El, I began studying the book of Hosea in *The Names of God Bible,* edited by Ann Spangler (Revell, 2011).

*Harry Mowvley, *The Books of Amos & Hosea* (London: Epworth Press, 1991).

If you're looking for a quick and meaning-ful synopsis of Hosea, look at chapter one in *The Names of God Bible.* (For further study, go to www.mesuandrews.com for free downloadable Bible study questions and a group discussion guide.) As is true of all prophetic books in Scripture, some of Hosea's prophecies were fulfilled in his lifetime, some were fulfilled later in Israel's history, and some will be fulfilled in the future. But one of my favorite lessons from Ann Spangler's research is found in Hosea 1:9, when Yahweh refuses to be called *Ehyeh* — I Am — by the Israelites anymore. He refuses to be known any longer as their mighty, desert-wandering God. How devas-tating, right? But in the very next verse, He promises to someday be *El Chay* — their living God. My heart just soars at those words! That's my Jesus! He's no longer the distant, dry, desert God of Sinai. He's the resurrected Savior — the merciful, holy, *liv-ing,* gracious God of the New Testament — right there in the first chapter of Hosea.

Second Kings 14:1–18:12 gives the bibli-cal accounts of both Israel's and Judah's kings. Second Chronicles concentrates on Judah's kingdom in far more detail. You can read about the reigns of King Amaziah, Uz-ziah, Jotham, Ahaz, and Hezekiah in chapters 25–32.

One final comment on the list of kings in Hosea 1:1. Though Hosea was an Israelite, this verse mentions four Judean kings and only one Israelite king. My story depicts Hosea's life as most commentators suggest. Hosea (or his scribe) is believed to have recorded his prophecies after he was safely out of Israel and living in Judah. Several experts went a step further, however, saying the writer of Hosea likely added Judah to many of the prophecies that Hosea originally spoke only to the people of Israel. They reasoned that during Ahaz's reign, Judah's idolatry became at least as vile as Israel's had been. Hosea's words to faithless Israel were equally relevant to the idolatrous nation Judah had become under Ahaz's reign.

As I read those comments, I realized Hosea's words to faithless Israel were just as relevant to our world today. I have broken God's heart too often as well. May we all return to Yahweh and say, "Forgive all our sins, and kindly receive us. Then we'll praise You with our lips. We will never again say that the things our hands have made are our gods."

ACKNOWLEDGMENTS

Writing this book was a little different than it was for my first two novels. I knew it was going to require more research, and I had half the time to write it. Fortunately, Jesus knew all that as well. My prayer team worked overtime on this one. I sent out multiple red alerts when I hit a wall on the plot or felt overwhelmed.

Multnomah University Research Librarian Suzanne Smith was an incredible resource in the process. I gave her a time period, a topic, and a few details, and she'd return with lists of books and periodicals that kept me reading for weeks. And when I kept books *way* past due dates, Pam Middleton rescued me and offered grace.

Another blessing came in the form of my first ACFW National Conference. Besides the incredible people I met there (way too many to name), I attended crucial workshops that streamlined this book's process.

Jeff Gerke's continuing class, "Plot vs. Character," was worth the whole conference fee, but Karen Ball's encouragement to seat-of-the-pants authors was also a godsend. Mary DeMuth gave me incredible insight for Gomer's broken childhood. Thank you for your beautiful and transparent ministry.

To my faithful critique partners, Meg Wilson and Michele Nordquist — you two are perfect editing harmony. When I click "Combine" on that MS Word Review tab, I get grammar, plot, characterization . . . I love your encouraging comments, and your nitpicking gives me indigestion — and always makes the story stronger. "Thank you" is never enough for what I put you through.

To Vicki Crumpton, my editor and champion. I've never met anyone who can say the hard things so gently. I love your wit, and you always seem to find the heart of a trouble spot I can't quite explain. You are incredibly talented and the most humble person I've ever met. I admire you deeply, my friend.

To Jessica English, Michele Misiak, and the whole Revell team — what a privilege to finally have met so many of you in person! You're fabulous at what you do, and you've spoiled me rotten! I so appreciate the heart and soul you put into your work, the joy with which you encourage and serve. Thank you beyond words.

To my family. Thank you for patiently giving up time during the holidays so I could run off to a hotel and write. Thanks to my son-in-love, Brad King, for his work on my book trailers. To my sweet mama, Mary Cooley. She loves to talk about *anything* having to do with her God, and she always has special insight when it comes to loving Jesus.

Finally, to my husband, Roy. I would not know real love unless I knew you. I adore you.

ABOUT THE AUTHOR

Mesu Andrews has devoted herself to passionate and intense study of Scripture. Harnessing her deep understanding of and love for God's Word, Andrews brings the biblical world alive for her readers. She and her husband enjoyed fourteen years of pastoral ministry before moving to the Pacific Northwest to pursue the next step in God's calling. They have two married children and live in Washington, where Mesu writes full-time. Visit Mesu at www.mesu andrews.com.